Mer

Singleman

Mentoring Mr Singleman

A Cornish Romance

Kim Sancreed

ISBN 978-1-5272-5712-2

Cover Design www.kaspar.co.uk

For my former colleagues.

Chapter One

"The stray tendril of a tattoo"

The September sunshine fell softly through the tall windows of the staffroom of St Petroc's School, turning the light oak panelling a mellow gold. The room was alive with animated chatter as teaching colleagues, tanned and rested, greeted one another warmly after the long summer break. Most wore relaxed clothing. A few were dressed down to such an extent they seemed merely to be swinging by on their way to the beach - a look that was not entirely misleading.

It was In-service Training day, when the students were still on holiday, but the staff were required to attend a series of dispiriting and entirely counter-productive senior management briefings. The pleasure of renewing acquaintance with old friends was therefore tinged with resentment. Nonetheless, thought Dave Singleman, as he chewed on the *pain au chocolat* provided for the occasion by the Governors, this precise moment – the greeting moment – was the high point of the term. From here, things would only get worse.

The Head, in a concession to the ambiguous nature of the day, was also in relaxed rig, his higher status detectable in the razor-sharp creases of his chinos and the stiffness of the collar on his open-necked shirt. The only suited figure in the room was Killick, the most nakedly ambitious of St Petroc's three deputies. He showed interest in neither pastries nor bonhomie but sat alone, a black coffee untouched at his elbow. In his hand was a file of papers, and these he studied with an expression of forensic rigour. In Killick's view education was a serious enterprise, and exam results the only acceptable evidence of its success or failure.

Although to all intents and purposes a comprehensive, St Petroc's carried itself with an air of dignity. Half a century ago it had been the grammar school that served one of Cornwall's most westerly conurbations, and it had buildings and grounds more imposing than the glass and concrete structures that sprang up in the seventies. More recently, it had bowed to government and financial pressure, and embraced Academy status.

As nine o'clock approached, the melee began to throng its way through the double doors in the back of the staffroom and to drift, without any evidence of urgency, towards the theatre. Dave fell into step alongside Mark Armitage, his closest friend at the school and a fellow member of the English department.

"And so it begins," he murmured, half to himself.

"May it be a good one," said Mark. "How was your writing course?"

"Good, thanks. Really good, actually. *Mousehole!* is up and running."

Dave pronounced it "Mowzle", for his embryonic novel was not intended to be a study of domestic rodents, but a swashbuckling epic, loosely based on a Spanish invasion of the Cornish village of that name in the sixteenth century. He was fond of his working title, and in particular the exclamation mark, but he worried from time to time about the challenges it might present to a marketing department.

"Meet anybody interesting?" Armitage's tone was neutral, but Dave didn't take the bait.

"You mean famous authors of the future?"

"I mean fabulous women of the here and now."

"Ah yes. Fabulous women. Show me everything you have in stock."

Mark smiled. "Never mind. Enjoy the single life while you can. Some of us come back to school for a rest."

Armitage was five years older than Dave, happily hitched to a blonde matriarch who had produced three small Armitages in rapid succession. Dave was an occasional supper guest of Mark and Hermione, and gentle ribbing of his bachelor status was an unspoken condition of their hospitality that he didn't entirely resent. He saw his friends, with their comfortable, chaotic household and easy-going affection, as role models of a sort for some possible, if remote, future existence.

"It's my birthday today, you know," he said.

"Yes of course it is! Many happy returns! Twenty...nine?"

"I wish. It's the big three-oh. I am, officially, no longer young."

"Anything planned?"

"A bit of surfing after school. Then the Idlers are taking me for a beer and a burger."

"Ooh-er. Hang on to your trousers."

The Idlers Club was a loose cabal of four or five single male members of staff who dedicated themselves, only partly in jest, to the pursuit of pleasure and to keeping schoolwork to the bare minimum. At lunchtime, while other colleagues caught up on marking or replied to parental emails, the Idlers ostentatiously played poker. They organised occasional "Sunday School Outings", lads' weekends upcountry which generated unsubstantiated rumours of outrageous behaviour. Ineligible to join himself, Mark enjoyed teasing Dave about his association with the closest thing St Petroc's possessed to a resistance movement.

They took their seats at the back of the auditorium, where three of the Idlers were already established. It was a tactic shared by a good three quarters of the staff, so that the senior management team, who liked the stage to be atmospherically lit, found themselves addressing their remarks on safeguarding and value-added indices to a dozen or so newcomers and loyalists in the front row, beyond which lay a gulf of blackness. On a medieval map it might have been marked "Here be Indifference." It always puzzled Dave that they didn't simply tell everyone to shift down to the front, as any teacher would have done had Year 11 tried the same tactic. But familiarity with the classroom and the realpolitik of behaviour management was not the Head's strong suit.

He settled himself in his seat and concentrated on finding the right mental attitude to carry him through the next ninety minutes. This was essentially one where 90% of his focus was on his own affairs – Chapter 2 of *Mousehole!;* Plymouth Argyle's prospects for the season; the disappointingly few birthday cards he had received. Like a faithful Doberman snoring on the hallway rug, however, he kept one ear cocked, alert to any vital information that might be buried in the dreary Powerpoint presentations that would constitute the first part of the day.

On the stage, the Head was seated between his two senior deputies – Killick on his right, still studying his sheaf of papers, and Emily Flowerdew on his left. Dave, who had no time for Killick, had an enduring fondness for Emily, who was responsible for pastoral matters, a brief she addressed with great compassion and a will of iron. Behind this trio the third deputy, Anderson, who was burdened with the title of Director of Digital Strategy, fiddled with the laptop that sat on its own small podium in the centre of the stage. This device was as important to proceedings as the control console of the Starship Enterprise, yet somehow preliminary fiddling seemed always to be required. Eventually Anderson straightened himself and nodded to the Head, who rose to his feet and cleared his throat.

"Welcome back everyone, I hope we have all had a restful break. We have a number of new faces to welcome." Dave sat up slightly. New staff these days were invariably young and often female.

The new teachers were welcomed in order of seniority, and each felt obliged to half-rise and make some sort of acknowledgment to the invisible host behind them. First to be introduced were three new Heads of Department, and it didn't escape Dave that they were all around his own age. His own progress up the management ladder to date was limited to a small responsibility allowance for running the Year 8 Shakespeare festival. He knew that in order to maintain what the websites called his arc of ambition, he should be applying for more senior positions himself.

The Head moved on to the more junior of the new arrivals.

"Kate Porteous will be joining the English department…"

A neat, compact brunette with John Lennon glasses stood and raised what might have been an ironical hand before dropping back to her seat. Dave glanced at Mark, but his friend was staring up at the redundant mirror ball in the centre of the lighting grid with a wry smile, musing perhaps on his own lost days of dancefloor derring-do.

Introductions over, the floor was given over to the coiled spring of pedagogical potential that was Anton Killick. Killick had come to them the previous year from a prominent London academy, and had been touted at the time as a bit of a catch. A clean-cut, powerfully built man of little obvious imagination, he maintained a scrupulous but faintly remote politeness to all colleagues, and always signed his emails "kind regards", a salutation that Dave considered to be at best passive-aggressive and at worst downright deceitful.

Killick embarked on an efficient dissection of the recent GCSE and A level results, with complex extrapolations based on an obscure national metric of added value. These apparently showed, via a series of intricate graphs, that while the staff of St Petroc's might feel that they had done a perfectly decent job by their students, they were in fact lagging a point or two behind similar schools elsewhere in the country.

"As a consequence," explained Killick, "we will be including an element of Value Added in the school's appraisal programme going forward."

The callow enthusiasts in the front row leaned forward attentively, some nodding. Up in the cheap seats a perceptible wave of unease rippled through the darkness, accompanied by a barely audible "Jesus wept!" from one of the Idlers.

Appraisal was one of those ideas that stubbornly refused to go away, despite the failure of successive attempts to implement it over recent years. The idea was that teachers should be observed regularly and given some sort of report, including targets for development, with the process repeated at regular intervals so that the entire school maintained a continuous upward spiral of improvement, efficiency and value for money. It didn't work, however, merely stirring up fears and resentments related to the spectre of performance-related pay among staff who were already – with the possible exception of the Idlers - working to the maximum.

Dave closed his eyes again, confident that when the time came to worry about appraisal, somebody would tell him what he needed to do. He knew he was a solid classroom teacher, popular with his students and thorough where thoroughness was required, and his results that summer were among the best in the department. He returned to his reverie, but found himself strangely irked by the earlier image of the three new thirty-something-not-very-much Heads of Department. How might he feel if he were in their shoes right now? A little excited, perhaps, at the prospect of a new start, with a department of his own to steer and manage? Looking forward to the extra few hundred that the monthly pay-check would bring into his bank account? Or petrified at the weight of responsibility for implementing the latest daft initiative to emanate from meddlers like Killick, hobbled by the requirement to pay attention to those jazzy graphs? He shuddered.

They were lucky in their own departmental head. Frances Fivey was a platinum-haired goddess in her early forties with a formidable intellect, a deep love of literature, and a live-in girlfriend who happened to be an Ofsted Inspector. Frances seemed able to float above the petty irritations of school life, buoyed up by the enthusiasm and love of her students and the great literature in which she immersed herself. She was already a legend at St Petroc's, and the daunting thought of attempting to emulate her in a new and unfamiliar school was another reason (so Dave told himself) for his lack of ambition.

"But at my back I always hear, time's winged chariot hurrying near"

The line, from a seventeenth century poem in the previous year's GCSE anthology, came unbidden into his head.

Get a grip, Singleman, he told himself. People died young in those days! Yet thirty, even at a generous estimate, was a third of his life gone, with precious little to show for it. A few grand in the bank, supposedly the deposit for some future investment in property; a 1970's MG that he suspected was beginning to make him look more like an old fogey than a young one. A couple of half-hearted attempts at a serious relationship that had fizzled out within a few months, and the first chapter of a novel with an inconvenient title. It wasn't an encouraging audit.

With a start he realised that the presentations were over, and the disillusioned masses were rising and shuffling their way towards the foyer, the shiny newness of the day already substantially diminished. He saw Frances waving to him, and made his way through the throng towards her. As always, she looked at ease with herself and the world.

"Hello Dave! Happy Birthday! There's a card in your pigeon-hole."

That makes four, thought Dave as he murmured his thanks.

"I don't think you've met Kate." Standing next to Frances was the brunette with the geeky glasses, a feature offset by a small nose stud and the stray tendril of a tattoo on the left side of her collarbone. It was difficult not to speculate upon where it might begin or end.

Dave shook her hand. "Good to meet you. Kate. Ignore the nonsense about appraisal – it'll never happen."

Her hands were neat, and her grip was cool and firm. Her voice was cool too, the accent a bit northern.

"It's got its place. It worked quite well in my last school."

Dave raised an eyebrow. "Don't tell Killick. He'll have you on the steering group."

"I've already offered."

No evidence of irony there. Either she had drunk the Kool-aid, or she was chronically ambitious. Through the glasses her gaze was clear and direct. She was pretty, in a no-nonsense, unadorned kind of way. Clear skin and white, even teeth. No visible make-up.

"I've got the programme here." said Frances. "Room 61 next, I think, for the workshop on differentiation."

The four of them moved out into the sunshine.

Chapter Two

"Please. Not. Donkey."

The following day marked the start of term proper at St Petroc's. The playground, empty and largely silent for the previous six weeks, filled once more with the milling blue blazers and arcane banter of a thousand students at their various stages of adolescent development. In the Year Seven compound undersized newcomers in box-fresh uniform stood around in self-conscious knots while the more seasoned middle school returners kicked footballs or marked out their territory. Titans of the Upper Sixth reminisced slyly on the summer's parties and checked out each other's take on the new "business" dress code, introduced by Killick the previous term.

Sammy Pascoe and Isadora Brunel, who occupied a position around the lower middle of the student hierarchy, walked together up the hill to the school. They made an incongruous pairing. She was tall for her age, honey-haired and tanned, with a loping confident stride, while he was skinny and a little undersized, his uniform clean enough but frayed at the edges. His complexion was pale despite the long summer that now lingered tantalisingly into the start of the new school year. Each carried a backpack that on this first day of term was light and shapeless, but which would in the course of the week become freighted with books, folders and PE kit, as their teenage worlds would be burdened with anxiety, deadlines and coursework. They didn't speak, but there was something in the way they kept step that suggested they were companions – not an item as such - almost certainly not that - but something more than mere classmates.

The silence between them this morning was uncharacteristic. Sammy and Issy lived within cycling distance of each other, though in differing circumstances, and had been friends since junior school. They had maintained their close companionship throughout the first two years at St Petroc's, during which they had shared a form group and most of their classes. But Issy had spent the last four weeks of the summer on an extended family holiday, so that Sammy had barely seen her, and in this time some subtle change had clearly taken place in his friend. He noticed the height difference between them more now, and there was something new in the way she moved. She had sat with him on the bus, as she always did, and had been friendly enough, but there was a slight reserve between them that Sammy was uncertain how to address. She had several times checked her phone, without offering to share with him what it was that interested her.

There was another reason on Sammy's part for silence. They were now in Year Nine, when the forms groups were re-jigged. The new classes had been communicated to parents and students at the end of the previous term, and Sammy had been dismayed to find himself moved from the form he had happily shared with his friend for the past two years. A further blow was that his old form was to be tutored by Mr Singleman, who had taught them English the previous year, and whom they both liked.

Sammy was resilient by nature and upbringing, and he had declined to make a fuss. His parents had more than enough to cope with at home, and in any case took an old fashioned "Teachers know best" approach to relationships with the school authorities. But now, as the moment of separation approached, he felt keenly the change in his circumstances.

It was Issy who finally spoke as they reached the top of the hill that led up to the school.

"Who have you got again?"

"For my form tutor?"

"Yes. For your form tutor."

"Some new woman. They did tell us. Miss Porter or something."

"I've got Mr Singleman."

"I know. Wish I had." Meaning – *I wish we were still in the same form, don't you?*

"You'll be fine. I like Singleman, but he can be a little casual at times."

"How so?"

"Well, you know. He's not quite as *focused* as he could be. It's not always clear what his learning objectives are."

Sammy absorbed this. Issy continued.

"Admittedly the Shakespeare festival was good. I'll give him that."

Sammy was finding this conversation slightly odd. Learning objectives had become a bit of a thing the previous year, with teachers putting them up on the whiteboard at the start of each lesson. Mr Killick, who had taught them science, liked to embed his in a power point presentation in a variety of unexpected ways, so that they made regular appearances throughout the hour, trailed on banners behind aeroplanes, or bursting out of cakes. They seemed to Sammy a bit of a gimmick, and he didn't recall Issy expressing much enthusiasm for them.

"Anyway," she resumed briskly. "Here we are. See you later."

She turned and gave him a brief hug. He was too surprised to respond.

"You'll be fine," she said again, then she turned and loped off in the direction of her form room.

"Breaktime?" called Sammy after her half-heartedly as she joined the throng of students milling around the bottom of the English stairwell. But she didn't seem to hear, and soon her bobbing lime-green back pack disappeared into the crowd.

Freshly showered after his morning's workout in the weights room, Anton Killick stood at the top of the main playground steps, legs apart, hands on hips, narrowed eyes scanning the incoming stream of students. Aficionados of Hollywood westerns might have seen something of Jack Palance in his Slavic cheekbones. There however the similarity ended, for Jack Palance in his many avatars was a man of few words, and would never have engaged in the superficially benevolent monologue of greeting, encouragement and admonition that was Killick's manner on these occasions.

"Good Morning Students, Welcome back! Good Morning Becky. Good Morning Alice. Welcome back! Are we ambitious? Are we committed? Good morning Bilal. Tie please. Good Morning. Harry. Jonny. Ah… Jonny, can I just have a look at these shoes? I don't believe these accord with our rules. Just drop by my office at breaktime and we'll discuss those further. Good Morning Sneha. Morning Megan. Earrings please. No – now. Thank you. You can have them at four o' clock. Good Morning, good morning. Are we goal orientated? Are we reaching for the stars?….". And so forth. Despite the jocularity, there was something mechanical in the tone, a lack of warmth which the pupils were not slow to pick up.

Killick was nonetheless accorded a grudging respect by the student body, partly because it had got about that he was a blackbelt 2nd dan in Taekwondo and could do one handed press-ups with ease, and partly because he delivered his subject with clarity, and determination, and, to be fair, a considerable degree of patience for those who struggled to see the relevance of Newton's Third Law to their life chances. The staff were less sure about him. His primary area of responsibility was the curriculum, but he was a rigorous enforcer of the school rules and had quickly become the "bad cop" to whom malefactors were sent by those who considered the gentler promptings of Emily Flowerdew to be insufficient. Killick was rumoured to survive, and even thrive, on five hours sleep a night and two hours in the gym each day. Whatever their reservations, most colleagues would acknowledge that things had needed tightening up a bit, and as Killick had as yet done nothing to cause major offence, they were prepared to give him the benefit of the doubt for the time being.

Sammy sat at the back of his new form room. It was in the English block, only a few yards from where Mr Singleman had his own form, and this made him feel less of an outcast. And he knew most of the kids at least by sight, though few of them were what you would call mates. On his left there was a sturdy boy called Hardeep who was a good cricketer and pretty sensible. A couple of lads that he knew from the theatre tech-team sat a few desks down. The seat on his right was empty.

Their form tutor – the new member of staff that none of them knew - was sorting through the box of administrative bits and pieces that were always required at the start of the new year: timetables, fire regulations, lunch rotas and homework diaries. She looked youngish – neatly dressed, compact, not obviously fazed by this first contact with her new class, many of whom were still chattering noisily.

Sammy vaguely registered this as a positive first impression. He liked a laugh as much as the next boy, but he also wanted to learn. He knew, because they regularly reminded him, that his own family had not had much in the way of education. His father was a jobbing builder, and his mother had been a care assistant until chronic arthritis put her in a wheelchair. He had an older brother in the army. All the males in the household were dyslexic, but Sammy's teachers had identified the intelligence and curiosity that lay beneath his scrawled and chaotically-spelled written work, and his generally sunny nature had won him supporters.

A distant bell signalled the formal start to registration, and gradually the chatter died away, not because the teacher had demanded it verbally, but because one by one the students became aware that she had risen to her feet and was eyeballing the talkers through her small round glasses, her face expressionless. The room settled into silence, and she smiled briefly. She had a nice smile, but once it was gone, it was gone.

"Good morning 3G. I'm Ms Porteous and I'm your form tutor this year. I'm new to the school so I'll be looking to you to help me out if I get stuck. Now we have some basic administrative tasks to deal with…"

The form room door burst open at this point and a lanky, blazer-less youth with a tie at half-mast strode in. He marched past Ms Porteous and flung himself into the seat next to Sammy, whose heart sank.

Please. Not. Donkey.

A titter went round the room.

"Wha'?" The youth stared round. Then,

"Sorry I'm late miss. I missed the bus." This in a tone that did not suggest contrition.

More tittering. Donkey was well known to live a quarter of a mile from the school, on the Penhale council estate.

Ms Porteous, momentarily taken aback by the interruption, removed her glasses and began polishing them. The class looked on with interest. She looked up.

"And do you often miss the bus?"

"Eh? No. Just with it being the first day. I wasn't used to getting up, see."

"Well, we're all in the same boat in that regard. Are you quite settled now?"

"Yeah you're all right miss. You crack on."

The briefest of pauses. Enough to make clear that the impertinence had been noted.

"What's your name?"

"Donovan. My mates call me Donkey."

More tittering. Ms Porteous's face remained expressionless.

"Well as I'm not one of your mates, I'll stick with Donovan. I'm Ms Porteous, Donovan, and I'm your new form tutor. Now if you're ready, we'll continue." There was a brief pause during which the clear steady stare encompassed and silenced not just Donkey, but all would-be titterers. One or two sympathetic members of the class shuffled respectfully into a listening attitude.

Across the landing in Room 32, Dave Singleman was enjoying the advantages of several years' tenure – of students who had never known the school without him, and a classroom that fitted him like an old tweed jacket. He had taught many of the group the previous year, and had had the opportunity to horse-trade a little around the newcomers – volunteering to take on one or two rogues whom he knew he could handle, thereby avoiding anybody particularly odious. (He had drawn the line at Donkey). He had scanned the form list in advance and identified his first choice form prefect. Issy Brunel - scholarly, cheerful and always well turned out - would do nicely. His book choices for the term had been squirrelled away in the cupboard at the back of the classroom, and he had a range of tried and tested starter activities lined up that should see him comfortably to the end of the week. So far, so straightforward.

Much of this work had been done weeks earlier, so that after yesterday's predictably tedious Inset he had been able to jump in the MG and head for the beach, the roof down and his surfboard jammed in the passenger well. Colleagues whose preparations were less advanced watched him go with an envious smile. There had still been warmth in the sun, and a couple of hours on the surf had greatly improved his mood. The Idlers, as good as their word, picked him up from the Engine House at seven, bought him a burger and a couple of beers and dropped him back again, so that he felt his birthday had in some measure been marked. Today he felt rested and ready for the term.

And so, all across St Petroc's, another year got under way, in a fashion shared by schools the world over, and not perhaps so greatly changed over the years. On the playing fields, fresh white lines marked out the rugby and hockey pitches. In the kitchens the vegetables were already being chopped for the day's lunch. In fifty classrooms across the school estate the rituals of Sammy, Issy, Dave Singleman and Kate Porteous were being enacted in much the same style, give or take one or two variations of circumstance and personality, as they were in a thousand schools across the land. The start of the autumn term offers up a clean sheet, so that all but the blackest of past misdemeanours are forgotten and annulled by the bright optimism inherent in a new school year. Everyone feels this, staff and students alike. It is one of the joys of teaching, and if all goes well, it can last for several days.

Chapter Three

"An expression of comedy bewilderment"

After school Kate had an appointment to view an apartment. The bed and breakfast that she had booked into for her first week in her new post was comfortable but pricey, and she was keen to find a place of her own.

Her smart yellow Fiat 500 chirruped its greeting as she approached it. Like many young professionals she was prepared to spend good money on clothes, accessories and a smart car, as homeownership, at least in the short term, was out of the question. The Fiat was only a couple of years old, and she felt good every time she got behind the wheel. She slipped off her suit jacket and hung it on the peg behind the driver's seat, swapped her Trotskyite glasses for a pair of designer shades, and programmed the satnav with nimble, competent fingers.

The apartment was apparently some kind of converted mine building, five miles beyond Newlyn on the coast road. She opened the sunroof and breathed in the still unfamiliar scent of the sea air as she drove, reflecting on her first proper day in her new job. So far, so good - the students she had met seemed friendly and reasonably interested in learning, or at least in enjoying their work. They were perhaps a little laid back, but she could cope with that. Her last school had been a boys' grammar in Yorkshire, a testosterone fuelled hothouse where academic excellence was valued second only to selection for the first fifteen. St Petroc's, situated as it was in the far southwest, felt notably more relaxed, two or three years behind more metropolitan establishments in the degree of its enslavement to the doctrine of continuous improvement. Not that she had come here to slack – Kate Porteous was not one of nature's slackers.

The staff she had met so far, particularly in her own department, had welcomed her, and Frances Fivey was clearly going to be a supportive and inspirational line manager. A few years here and she'd be well placed to apply for her own departmental headship. That said, as she drove out of town and onto the coast road, the sea a sparkling sapphire, and the heather on the cliff tops still magnificent, she could see how even the most determined careerist might be tempted to linger and settle.

She swung round a sharp right-hand bend just as the satnav informed her that she had reached her destination. The road ran downhill at this point, with the sea suddenly quite close. She had to brake heavily to pull off onto the gravelled parking area on her left, on which a red Range Rover was already standing. A girl in a St Petroc's blazer was in the passenger seat, long fair hair tumbled forward over a book, or more likely her phone.

Kate got out of her car and took in the tall, square granite structure that dominated the site. There were arched windows on three floors in each side, and at one corner of the building was the stub of a chimney. Wooden steps led up to a solid looking balcony at first floor level, providing access to the upstairs flat. Next to where she had parked there was a smaller, windowless, stone building, some kind of outhouse. She had seen many of these engine houses scattered across this end of Cornwall, most of them in ruins. This one had been renovated, and the ground floor was available at a rent she could afford.

A tall woman in a striped top, an older version of the girl in the car, came out of the ground floor flat.

"You must be Kate?"

Kate nodded and shook the woman's hand.

"I'm Sue Brunel. Welcome to Wheal Prosper."

"Thank you. Well. This is different. Is it very old?"

"Mid-Victorian. It was built to house the steam engine that drove the pumps. Many of the mine shafts and tunnels run out several miles under the sea bed, and they had to be kept free of water."

They stood together while Kate took in this information, and the extraordinary setting. They must be fifty or sixty feet above the shoreline, and beyond the buildings she could see what looked like a path that must lead down to the beach. On the other side of the road the rolling green and purple carpet of the heather was split here and there with golden flashes of gorse. From time to time a car sped by on the main road, but other than that she could hear only the cry of the gulls, and faintly in the background the steady beat of the surf.

"This is the rush hour," said Sue, "or what passes for one. Most of the time it's pretty quiet."

Kate nodded.

"There's a café down on the beach that stays open for about three quarters of the year. They'll sell you milk and eggs and things if you're short. Otherwise there's a Tesco back in Newlyn. Do you surf?"

"Not yet."

"Well the outhouse is yours to keep any gear in if you want to. There's a washing machine in there too. Shall we go inside?"

The walls of the Engine House were almost a metre thick, so that the floor space was considerably smaller than she was expecting. One square room about four metres across constituted the living area, with kitchen surfaces and appliances set around one corner. In the back wall a door led into what must be a lean-to structure, providing a small bedroom and a shower room. It was basic, but in good repair, the interior walls left un-plastered to show off the stonework. The furnishings, such as they were, looked good quality, if a few years old.

"Must get cold in winter?"

"It's centrally heated," said Sue. "Oil fired of course, out here. It's fairly snug. The damp tends to be more of a problem in Cornwall, but the Engine House was all treated a couple of years ago."

It was true that it didn't smell at all musty.

"And it's available now?"

"Yes. We let it out short term during the summer, but if we can pick up a long let in September, we take it. We've had a few St Petroc's staff over the years. They generally make good tenants."

Kate looked around, trying to imagine herself seeing out the winter surrounded by these ancient stone walls, hearing the sea on January nights crashing onto the beach below. She had hoped to get more space for her money, and she had originally envisaged herself living in the town, but she was keen to get established on her own. She had a bit of furniture in storage, but nothing she wasn't prepared to sell. It could work. It could be fun. It was certainly different. She glanced again at the schedule in her hand, but she had already done the sums.

"Yes," she said decisively. "I'll take it."

"Excellent!" said Sue. "The letting agent will deal with all the paperwork, and give you your keys. I can wait a bit longer if you want another poke around?"

"I need to get back, thanks. Could I move in at the weekend?"

"Shouldn't be a problem. I'll let the agent know. Normally we would do reference checks and so forth, but we don't bother if it's school staff."

"Great!"

They shook hands again, and Kate took a last look around as Sue locked up. It was idyllic. What a find! She wandered over to where the path led down towards the beach. It was steep and narrow, but not impossibly so, and below on a strip of golden sand the last of the season's holidaymakers were enjoying the Indian summer, a few surfers still putting on a bit of a show. She might try surfing. A shame not to, when it was on her doorstep. She could see the café off to the left. That could be a nice place to chill out at the end of a busy day. Feeling increasingly pleased with her decision, she walked back to her car as the Range Rover pulled out and accelerated down the hill, spitting gravel as it went.

The bend in the road that had nearly caused Kate to overshoot on her arrival made the exit a difficult one for anyone heading back towards Newlyn. She considered following Sue in the opposite direction, but it would take her away from where she wanted to go, and she had things to do. There was nothing coming from the downhill side, where she had a clear view, and she could see perhaps forty yards up the hill to her right before the bend obscured all oncoming traffic. She let a couple of cars come round the corner, judging the amount of time she would have to safely get across. It was tight, but do-able. At the next gap she dropped the clutch and swung out across onto the far side of the road.

As she did so a small blue sports car came fast round the bend. She was just about safely in her lane but still in the process of straightening up, and there was a sharp crack as the other car shot past and the wing mirrors of the two vehicles made momentary contact. She had a brief impression of a man of around her own age wearing sunglasses and an expression of comedy bewilderment as he disappeared down the hill.

"Bugger!" muttered Kate. She continued driving slowly round the bend that had caused the problem. There was a layby a hundred yards further on, and she pulled in to inspect the damage. The mirror, which was electrically adjustable, had been knocked from its socket, and now hung useless by its wires. Its casing was cracked, and the paintwork was scuffed where it had knocked against the door.

It occurred to her that the driver of the sports car might also have stopped. She locked the car and gingerly, hugging the verge, picked her way back round towards Wheal Prosper. The road stretched away from her down the hill, empty.

She stood on the grass verge, listening to the mocking cries of the gulls. That was an offence, wasn't it? Failing to stop after an accident? All right it wasn't a serious accident, but her vehicle had been damaged. Could he have failed to notice the impact? Impossible! She had heard it clearly, and his roof had been down. Should she go to the police? She didn't think she'd even seen a policeman in the week or so she had been in Cornwall. It would be her word against his. Damn! And the day had been going so well!

Back at the car, she inspected the damage once more. Kate was resolutely self-sufficient when it came to basic maintenance, but the mirror was clearly beyond repair. She identified a plastic clip that could be disconnected, allowing her to separate the mirror from the car, so that at least it would no longer knock against the door as she drove. She put it on the back seat and headed, a little dolefully, back to town.

Dave Singleman pulled into the petrol station a mile down the long hill beyond the Engine House and got out to inspect the damage. What the hell had the stupid woman been doing so far over? The MG had old fashioned fixed chrome wing mirrors, and while the one on the driver's side now bore a slight dent, it wasn't too severe. The car in any case carried its share of battle scars, as befitted a Cornish runaround whose main purpose was to carry its owner and his surfboard from home to school to beach.

He filled up with petrol, picked up a cook-chill lasagne from the shop for his supper, and drove back up to the Engine House, parking next to the outbuilding. He pulled the roof back up and secured it with the two clasps, and picked his briefcase off the seat. He didn't pause to admire the view, as Kate had twenty minutes earlier, but bounded up the wooden stairway that gave access to his apartment and let himself in through the balcony door, flicking the oven on as he passed. He climbed the ladder to the mezzanine sleeping deck and changed quickly into jeans and a fleece, and returned to the kitchen, where he inspected the instructions on the cardboard sleeve of the lasagne. No stranger to cook-chill meals, it always puzzled him that there appeared to be no consistency to whether you left the film lid on, peeled it off, or poked holes in it. This particular brand called for the poking of holes, which he duly did with the tip of the vegetable knife, producing a series of satisfying pops. He stuck the lasagne in the oven, picked a beer from the fridge, and returned to the balcony, pulling the battered sun-lounger round to face the setting sun.

He considered once more the incident with the wing mirror. Ought he perhaps to have stopped? There had seemed little purpose. He had glanced in his rear mirror immediately after the collision, but the Fiat 500 had disappeared round the bend. It wasn't a particularly safe place for either of them to stop, and in any case, it was a knock-for-knock incident – just one of those things. He would either disregard the damage to his own car, such as it was, or pick up another mirror from a scrapyard.

He pushed to one side the thought that the yellow car, which had looked rather new and shiny - might not be so cheaply repaired. He had never owned a new car, regarding them as poor investments and only likely to lead to distress over exactly such incidents as these. He determined to think no more of the matter, and settled down to enjoy his beer and the sunset, and to think a little about the new colleague in the English department, whose geeky good looks, he was bound to admit, had more than a little appeal.

There had been no hug between Sammy and Isadora when they parted at Eglos bus stop at the end of that first school day. Issy said she couldn't hang around as she had to help her mum with a viewing, and sure enough the Brunel family SUV was parked across the road from the bus stop. Issy's Mum smiled and waved to him as he watched her cross and climb up into the car, and Sammy waved back before turning up the lane that led into the village. The Brunels didn't seem to have what Sammy regarded as actual jobs, but owned property, mostly holiday lets, which Sammy's mother didn't approve of. In a part of Cornwall where London money had pushed property prices out of reach of many young locals, incomers were tolerated rather than welcomed. His father was less antagonistic, recognising that for tradesmen such as himself it brought good work. He had a contract to carry out maintenance for the Brunels on a number of their houses.

Sammy pushed open the door of the small terraced miner's cottage he had lived in all his life. The front door gave straight onto the living room, whose whitewashed walls were hung with an odd collection of musical instruments – mandolins, banjos and hand-drums. The room was dark after the sunshine of the early evening. His mother was in her wheelchair by the fire that they kept in all year round, fuelled by an apparently limitless supply of wood to which Viv Pascoe had mysterious access. A tray on her lap was spread with papers relating to her work as a parish councillor.

"Hello sweetie, How was it?"

"Yeah, it was ok. We didn't do much. Do you want a cup of tea?"

"What do you think?"

He smiled and went through to the cramped kitchen to fill the kettle.

"How's your new form? Have you got some of your friends there?"

"There's a few kids I know. Hardeep's all right."

He stuck his head back round. "Donovan Doggett's sitting next to me though."

His mother made a face. "Maybe he'll have grown some sense over the holidays."

"He's grown about six inches, I know that. Mind you so's Issy."

"So will you, soon enough. Your brother was small at your age."

He added milk to the mugs, and a spoonful of sugar to his mum's, and poured in the water.

"There you go. Nice cardy, by the way."

She smiled. She liked that he noticed things like that, that he made the effort.

Chapter Four

"A gel pen poised for action"

On Thursday afternoons the English department had their weekly meeting, and Frances Fivey's team were seated around an island of desks in the middle of her classroom. Frances's classroom was an extension of her personality, and as such its wall space was unfashionably free of the work of students, being covered instead with Shakespeare sonnets, William Morris fabric, Arthur Rackham illustrations and other expressions of the human creative spirit that met her exacting standards of excellence. Dave wasn't sure how she got away with it, except that she did it so well.

The meeting had not yet begun, as Frances and Kate were still engaged in conversation in the workroom. It was good to be back once more with his English colleagues, who under Frances made a disparate but broadly united team who liked and respected each other, and tolerated each other's foibles. With the exception of Kate, they had been together since Dave's arrival five years previously. There were seven of them who taught in the department more or less full time. Mark Armitage was Frances's deputy, and seemed happy to remain in that role while the currents of family life carried him through to his middle years. His wife was a GP when she was not having babies, and they were comfortably situated. Jenny

Skinner was an outwardly disorganised and perpetually flustered single mother with a penchant for diaphanous scarves and a heart of transparent goodness. When the occasional crises of her chaotic life impinged upon the department, they were readily absorbed and covered for. Raphael d'Allesandro taught drama. He was trim, dark and wiry, and took the teaching of his subject with the utmost seriousness, while treating the requirements of the wider school with such disdain that he would rarely acknowledge them. As always he carried a black Moleskine notebook, in which he made jottings crucial to whatever theatrical project was engaging his interest at the time.

Bar one or two minor contributors (Emily Flowerdew taught a small timetable of Junior English) that left only the Eldest Member. Edward Tremenhere had been Head of Department decades previously until an un-named indiscretion led to a lengthy leave of absence, and, it was rumoured, a spell in a monastery. He was a tall, spare ascetic man in his middle fifties, a classical scholar originally, and a published poet who claimed to have read everything in the canon before 1950, and nothing after that date. Previous Heads of Department had found him difficult to manage, but Frances held him in high regard, and Dave had the impression that the respect was mutual.

How would Kate fit in with this lot, he wondered? From the initial impression of her brisk efficiency, he suspected she might find them all a bit casual. Did she have a sense of humour? Would she find Jenny unbearably disorganised? How would Edward, whose mild donnish misogyny would probably not have been denied had it been put to him, regard her, and she him? Mark Armitage would of course embrace her with his usual genial good nature, and Raphael treated everyone with the same courteous indifference.

Frances glided in, followed by Kate.

"Hello everybody, sorry for that slight delay. Now Kate - I don't think you've met Edward, our father confessor, or Raphael, who spends most of his time in the Theatre, where he is the school's unofficial Lord of Misrule."

Edward Tremenhere inclined his head graciously. Raphael looked up from his notebook, flashed her a dazzling smile, and returned to his scribbling. Kate murmured a greeting as she sat down and rummaged in her pencil case.

"So… lots to get through, and I'd like to finish by five fifteen. We've been asked to discuss GCSE results in relation to Anton's *lovely* graphs, but I don't really see the point and I'll chat to one or two of you individually anyway, so can we all agree that they have been discussed in as far as was found useful, and that we have absorbed such lessons as are there to be absorbed?"

Nods and wry smiles around the table. Dave glanced at Kate, whose expression remained neutral. She had her planner open and a gel pen poised for action.

"I'll be here for thirty minutes or so after the meeting, so if there are any qualms about set lists or anything else that the first week has thrown up I'll deal with those then. As you know it's a busy term…"

"As they all are," said Mark.

"Indeed so. But this one has a lot of extra bits and pieces, notably the Shakespeare festival, which is happening on Thursday 15th November – Raphael and Dave - anything you would like to say at this stage?

Raphael looked up from his notebook and glanced at Dave.

"Not a great deal from my side of things. Dave's running the programme which I'm sure he'll do with his customary attention to detail. I'll try to keep the theatre as free as I can for rehearsal."

"We really do need as much access as possible to rehearse in the space, Raph," said Mark, the mildest note of reproof in his tone. "Last year was a bit of a disaster from that point of view."

"Yes, everybody wants the space," said Raphael. "I understand that. The GCSE practicals are after half term so once they're done you'll have a clear fortnight. Senior Management will no doubt want it from time to time but I'll keep it as clear as I can."

"Good. It's a little way off yet but I wanted to make sure it was on everybody's radar. Now the other big event this term is the Year 9 London trip, which is the weekend before half term. I've booked tickets for Macbeth at the Globe on Friday evening with the V and A in the afternoon if we're up in time.

Saturday morning it will probably be the Tate Modern, returning some time Saturday evening. We need four members of staff from this department, and Edward has kindly said he'll come, so I'm looking for a couple more."

"I'd be happy to help," said Kate. "I've got a Year 9 form."

"Excellent. Room for one more…"

Glances were exchanged around the table. The Year 9 London trip, which was a joint venture with the Art department, could be hard work and involved several hours each way on the coach. There had been an unfortunate incident the previous year in which some brightly coloured condoms had had to be retrieved from the fountains in Trafalgar Square with Dave's golf umbrella.

"Starting junior play rehearsals, I'm afraid," said Raphael.

"Tricky for me with family," said Mark.

"Pretty well impossible for me, for the same reason, I'm afraid," said Jenny apologetically.

"Dave? I wondered if you might?"

"I probably could," said Dave. "Though it's not my favourite gig…"

"I'd be very grateful," said Frances winningly. "And it will look very good on your appraisal documentation."

"Does my appraisal documentation require adornment?"

"No more than anybody else's," said Frances smoothly. "But will you, please? We could do with your heft."

"Oh well if it's my *heft* you're after that's different. I'll check my diary. There's also the inter-schools debating competition, by the way – that's the week after the Shakespeare festival, and we usually try to do a bit of class debating in the run-up."

"Yes of course. I should have mentioned it."

She smiled at Dave indulgently. Debating was one of his hobby horses.

"Moving on then. I wanted to have a bit of an open discussion about our language strategy at Key Stage Three…"

The meeting drifted on more or less purposefully and wound up shortly after 5pm. The room emptied quickly and Dave was about to follow his colleagues to the car park when Frances looked up from her desk.

"Are you dashing off? I wouldn't mind a quick chat if you could spare a minute or two."

"Sure." Dave turned and sat down again at the island of tables. Frances finished tidying some papers.

She looked at him directly.

"Were you aware that Sheila Abbot is retiring this year?"

"Really? I thought she had a while to go yet." Sheila Abbot was the Head of Year Nine.

"Well she could go on longer if she wanted to, but her husband's apparently not well. So she's going to take early retirement. Which means a vacancy for a pastoral Head."

"Right."

"I wanted to encourage you to consider applying. I think you'd have a good shout of getting it if you did."

"I see. Well. I suppose I had thought… maybe if she went in three or four years time…"

"Well she's going now. You'd make a great Head of Year, Dave. You're smart and capable, popular with the kids…"

"Thanks for that. It's just that I'm fairly comfortable with the route I'm on."

Frances smiled.

"OK so it's less of a route and more of a...meander, or something. But meandering suits me. I'm not, as you may have noticed, particularly ambitious. I'm quite happy in my own classroom, getting down with the kids, having some time to surf and play golf…"

"Work on your novel…"

"You surely don't disapprove of that?"

"Absolutely not. In fact right now your mode of meandering has considerable appeal. Well, maybe not the golf. It's what you've been doing for the past five years and you clearly thrive on it. But you're now in that zone where you either make a move, or you're going to be meandering for the next thirty years. And this opportunity is coming up now. I just wanted to make sure you were thinking about it."

"Well I appreciate the heads up. It's just…I really haven't much sympathy for the direction education is heading right now. I suppose I feel that if I keep my head down I can keep doing more or less what I like, and so long as the results keep coming in I can ignore all the sound and fury from Anton and Co."

"But this is a pastoral role. You'd only have dear old Emily to keep happy. And, you know, she won't be around forever."

"Well let's not hurry Emily into an early grave for the sake of my brilliant career."

"No indeed. But Dave, I wouldn't encourage you if I didn't think you'd do a really great job. And there will be others going for it. You'll need to look like you want it."

"Oh Gawd!"

"Maybe time to quietly step away from the Idlers Club."

Dave looked at her, mock sternly. "Frances, You know I can't discuss the Idlers Club, if indeed such an organisation exists." He rose. "Look, thanks for the encouragement. I will give it some thought. And…you can put me down for the London trip."

"Ah, you're a star. We'll have fun. There will be larks. But no condoms."

In the kitchen of their council house on the Penhale estate, Donkey Doggett faced his older brother Jason across the kitchen table, while his mother, a thin woman with a pinched face, paced around them anxiously. A squat Staffordshire bull terrier was snuffling at a bowl of meat in one corner.

"It's straightforward enough Donny," said his brother softly. "You get alongside someone – someone who ain't goin to squeal to the teacher, and you make friends. You get on their insta account, or their snapchat, or whatever, and you start to share stuff. That's all you gotta do."

Donkey squirmed uncomfortably.

"It i'nt that easy, Jase. I've got mates from the estate. Loads of them. It'll look a bit weird if I start cosying up to other folk."

"It's gotta be somebody who doesn't live on the estate," said Jason. Somebody you're not going to worry too much about putting a bit of pressure on, when the time comes. So it's not got to be any of your real mates."

"What's this all about anyway," said Mrs Doggett plaintively. "Why don't you just leave the boy alone?"

"Keep out of this, won't you ma? I've got a business opportunity I'm being offered by the Bristol guys, but I need to recruit a team. Donny's going to help me, is all." He turned back to Donkey.

"Well do you want to give it a try, or don't you?"

"Isn't there something else I can do? Be like a courier or something?"

"Well that's a possibility too. But we start with the simple stuff. You know what the old man says. Them as are faithful in small things will be trusted with greater things."

Mr Doggett, who was at that time detained in Exeter at Her Majesty's pleasure, had had a strict Methodist upbringing, and unexpected fragments of biblical wisdom had found their way into the family's shared discourse.

"Well…I'll give it a try."

"Good," said Jason. "Good lad. What's for tea, ma?"

Chapter Five

"The genial manner of Mr Singleman"

"Guess what?" said Issy the next morning, as the bus swung out onto the main road.

"What?" Sammy perked up. This conspiratorial tone was more like the old Issy.

"Mr Singleman and your form tutor are going to be neighbours." She kept her voice low. Her parents had drummed into her the importance of confidentiality regarding tenants, particularly those from the school, and it was a mark of her faith in Sammy's discretion that she was sharing this intelligence at all.

"At Wheal Prosper?"

"Yup. Your Miss Porteous has taken the ground floor flat."

"It's Ms Porteous."

"Ms then, whatever. Actually I approve of Ms. I'd be a Ms if I was a teacher."

"Doesn't really work though. Everyone just calls her "Miss", Same with Miss Fivey."

"Well I'm going to try and remember to call her Ms. You should too. You said you were a feminist."

"I am. I've got a tee shirt."

"You should wear it more often."

"I wore it last own clothes day. Didn't half get the piss taken out of me."

"Anyway. Porteous and Singleman. What d'you reckon?"

"How do you mean?"

"As a thing. He definitely needs a girlfriend. But would they make a good couple?"

Sammy laughed. "I don't know. I don't really know what she's like yet. She seems OK."

"Would you say she was nice-looking?"

Sammy pondered this. They had never before discussed the attractiveness of an adult, or for that matter anybody their own age.

"Yeah I guess she's all right. Maybe a bit…forbidding."

"That'll just be a teacher thing. If you're a new teacher you're not meant to smile till Christmas."

"I've got Singleman for English again."

"Yeah me too. I think we're in the top set."

"Cool."

The bus swung onto the hard standing at the bottom of the hill, bringing an end to their discussion, and the gaggle of students who shared their journey disinterred their back packs, games kit and musical instruments from beneath their seats, and resolved themselves into a more or less orderly queue for disembarkation, and the steady unenthusiastic plod up the hill.

In the staff car park, Kate Porteous stood beside her car, her brow furrowed. She had come in early that morning to visit the gym, spending twenty minutes on the running machine and doing a bit of stretching. It was a small but reasonably well equipped facility that was open to staff and sixth formers before and after school. That morning it had been quiet, though Killick, the deputy, had been there, performing a series of impressive looking kung fu type exercises. She hadn't particularly taken to Anton Killick at her interview, though he had been courteous and professional throughout, but there was no denying he was in great physical shape. She had her ear buds in, and faced determinedly to the front as she pounded away on the conveyor, but it had been difficult to entirely disregard the high-kicking and posturing in the periphery of her vision, and the sculpted triceps.

By the time she returned to her car to deposit her gym gear and collect her briefcase it was nearly time for registration, and the car park was full. What gave her pause now was the car that had parked next to her – a slightly battered blue MG. Its roof was up, but she was fairly sure it was the same colour and model as the vehicle she had had her near miss with two days ago. She crossed to the driver's side and inspected the wing mirror. The dent was not large, but it was unmistakable. There was even a scuff of the Fiat's distinctive yellow paint.

Kate glanced around, but there was nobody nearby. She took out her phone and, keeping it discreetly at waist level, photographed the mirror. She took another picture of the number plate. Then she headed for the staff room, deep in thought. She was unsure as to whether anything was to be gained by confronting the owner of the car, who it now appeared was one of her teaching colleagues, or perhaps a member of the support staff. Yet it felt like unfinished business, the more so now that there might be a professional connection. Was it worth a confrontation? What, if anything, would be achieved? The owner of the MG would almost certainly be defensive, or worse. She tried to put the matter from her mind as she collected her registration folder and headed for her classroom.

She arrived a minute or two late. The form seemed happy enough to see her however, and the knot of girls who sat on the left greeted her cheerfully. Donkey was missing once more. She made a mental note to check his file and his previous reports.

"Year group assembly this morning miss," offered Sammy from the back of the form.

"Ah, yes so it is. Thank you. In the theatre, isn't it?"

"Yeah but we need to go now, miss. Or we'll have to sit on the floor."

Kate checked her watch. There was still the register to take, and one or two notes to pass on to individual students.

"Right, let's just do a quick head count...twenty seven. Three missing. And they are?

"Donkey!"

"Hardeep's got elite sports mentoring."

"Anna wasn't on the bus…"

"Okay – Hardeep, Donovan and Anna - thank you. I need to see Sammy briefly and Anoushka, please. The rest of you can head for assembly."

There was a scraping of chairs and a general exodus, while Sammy and Anoushka made their way to her desk.

"Just learning support reminders for you two."

She passed on the green reminder slips, and the two students followed their classmates out of the door.

"Oh Sammy. One other thing."

He turned back. "Yes miss?"

"You wouldn't happen to know who owns the old blue sports car in the staff car park, would you?"

"The MG?"

"If that's what it is."

"That's Mr Singleman's. He's 3M's tutor."

Through the door she could see Dave following his form down the stair.

"Ah yes, of course. I know Mr Singleman. Thank you. You'd better get on."

Kate busied herself with noting the absentees while Sammy hurried off to the theatre.

So it was Dave Singleman who had sped round the corner in that reckless way, and damaged her car as a consequence! Well, well. As she followed her form along to the theatre Kate reviewed her impressions of him so far. He seemed a decent enough bloke from what she'd seen of him. Nice eyes. Bit of a professional cynic, maybe. He had been pleasant and friendly on the Inset day, and his colleagues seemed to like him. The question was, where, if anywhere, she should take the matter from here.

She might of course just let the whole thing go – get the damage repaired and put it behind her. Or she could, in a non-threatening, perhaps even in a jokey way, bring it to his attention, and see how he reacted. That was assuming he didn't know already. What if he did? What if he had recognised her and was just waiting for the right moment to apologise? Or had clocked the damaged Fiat on the way in, and was even now wondering who it belonged to and what he, in his turn, ought to do. Maybe he would offer to make good the damage. Unlikely, but not out of the question. He must know he had been going faster than he ought.

In the theatre the staff sat on the balcony that ran along the side wall, where they were well placed to eyeball their charges should the need arise. As she made her way along she could see Dave Singleman, one seat from the end – and the end seat was vacant. She slipped in next to him. The students were still finding their places, and Sheila Abbot was busying herself with the laptop and a memory stick.

"Morning," said Kate, cheerily.

"Morning Kate. All well with you? Which form have you got then?"

"3G are mine."

"What are they like? They were all re-jigged last year."

"Yeah they seem OK. One lad who wants me to call him Donkey seems to have punctuality issues."

"Ah yes. Donovan Doggett. Crown Prince of the Penhale estate. He was quite a handful last year, but who knows – he may settle down a bit in year nine."

"Like they usually do?"

"Well… I take your point. Anyway – don't hesitate to give me a shout if you need a hand with anything. I'm just across the corridor."

Further conversation was prevented by the Head of Year calling the theatre to order, and embarking upon a litany of encouragement and warning appropriate to the first assembly of the year. Teacher and pupil alike listened attentively, or at least gave the impression of doing so.

Fifteen minutes later, the assembly over, they were once more standing in a throng of students as the theatre emptied itself and the various classes headed for lessons. Kate deliberately avoided Dave on her way out. The conversation in the theatre had reinforced two impressions in her mind – Dave Singleman was essentially a pleasant, well-meaning colleague who wished to be friendly and supportive, and he was entirely oblivious to the fact that he had damaged her car.

She had a free lesson after the assembly, which she had intended to use to read up on some policy documents. Up in the staff workroom, however, seated at the computer, she found it difficult to concentrate. She googled the local Fiat dealer but could find no information about the cost of mirrors. The workroom was empty, so she rang the dealer and explained the issue. She was told that it was impossible to give a quotation without a visual inspection, but it could easily be a couple of hundred pounds, depending on the extent of the damage. She was welcome to come in that afternoon and they would look at it for her.

Two hundred quid was a big ask in her current circumstances, and she was due to sign the lease for Wheal Prosper after school. Bugger! Decent he might be, and ignorant of the damage he had caused, but she found her irritation rising at the genial manner of Mr Singleman. And thinking about it, what was all that patronising bollocks about "give me a shout if you need a hand with anything"? If you can't handle your difficult students, was the clear implication.

She glanced at her watch and realised that half her free lesson had already gone. She hauled her attention back to the task in hand.

An enjoyable lesson with an enthusiastic Year Seven group improved her mood considerably, and she headed to the staffroom at breaktime in a more settled frame of mind. If her first week wasn't to be hijacked by this silly business there were two things she needed to do. Find exactly how much the damage to her car was going to cost to repair, and square things off with Singleman. There was no virtue in falling out with a colleague with whom, in all probability, she would benefit from maintaining friendly relationships, especially if he was completely ignorant as to the reasons for her hostility. The first opportunity she got, she would put him in the picture, without making any assumptions as to what his response might be.

Dave had had his free lesson immediately before break, and when Kate arrived in the staffroom with her good intentions he was already there, chatting to a couple of the Idlers. They were discussing the chances of getting a game of golf that weekend, the weather being forecast to break.

"To be honest," said Dave, it would suit me to give it a miss. "I had a minor prang in the MG the other day, and I need to get round the scrappies."

"Much damage done?" This was Robbo, who taught PE.

"Nah, just a dent in the wing mirror. Some crazy woman came round the bend at Wheal Prosper on the wrong side of the road. Actually, to be fair, I'm just assuming it was a woman from the car. I was too busy avoiding instant death to notice who was driving."

Kate had made herself a coffee and positioned herself strategically a few feet behind the group, with the aim of catching Dave's attention if the chance arose. Consequently she heard, quite clearly, his brusque and partisan account of the accident. She bristled with indignation, but what came next was worse.

"What kind of car was it?"

"Fiat 500."

"Deffo a woman's car," opined Stubbsy, an angular, acned young man who had joined the history department the previous year as an NQT.

"Yeah, well it would figure."

Hashtag everyday sexism, thought Kate indignantly.

"Anyway, we knocked wing mirrors, and mine's got a bit of a dent."

"Won't have done hers much good."

"Well that's her problem. If anyone was in the wrong she was."

"She didn't stop then?"

"Nah – shot off round the bend, never to be seen again."

"I wouldn't worry. Her hubbie will pay for a new one."

"Yeah – no scrabbling around scrapyards in the rain for her."

Kate got up and left, her coffee undrunk. Robbo looked up as she rose, and watched her head for the door.

"That your new English colleague?"

"Where?"

"Just gone out. She was sitting behind you."

Dave turned round in time to see Kate disappear into the corridor.

"Yeah – Kate Porteous."

"She's not bad looking."

"Neat little ass," said Stubbsy.

Dave grimaced. "Please. We're not in the pub now."

The bell rang at that moment and they rose to begin the second half of morning school.

Chapter Six

"Not exactly bosom mates"

At lunchtime Kate sat alone in a corner of the dining hall, reflecting upon how quickly you could go off people, and indeed places. This was exactly what she had left her last school to get away from – dinosaur male colleagues who didn't make too much effort to hide their sexist assumptions. The lesson before lunch had been difficult, too – a low set Year Nine group with, among others, Donkey Doggett and a group of his mates, in uncooperative mood. That was clearly a class that was going to take some thinking about, and possibly an industrial grade bollocking in the not too distant future if it wasn't to become the bane of her Friday, week after week.

Jenny Skinner had sat with her over lunch, and while Kate could see that Jenny was a good and sweet person, just at that moment her light, self-deprecating chatter was not what she needed. Jenny's long story of the difficulties she faced that weekend with getting her children to two different parties and finishing her marking - what with the washing machine having packed up too - had been met with monosyllabic politeness on Kate's part, and Jenny had made her excuses and left. Kate knew she had been not far short of rude, and now she toyed miserably with her dessert, a comfortless concoction of butterscotch paste on top of a digestive biscuit.

At that moment Frances Fivey glided into view and waved at her. Something in Kate's response must have communicated her mood, and Frances altered course to join her.

"All right? You look a bit pissed off."

"Guilty as charged."

"Oh dear! What's happened?" Frances descended elegantly into the seat beside her. "Were your year nine a bit restless? Mine were."

"Well…yes they were hard going."

"You've got the bottom set, haven't you? I remember we did think long and hard about who we put in there. We can take another look at it if you've got some really tricky customers."

"Well – give me another couple of weeks with them. I ought to be able to sort them out. It's just been a full-on week – lots of new things, you know, then I had a bit of a prang in my car…"

"Oh no! is there much damage?"

"Just the wing mirror. But it turns out…you won't believe this but I'm pretty sure it was a colleague that ran into me." And she went on to explain the whole story to Frances, including the casual banter of Dave and his mates in the staffroom.

"…and I'm afraid I haven't much tolerance for that kind of thing. I came from a Boys' Grammar school, as you know, and attitudes like that were run of the mill there. I suppose I expected it to be different here."

Frances listened in sympathetic silence until she sensed the story was done.

"Yes, well. Lads will be lads, even in lovely Cornwall. They're not my thing personally but some people seem to like them. But look – I might be able to reassure you. I've worked with Dave for the last five years, and he's a genuinely nice guy. I'm sure he's got his blind spots but fundamentally he's sound. I certainly wouldn't describe him as sexist. Who was he talking to?"

"I don't know. A tall bloke in a tracksuit and a spotty kid who looked like he's just out the sixth form."

"Ah. You've just encountered the Idlers– the staff room chapter of the Jeremy Clarkson fan club. They are, almost certainly, the embodiment of everything you despise, but personally I just find them amusing."

"And Dave is a member of this group?"

"Well – he's a bit semi-detached, I think. And he knows they represent his worst self. It's just – he's a single bloke, and they're all into the same kind of stuff – surfing, golf, cars. He's not really like them. And to be honest, Robbo is quite a decent guy too when you're dealing with him on a practical level – he's in the same year team as me. The one they call Stubbsy I don't really know. He's not been here long."

"I suppose, to be fair, Dave wasn't the one making the really crass comments. But he clearly thinks the accident was my fault. Is there such a thing as a woman's car?"

"Probably, sadly. Anyway, you need to put this behind you. What are you doing tonight?"

"Nothing much – I've got to sort out the paperwork on a flat I'm renting. And maybe get the garage to look at my car."

"Come round to mine. We're planning an evening of gin-research. All girls, all good fun."

"Oh. That's really kind. I'm not much of a gin-drinker…"

"It's never too late to start. And anyway, there'll be tonic, so you can dilute to taste. 4 Union Place. Just behind the town hall. About 8?"

"Well – yes, thank you, that would be lovely."

"Excellent! Now I must go." Frances rose, and briefly resting a hand on Kate's shoulder smiled dazzlingly before sweeping imperiously out of the dining hall, past a knot of latecomers who were peering hopefully into the custard urn. Kate stacked up her dishes and rose from the table.

Up in the English departmental office, Dave Singleman was pondering the best approach to the last lesson of his teaching week. He had his Upper Sixth A level group – a cheery enough bunch whom he had taught last year, and with whom he had a strong and productive relationship. The question was, this being last period on a Friday, was it worth beginning the new text they would be studying that term? Or might there still be one or two late back from holiday, or indeed bunking off on the assumption that work would start in earnest the following week? There was a rather good DVD about Thomas Hardy on the shelf – that might serve as a worthwhile but undemanding introduction to the unit…

The door opened and Frances came in.

"Almost the weekend!" she said brightly. "All good so far?"

"Fine thanks, said Dave. "Just debating what to do with the Upper Sixth." They shared the group, so Frances knew them well.

"You might find there's one or two missing. I had them earlier in the day."

"Really? That settles it then. I've got them Monday morning – we'll hit the ground running then."

"I think that might be wise."

Dave picked the Hardy DVD off the shelf, and was about to head for the door, when he noticed Frances looking at him oddly.

"Everything all right?"

"Well…it's our new colleague. She's had a bit of a week. Somebody knocked the wing mirror off her car."

"Well I can sympathise. Something very similar happened to me."

"Yes. I don't think that's as much of a coincidence as you might assume."

Dave sat down at the table. "Really? What kind of car does she drive?"

"Oh I don't know- she did tell me but I've no interest in cars. It's bright yellow and it's quite new."

"Shit. Did she say where it happened."

"Out by Wheal Prosper. She's clocked your car and put two and two together but she's not sure what to do. I don't think your breaktime conversation with the Idlers did much to reassure her."

"Eeurghhh! They – ok make that *we* – were being a bit laddish. Damn! The accident was probably her fault if it was anybody's, but if I had known it was a colleague I'd at least have said something. What do you think I should do?"

"Well I think if you were able to just let her know you're aware of what happened and maybe be really nice about it, that would be one thing she could cross off her worry list."

"Right. Yes of course. But…did you say the mirror was knocked right off?"

"Apparently so. What about yours?"

"Just a dent. That Fiat was quite new and shiny too, now you mention it. Bugger!"

At that point the bell rang for the start of the next lesson, and Kate herself came into the workroom. She stopped and looked at them both. Frances smiled winningly, but Dave's face told its own story. She reddened, turned and went straight back into the corridor.

Dave turned to Frances and made a face like an ancient Greek tragedy mask.

"What now Boss?"

"She's got to teach now. How about you come back here after school and we'll try to patch things up before the weekend."

"My lot are going to be watching a DVD, so I could come out of the lesson if I had to."

"OK that might work. Leave it with me." She smiled at his crestfallen expression. "It'll be fine. It's only a wing mirror. You're both sensible people."

In his classroom Dave set up the DVD and did his best to greet his students in something like his usual manner. As Frances had predicted, there were a couple of absentees.

"Are we watching a DVD, Sir?"

It was a stock question, uttered as a matter of course by students of all ages when they detect the slightest evidence of such a possibility. In the current circumstances it provoked Dave to his first descent into sarcasm that year.

"No, we're going to make pancakes."

"Are we really Sir?"

"I think he's kidding."

"Of course we're watching a DVD, bozo! Which one is it Sir?"

"Is it the Tempest with the naked men?"

"Did you have a good summer Sir?"

"Yes thank you Jonathan, I had a good summer. It seems a long time ago. No Jasmine, it is not the Tempest with the naked men, that was last year, although it is possible we may return to it in the summer for revision purposes."

"Please no sir, it grosses me out."

"It is in fact a DVD about Thomas Hardy, whose poetry, as I think you are aware, we are studying this term. It contains no nudity, violence or bad language. You could watch it with your grandparents. No need to take notes – just sit back and absorb what you can. The hard work begins next week."

"Cheers Sir."

"Good move Sir."

"You're a gent!"

Well I like to think so, thought Dave as the DVD began and the class settled down to watch.

Twenty minutes later Frances stuck her head round the door. Dave rose and went over to her.

"How about you leave this lot for ten minutes and swing by the workroom? I'll look after Kate's class and you two can have a chat about wing mirrors."

Dave thought about it. "I'm not sure what I'm going to say. It's kind of awkward."

"It's not going to get any less awkward."

"True." He paused. "OK. Now?"

"I think so. This lot look reasonably absorbed."

"Fine."

He considered saying something to the class but decided against it. There was a kind of fragile bubble of concentration in the room that it seemed wiser not to break. He followed Frances into the corridor and slipped into the workroom.

Should he sit down? Or stand? Standing might appear threatening. But sitting, when he was first in the room, might look like a power play. He decided to try sitting in a relaxed and disarming manner.

A minute or two passed. The chairs were made of hard moulded plastic, and not conducive to a relaxed posture. He picked up a Year 9 reader that was sitting on the table, and leafed through it aimlessly.

The door opened, and Kate entered. She looked composed. Dave immediately felt profoundly awkward and rose to his feet. Kate sat down, so Dave sat down too.

"Um, right," he began, but she had started to speak at the same time.

"Sorry, you go first."

"No, you."

"OK." He cleared his throat. "Frances has explained that it was your car that I knocked mirrors with yesterday out at Wheal Prosper. She says it's quite badly damaged."

"Well, the mirror's now on the back seat."

"OK, and I appreciate it's a newish car…"

"It's two years old."

"Sure, sure. I've never had a new car myself but I can imagine that's quite upsetting."

"Only in that it's going to be expensive to fix."

"Shit."

"You said it."

"OK." Dave swallowed. "I think I'd like to say, in the manner of two people who bump into one another in a supermarket, when it's not really anybody's fault, but somebody's shopping ends up on the floor, that I'm really sorry. But having said that…"

"You don't accept any responsibility?"

"Well… you were quite far over…"

"I was on my own side of the road…"

"I'm not 100% sure you were…"

"I am. And I wasn't going fast – I'd only just pulled out from the parking area."

"At Wheal Prosper?"

"That's right. You on the other hand came flying round that bend."

"You think I'm responsible?"

Kate hesitated. "In part, yes."

"I know that stretch of road fairly well. It's a forty limit and I was doing thirty-five tops. So you might have felt I was flying round, if you weren't going fast yourself, but that doesn't mean I was driving dangerously, or even breaking the speed limit. And…" he paused. "You said you were coming off the parking area at Wheal Prosper?"

"Yes."

"Do you mind me asking what took you there?"

"I don't see that that's got any relevance."

"OK…it's just generally speaking people don't turn right off there, because of the bend. They go left, and cut back round via the lanes."

There was a pause, Kate had a vision of Sue Brunel's Range Rover turning left down the hill, spitting gravel from its back tyres as it went.

"I wouldn't know what people usually do."

Their eyes met. She held his gaze but said nothing further. Dave spoke into the gap.

"Look, I think there's two issues here. One is the question of the damage to your car and whether anybody is at fault. I'm not sure how that gets resolved. The other is, you're a new colleague and we're going to be working together and I'm sure neither of us wants to get off to a bad start."

"I think that ship might have sailed."

"Well I appreciate it's not a nice way to end your first week. But surely we don't need to fall out over it? Let's put the damage issue to one side at the moment. Can we at least agree we're not enemies?"

Kate suddenly felt very tired, and outmanoeuvred.

"I guess…" she paused.

"Please? And I'll give some thought to what we do about the damage."

"OK. Not enemies." She paused. "I should have asked if your car was damaged."

"Nothing I can't fix myself."

"Good. OK. I'd better get back to my class."

"Me too."

She rose and turned, leaving the room without looking back at him.

Not enemies, he thought, as he walked the few yards back to his classroom. But not exactly bosom mates either.

Chapter Seven

"His aspirations to the writing life"

Kate headed to the letting agent after school, to finalise the arrangements for her new flat. This proved straightforward enough, and left her enough time to visit the Fiat dealer on the outskirts of town. The service engineer looked sceptically at the mirror, and ran his fingers over the bodywork at the top of the door.

"Well your mirror's had it, but the paintwork's not too bad – that little bit of scuffing where it's knocked against the door will come up nice enough with some T-cut."

"The guy I spoke to said it could be as much a couple of hundred."

"That would include fitting, but to be honest it's not too tricky, if you've got a fella that could do it for you."

"I've got a socket set, and I'm reasonably intelligent," said Kate. "Would that be enough?"

The mechanic looked a little discomfited.

"I guess so. No offence meant."

"None taken," smiled Kate.

"Come into the office and I'll give you a price."

Kate followed him into the service office and waited while he scrolled through some pages on his computer.

"What's the registration please?"

Kate told him. The man made a quiet popping noise with his lips as he tweaked his mouse. It was hard to tell if it was pessimistic popping or just something to fill the silence.

"£145.75 including the VAT for the mirror unit and the casing. Have you been to us before?"

"No – I've just moved down."

"We can do you a new customer discount if you provide us with your email address and the date your next service is due."

"I'm happy to do that."

"Then that'll be £131.25, if you're fitting it yourself. We don't have the part in stock but it should be here by Monday if I order it now."

"Great!"

She left the Fiat dealer feeling lighter in spirit, as one does when an apparent disaster turns out to be less serious than it first appeared - a hundred and thirty quid was steep, but bearable. While her workroom meeting with Dave Singleman had left her feeling slightly bruised, and in some obscure way tricked out of any realistic possibility of recompense for the damage, it had at least drawn a line of sorts under the affair. Tonight she had her evening at Frances's to look forward to, and her new home to move into in the morning. Things were getting back on track.

Dave had not been entirely straight with the Idlers when he made his golfing excuses at breaktime. He did not intend to spend his weekend combing the scrap yards, but he had other business that would take him out of the county until Sunday. He was heading to Somerset for a weekend house-party at the home of one of the would-be writers he had met on his course that summer. *Mousehole!* and his aspirations to the writing life were not things he cared to share with the Idlers. Now he was sitting in stationery traffic on the M5 as the world turned slowly to indigo. He was still at least an hour from his destination.

He shifted in the less than generously upholstered driver's seat of the MG, and snapped off the radio, having heard as much as he wished to hear of the day's news. His mind drifted back to late July, to the golden week he had spent a few miles from Glastonbury, and the friends he had made. The course had been intended to kickstart his novel, a project to carry him through the quiet, surf-less evenings of the coming winter, and while it had achieved that objective, he had since added little to the 2000 words or so that he had produced that week. He was determined however that come the change of the clocks at the end of October, he would see it through, not because he was convinced of its literary value, but because writing professionally was one of the few things he could see himself doing to earn a living outside teaching.

He had been reluctant initially to apply for the course. It was not cheap - he could have had a week surfing in Morocco for the money – and he knew that he was not really a sit-in-a-circle-and-bare-your-soul kind of writer – more the solitary, sit-in-an-attic-and-freeze-your bollocks-off variety. However, from the moment the MG had swung into the yard of the medieval manor house where the course was taking place, something told him the experience was going to be worth it, whatever the consequences for his *meisterwerk*.

There had been a dozen students, split evenly between the sexes and spread in age from twenty to seventy. They came from all walks of life – some already earning reasonable money from writing while others, like himself, had never had anything published. There had been a tax inspector and a taxidermist, a pole-dancer and former soldier. But their working lives were the one thing they didn't much talk about, as if they all knew they were there as part of a grand scheme to get away from all of that crap.

Each of them had a cell like study bedroom in what had once been the piggery, but they cooked and ate together in the manor house, sitting round a vast refectory table, surrounded by books. In the mornings two resident tutors, themselves successful writers, led workshops and set exercises, and in the afternoons they wrote in their quarters, reconvening in the evenings to drink wine, play literary games, and share their work. Over the five days Dave had got *Mousehole!* out of the blocks, and picked up numerous useful tips, but more importantly he had just had a bloody good time – possibly more fun even than he would have had at Magic Bay.

Most of them were west country based, and as they had gelled so well, the offer from one of the group to host a follow-up weekend had been enthusiastically received. Candice had already published one work of erotic fiction, and though she said there was no money in it she had rocked up in a massive Audi, and she assured them that there was "loads of room, darlings," at the old rectory she shared with her stockbroker husband and three Rhodesian ridgebacks.

Whatever obstruction had brought the northbound carriageway to a halt resolved itself, and the traffic began to move. The MG climbed through the gears and Dave became aware that he was hungry. Supper was scheduled for 9, and at this rate he might just make it.

Sammy helped his Mum into the passenger seat of the pickup, while his dad folded the wheelchair and heaved it into the back with the wheelbarrows and spades. A guitar in its hard case completed the incongruous cargo. The rain wasn't forecast to come in until Saturday afternoon, so there was no need to fix the tarpaulin. Sammy climbed in the driver's side and shuffled along the bench seat next to his Mum. She had already fastened her seatbelt, and he attended to his own lap-strap. Viv Pascoe jumped in and pulled the driver's door closed with a bang.

"Got your whistles Maisy?"

"In me bag. Drum's at me feet."

"Right on!"

The ancient Nissan coughed into life and they swung out into the lane. They weren't going far. Once a month there was a folk night at a pub in the neighbouring village, and folk music, particularly Cornish songs and tunes from an age when mining and fishing were the mainstays of existence for local communities, was one of the things that bound the Pascoe family together.

Dusk was falling as they arrived and parked, and already music and chatter floated out from the bar. Sammy pushed his Mum in the wheelchair, struggling a little to manoeuvre her up the step and through the narrow doorway. She had a brightly coloured knitted bag with her whistles and the flat circular drum across her knees. Viv Pascoe brought up the rear with the guitar. They were greeted warmly as they entered. Willing hands were extended to assist, and space made in the crude circle that those who had come to perform or share in the music had made around the room.

Among all this, other drinkers stood and chatted, though a degree of respect would be shown during the songs. In any case, once the evening got going properly, and the Betty Stoggs was flowing, they would be onto the favourites that they all knew by heart, and the talkers wouldn't have a chance. Viv saw his family settled, then made his way to the bar to get the first round in. A girl in the corner by the fire was coaxing a tune from a battered melodeon. Sammy looked around at the familiar, friendly, lived-in faces and wondered, as he often did on these Friday nights in the pub, what Issy and her family were doing.

Issy and her family were at home, finishing their supper. The Brunels lived a mile outside Eglos, in a handsome modern property with an abundance of decking and bi-fold doors that her parents had built ten years ago, when her father had sold his successful printing business in Surrey and they had come down to pursue the good life. Issy could remember as a small child being shown the site, and the plans, and the long journeys down and back to Cornwall while it was being built. Her little sister Pheobe had been born not long after they moved in, and the four of them sat now round the light oak table in the cathedral-like kitchen.

Mr Brunel divided the remains of a good bottle of Sancerre between his own and his wife's glasses, elegant, wafer thin globes, two of which could have held the entire contents of the bottle at first pouring. Issy, who was permitted an inch or so of wine for her own consumption on a Friday night, was already aware that this was not, of course what one did.

"Please may I leave the table?" Her phone, which was set to silent, had buzzed in the back pocket of her jeans.

"You may," said her mother. "But I'd like a hand with the clearing up."

"Can I do it later? I need to do my piano practice."

"Does the piano practice need to be done right now?"

"Well…I'm kind of in the mood just now."

Her mother looked at her. Isadora was reasonably keen on her piano, working towards Grade 5. It was true that she probably wasn't quite so keen on stacking the dishwasher.

"You go and do your practice now," said her father. "I'll help your mother clear."

"Cheers dad!" She got down from the table and left the room.

"Please may I leave the table?" said Phoebe.

"Yes of course. Have you packed your ballet things?"

Phoebe made a puzzled face, finger to lips as if this were a complex question that required a considered response.

"Sort it out, please, Phoebes," said her father. "I'm taking you tomorrow morning and I don't want any last-minute faffing around."

"OK" sang Phoebe, jumping down from her seat and disappearing into the hall.

In the music room Issy was studying her phone. Finally, finally, he had got in touch.

Hi babes I is missing you. Luv Enrique xxxxx

She studied the message, committing it to memory, then texted back.

Missing u 2. Loads of Luv. Issy xxxxx

In a moment or two a passably competent rendering of Fűr Elise could be heard coming from the music room. Sue Brunel smiled at her husband over the last of her Sancerre.

In a layby off a B-road somewhere in the Somerset Levels, Dave was peering at a map by torchlight. By his reckoning he had missed a turning about two miles back. He didn't possess a satnav, and the battery on his phone was low. He wanted to save it in case he needed to call Candice, and in any case he liked maps. A satnav was useful in getting you to your destination, but you never had a sense of where you actually were. He folded the map so that he could check it again easily if required, and threw it and the torch onto the passenger seat. He arched his back and stretched, then got back into the car and executed a neat U-turn before accelerating off into the darkness.

In a white, square, largely empty room of modest proportions, on an anonymous housing estate on the other side of town from St Petroc's, Anton Killick sat cross legged on a mat. He had been sitting in this position, back straight, head erect, eyes closed, for an hour. It was one of his spiritual exercises. He wore loose fitting black linen trousers and a white tee shirt. He felt completely calm. The only sound in the room was a faint scratching from a cage on the sideboard, where two white rats rootled busily among their wood shavings.

Killick opened his eyes slowly, and allowed himself to register what the small digital clock on the windowsill had to tell him. He smiled. It was one of the indicators of mastery that one's unconscious was capable of signalling when it was time to emerge from the meditative state.

It was nine o'clock, but he had not yet eaten. He would permit himself a bowl of yoghurt, with some of the berries he had had shipped in from South Korea, before he went to bed. Saturday morning was the Taekwondo session at the gym in Plymouth, and he wanted to be in the best possible state for that. There was a club in town that he attended on Wednesday evenings, but it was populated by just the kind of amateurs one would expect in the provinces, dilettantes who had no interest in the pursuit of mastery, whose participation in the martial art was an act of self-indulgence and self-aggrandisement. For Killick, Taekwondo was one element in a total programme focused on the betterment not just of oneself (although that was a by-product, and not one to be in any way ashamed of) but of the world.

Darkness fell over the housing estate. Five miles away the same darkness wrapped itself around the Brunels' brightly lit home on the outskirts of Eglos and settled outside the windows of the little inn in the next village, from which came the sound of Cornish voices raised in song. In the brightly lit heart of the town, where a group of women in the prime of life drank gin together and roared with laughter at the follies of men, it went entirely un-noticed.

Chapter Eight

"She deserved not to be spurned"

The Old Rectory at Norton Fitzpiers was a sprawling Gothic confection set in generous gardens. Where exactly the flock of the one-time incumbent resided was unclear, as there had been barely a light for miles around as Dave approached. He paused now on the doorstep, breathing in the night air, and enjoying the anticipation of the evening to come. Inside he could hear voices, high laughter, the occasional chink of cutlery.

He gave a tug on the heavy brass bell-pull to the right of the front door. There was a low jangle of chimes, followed by a deep growling and a skittering of claws on tiled floor, then a crash, as the door itself – not a lightweight affair- vibrated visibly under the weight of what was presumably one of the Rhodesian ridgebacks. A second later this growl-skitter-crash crescendo was repeated. Dave took a step to the side and waited for the third. It didn't come. Instead the door opened a couple of inches.

"Daaave! Hi! You made it!" Candice's low husky voice came through the crack. "Now listen darling, I'm going to let Hughie and Dewey out, so you must just stand to one side or you'll get knocked over. They wouldn't harm a fly, but they are a bit *boisterous,* I'm afraid..."

Dave did as he was told. Candice opened the door and two enormous lean tan coloured dogs shot past him and bounded down the steps, disappearing off into the darkness. Where the hell was Louie?

"Darling!" Candice formed herself into a tableau of the greeting hostess, glass in one hand, other extended towards him, eyes closed and chin arched forward to receive his one-two kisses. She was wearing a black cocktail dress that accentuated her still impressive figure, and Dave felt travel-grimy and underdressed.

"I thought tomorrow evening was the smart bit," he said apologetically.

"Well yes, but I'm the hostess, darling. I make and break rules at will." This was accompanied by a smoky chuckle that was vaguely indecent. "Now look, we've just begun to eat but it's a buffet so people are drifting around all over the place. Do you want me to show you your room now, or would you rather just join the party? Just join the party! What would you like to drink?"

"A beer would be great thanks – whatever you've got."

She led him across a high square hall in the direction of the laughter.

"Look who's here, everyone!"

"Dave!"

"Hullo mate!"

"Hi Dave! Come and sit here - look we've saved you a space."

The room was brightly lit. He crossed to join a group of three familiar faces on a large comfortable sofa. The third ridgeback, presumably of a less excitable disposition, was spread in front of the fire, legs out at right-angles to its body in a posture that lent it the substantial elegance of a piece of good quality furniture. It was slightly overwhelming, after the capsule-like darkness of the MG's cockpit, to be thrust among these friendly, smiling revellers, whom he realised in that moment he barely knew. Most were by now on their second or third drink. All had plates of food. Some, thankfully, were in jeans. He gathered himself.

"Hello, hello, everyone. Sorry I'm late! Great to see you all! Look just let me grab a beer and some food…"

"Here's your beer darling," said Candice. "You sit down and I'll fill a plate for you."

He joined the group on the sofa. After a few routine enquiries as to his journey the chatter moved on from the novelty of his arrival, and in the space this made, fortified by the beer and a groaning plateful of food, he was able to recalibrate to match the pace and intensity of the party. Within twenty minutes or so he felt once again at ease.

He awoke late the next day, in a small attic bedroom with a sloping ceiling and a tiny dormer window. The bed linen was expensive, as was the Egyptian cotton bath towel draped over a stripped pine rocking chair in the corner. After the initial dislocation of his late arrival, the evening had settled into a pleasant session of catching up and general chit chat – book talk, or gossip column stuff that he could negotiate either through his relatively superficial knowledge of such things, or by declaring his ignorance and pleading for enlightenment. Just as in summer they had spoken little of their professional lives, so last night they had by tacit agreement avoided discussion of their works in progress. That was scheduled to take place over morning coffee, according to the rough programme that had been proposed, and from which Candice might presumably depart at any point.

He showered and dressed in clean clothes, and made his way downstairs. In the daylight his impression of the size of the property was confirmed. There were three floors, including his own on the attic level, which had its own bathroom and two other bedrooms. A galleried landing with several bedrooms – and presumably bathrooms - ran round the large hall, and on the ground floor there were three or four stately square rooms, decorated in a style and palette popular a decade or two previously – deep greens and crimsons; Laura Ashley or Liberty curtains with matching tiebacks. Clearly Candice was a stranger to the Ikea catalogue.

He found his way to the kitchen where a small knot of guests was negotiating a rotation of kettle, toaster, fridge and microwave.

"Morning all."

"Good Morning Dave. Did you sleep well?" This was Colin, a lean ex-Marine in his fifties who had spent a lot of time overseas.

"Yes thanks. I take it we just help ourselves."

"Apparently so. Candice floated in earlier and waved her hand vaguely in the direction of the fridge and that cupboard, which is where most of the cereals are to be found. There's bread and pastries in a basket on the table. She's gone off to walk the dogs."

Colin moved off with his croissants. He walked on the balls of his feet, as if ready at any time to dive for cover. Dave moved to the front of the toaster queue where Marina, who was writing something bleak set in a Newcastle abattoir, was nursing a mug of black coffee.

"Any idea how this works?" The toaster had a set of controls that would have graced the dashboard of Howard Hughes's speedboat.

"You press that one down first – then set the dial, then pop the bread in – there,"

"Cheers Marina."

"The coffee maker's worse. But there are some cafetieres."

"I'm happy with instant."

"Candice doesn't do instant. Or PG Tips."

"Lucky old us. I don't think I've met Mr Candice yet. Is he here?"

"Henry's been packed off to town for the weekend. Apparently he's very understanding."

"As in, he's happy to have his home taken over by writers?"

"As in he and Candice lead parallel lives. I believe there are others involved."

"I see." He paused to absorb this, connected it briefly with the little black number, the smoky, indecent chuckle. "We're meeting at 11, is that right?"

"That's the plan. Circle time to share where we're all at with our writing, then free time until supper at 7, and after that we read from our work. Then - general hilarity."

Dave's toast popped up, looking much as toast did on emerging from more humble appliances. He reached for the butter.

"I'd better get some writing done then, or I'll have nothing new to share. What about you?"

"I've made some progress."

It transpired at the eleven o'clock sharing session that everyone except Dave had made progress. The body count had steadily risen in the crime thrillers; and the romances had all duly met their Act 2 setbacks. Colin's tale of mercenaries in Afghanistan had acquired another 5000 words, while Candice's pole dancing memoir continued to weave its sinuous course through the red-light districts of northern Europe. Even Nigel, the part-time taxidermist, whose pastoral novel set in the Lake District, to everyone's disappointment, was set to contain not a single episode of taxidermy, had added a chapter or two of cloudy wandering. Only *Mousehole!* remained stubbornly stalled, and he determined to spend that afternoon, which was looking wet anyway, in his bedroom with his laptop.

Thinking back, Dave couldn't remember when the wine started to flow. Around five, perhaps? He had toiled away diligently all afternoon, and had knocked off fifteen hundred words, leaving time to apply a bit of sparkle - it felt important to give a good account of himself. A coalition of the energetic had gone walking in the rain, arriving back dripping and noisily pleased with themselves. He remembered that distinctly enough. They had gone off to shower and returned in a mood to kickstart the evening. So yes, maybe around five.

The drinking had continued steadily through supper, which was served and efficiently cleared by two women drafted in from the village at Candice's expense. Bottles were carried through to the lounge to accompany the reading, and port appeared too. The reading itself went by in something of a blur – he remembered Marina's cool voice detailing a mechanical dismemberment, and finding Candice's smoky depiction of a Hamburg brothel unsettlingly erotic. In the end Nigel's gentle account of Wordsworthian ramblings, free of taxidermy as they were, had been rather welcome. His own contribution had not, he felt, stood out as being particularly remarkable, and he had stumbled over one or two of the place names.

Now they were playing some sophisticated variation of literary charades, the rules just a little too complex for the stage the evening had reached. Naomi, an athletic black girl from Birmingham, who didn't drink, was miming earnestly in the middle of the floor, but the room was losing its focus, the shouted offers of a solution increasingly bizarre and apparently well off the mark. Candice put on some music and shimmied over to Dave, her wine glass in her hand. She pulled him to his feet, and others were starting to dance. Naomi gave up her miming, laughing. "It was Mrs Rochester!" Nobody seemed to care, and the port went round again.

Candice moved well, which was perhaps not surprising given her history. He did his best to keep up. He didn't think he'd ever danced with a pole dancer before. He'd been missing out. She was, undeniably, quite sexy. Did it matter that she was a bit…well quite a bit really… older than him? Not in this day and age, he told himself firmly. The tempo slowed, and now her arms were round his neck, his round her waist. He could feel the heat of her body through her dress. This didn't feel entirely proper, but he couldn't for the life of him think why that should be. He realised he was quite drunk, but told himself this was just the writing life. A bit of Bohemia went with the territory…no…Bohemia *was* the territory. What was everybody else doing? What was Henry the stockbroker doing right now? There were others dancing, one or two close. Perhaps it was going to turn into an orgy! He'd never been to an orgy, wasn't sure he wanted…where were the Marines when you needed them?

The track finished and Candice still held him close. Disengage, Singleman, disengage! Candice picked up the signal, flashed him a winning smile and unpeeled herself. He wandered off to find the toilet. Probably that was about the right amount of Bohemia for one evening.

He urinated noisily and as accurately as he could, leaning against one wall. He splashed water on his face and paused to look at himself in the mirror. There was lipstick on his cheek, and he wiped it off, but it felt like somebody else's hand, or somebody else's cheek. Bed. That was the answer. He just needed to gather himself. Just for a minute or so.

He drifted back into the lounge and raised a genial hand, but there was only a knot of three people in a corner, talking. The orgy had either lost its energy or shifted its ground. He made his way to the stair and set himself to the challenge of reaching his attic room. Such a long way up – such an unreasonably long way up. He reached the first floor and rested on the galleried landing. Why was he in one of those pokey garret rooms anyway? Perhaps because he was a proper writer. He made his way round and as he approached the more modest stair to the next level one of the doors opened, and Candice stood in the doorway. Beautiful, wise, Candice, generous hostess, whom he had perhaps unkindly spurned. Had he spurned her? He hoped not. She deserved not to be spurned. No woman of such elegance, such compact, erotic dignity, no woman who had lived as Candice had lived…

She took his hand and pulled him into the room.

"Just a goodnight kiss, darling."

Chapter Nine

"Like the lost shadow of its owner"

Early on Saturday morning Kate sat in a café in town, her hands cupped around a large Americano, feeling pleased at the manner in which she had negotiated the previous evening. Her head was a little fuzzy, but nothing some fresh air and a coffee wouldn't shift.

She was not a great drinker - even at university in Durham she had led a fairly sober existence. The only child of mildly evangelical Anglicans, she had grown up with a deep respect for her moderate, warm-hearted and principled parents, and carried their values with her when she left home. When in her final year she had untethered herself from the intellectual strictures of their faith, that had seemed liberty enough. During her post-graduate years she had made one or two carefully planned excursions along the primrose path of dalliance, as much as anything to get the relevant boxes ticked before she embarked on her professional life. Thereafter she settled back into a staid and self-protective mode of living that she recognised as limiting, and not necessarily all that she wanted. Nothing that was on offer in her years at the northern grammar school, however, had tempted her to abandon it.

She had arrived at Frances's as instructed, and been mildly surprised to find Edward Tremenhere and Raphael the drama teacher in the hall with their coats on. Both greeted her cheerfully.

"We're not staying," said Edward, from what seemed like a considerable height. "We are moving to higher ground. We shall leave you to your gin."

"Oh," replied Kate, momentarily at a loss. "Is the higher ground nearby?"

"Just in town," said Raphael. "There's a lecture at the Miners and Mechanics Institute on Grotowski. It's not really Edward's thing, but I've persuaded him that he'll enjoy it."

"Higher intellectual ground," said Edward.

"I've not heard of Grotowski, I'm afraid," admitted Kate.

"None of us have," said Frances. "It's a theatre thing. A bit niche. Have a nice time, boys." She closed the door behind them.

"Men aren't allowed to do gin research. Their palates have been dulled by too much lager. Come and meet the others."

There were two others. Inga, Frances's partner, who looked and sounded Scandinavian, and Rona, a dark pretty woman in a vivid green dress who Kate recognised as the Head's PA, memorable for her broad Glasgow accent. She turned out to be Raphael's wife.

"We've not long finished supper," said Frances, and disappeared to the kitchen.

"So," said Inga. "You've been at school, what two days now? And how are you finding it?"

"Oh…fine, I think," said Kate. "The staff seem very friendly, and the kids too, mostly."

"Yes I think it is a friendly school. And I think that the academy trust seems to be adding a degree of rigour, without being too heavy-handed."

"Where are you living?" asked Rona.

"Oh…I'm just about to move into a flat, out past Newlyn. I picked up the keys yesterday."

"That's good", said Rona, "You want tae get settled."

Frances returned with a silver tray on which were a bowl of ice cubes, a bottle of tonic, a large sprig of mint and four glass tumblers.

"Aw here we go," said Rona, "What have ye got for us?"

Frances had three bottles of gin, all from small distilleries in Devon and Cornwall. She gave a short introduction to each by the simple expedient of reading the labels.

"Kate – which would you like to try first?"

Kate had, at Frances's insistence, abandoned her plans to drive home, but managed to keep her intake more or less within the bounds of moderation. As a consequence she had enjoyed the not entirely unfamiliar experience of being the only reasonably sober person in the room. The conversation had been lively and intelligent to begin with, but gradually slid into a hilarious exchange of anecdotes and observations in which men and their foibles, particularly those in the higher echelons of education management and policy making, came in for a particularly rough time. From here it was a short but inevitable step to scabrous and scatological bawdry to which she could contribute little. Eventually Raphael returned to collect Rona, and Frances and Inga, after a considerable degree of hunting, found Kate a sleeping bag and a spare pillow. The sofa had been perfectly comfortable and she had awoken, with a relatively clear head, to a silent house. The bottles, alarmingly depleted, still stood on their silver tray. She found her coat, scribbled Frances a brief note of thanks, and left in search of a café.

The evening had come at a good time. The laughter had been therapeutic, and the friendship genuine, and maybe getting a bit tipsy was as good a way as any of putting the seal on that awkward first week. Now she was going to move into her new flat above the beach. The keys were back at her digs, and she still had to settle up there, and pick up some things. She needed to buy some T-cut. She had some furniture in storage on an industrial estate outside town - she would need a van to bring that over, and perhaps some assistance to get it in, though they were mostly light pieces. The flat already had the basics, and there wasn't room for that much more. Probably the smart thing was to drive over there, get the feel of the place, make sure she had bedding sorted and groceries in for the week, and leave the furniture till another day. The rental on the storage unit was paid till the end of the month anyway. She drained her coffee and moved her head from side to side experimentally. A few twinges, but the fresh air was definitely helping.

Once more, she drove out the coast road beyond Newlyn. It wasn't sunny any more, and someone had said rain was expected. As she approached the bend before Wheal Prosper, she glanced at the speedometer. She was doing over thirty, less than on her first visit, because she knew she had to slow down to pull off. It didn't seem that fast. Forget it, she told herself. That's last week's stuff.

She pulled onto the parking area and got out of the car. The damp breeze tugged at her hair, but the air still felt mild. The sky was dull, but the rain didn't look imminent. She checked the forecast on her phone. Rain from two o'clock. Plenty of time to get her stuff in.

She didn't go straight to the flat, but wandered round the perimeter of the site. There was a grassy border around the gravel that ended a few yards beyond the outhouse on the left, and a similar apron of green at the back of the Engine House. She noticed a clothes line, empty but for a few plastic pegs. That would be useful. She walked over to where the path disappeared over the edge of the higher ground – it was almost steep enough to be called a cliff – and looked down on the beach once more.

To her surprise the beach had largely disappeared, leaving only a narrow strip of sand, and the grey waves, instead of rolling in gently, were slapping down in a manner that seemed vaguely hostile. The scene was almost deserted. though a solitary dog walker was picking his way along the foot of the cliff. There was no sign of life at the café. She made a mental note to buy a set of tide tables.

Kate glanced back at the Engine House and noticed an empty beer bottle on the balcony rail. For the first time it occurred to her that she might have a neighbour, and the realisation momentarily punctured her mood. Sue hadn't said who, if anybody, would be living above her. Perhaps it was still being kept as a holiday let. Hers was the only car, after all.

She decided to check out the outhouse first, to delay the moment of crossing the threshold of her new home. The door was heavy and secured with a sturdy bolt, but it slid back easily enough. She pushed it open and felt for a light switch. The bare, low-ceilinged room contained a washing machine, rusting a little at the edges but apparently in recent use, given the bottle of detergent on the shelf above. There was also a surfboard propped in the corner, and a wetsuit hanging on a hook. Kate knew nothing of surfboards, but it looked rather faded and battered, so perhaps it was just something for the summer visitors. She ran her hand over its dry, scratched surface and tried to imagine what it might be like to be crouched on this sliver of fibreglass, combing a path across the waves.

She turned her attention to the wetsuit, a man's by the look of it. There was something odd about it hanging there, like the lost shadow of its owner. She pinched the cuff, and a trickle of water squeezed out. Ah well. Surfers, one imagined, were generally benevolent, ecologically aware folk, and probably quite nice to have as neighbours. If you had to have neighbours.

She bolted the outhouse door carefully behind her and crossed the gravel to the Engine House. She fished out the key the estate agent had given her, turned it in the lock and pushed.

The first time she had seen the flat, two days previously, it had been hard to take in the detail, absorbed as she had been in the binary question of whether it was or wasn't suitable. Now she noticed things – the sofa, which was deep in the seat, good for curling up on. The broad window on the seaward side in front of which she could put her desk. She pulled an upright chair from its place in the corner and sat as she would when working, and was pleased that even from this seated position a thin grey bar of sea-horizon was visible.

The granite blocks that formed the walls were two feet across, deep grooves between them where the pointing had been left exposed. Strange to think what primitive machinery this room must once have housed – power and potential dramatically above anything people had known before. She looked on the floor for signs of where it might have been, but the stripped pine was a later addition. A couple of bright rugs would work well.

She opened the door into the bedroom and lay experimentally on the small double bed. It was comfortable enough. There was a wardrobe and a chest of drawers, both pine, and she opened these, alert to damp. A few wire hangers rattled in the wardrobe, and one of the drawers was a bit stiff. But they were fine – she could put her clothes straight in. The shower room was clean, the toilet spotless. The water pressure when she tried it seemed sufficient.

She wandered back into the living area and inspected the kitchen. There was an induction hob, which might take a bit of getting used to, and a fridge freezer. No dishwasher, but that was all right. Not all that much cupboard space, or work surface for that matter. The drawers contained the basics, but she had her own stuff anyway – she might move that in and see if Sue would store the rest.

She put the kettle on and went back out to the car. There wasn't much to unload – her duvet and bedding, a couple of bags of clothes and toiletries and her favourite books. She had bought fresh milk and coffee on the way, and planned to do a more substantial grocery shop later. She changed the bedding while the kettle was boiling.

She set up her Bluetooth speaker and selected some music on her phone. She had eclectic taste, and having scrolled through the bands of her teenage years, including the ones she had inherited from her parents, she settled on some jazz. Something to have on in the background, that wouldn't intrude too much. She found a cafetiere in the cupboard and settled down with her coffee to make a list.

A knock on the door made her look up sharply, for she hadn't heard a car. She rose to open it and a tall girl of about fourteen stood holding the handlebars of her bike in one hand and a backpack in the other. Long honey-coloured hair spilled out from under her cycle helmet.

"Hello," the girl said. "Mum said to give you this."

She rummaged in the back-pack and handed over an envelope.

"It's the inventory. She said just to check and sign, or make a note of anything that's not right. It should be fine though. We went through it after the holidaymakers left."

The envelope was unsealed and Kate peered inside. There were a couple of stapled sheets of A4.

"Thank you. You're at St Petroc's, aren't you?"

"Yes. I'm in 9M. You're my friend's form tutor." Her manner was direct. She was unafraid to meet Kate's eyes.

"Who's your friend?"

"Sammy Pascoe."

"Oh yes, I know Sammy. And what's your name?"

"Isadora Brunel."

"Like the famous engineer."

"Yes, he's my great-great-great-great uncle." A statement, not a boast.

"I see! Are you interested in that kind of stuff? As a career I mean?"

"Not really. I'm going to be a barrister."

Something in the girl's direct gaze and the economy of her speech made this seem a perfectly likely outcome.

"Well thank you, Isadora."

"Most people call me Issy."

Kate smiled. "Thank you Issy. I'll deal with this over the weekend."

The girl nodded and turned her bike around. As she cycled out towards the main road, Kate called after her. She stopped and looked back. Kate hesitated. She had been going to ask her if she knew who had the flat above, but the question seemed suddenly a bit needy. Instead she said.

"Careful on the road!"

The girl nodded. It's fine so long as you go left," she called back, and with a careful glance towards the bend she set off down the hill.

Chapter Ten

"If this is your idea of revenge..."

Dave awoke on Sunday morning in the attic room, and for a moment or two the fact that his brain seemed to be suspended on rusty springs inside his skull was his only cause for concern. Then he remembered, or at least he thought he did. He remembered the slow ascent of the staircase, the opening of the bedroom door, and Candice, shorter than usual because she was barefooted; skinnier than usual because she wasn't wearing very much. He remembered her hot tongue in his mouth, and falling onto a bed the size of a small Scottish island. He couldn't be one hundred percent sure what happened next, but he had a good idea. Then there had been another staircase, hands pushing him this time. How on earth had he got back up to his room?

He stood under the shower until it was clear that hot needles of water could do no more for the misrule in his head. It wasn't that he had never woken up in a relatively strange woman's bed, back in the day before responsible adulthood tightened its grip, but not a married woman in whose house he was a guest. Not a married woman of, God, what…forty eight? Fifty even?

He dried himself thoughtfully, and set himself to identifying mitigating factors. Probably, Candice did this kind of thing all the time (although that in itself raised other worries). Probably, hopefully, she wasn't so daft as to risk pregnancy, if such a thing were possible at her age. He was hazy on the reproductive biology of middle-aged women. Probably she saw it all as a merry diversion, and wouldn't attach any meaning or obligation to the encounter.

There were, however, too many unknowns for comfort. He dressed and packed his things, undecided whether to make a quick and discreet exit, or to seek a brief conversation with Candice to establish what precisely had happened and to clarify expectations. It was a quarter past nine, and he was desperate for a coffee. And it would be undignified to bolt. A brief call into the kitchen then, to make his excuses to whoever might be there, then he would hit the road, provided he felt ok to drive.

The only occupant of the kitchen was Colin the Royal Marine, who was at his post by the toaster, looking trim and at ease, as if he had run five miles before breakfast.

"Morning, old boy. Good night's sleep?" If there was mischief in his tone Dave decided it was subtle enough to be ignored by a man with a hangover such as his.

"Yeah… might have overdone it a bit last night," Dave mumbled. He avoided the older man's eyes. He filled the kettle and rinsed out a cafetiere. Colin whistled "A Life on the Ocean Wave" as he buttered his toast.

Candice came in, yawning, dressed in jeans and an expensive looking top. If she had make-up on it was discreet.

"Good morning darlings. Got everything you need? I did ask the girls to bring in fresh milk. The Sunday papers are in the lounge."

Nothing in her tone implied favouritism, nor for that matter a recent history of drunken copulation. Dave once more tried to work out how old she might be, although this was difficult as he didn't want to be seen staring. Come on, Colin, he thought. Bugger off and do some press-ups or something. And stop that bloody whistling.

Whether to do press-ups or to read the Telegraph, Colin did indeed wander back out of the kitchen, leaving Dave fumbling with the cafetiere while watching Candice out of the corner of his eye as she cleared some mugs into the dishwasher.

"Make some for me will you darling?" said Candice.

"Uh, sure. Look, Candice… last night...." He measured out the coffee carefully, using it as an excuse not to look at her.

"Mmm?"

"I'm not sure what actually, I mean…"

"You were very drunk darling."

"Yes, yes I was."

"But fortunately not *too* drunk."

"Oh."

"We had ever such a job getting you back up the stairs. That was around 4 am I think."

"Ah, right. Sorry about that. We?"

"Colin gave me a hand. He's very strong for a man of his size."

Colin. Oh God! So he had, in the end, been rescued by the Marines. He handed her the coffee, and their eyes met briefly. She smiled a winning smile. Could those even, pearly teeth really be fifty years old?

"Don't worry darling. I look after myself and Henry is very understanding. You're unlikely to meet him and if you do you'll find him perfectly affable."

Something about this bothered Dave, although it was clearly intended to be reassuring. If he could just engineer his departure now, it might feel something like a clean break.

"I have to head off, fairly soon," he said. "Got a bit of work to do for school tomorrow." Then as an afterthought, and not entirely sincerely, "If there's anything I can do before I go, clearing up, I mean…"

"It's all taken care of."

"Yes well…" he drained his coffee and gathered himself, met her eyes again. Whatever her age, she was a damned good-looking woman. "It's been a very memorable weekend, Candice. Thank you…for…um… everything. " He was not at his rhetorical best when hungover.

"All a pleasure darling. Now I must walk the dogs." She leaned forward and kissed his cheek, more like a mother than a lover.

He dropped the hood on the MG and took the sixty miles to Exeter Services slowly. The rain clouds had cleared and a watery sun made for pleasant motoring. At Exeter he ordered a large cooked breakfast and a second cup of coffee, and began to feel more human. The motorway gave way to the A30, which was blessedly quiet, and forty minutes later he was negotiating the dip at Dunheved Bridge that marked the border between Devon and Cornwall. His thoughts returned to the week ahead, and he revisited for the first time Friday's rather awkward conversation with Kate Porteous.

Ought he to have made some concession on the wing mirror? He had the impression that was what she had been looking for. It certainly wasn't his fault - at the worst it was knock for knock. It had been, perhaps, a little tactless to imply that she was to blame, but she had started that game, and he couldn't be too hard on himself for being defensive. If it *was* knock for knock, that left two options. Either each of them paid for their own damage, or they split the combined cost. Unquestionably the former course favoured him, the latter her. She had said two hundred quid. That seemed a lot. Maybe he could offer to make a contribution, as a goodwill gesture.

Something else bothered him. What had she been doing at Wheal Prosper? Holiday makers occasionally treated it as a layby from which to access the beach, but the more likely explanation was that she was looking at the ground floor of the Engine House. Sue Brunel had said they might try to find a winter tenant. Of course, that didn't mean she would take it – it wasn't everyone's cup of tea, and she struck him as the kind of girl who liked things a bit less rustic, a bit more chic. But what was he basing that on? The Fiat? That had to be balanced against the tattoo and the nose stud. So he had to face the possibility that they might be neighbours.

What did he make of her anyway, this Kate Porteous, leaving aside the unfortunate incident of the wing mirror? Aesthetically, she was his type – neat, dark, really quite good-looking in an un-fussy way. Not exactly drop-dead gorgeous, but he'd take a sense of humour over that any day. Was there a sense of humour, though? The jury was still out on that one. Mind you, given his experience over the last twenty-four hours, fun was perhaps a bit over-rated. Maybe fun was something you had in your twenties. And then again in your fifties. Right now, a decent looking, serious minded girl of around his own age was an appealing prospect.

When eventually he pulled onto the parking area by the Engine House, it was empty. The clothes line too was as he had left it. There were definitely some tyre tracks, but how fresh was unclear. Out of habit, he walked to the top of the path to check on the surf. The tide was receding now, and the surf was coming in at couple of feet and pretty clean. Surely lesson preparation could wait till the evening. Right now what he needed was his board and his wetsuit. He picked his weekend bag out of the boot of the MG and climbed, still a little gingerly, up the stairs to the balcony, casting a surreptitious glance into the window of the ground floor flat as he passed. There were signs of occupation – mugs on the draining board, an unfamiliar throw on the settee. He changed into his shorts and walked barefoot and bare-chested down the stair and across to the outhouse.

He left the door slightly ajar to save turning on the light and eased himself into his wetsuit. He was pulling on his boots when he heard the car pull up outside, and faced with the immediate decision of whether to hop out into the daylight half-clad in neoprene just as the occupant of the car alighted, or remain in the outhouse, he chose the latter course. He took a step back into the shadows and waited, one rubber boot on his foot and one still in his hand.

Kate saw the MG as soon as she pulled into Wheal Prosper. Looking back, she did wonder that she didn't immediately pull together the various threads of evidence, and realise that Dave Singleman was the occupant of the upstairs flat. Instead, her first thought was that he had returned to the scene of the crime to reassess his own culpability, or that he was using Wheal Prosper as a convenient parking spot for the beach. She sat in her car for a moment and considered. If he had come back for a second look at the scene of the accident, then that was to be cautiously encouraged. If he was merely parking on what was in effect her land, then that was a bit of a cheek.

Either way, he was the last person she wanted to bump into right now. She had been shopping for various essentials, and had picked up a pasty for lunch, the aroma of which was calling to her from her shopping bag. She got out of the car and was about to go indoors when the outhouse door caught her eye. It was slightly ajar. Tutting, she pulled it closed and shot the bolt.

In the outhouse, as he listened to the car pull up, it occurred to Dave that remaining unseen might have been the wrong option. But how should he now reveal himself? With a self-deprecatory cough? Or a polite good afternoon? By the time he had started to form the words, the door had closed, and the bolt slid home, plunging him into darkness. He would have called out, but in his hungover state he was absurdly at a loss for the right words. He realised that he had only a brief span of time in which to alert whoever had closed the door that he was now a prisoner, before they disappeared to do whatever they had come to do. He hopped cautiously over to where his retinal memory told him the door had been and felt for its surface.

The hammering of Dave's fists on the heavy outhouse door coincided with Kate pulling shut her own front door, so that she heard nothing. It was half an hour later that she remembered she had left her phone in the car and once again emerged from the flat. She heard a muffled calling (he had given up on the banging) and realised immediately that she had inadvertently made somebody a prisoner. She approached the outhouse cautiously.

"Hello," she said to the door. "Do you mind just identifying yourself?"

"Identify myself? I flaming live here!" replied the door.

"You live here? At Wheal Prosper?" She recognised the voice immediately, but was momentarily confused by the implications of the statement.

"Yes! I live here! Look, can you just open the door – I'm desperate for a pee."

"It is Dave, isn't it?"

"Of course it's Dave."

Kate slid back the bolt and stepped to one side. The door opened and her neighbour emerged, still half-clad in his wetsuit and clutching one neoprene boot.

"So… you live upstairs?"

"If you now live downstairs, then yes, I live upstairs. And if this is your idea of revenge for your car getting damaged then I think it's a bit childish."

"Don't be ridiculous. I had no idea you were in there!"

"You're telling me you bolted the door by accident?"

"Of course not by accident. I'm just…tidy by nature. I certainly didn't mean to lock you in." She paused. "I'm sorry."

"OK," he said, rather huffily, and walked with as much dignity as he could manage across the gravel to the balcony steps. Kate watched him go, then closed and bolted the outhouse door, suppressing a smile. It hadn't, of course, been a deliberate act of revenge. But it would serve the purpose.

Chapter Eleven

"It's nice to get on with your neighbours if you can"

Three weeks into the Autumn term, which nobody any longer regarded as new, Kate was sitting next to Dave in the staffroom at breaktime, listening attentively to the Monday briefing. Blots large and small had by this time besmirched the once clean copybooks of various students, and the Senior Management Team considered that everybody had had a chance to settle in and could cope with a little extra pressure.

Initially, following that first weekend, relationships between the occupants of the Engine House at Wheal Prosper had been frosty, and for the first few days their interactions consisted of rather stiff exchanges of necessary information, or polite acknowledgements of the other's presence when they met on their way to and from school.

It was the school relationship that thawed first, as if each acknowledged that this was the bit that mattered – a kind of "not in front of the children", nine-to-four suspension of hostilities. Each was sufficiently generous to recognise in the other a capable and committed teacher, although their styles might be different. After a week or so they were able to engage in quite sensible and productive discussion in the workroom or even over lunch, but they returned to their separate levels of the Engine House each evening, where a strict curfew was maintained until the following day. Each kept their music at low volume, not out of consideration for the other, but in order to avoid any possible cause for complaint.

The first couple of weekends after the outhouse incident, Dave made sure he was on the golf course or the beach, while Kate took herself off to explore the coastal paths. As the washing machine was a shared facility, each contrived to do their washing while the other was known to be from home. In fact it was laundry, on the second Sunday of their localised cold war, that brought about the first truce. Kate had put a load on in the morning while she went to the shops, and Dave took advantage of her absence to engage in some necessary tinkering with the MG's carburettor. He was just completing this task when the yellow Fiat swung in from the main road.

Kate got out, said hello politely enough, and disappeared into the Engine House with her shopping. Dave closed the bonnet of the MG and began cleaning his hands with a rag. Kate re-emerged with her laundry basket and peg bag and grimaced up at the sky. It had clouded over in the course of the morning, and the first drops of rain were beginning to fall.

"I was hoping to get this load on the line – what do you reckon?"

"I wouldn't," said Dave. "This will be on for the day. Have you got a tumble drier?"

Kate admitted that she hadn't.

"You can use mine if you like. Just let me finish cleaning up."

Kate was momentarily nonplussed.

"Oh. That's decent of you. I…I thought I might dry it over the bath."

"Do you have a bath?"

"Well no. I suppose I meant metaphorically."

"Well – the offer's there. It'll only take half an hour."

Again Kate hesitated, and Dave, feeling her reluctance and taking it, in part at least, personally, closed the boot and began walking back to the Engine House.

"Thanks!" said Kate. "I will, if you really don't mind. I just didn't want to put you to any trouble."

"No trouble," he called back over his shoulder. "Just bring it up when you're ready."

When Kate appeared a few minutes later at the top of the stair with her basket of damp washing, the kettle was coming to the boil.

"Come in," said Dave. The tumble drier's over there. I'm making a coffee if you want one."

"Oh. Um, OK, thanks. That would be nice. Actually, I've got some biscuits here – I've just been to Tesco." She produced a packet of chocolate digestives and put them on the worksurface. She had brought them to reduce the extent to which she would be in his debt.

"Jolly good."

Kate put her washing in the drier while Dave made the coffees.

"How do you take it?"

"Just black, please."

He brought the mugs over to the low coffee table, and pulled up a kitchen chair, leaving the small battered sofa for his guest. He brought the biscuits too, but he didn't open them.

Kate came over and perched on the edge of the sofa.

"You've got an upstairs!" she said, gesturing to the steep wooden stairway that led to the sleeping deck.

"It's only a mezzanine. But you get a great view through the big window."

A pause. Kate opened the biscuits and offered them to Dave. He took one.

"Thanks. So…how are you settling in?"

"At school? Or downstairs?"

"Well, both, really. You seem to be doing fine at school."

"Yes – it's odd though, starting again somewhere new. I'd forgotten what it's like. Nothing's at your fingertips, you know? The batch photocopying routine; who to see if the whiteboard's not working; that kind of stuff."

Dave nodded. "I remember it well. But it all becomes second nature soon enough. And the kids down here aren't generally malicious. Too laid back, most of them." He paused. "And how's the flat working out?"

"It's comfortable enough. A bit basic, but the location makes up for that."

"Neighbours OK?"

The question was put so innocently it caught her off guard. She paused then said,

"We got off to a bit of a rocky start, but things seem to be improving."

"That's good," said Dave. "It's nice to get on with your neighbours if you can."

They both seemed to feel this was a moment to study the remains of their coffee.

Kate broke the short silence.

"Well look, thanks for the drink, and the use of your drier. I'll just go down and put my shopping away – by that time it should be done. Hang on to the biscuits if you like."

"I will, cheers for that." He stood up and walked to the door with her. "See you shortly."

So far, that was the only time she had been in his flat, and she hadn't invited him into her own apartment. But the atmosphere at the Engine House was distinctly warmer from that morning, and the difficulties of the first week of term appeared to be behind them. During the first week of their joint occupancy Dave had watched with interest from his balcony one evening as Kate, with impressive competence, fitted the new wing mirror to her car. He had considered enquiring as to the cost and offering to make a contribution, but the moment had come and gone, and the matter had not been mentioned again.

Now it felt quite comfortable to be sitting next to her in the Monday briefing, knowing that she was his neighbour as well as a departmental colleague.

To Dave's mind, the Monday morning briefing had changed in character over the past year. At one time its principle function had been pastoral – an opportunity to acquaint staff with the changing circumstances and temporary frailties of various students – whose much loved family pet had passed away; which pupil now wished to be known as Demelza rather than Daniel; who would be on crutches for the next six weeks. Recently however it had been announced that such information would be circulated by email, and the briefing had become instead an opportunity for senior staff to remind teaching colleagues of the latest initiatives designed to move St Petroc's from its current rating as a "Good" school, towards the educational gold standard represented by "Outstanding". An Ofsted inspection was expected sometime in the spring term, which Killick clearly regarded as a challenge to be risen to with all the gusto of a crack unit of venture scouts constructing a rope bridge across a chasm.

Another recent feature of the briefing was that staff who went the extra mile in terms of after-school or weekend activities were ostentatiously congratulated. State schools generally had limited expectations in this line, but the Head had recently become fixated upon competing with the independent school in the cathedral city that lay a forty minute train journey to the east – a journey that several parents with the means to do so were apparently quite happy to subject their children to, in the interests of giving them a head start in life's race. Improving the school's offer in what he liked to call "the co-curricular realm" was one of the Head's pet projects.

The briefing was nearly over, and Killick was on his feet.

"I want to share with you some exciting news about an opportunity that has arisen as part of the support offered by Marcato."

Marcato was the Academy trust of which they were a member. It was bankrolled by a prominent west country car-dealer, and its headquarters were in Bristol, which at 200 miles away Dave considered too near by half.

"St Petroc's is going to be setting up its own mentoring programme for aspiring middle and senior managers." He paused to let this sink in, and indeed a frisson of interest was detectable.

"We'll be forwarding the full details to staff by email, but I wanted to outline briefly what will be involved. The programme will run for one year, beginning shortly after October half term. It will consist of regular seminars to reflect upon educational practice, plus one-to-one career development sessions with a management consultant, and it will lead to the submission of a formal presentation on an aspect of each staff member's work at St Petroc's. There will be eight places available on the first tranche, and we expect uptake to be competitive. The email will detail what you need to do should you wish to apply."

The frisson grew to a hubbub. Teachers, when they find themselves on the opposite side of the classroom, behave remarkably like students. One or two hands went up. Killick looked pleased at the animated response, and took the questions with an air of patient indulgence.

"Will the seminars take place out of school time?"

"Some of them may do, but Marcato are funding cover for the participants for three days each in total over the duration of the course."

"Can anyone apply?"

"The course is open to all staff who have successfully passed their NQT year, and you will have the opportunity to make clear on your application why you feel you should be selected, but precedence is likely to go to those who are actively seeking promotion to middle or senior management positions."

Dave put up his hand, and Killick nodded.

"How is the school likely to view applicants for internal appointments who have chosen, for whatever reason, not to apply for the course?"

Killick glanced briefly at the head, then replied smoothly,

"It is the school's policy to assess all applicants for positions on their merits, and nobody should feel unable to apply for a post simply because they have chosen not to take up this mentoring opportunity, or indeed been unsuccessful in applying for it. As I said, we expect it to be competitive, and there may well be some very worthy applicants who don't make the cut first time round."

Glances and murmurings among the teaching body, who were not fooled for a moment by this glib response. Fairly evidently, if you had any ambition for promotion, this was an opportunity to signal it, and the failure to do so would not go un-noticed. Three days' cover, though, was not to be sniffed at, and suggested that this was not necessarily an entirely cynical SMT ploy.

The bell signalled the end of break, and the Head drew the meeting to a close. As they filed out, Frances Fivey leaned close to Dave and whispered, "I would support your application, Mr Singleman."

"I'd support yours," he replied, and she laughed.

The Monday briefing meant that the normal staff duty team was scaled down to skeleton levels, the thinking being that the students' capacity and inclination for mischief was low on the first breaktime of the week. In the middle school playground, Edward Tremenhere was the only member of staff on duty, and he was seated on a bench in the sunshine, a mug of coffee in his right hand and one long leg crossed over the other. He exchanged occasional kindly words with the students who knew him well enough not to be intimidated by his size and his patrician demeanour, and in between these brief conversations he read from a volume of Demosthenes in the original Greek. He was also keeping a discreet eye on a far corner of the playground where Donkey Doggett was deep in furtive conversation with two boys from the year above.

The conversation, had he been able to overhear it, might have presented a greater problem to his skills of translation that the slim book in his hand. It was conducted in a kind of dialect that combined teenage slang with broad Cornish idiom, and concerned the availability of Class A drugs (a topic with its own unique vocabulary) on the estate where Donkey's family had held sway for a decade or more. This was a matter on which Donkey was held to be an authority, thanks to his brother's connections with the Bristol criminal fraternity, and his father's current residency in Exeter Prison, although this was in fact for burglary. Edward Tremenhere knew little of this, but he had worked around young people long enough to recognise unhealthy alliances, particularly across year groups, and he made a mental note to pass on the intelligence. The bell rang and he rose to his feet, slipping the book into his jacket pocket.

Chapter Twelve

"He's a bit cynical, isn't he?"

That breaktime Sammy Pascoe was in the theatre, hanging out with the tech team. This was a small cohort from a variety of year groups who met to learn the skills of sound, lighting and stage management from the school's technician, one Harrison Roche. Roche was a morbidly obese young man who could barely squeeze into the cramped lighting box at the back of the theatre, but he was kindly, and had great patience with his young charges, who respected his encyclopaedic knowledge of lighting systems. Harrison in his turn reported to Raphael D'Allesandro.

As well as offering a pool of trained labour to support Raphael's programme of school shows, the tech team performed a valuable pastoral function in providing an extended family, and access to a safe and privileged breaktime hangout, for various oddballs and misfits. Some were highly intelligent, some less so, but most, for whatever reason, found the school's other social networks difficult to penetrate. Like all extended families, the tech team had its own pecking orders, running resentments, and occasional spectacular bust-ups, but such was the combined respect in which Raphael and Harrison were held, these differences were always suppressed when it came to show time.

Sammy's particular interest was in sound engineering. His father played in a local band, and he sometimes helped out at gigs, operating the relatively unsophisticated mixing desk that the Kernow Dixies carted around from pub to village hall. The tech team frustrated him at times, and he was something of a part-time member, but lately Issy seemed keen to hang out with some of the other girls in Year 9, members of the earring and make up brigade led by Lily Tregunna, around whom Sammy never felt entirely comfortable. He had not yet settled into any solid friendships in his new form, so he had gravitated back to the theatre, where Harrison at least had been pleased to see him.

"Right me 'ansomes," called Harrison from the back of the theatre. "Thassa bell. Back to lessons."

Sammy finished coiling the cable he was dealing with and hung it on the appropriate hook. As he picked up his bag from the pile in the wings, another of the year nine techies said,

"Donkey was looking for you earlier."

"Well I'm in his form," said Sammy. "If he bothered to come to registration he'd find me in the next seat along."

"Tell him that, shall I?"

Sammy shrugged. "Tell him what you like."

It was English next, with Singleman. As he filed in, Sammy caught sight of Donkey leaning against the wall outside Ms Porteous's room. He felt uneasy. While not deeply malicious, Doggett was not above throwing his weight about, and while Sammy had managed to keep out of his way during his first two years at the school, he was uncomfortable at the proximity brought about by the mixing up of the forms. Donkey hadn't shown much interest in him up to now, and Sammy was keen that it should stay that way.

He took his seat next to Issy, who gifted him a smile of greeting. Singleman was at the front, hands on hips, waiting for the class to settle, bags to be removed from desks.

"Good morning, everybody. Are we all here? Excellent. We're going to be looking today at competitive debating, which as you know is something the Head is very keen on, and for good reason. Debating is at the heart of a civilised society. It is a formalised means by which we can discuss and indeed disagree about important subjects without coming to blows. It is the basis of our parliamentary process, though, as you will see in the short clip from Prime Minister's Questions that I'm going to show you today, the reality isn't always as civilised as we might wish.

"Debating also teaches us the value of rational thinking – engaging with arguments on a logical, rather than an emotional level. That's why, in debating competitions, you don't get to choose which side of the argument you are on – your job is to present the best possible case for or against that subject, whatever your personal views. So, for example, are there any vegans in the class?"

A number of hands went up. Veganism was trending spectacularly.

"Right. So, Connor, would I be right in thinking you are also opposed to fox-hunting?"

"Totally," acknowledged Connor.

"But in a debating competition, you might find yourself speaking in favour of a motion such as 'This house believes that the ban on hunting with hounds should be repealed.'"

The veganist tendency turned to one another in collective bafflement.

"That would be really hard, Sir."

"Emotionally, yes, I can absolutely accept that it would be hard. But as there are many thousands of perfectly sensible people who ardently believe that the ban should be repealed, there must presumably be some arguments for that position. Yes, Issy?"

"It's a bit like a lawyer having to defend someone who might have committed a murder or something."

"Exactly so…excellent point. However likely it is that the accused is guilty, the case for the defence must be heard. That way, justice is done. Similarly, to bring it back to fox hunting, Connor can only be more secure in his opposition if he has fully examined all the arguments of those who support hunting."

The class were fully engaged. It was a top set, and the idea of verbal swordplay in the interests of intellectual rigour had some appeal.

"You may also be aware," continued Mr Singleman, "that each year we enter a Year Nine team for the West Cornwall Debating Competition, which takes place later this term. It's a lot of fun, and last year we were runners-up, so this year I'd like to win it."

Across the corridor, in Kate Porteous's classroom, a similar lesson was in progress, although the tone was notably different. Dave and Frances had encouraged all Y9 teachers to use the occasion of the competition to introduce their groups to debating, and Kate was willing enough to give it a go. Her bottom set were, as was to be expected, a rather mixed bunch. It was only about half the size of the larger groups, as a concession to the challenges that it presented, and it contained a much wider spread of personalities and abilities that Dave's high-fliers. Relatively able idlers shared the class with inveterate rogues and students with significant learning difficulties, one of whom had a dedicated teaching assistant.

It was the group that had been difficult when Kate had first encountered them on a Friday afternoon in early September, and since then she had put a considerable amount of thought and effort into her approach to teaching them. She had checked back on the records of the students to get a sense of why each was languishing in this bottom set, and made a point of greeting them when she met them outside the classroom. Two or three were in her form, including Donovan Doggett, and with these in particular she had made an effort to build relationships.

"What happens," asked Kate, "when you disagree strongly with somebody about something?"

The class were arranged round a large rectangle of desks, facing in towards each other. Donovan Doggett was on her left. Ryan, who used a wheelchair, was in a gap she had created at one corner, his teaching assistant next to him. There were several girls in the group. Inevitably, it took longer to settle them that it did with her other classes, but now they were reasonably attentive, and the question drew in those who had been inclined to quietly switch off.

"You have, like an argument."

"Depends what it is."

"You scat 'en!"

"Explain, please, Donovan?"

"You beat them up."

"And what if they're bigger and harder than you are?"

"They beat you up." Several of the class laughed.

"So," Kate said patiently, "The strongest person gets to make all the decisions?"

"Tha's how it works on my estate."

"OK maybe it feels like that, but probably not all decisions are actually taken that way. Suppose, for example there's money available to provide a skateboard park. It could go on your estate, or it could go somewhere else in the town. How does that decision get made?"

"That'd be the Council, Miss," said Lily Tregunna without looking up from her nails.

"Correct, Lily, it would be the Council. And how do you think the Council decide, if, say, there are three possible locations for the skatepark, one of which might be Donovan's estate?"

"They kind of sit down and have a big discussion."

"Exactly so. But a discussion works better if you have rules…"

And so, with even Donkey paying a degree of attention, the class inched towards the idea of a formal debate.

At lunch she was sitting with Frances. The staff tables were at one end of the large panelled hall, which had something of the atmosphere of a Victorian workhouse. A soundscape of clattering and chattering, underscored by the scraping of chairs and of plates, meant that conversation with anyone but one's nearest neighbour was impractical.

"So how did the introduction to debating go?" asked Frances.

"Quite well, actually. Even Donkey wanted to get involved, particularly when we decided to debate the legalisation of cannabis."

"There's a surprise."

"He did bring a considerable level of knowledge to the discussion."

"Most of the weed on the Penhale estate comes via the Doggetts. And some of the class A stuff too, by all accounts. I've never taught him, but I've heard he's not as bad as his brother was."

"I wonder how far he's caught up in all of that. I guess it's inevitable."

"I don't know. It would be worth talking to Emily. She's generally got a handle on that kind of thing. I'm afraid with the likes of Donkey it's pretty much going to be damage limitation."

Kate made a face. "I'd like to try and do a bit better than that. He's in my form as well. And I don't think he's as stupid as he makes himself out to be. I'll have a look at his scores."

"Well I commend your open-mindedness," said Frances, "but if I were you, I'd make sure you were up to speed on the sanctions regime too."

Dave Singleman came weaving towards them with a loaded plastic tray and took a seat on the other side of the table.

"Well that was fun," he said as he transferred his plates from the tray. "We're all geared up for a preliminary team selection debate on whether there should be a tax on second homes. I've got Issy Brunel and Sammy Pascoe proposing, and Connor Pendarves and Mo Maxwell against.

"How does Issy feel about that? Her parents make a living from property, don't they?"

"Well that's the interesting thing," said Dave, attacking his pasty with the vigour of a man who feels he's earned it. "She wants to be a criminal barrister when she's older, and she completely gets that you have to be prepared to take on unpopular briefs. So she's testing herself out, I guess. Quite impressive really."

"What's Sammy like?" asked Kate. "He's one of mine."

"He'll be good," said Dave. "He's sharp as a tack."

"Sammy was borderline for the top set," explained Frances. "His written work's all over the place. But Dave put up a strong fight on his behalf."

"He'll come through," said Dave. "You mark my words. He's got a good brain and a good work ethic too."

"Well," said Frances, "I'm pleased to hear debating is going down well. What do we all make of the SMT mentoring programme?"

"I think it looks quite good," said Kate. "Useful to have on your CV. The three hundred and sixty degree feedback is an interesting idea."

"I thought it sounded like it was there for the Ofsted inspectors," said Dave through a mouthful of pasty. "And what's three hundred and sixty degree feedback when it's at home?"

"You get a kind of structured report from a complete range of people that you work with, or for, or alongside. Pupils too. It's all in the email."

"Bloody hell" said Dave, "That could be revelatory. Do you get to choose them?"

"I'm not sure."

"Do you think you might apply," asked Frances, directing the question at Kate.

"Well I don't know. I was going to ask you about it. I mean I've only just got here, but I do want to progress…"

"The applications don't have to be in for another couple of weeks. That's long enough for people to have formed an opinion of you. And you can probably get some input from your previous school if you need it. What about you, Dave?"

"Not really my cup of tea," said Dave. "Navel-gazing and psycho-babble. It's got Killick's fingerprints all over it."

"I thought you asked a very sensible question in the meeting," said Frances, innocently.

"Someone's got to ask the sensible questions," said Dave. "Right then. I've got a meeting with Raph about the Shakespeare festival at 1.30. Have a good afternoon, all."

They watched him go.

"He's a bit…cynical, isn't he?" said Kate. "Does he want to be a classroom teacher all his life?"

"I don't think he knows what he wants at the moment," said Frances. "The cynicism is a relatively recent phenomenon. I'm afraid he's rather allergic to Anton and his enthusiasms. But I think your arrival will do him good – we're all a little too comfortable in our various niches. And I understand you're neighbours."

"That's right," said Kate. It seemed there ought to be something to add to this, but she didn't feel inclined to elaborate. She wasn't sure she wanted to be linked with Dave Singleman in the mind of teaching colleagues, either as his neighbour or his reforming spirit.

Frances changed the subject.

"Anyway. I'd be very happy to support an application for the mentoring scheme if you did decide to apply."

"Thank you," said Kate, rising from the table. "I'll give it some thought."

Chapter Thirteen

"What's got into Singleman?"

One evening later that week, as Kate cleared away her supper things, there was a knock on the door. It was now the end of September, and the bands of cloud that had periodically punctuated the otherwise fine weather had become more frequent, so that lowering, slatey skies and fine drenching rain from the southwest became the norm, and the occasional hours of sunshine were a welcome relief. A fine drizzle was falling now, and although her flat was not cold, she was tempted to put the heating on to take the feeling of damp out of the air.

The knocking had been preceded by the sound of footsteps coming down the outside stair, so she was unsurprised to find Dave Singleman hunched on her doorstep, fleece collar turned up against the weather. Although it was not quite dark she had turned on the outside light before opening the door, and it picked out fine drops of moisture on his clothing and on the ends of his long lashes.

"Hullo," she said. "You'd better come in."

"Cheers." He wiped his feet. "It's not very nice out there."

They were both standing in the kitchen area. Kate's comfortable seating, such as it was, was already occupied by a combination of her briefcase, a basket of ironing, and her laptop. She didn't offer to move any of them.

"I'm afraid it's a bit of a mess," she said, by way of excuse.

"Well I won't stop. I just wondered if there was any chance you could give me a lift to school tomorrow? The car's in for its MOT. I could get the bus if it's inconvenient, but it's forecast to be even wetter than this in the morning."

"You're welcome to a lift," said Kate. "But I'll be leaving at 7.30."

"Bloody hell. You're keen."

"I like to go to the gym in the mornings."

"Right. Are you in training for something?"

"Not particularly. Do we need to go via the garage?"

"No, I dropped the car in on the way home from school. It's only down the road."

He didn't seem in a hurry to leave. Kate was reminded that the balance of hospitality was currently in his favour, but she couldn't afford to fritter the evening away in chit-chat.

"Look, I've got a ton of marking to do, but if you want a quick coffee…"

"No, sorry – I said I wasn't going to stop and I won't. I've got marking to do too. 7.30 tomorrow, then."

"Yes please."

"Thanks, that'll be a big help."

He left, and Kate listened to his footsteps as he climbed the wooden stair to the balcony above. She dropped the latch on the door and returned to the dishes. She could hear the creaking of the floorboards overhead, and she turned on the radio. She noticed again that the Engine House felt colder, and resolved to buy some sort of electric heater to stave off the moment when she would have to turn on the radiators.

At 7.32 the next morning she was sitting in the Fiat, tapping her fingers on the steering wheel. It was raining steadily. She adjusted the electric door mirror so that she could watch the top of the stair. (A hundred and thirty-five quid, she reminded herself – and no contribution forthcoming). There was still no sign of Dave emerging from the upper flat. She was damned if she was going to go up and knock on his door, and get soaked in the process. She pressed twice sharply on the horn. One more minute and I'm leaving, she resolved, and at that point there was a blur of movement in the rain-streaked mirror. Dave locked his door, came strolling down the stairs, whistling, and crossed to the car. He slung his bag in the back beside Kate's.

"Morning! Grotty day. Thanks for this."

Kate said nothing, but pointed at the clock on the dashboard.

"Sorry," said Dave, altering his expression to one of contrition as Kate put the Fiat into gear. "It's a bit earlier than I'm used to."

Kate's irritation was compounded by having to wait for a small convoy of tractors to pass before turning left out of Wheal Prosper, a manoeuvre she felt sure Dave would be noting, and might even comment on. In fact her passenger maintained a tactful silence, but even this was annoying, and once they were on the main road Kate pointedly turned on the radio. The rest of the journey proceeded without conversation.

By the time they reached the school, only a minute or two later than Kate would have wished, she was as cross with herself for her ill-humour as she had been with Dave fifteen minutes earlier.

"Right," she said, as they pulled up. "I take it you would like a lift back?"

"Only if it's convenient," said Dave, still markedly subdued. "And I'm really sorry for being a bit late this morning."

"Forget it. I'm sorry I was grumpy. It's just…I like my routines."

"God yes…where would we be without routines?" said Dave. "So…what time back?"

"Well I would normally leave at six," said Kate, "but perhaps that'll be too late for you to pick up your car."

"No that's fine," he said. "They'll leave it outside. Assuming there's nothing needing doing, that is. I'll be here at five to six sharp. Scout's honour!"

With that they both got out of the car, and Kate headed for the gym. Dave briefly contemplated some advanced lesson planning, then decided he had time to nip into town and grab some breakfast instead.

It was a ten-minute walk through the rain, and by the time he arrived at Costa he was distinctly damp. He sat quietly steaming in a corner seat with his coffee and bacon muffin, pointedly ignoring the gaggle of St Petroc's kids at the table by the window, who for their part were pointedly ignoring him – the coffee shop was in theory out of bounds following an incident of anti-social behaviour earlier in the term. He found himself oddly moved by Kate's admission, or near admission, of inflexibility, and the more contrite at having messed her around. He enjoyed the professional interaction they had over school matters, and even quite liked the fact that she was a bit of a keen bean. In his head he often teased her about it, as he might have done with a colleague he knew better, but this banter was kept entirely internal - he was not confident that Kate would respond kindly to teasing, however gentle. He reflected that if none of the other stuff had happened - if, say, she had simply taken a flat in town, then he would have found her an intriguing and not unappealing prospect. The Door Mirror Incident and the Outhouse Incident however, not to mention the complication of her continuing proximity at the Engine House, muddied the water, and made it easier to categorise her as Undeniably Attractive but a Little too Spiky for Comfort, and therefore probably of no further interest.

He was aware, however, that this might not be the whole story. Much depended on which of two contrasting versions of himself he was setting Kate Porteous alongside. This theme of Dave One and Dave Two, as he had come to think of his two selves, was occupying him increasingly in his contemplative moments, largely as a result of the information Frances had imparted regarding the possible vacancy at the Head of Year Nine. Dave One was essentially his twenties self, which clearly could be allowed to drift onwards seamlessly into his thirties if he so wished. Indeed there was a case for such a laissez-faire approach, namely that he had, up to now, been reasonably content.

Dave Two was a quite different Dave – a more focused, even a more *responsible* Dave. One whose easy and positive relationships with his students, given a little sharpening at the edges, could make him an effective pastoral head, without tying him in too closely to the more tedious, transactional aspects of the middle management treadmill. One who might have more appeal to his career-focused neighbour.

It was by way of trying out Dave Two that he finished his coffee, wandered over to the St Petroc's group in the window, and gently but firmly reminded them of the as-yet-unlifted embargo on Costa.

"I'll let you finish your drinks," he said, "and I won't take this further, but I'll be dropping in over the next few days, and if I find any of you here again you'll be in detention." He turned and left the coffee shop without smiling.

The students exchanged puzzled glances.

"What's got into Singleman?"

At lunchtime there was a voicemail on his phone informing him that the MG needed two new tyres and some welding work on the subframe, which would be carried out the next day. There was also a text from a number he didn't recognise, though when he opened it it was obvious enough who had sent it.

Darling will be in Cornwall for a couple of days next month would be lovely to get together C. xxxx

This was not welcome. He had managed successfully to banish the Candice affair from his thoughts, telling himself that the details were hazy, the circumstances extraordinary and the distance between their respective orbits considerable. In his mind the drunken evening at the Old Rectory had something of the character of an erotic curio brought home by a seafaring uncle, to be locked in a cabinet, taken out and examined once in a while perhaps, but not to be left on public display. The text message was unsettling in its lack of specifics, and he wondered if this was deliberate. Perhaps Candice was testing the water. It was hard to formulate an appropriate response when there were few details on offer. What exactly did "getting together" involve? The phrase had a hippy-ish flavour that was somehow very Candice.

He was as good as his word to Kate, and was standing by her car when she appeared at six o'clock that evening. He explained the situation with the MG and to his relief she readily agreed to run him in again the following day. She had apparently had a good teaching day, and was inclined to chat on the way home. It was Dave whose responses were muted, burdened as he was by the implications of Candice's text and the prospect of a hefty bill for the MG. In his mind the two became conflated, symptoms of a deeper malaise, a certain looseness in his whole approach to life which was at odds with this shiny, perky little car (its welding undegraded and its tyres unworn) and its neat, confident driver.

By the time they got back to Wheal Prosper the rain had passed through, and the sky was clearing. A thin band of gold in the west promised a fine sunset. It was colder, but the air and the grass smelled fresh.

"You know what," said Dave. "I fancy a beer. The café will still be open. Why don't you let me buy you a drink by way of a thank-you."

"Oh…well – that'd be nice. Maybe not a beer…"

"A coffee then. The evening's too good to waste."

She smiled. "You're right. I'll just stick my bag inside."

Ten minutes later they were settled in the window seat of the beach café, Dave with a beer, Kate with her coffee. The café faced south west, and the sun sat a little above the horizon, still just clear of the line of flat cloud that would bring the next band of rain.

"This is nice," said Kate. "I should do it more often."

"Take the chance while you can," said Dave. "They close in the evenings after half term. Then it shuts altogether in January and February. In the summer, though, there's a bit of a scene - bands and comedy nights."

"And all on the doorstep."

"Yeah. I mean there's more going on in town, but I wouldn't swap it."

"How long have you been out here?"

"Three years. It won't last for ever, though. Sooner or later the Brunels will want to do up the Engine House – it's a bit scruffy as holiday lets go, and if they spent a few grand on it they could ask top dollar, given the location."

"It suits you then?"

"Yeah, it suits me. What about you?"

"I'm enjoying it. I mean, it's kind of living the dream, isn't it? I'm not sure what it'll be like in the winter though."

"I love it in winter. It never really gets that cold, but on wild nights it's amazing. Like Wuthering Heights by the sea."

Kate laughed. "You know how to sell it to a Yorkshire lass."

"Have you been in the sea yet?"

"Yeah, I had a dip a couple of weeks back. I used to do a lot of swimming, when I was younger, but all indoors. The waves make it exciting, much more dynamic, but sometimes I long for a 50m pool and a clear lane."

"You swam competitively, then?"

"As a teenager. Then it was clear I wasn't going to grow any more. There's a limit to what you can achieve in the pool when you're five foot four."

"What about surfing?"

"I'd like to give it a go. It's just finding the time."

"This is a good time of year to learn. The water's still warm and the tourists have gone home. The surf's good too."

"Does the surf school run in the winter?"

Dave looked at her. "You don't need to pay the surf school. I'd be glad to teach you."

She laughed. "That's kind. But I might prefer to make a fool of myself in front of someone I don't know."

"I guess."

They were quiet for a moment.

"Well – thanks for the coffee" said Kate. "Good call. I ought to be getting back."

"I might just grab a burger down here," said Dave. "I can't be bothered to cook."

"I've got some leftovers to use up. I'll see you same time tomorrow morning."

"On the dot," said Dave.

As he watched her leave he wondered if he had crossed a line of some sort, or merely moved along one. That morning he had been happy just to have a lift to work. Now he was a little disappointed that she hadn't jumped at his offer of a surfing lesson, or agreed to stay for some food. It would have been nice to have had his second beer sitting across from Kate, as dusk crept along the beach.

Chapter Fourteen

"Perhaps he moonlights as a porn star"

Sammy and Issy sat on the bus. The journey from Eglos took fifteen minutes, which seemed to Sammy quite a long time to sit next to a friend in silence. Silence this morning seemed to be what Issy wanted, however. She had greeted him perfunctorily and put in her earbuds as soon as they sat down. It would be easier in some ways, Sammy thought, if they could just agree that for whatever reason, the character of their relationship was changing, but nothing was being said. Sometimes Issy seemed to be her old self, full of quick-witted chatter and strong opinions. They were not always opinions he agreed with, but that was half the pleasure in the friendship. She was not a girl who got irritated by what he had learned from Mr Singleman to call rational argument. These days however, she seemed remote, her thoughts elsewhere. Sammy didn't feel rejected as such, just temporarily side-lined.

There was, apparently, a boy involved – someone she had met on holiday. He had learned this from Hardeep, who had got it from Amy, who was mates with Lily Tregunna, who was an accepted authority on matters of that nature. Sammy was not particularly put out by this intelligence – Spain was, after all, a long way away, but he was disappointed that the news had come to him third hand. He acknowledged that at this point, he and Issy were probably not quite on the same track of adolescence. His own developing interest in sex was at an experimental and abstract stage, and he found it hard to make the connection between the urgent physical excitement that images could arouse, and the real world of friendship with someone like Issy, whom he liked deeply and for whom he had a kind of respect that might be regarded as old fashioned. The debating competition offered a crumb of comfort – Mr Singleman had paired them together, and he thought it could be fun to work with Issy on researching a topic and constructing an argument, discussing how they would divide up the responsibilities.

His thoughts turned to Donkey. Donkey wanted something from him, but it wasn't yet clear what it was. He had accosted him in the playground at the end of lunchtime on Wednesday and demanded Sammy's snapchat details. Sammy had told him to eff off, and for a moment he thought Donkey was going to hit him. The question was, why did Donkey want to be mates with him all of a sudden? There was nothing he could do about him physically – Doggett was four inches taller than him, and had a stringy, athletic build, but Sammy had a toughness to him that could endure a fair degree of persecution, and a contempt for the bigger boy that provided a measure of psychological defence. He would keep his distance as best he could and sit it out until Donkey decided there were more rewarding victims for whatever he had in mind.

The bus was at the last set of traffic lights before the school hill when Issy pulled out her ear buds and said, as if they had been deep in conversation since they left the village,

"They're sharing lifts now."

"Who?" asked Sammy, purely to prolong the conversation. He knew perfectly well who she meant.

"Singleman and Porteous. I saw them after hockey practice yesterday. They looked quite... matey."

"Well if they're neighbours…"

"I reckon they'll have got it together by Christmas."

"Can't they just be friends?"

She looked at him and grinned.

"Oh Sammy. You're very sweet."

"Cheers, for that," he said, and turned to look out of the window.

In English, Mr Singleman gave out the letters for the London trip. This had been a feature of the autumn term of Year 9 for some time now, and was greatly looked forward to by the students. For many of them it would be their first visit to the capital. The trip had its detractors – the price tag made it a challenge for many parents, although there was a fund, underwritten by the Acadamy Trust, to which families could apply for support. Killick was said to be sceptical, and had made noises about suspending the trip altogether following the condoms incident the previous year, but he had been over-ruled. Emily Flowerdew was a strong supporter.

The trip was scheduled for the weekend before half term. They would leave early on the Friday morning, to allow time for a visit to the Victoria and Albert Museum, then they were to see Macbeth at the Globe in the evening. There was more culture scheduled for the following morning before the long journey home. Most exciting from the point of view of the students, however, was the night spent in a London youth hostel, around which had grown an entire mythology of nocturnal misdeeds.

Mr Singleman gave them a minute to absorb the contents of the letter before he started the lesson. Issy read hers carefully and didn't see Sammy glance briefly at his and jam it without ceremony in his bag. When they moved on to work on their debating speeches, however, she did notice that he was subdued, and remembering his slightly huffy response to her gentle teasing on the bus, she resolved to be nice to him on the way home.

At lunchtime Dave instinctively looked for Kate in the crowded dining hall, but she was nowhere to be seen, so he sat next to Jenny Skinner and asked her how her kids were doing, in a conscious attempt to store up good karma. In fact he got on well with Jenny, whose very public abandonment by her husband, a teacher at a neighbouring school, had aroused the sympathy of most of the staff. Dave occasionally helped her out with practical household matters, a service Jenny accepted with uncomplicated gratitude.

He had not yet replied to Candice's text.

Kate wasn't in the dining hall because she was in Anton Killick's study, at the first meeting of the appraisal steering group. Lunch had been provided by the canteen in the form of a tray of limp ham sandwiches, made from white bread that resembled something that might be bought in bulk at a DIY store. One or two pale lettuce leaves garnished the platter in a nod to the concept of five-a-day.

The steering group, which was seated in a tight circle in what little space the office afforded, consisted of Anton, Kate, Emily Flowerdew, and a bun-shaped woman in a white coat called Morwenna Barnes. She was introduced as the Head of Chemistry. To Kate's surprise Robbo, Dave's buddy from the Idlers Club, was also present.

Anton's study was notable for the plainness of its décor. The walls were white and bare, the desk clear save for a wafer-thin MacBook and a small bronze statuette of a figure in kung-fu pyjamas executing a roundhouse kick. The only other features were functional, though not in an obviously educational sense. A large red cylindrical punchbag was suspended in one corner and there was a horizontal steel bar set into the door frame an inch or two below the lintel. Robbo, who was six foot four, had to duck his head on entering.

Killick's crisp white shirt sleeves were rolled up to reveal sculpted but oddly hairless forearms. Perhaps, thought Kate, he moonlights as a porn star. It was a distracting idea, and she had to shake her head briefly to clear it when Killick opened the meeting.

"Thank you all for coming. I want to begin by laying out what I see as the particular challenges we face in implementing a satisfactory appraisal system, and why I think that it is necessary, despite these challenges, that we push through on this. There should be time for everyone to give their views before we go, but that may be all we can do in this first meeting.

"The biggest challenge we face, clearly, is a degree of cynicism from some members of staff. I find this regrettable, and in many ways incomprehensible. It seems to me to be rooted in some rose-tinted vision of the education system of the last century, when there was no National Curriculum, no league tables, no attainment tests. Now obviously I'm not old enough to have taught under this system myself, but anecdotal and indeed documentary evidence suggests that this approach, while it undoubtedly afforded teachers a considerable amount of professional freedom, resulted in complacency, a slide in standards, and outcomes that varied wildly from school to school."

Kate stole a glance at Emily Flowerdew, who was the only one senior enough to be held responsible for the slide into complacent mediocrity, but the older woman's face was impassive. Killick continued,

"I have no time for cynicism. It has no place in education, and it certainly has no place at St Petroc's. I do not intend to allow it to prevent us from doing the right thing by our students."

He paused to allow this noble avowal to sink in. Robbo shifted in his seat, as if about to comment, but thought the better of it.

"The second challenge we face is one of resources. I do accept that the pressures we are under, in terms of time and budgetary restraint, are considerable. I'm hopeful that this group will assist me in coming up with proposals that will deliver the outcomes we are looking for without placing an intolerable burden on staff.

"Colleagues are resistant to the idea of working harder – I get that message loud and clear. In some, though by no means in all cases, this is understandable. However we are all, I believe, capable of working *smarter*." Again a slight pause, to allow the room to catch up with his thinking.

The room had heard this trope before. Killick altered his body language, sitting back in his seat and spreading his arms, palms upward like a supplicant.

"So why are we doing this?" He leaned forward again, eyes widening slightly. "Put simply, without it we shall never improve. At best we will tread water, comfortable with our assessment as a "good" school, knowing that, generally speaking, unless parents have fifteen thousand a year to send their children up the line, we are the school of choice in the area. Well that's not good enough for me. As long as there is room for improvement – and I think that we can all acknowledge that there *is* room for improvement – we should be determined to make that improvement. As long as there is a standard above that which we are currently deemed to meet – and let us be clear, this is not an impossible standard, many Marcato schools achieve it - we should be striving to attain that standard. We owe it to our students and to their parents. We owe it to *Cornwall.*"

Robbo and Morwenna Barnes, who were both Cornish born and bred, exchanged the briefest of glances. Even Kate, who up to that point had been quite impressed by the clarity and passion of Killick's speech, thought that this was perhaps laying it on a bit thick.

Anton, however, was apparently pleased with this conclusion to his remarks. He sat back in his seat and spread his arms again.

"Colleagues – over to you."

There was a perceptible adjusting of posture, like the break between the movements of a symphony. There was, briefly, the same awful possibility that someone might applaud. There were deferential glances at Emily, but her mouth remained firmly closed. Perhaps she didn't want to make this too SMT led. Morwenna Barnes spoke first.

"Anton I think you mentioned on the Inset day that you wanted to include value-added as an element in appraisal…"

"Thank you, Morwenna, an excellent point…" cut in Killick.

"I haven't actually made my point yet," said Morwenna.

The Deputy Head looked wounded. "I do apologise. Please continue."

"I think most staff understand the need for appraisal, and many would welcome a workable system that felt like part of a professional development strategy. Sticking value-added in there is a whole different ball game. It smacks of payment by results. It will just add extra pressure."

"Morwenna's right," said Robbo. "There are far too many variables beyond the individual teacher's control."

Killick was momentarily nonplussed.

"I find this difficult to understand," he said. "Exam results, surely, are our gold standard. They're what we are here for…"

"Well not entirely, Anton," said Emily, speaking for the first time. "We serve our students best when they leave us fully equipped to achieve their potential; ready, hopefully, to move on to the next stage of life. Exam results are an important aspect of that, of course, but there are many other ways in which we help our students to prepare for the outside world."

"And these other ways are recognised by Ofsted," put in Robbo. "Our last report praised the quality of relationships between staff and students, the breadth of the educational experience we offer, and the general levels of well-being of the kids."

"Our last report wasn't quite so complimentary about our exam results," said Killick. "And all these other things, which are of course important, are easier to recognise than to measure. What I want us to do is to address ourselves to the shortcomings of the one area for which we have hard data, and that is academic achievement."

"Kate, you've come from an academic school," said Emily. "What's your take on this?"

"Well," said Kate, hesitantly. "My last school *was* an academic school, and we did measure value-added fairly rigorously. I have to say for me it produced a rather sterile environment, and one that the teachers found quite stressful. I've only been here a few weeks, but I already get a different vibe from St Petroc's. It's clearly a school that cares about the wellbeing of its students, and that seems to me a very healthy approach." She paused. She was aware of Killick watching her, poised to interrupt.

"Having said that, I also have sympathy for Anton's desire not to let the academic element slide out of sight. I'd be interested in trying to come up with a way of including academic attainment of students in the appraisal package, but doing it in a manner that avoids this kind of ratchet effect - where all a good set of results does for a teacher is make it harder to show progress next time round."

"Well, quite," said Robbo. "Well put."

There was a pause. Killick looked at his watch.

"I think I'd like to draw it to a close there," he said. I'm sure we'd all like five minutes before afternoon school. Is everybody good to meet at the same time in a fortnight?"

There were nods all round.

"Then can I ask that we all apply ourselves to the matter as Kate has helpfully framed it? That we think about a means of including academic value that avoids – I'm not sure I like the word "ratchet", but let's hang onto it for the time being – that avoids the *perception,* shall we say, of any kind of ratchet effect."

There was a scraping of chairs and a murmuring of platitudes that Killick could, if he wished, interpret as assent. One by one they filtered out into the corridor, leaving the Deputy Head standing behind his desk, sculpted arms akimbo. Nobody had touched the sandwiches.

Chapter Fifteen

"The interior of the Fiat was quiet, like a confessional"

Killick watched them go through the vertical vision panel set into his office door, then he turned and crossed to the corner of the room where the red vinyl punchbag was suspended. He paused in front of it, feet hip-width apart, and breathed slowly and deeply, waiting for the footsteps in the corridor to recede. Then, in a fluid movement that seemed to begin from somewhere within him, he struck it three times, left-right-left, with considerable force. He breathed again, slowly and calmly, and bowed his head briefly before returning to his MacBook, and the spreadsheets that demonstrated with such clarity what his colleagues seemed unable to see.

In the next-door office Emily Flowerdew, already seated at her own desk, heard the rapid triple smack of Anton's combination punch. She looked up and pursed her lips thoughtfully. She was familiar with the sound, and knew what it signified, knew that if she were to put her head round Anton's door now, she would find him calm, professional, polite. She shook her head and returned to the pile of buff cardboard files in her in-tray, one of which bore Donovan Doggett's name.

Dave Singleman's Year 8 group were in excitable mood that afternoon. They were in the early stages of their preparation for the Shakespeare festival, and what might optimistically be called the creative tension was building rapidly.

The Shakespeare festival, or Shakeyfest as it was known, took place over two nights, and had been an early brainchild of Frances's. The idea was that each Year 8 English group would perform a short piece, between ten and twenty minutes in length, either from or about a Shakespeare play, or about some aspect of the Bard's life and work. The festival was not without its advantages for the hard-pressed English teacher - it occupied the best part of a half-term's work without generating much marking, and now that they were a few years into the project there was a bank of scripts in the department that meant little was required in the way of writing. Parents, students, governors and senior staff all loved it, or professed to, and invariably at Sixth Form leaving assemblies it was one of the collective memories everybody wanted to revisit.

It would be fair to say, however, that most members of the English department regarded it with a degree of ambivalence, and some quietly loathed it, while the theatre staff saw it as an unwelcome intrusion on an already busy programme, and invariably a source of loss and damage to the theatre stock. Organising 180 thirteen year-olds (it was an unwritten rule that everybody had to have a part) into six playlets in a language most of them barely understood, with the attendant challenges of costuming, rehearsal and casting, generated a peculiarly intense if entirely foreseeable set of anxieties. The logistical organisation on the night, for which Dave was responsible, was a significant challenge, with the theatre full to bursting, and the various groups, each with their peculiar baggage of props and costumes, and high on a combination of Haribo and adrenalin, vying for limited backstage space.

The lesson began with a predictable flurry of urgent questions and problematic pieces of information.

"Sir have you decided who's going to be Juliet?"

"Sir I've left my script at home."

"Sir, I'm not going to be here for the festival."

"Is it true we're going to have real swords?"

"Real swords? We're gonna have real swords!"

Once these details had been dealt with, a reasonable level of order imposed, and spare scripts found for those without, things proceeded in a more or less orderly fashion, the pace dictated by the need to translate the more complex speeches as they went along. It was acceptable for scripts to partially paraphrase, and indeed to invent entire scenes for the purposes of giving manageable speaking parts to the less confident, but Dave was something of a purist in this regard and kept such modifications to a minimum.

The lesson required considerable energy, the more so for being the last of the day, and it was with some relief that he escaped to the staffroom. He had couple of hours to fill before meeting with Kate, who was going to drop him off at the garage. There was marking to do, and before that a meeting of the Idlers Club to discuss the next Sunday School Outing. He made himself a cup of tea and wandered over to where Robbo and Stubbsy were already seated, along with Mike Pengelly, who taught maths.

"Afternoon chaps."

"Alright?"

"Not so bad."

"God the term's dragging."

"Is Matt coming?"

"Matt's taking detention. We expecting anyone else?"

There were around half a dozen fully paid-up Idlers, though they were rarely all in attendance at one time. Robbo was the unofficial Chair. He was second in the PE department, a tall athletic man with an impressive moustache and a serious demeanour that masked a deep-seated commitment to the idling lifestyle.

"Right. There's four of us going so far. We're all agreed that it'll be the first weekend of half term, and that there needs to be at least one round of golf involved. Question is – what else, and where?"

"I think we should go for Bristol again. Hit the clubs on Saturday night."

Dave made a face. "Am I the only one who's feeling a bit old for clubbing? I'd favour just booking into a decent hotel with a golf course. Get an all-in weekend package, and those who wish can get quietly pissed in the evenings."

"Dear, dear," said Mike. "Is this what happens when you turn thirty?"

"It appears so," said Dave.

"I'm for Bristol, deffo," said Stubbsy. "This is a chance to pull someone you won't bump into in Poundland."

Dave allowed himself the unkind thought that Stubbsy was unlikely to pull anyone until he'd sorted his acne.

"Put it to the vote, then," said Dave.

They did, and Bristol won by three to one. It was agreed that those who favoured Bristol would research hotels in the coming week, and Dave, by way of a consolation prize, could choose a suitable golf course for the daytime activities. Robbo changed the subject.

"I can also report back on the appraisal steering group meeting, not that there's a great deal to say. Basically nothing is up and running yet. Killick is determined to get academic attainment in there somewhere, but his only ally seems to be Kate Porteous. Emily's not keen."

"Can't you work on her, Dave?"

"Exercise some of that fabled Singleman charm?"

Stubbsy snickered.

"Kate's all right," said Dave. "She's keen, but she's not an idiot."

"No, she was only tentatively supportive," acknowledged Robbo. "But you know what Anton's like. He doesn't need much encouragement. I can't come out too strongly against, or he'll just dismiss me as a naysayer. I was quite surprised he let me on the working party in the first place."

"Keeping his enemies close," said Mike.

"I agree with Robbo," said Dave. "It's best to appear reasonably supportive, string it along slowly and maybe slip in a couple of ideas that we know won't fly. Maybe that's what Kate's doing."

Robbo looked at him sceptically. "I don't think so. She's pretty much on Killick's side. I wouldn't be surprised if he starts cultivating her."

"Nice work if you can get it," snickered Stubbsy.

God you are a knob, thought Dave. Mike and Robbo were good mates, but did he really want to spend a weekend of his half term with this guy? Come to think of it, was idling itself just a little bit passé?

"Well, good work, Robbo," said Mike. "Definitely worth having a man on the inside."

The meeting broke up, and Dave headed for the workroom. He contemplated the pile of exercise books on the table and decided he couldn't quite face them yet. He logged onto one of the PCs and scrolled down through his emails. He hovered the cursor over the one from Killick that outlined the details of the mentoring programme, and clicked. It was another small victory for Dave Two.

Dave Two was still ascendant on the way home in the car.

"So how was the steering group," he asked Kate as they cleared the town traffic and joined the coast road.

"Who wants to know?"

"Obviously, if it's *sub-judice,* I won't press you."

"I'm sure Robbo will fill you in on the details."

"Well you know Robbo – he's a great guy but he can be a touch cynical at times. I'd rather hear your account."

Kate glanced at him. "Are you winding me up?"

"No!" Dave contrived to look injured. "I'm genuinely interested."

"Well we're not really out of the blocks yet. The issue seems to be how to include some element of academic value-added in the appraisal process, without terrifying the teaching staff."

"It's a tricky one," said Dave.

"So, if you've any ideas, I'll be happy to relay them to the group."

"Well I might have some ideas," said Dave. "I might well have some ideas. But I wouldn't necessarily tell the steering group where you got them from."

"Really?" said Kate. "Why's that?"

"Well you know…I mean I think I'm regarded as a reasonably solid teacher and all that kind of thing, but maybe…"

"A touch cynical at times?"

He was rather enjoying this banter. Kate wasn't exactly laugh-a-minute, but she was quick. They had reached the garage where Dave's car, newly MOT'd, was sitting on the forecourt. He waited until she turned off the engine, and looked at her, deliberately. She met his eyes. The interior of the Fiat was quiet, like a confessional. It was well after six and the forecourt was deserted.

"OK," he said. "I have been, traditionally, a bit of a cynic. I hold my hands up to that. Frankly anyone at the chalk face has a right to be. But I am…reviewing my position." He was vaguely aware of Dave One stirring, turning to look at him, holding up his hands in disbelief.

"OK," said Kate, still meeting his gaze. "Tell me more." Her eyes behind the small round glasses were serious. Her eyes, when you saw them this close, were…rather gorgeous. He wanted to reach out and take off her glasses so that he could see them better. The thought struck him that it would be quite possible to fall in love with this woman, and it was rather intoxicating. He had fully intended to say something genuine and revealing of his vulnerability, perhaps share with her his intention, formed only that afternoon, of applying for the mentoring scheme, but instead he said,

"Can I kiss you?"

That's more like it, said Dave One approvingly.

"Absolutely not," said Kate. She sat back in her seat, looking forwards through the windscreen.

"I…" he began, but she cut him off.

"Looks like your car's ready." Still without looking at him she gestured through the windscreen towards the MG.

"Um…yes. Thanks for the lift. Again. And I'm really sorry if I…"

"It's fine," she said.

"You're not offended?"

"Just a bit taken aback."

"Yes. Of course. I'm really sorry."

"I said it's fine."

"OK. Good. I mean it's good that you're not offended. I'll, um, see you later."

Dave got out of the Fiat and closed the door carefully, patting the roof twice in what he immediately recognised as an unnecessary and patronising gesture. Cursing Dave One and all his works, he crossed to where the MG was waiting. The keys were on the rear wheel, under the wheel arch. He opened the door and got in, without looking back at Kate. By the time he had turned his car, the yellow Fiat was out of sight.

On the bus home that evening, it was Sammy who was silent in the face of Issy's determined efforts to be cheerful and friendly. She wanted to talk about the London trip, and he didn't.

She had no idea. She assumed that the £180 for the trip was, for him as for her, a simple matter of clicking a mouse, of making a marginal reduction in the seemingly limitless wealth available to the Brunel family for cars, houses, clothes, holidays, restaurants.

Sammy didn't think of himself as poor – the word had a Victorian ring to it – but he knew there wasn't spare cash for this kind of luxury. His mum's disability meant there were extra expenses of various sorts, and the state support she received didn't compensate for the loss of her wages as a carer. He had put the London trip letter in a convenient bin, and had no intention of mentioning it to his parents.

"Sammy, you are going to go to London, aren't you?" asked Issy, when a series of attempts to discuss the visit met with monosyllabic responses.

"Probably not."

"But it'll be awesome!"

"I think we're doing something that weekend."

"Really? Something nice?" To the best of Issy's knowledge the Pascoes rarely "did" anything, beyond going to the pub.

"It's a kind of family thing. It'll be OK."

"Can't you get out of it?"

Sammy shrugged. "I dunno. Don't think so."

In the Range Rover, on the short trip from the bus stop to her home outside the village, the penny, or rather the lack of pennies, dropped.

"I think I've been a bit of an idiot," Issy said to her Mum.

"Have you forgotten something?"

"I've forgotten that Sammy's family don't have much money. Mum is it possible they wouldn't be able to afford for him to go on the London trip?"

"I don't know. I suppose it might be tricky for them."

"I've just gone on and on at him about how much fun it's going to be, and how he needs to get his form in soon. Damn! I remember now there was some kind of issue in the junior school when we went to Bristol."

"I think the school has a fund of some sort…"

"Yes! Yes they do! He could apply to that."

"You need to be careful Issy. Sammy's family are proud people. They might not want to rely on the school's charity."

"No, I get that." She spent the rest of the journey in silence, thinking hard. She forgot that her phone had buzzed in her pocket on the way home, and it was much later that evening that she read the text from Enrique. It was different from the others, in a way that was both exciting and a bit scary.

Chapter Sixteen

"It's Candice by the way"

Back at the Engine House, Dave gloomily contemplated the culinary choices offered by his larder. He had intended to go to the supermarket on his way home, but in his confusion at the awkward parting from Kate, he had forgotten about this, and nearing the end of the week as it was, he was low on provisions. He was now faced with the prospect of a frozen pizza, which could be dressed up with the remains of a tin of baked beans at the back of the fridge, (though now he came to think of it, those had been there a while) or constructing something with pasta and lardons.

More in hope than expectation, he scanned the fridge for eggs, and found two in a box whose date was not dangerously prehistoric. A stub of Parmesan opened up the morale-boosting prospect of a spaghetti carbonara. Although he ate his fair share of TV dinners, Dave regarded them as a Bad Thing, and he felt better about himself if his meals were constructed at least partially from ingredients. At this moment, his thoughts still in something of a turmoil, he needed to persuade himself he was in control of events. He turned on Radio 3, another anchor for the orderly life that served the double purpose of declaring business as usual, while allowing space for thinking.

What exactly had he done? How big a mistake had he made? He had only known Kate four weeks, and they had been on good terms for less than half that. She was a new colleague and he was the old hand both at school and here at the Engine House. Did that alter the equation?

As he fried up the lardons and adjusted the heat beneath the spaghetti, he re-ran the sequence of events, and what had been said, so far as he could remember it. Clearly he had misjudged the mood and the moment. That was bad. But he had *asked* if he could kiss her, and while there was no denying she had looked a little shocked, she had said she wasn't offended. So hopefully, she wasn't going to lodge a sexual harassment claim, though he recognised that she was the type who wouldn't hesitate do so if she felt it was warranted. And anyway, he could look himself in the eye and say he wasn't trying to take advantage of her – he had simply been caught up in one of those delicate moments of enchantment that do, on occasions lead to kissing, and more, and which he had always considered as one of life's delights. Unfortunately the delight on this occasion was clearly one-sided.

Steady on, Singleman, he told himself. Don't panic.

Assuming no serious harm had been done to Kate's sense of wellbeing, or to his own career prospects, the question was, perhaps, where did it go from here? How should he now conduct himself towards her? The answer might have been more straightforward had it not been for the inconvenient truth that he was, it had to be acknowledged, falling a little bit in love with his spiky, self-contained, smart young colleague. That made it all considerably more tricky.

As Dave ate his way through his therapeutic supper, the spiky, self-contained, smart young colleague was sitting in the window seat of a quiet clifftop pub several miles from the Engine House, sipping at a gin and tonic, and contemplating much the same question of what form future relations should take. For Kate, however, the complication of romantic attachment was not an issue.

When she left Dave at the garage, she didn't go straight back to Wheal Prosper. He would only have been seconds behind her, and she wanted to avoid the awkwardness of parking side by side, and walking to their respective flats in embarrassed silence, or worse still stammering further platitudes of apology or absolution. She had turned off at the first opportunity, doubled back on herself, and driven out to the west.

It was true that she had been taken aback by Dave's unexpected request. It was also true that she had not really been offended, although she knew that she might have done more to convince Dave of this. Her thoughts were complex, formed of several strands. She had been steadily warming to her colleague. While he still had the capacity to irritate her, she had found herself increasingly convinced by Frances's early description of Dave as fundamentally a decent bloke – not necessarily entirely reliable in minor matters, but probably there when you needed him. And he was nice-looking – in an un-threatening, brown-eyed, long lashed kind of way. Kissing him might have been perfectly pleasant.

Was she therefore a little disappointed with herself for declining the offer? The truth was her response had been largely instinctive. After her initial scepticism at Dave's interest in the affairs of the steering group, she had accepted at face value the idea that he wanted to chat seriously about…what? His career prospects? His Battle with Cynicism? Whatever, she had been prepared to listen, and the "Can I kiss you" had come completely out of left field.

She didn't think anybody had said those words to her before. Her own calculated seduction of a fellow student on a PGCE ski trip had been largely unspoken, and since then she had avoided physical entanglements. She got offers from time to time, but not ones she felt inclined to accept. "Can I kiss you" was rather sweet, and had deserved, perhaps, with the benefit of hindsight, to be responded to in the affirmative, or at least a little less abruptly. She was not insensible to the kind of mental confusion Dave might now be feeling.

She looked out at the sea, which was calm, and losing its colour now to the dusk, and allowed herself to envision the counterfactual version of events, and what might have followed. Nothing there and then, presumably. They were hardly going to fumble their way through one another's clothing on the forecourt of Opie Autocare. The thought, though, aided perhaps by the gin, was diverting, and she shifted in her seat. A little unexpectedly, the idea of Dave Singleman segued into the idea of Anton Killick.

In a purely physical sense, Anton was…interesting. Those cheekbones. The strength in his hairless arms and presumably hairless chest. She could see that there was something lacking in the man – that porn-star soul-lessness - but soul was not a necessary ingredient of fantasy, and fantasy was so much less complicated than actual entanglement, particularly where neighbours and colleagues were concerned.

She drained her gin and tonic, picked up her bag and left the pub.

The subject of Kate's recent imaginings was at that precise moment seated cross-legged on a yoga mat in the middle of his empty, square, white living-room, settling himself prior to his meditation. The clock on the window ledge ticked quietly and the white rats snuffled in their straw. The emptying of one's mind, allowing the clutter of the day to float away into an airy distance, was for Anton usually a straightforward matter, but this evening he found that there were one or two details of the day's business that snagged at his attention. Chief among these was Kate Porteous, in whom he felt mildly disappointed. She had not been quite as enthusiastic an ally as she might have been. He adjusted his posture, shook his head gently as a horse might, and breathed steadily. Still the resistance. He stood and crossed to the window, resting his hands on the narrow ledge, and looked out over the twilit town. He would allow himself five minutes to explore, rationally and without attachment, how he wished to conduct himself in relation to this interesting and opinionated junior colleague, then he would return to his spiritual practice.

Back at the Engine House, Dave too was having difficulty in settling to his evening's activity. In his case it was not meditation, but progress with Chapter Two of *Mousehole!* that was proving elusive, the Spanish fleet still stubbornly becalmed in Santander. It would appear that for him at least, bold steps in the realm of romance were not the best preparation for the application of literary talent.

He decided that the best remedy for his restless mind, and perhaps also for the precarious position in which he had placed himself, was to push through on his original intention, which was to apply for a place on the mentoring scheme. That afternoon he had skim-read the pages of information that Killick had emailed to all staff, and now he turned to them once more. Even he had to acknowledge that the scheme amounted to more than just window dressing for the benefit of Ofsted. The commitment required was substantial, and would certainly cut into his leisure time, but perhaps he needed to recognise that the surf would always be there; that the golf courses of west Cornwall were not going to be given over to housing while his back was turned. *Mousehole!* might need to be put on hold, but wasn't his novel itself something of a displacement activity? He opened the online application form, and began to type his name, date of birth and qualifications. Outside his window the sea grew dark, and the lights of the channel buoys winked encouragement. Dave One seemed to have retreated for the time being, abashed perhaps at the trouble he had caused.

Dave Two was wrestling with the section that asked him to describe his ambitions as an educational practitioner when his phone rang in his pocket. He eased it out and glanced at the screen. A number, not a listed contact – the dialling code was familiar, though. He killed the call, and returned to the application form, leaving the phone on his desk. A moment later an urgent buzz signalled the arrival of a voicemail. He sighed and touched the screen. Might as well get it over with. The voicemail cycled through its tinny preliminaries, then came the familiar tones of Candice.

"Darling! You haven't answered my text you naughty thing! Now I'm not taking it personally because I know how frightfully busy you teachers are…but listen darling I'm going to be down your way on the 11th and 12th of October and I wondered if you could put me up for the night? We could have a lovely catch up and you can tell me all about how your writing is going. It's Candice by the way!"

Dave rested his head on his hands in the classic pose of weary resignation. Why, he asked himself, does my life need to be so flaming complicated?

Ten feet beneath him, Kate Porteous sat at her own window desk, her laptop open in front of her. In contrast to her neighbour on the floor above, however, her head was up and her mind clear. She too clicked on the email from Anton Killick, and went straight to the attachment that held the application form. She had fully absorbed the guidance notes the day the email came out. She began to type her details, undistracted by unwanted admirers. The one she knew about had been satisfactorily put on hold, and the one of whom she was ignorant was biding his time.

In the lounge of the town house in Penzance, Frances Fivey lay elegantly along the settee, her feet resting in Inga's lap. They had agreed upon a drink before Inga, whose turn it was, prepared the supper. That had been an hour ago, and they were on their third. A Verdi opera played softly in the background.

"So how is your new member of staff settling in? She is rather sweet I think."

"She's doing fine," yawned Frances. "She's resilient."

"She is maybe a little closed up on herself?"

"Maybe a little. I was rather hoping she and Dave might be company for one another."

"Like puppies."

"Just so. But they got off on the wrong foot. Or paw."

"Yes you told me. The wing mirror debacle. But it is all sorted now?"

"I think so. But I don't think they're about to fall into one another's arms. Did I tell you they ended up living next to one another?"

"Well. That explains it. Proximity makes the heart grow colder."

Frances rubbed Inga's lap with her stockinged toe.

"Not always. Are we eating tonight? Or shall I ring for a pizza?"

This was a provocation. Inga hated fast food of any sort, pizza especially.

"No, I am about to rise and attend to my duties. But there is something else I was going to ask you. This mentoring scheme…"

"Yeeees?"

"I think you should apply."

Frances wrinkled her nose. "It's really not my thing darling. I'm rather happy doing what I'm doing. And besides, I've been running around encouraging my staff to apply."

"That is because it is a good scheme and you are a good manager. But who is managing you? Who is developing your career?"

"I think you might be."

"Emily retires in three years' time, yes?"

"Assuming she goes when she's meant to."

"You would be so good at that job, Frances. You could build on the solid work that Emily has done, but add so much more. And from what I have seen of Anton, the school will need someone who can stand up to him, balance out his obsession with statistics and league tables."

"Says the Ofsted Inspector."

"I don't make the rules. And anyway, schools imagine we are much more obsessed with these things than we actually are."

"I'm getting hungry."

"Please think about it."

"I'll think about it. Now can we have some food?"

Chapter Seventeen

"The male ego is notoriously fragile"

The pace of the term picked up. The October break was unmistakably there on the horizon for any teacher who had time to lift their eyes and look, but there was too much to do before it could be contemplated as an imminent relief and pleasure. There were assessments to plan and mark, short reports to complete, and for the English department, the relentless onward march of the Shakespeare festival. There was also the London trip to be successfully planned and executed.

This busy-ness suited both Kate and Dave. The proposition in the car park of Opie Autocare had been mentioned by neither, but Kate had been careful to be friendly towards her colleague in their professional encounters, so that he knew he was not in disgrace. This concession was not lost on Dave, and he was grateful for it, but he nonetheless kept a respectful distance. Domestic interactions were few as a consequence of the MG being back on the road, allowing Dave to revert to his own, more flexible, commuting schedule. Kate now owned her own tumble drier.

She had also, with Frances's encouragement, submitted her application for the mentoring scheme. Dave had completed his, but for the time being it sat as a draft on his laptop. The deadline was still a week away, and he wasn't yet convinced that it was what he wanted to do. Dave One and Dave Two, such distinct and opposed characters only a week or so ago, seemed to have struck a truce, whereby it was accepted that a more settled and directed life plan might be contemplated, provided no drastic measures were taken without detailed consultation.

Dave's feelings and intentions with regard to Kate were similarly filed, for the present at least, in a tray marked "No Immediate Action", but she remained, unquestionably, a person of interest, and that surprising admission to himself that she was more than just appealing to the eye was nurtured and wondered at as she drifted in and out of his orbit. Sometimes in the evenings he was aware of her presence in the flat below as a source of warmth and positive energy, and he imagined he could sense her whereabouts as she moved around a few feet beneath him.

Kate was oblivious to the effect she was having upon her neighbour, assuming that his unexpected approach had been nothing more than a bloke trying it on, as blokes sometimes did. Her principle feeling at this point in the term was a kind of energising pleasure in the sense that she was no longer a brand-new colleague in unfamiliar surroundings. By now she knew by sight a good half of the staff, so that cheery greeting by name, and chatter around the coffee machine, became the norm. She was forming friendships with colleagues outside the department and had enjoyed one or two excursions and meet ups with single female staff of her own age. She was beginning to feel that she belonged, and she felt a growing certainty that the move she had made was a good one.

She was also getting to know her form, who were responding well to her consistent, no-nonsense, patient approach. She had had a long discussion with Emily Flowerdew about Donovan Doggett, and had read carefully through the inch-thick file of school and social worker's reports. She knew that it would be difficult to keep him on side, and probably, soon enough, difficult to keep him in school, but she was determined that if he did drop out it would not be for the lack of a supportive form tutor. She had made an arrangement to meet with him once a week at lunchtime, knowing that this would be virtually impossible to enforce, but interested to see if it was something he would see any value in. So far he had missed two of these meetings, and attended one, and she sat now in the pastoral office that was used for student appointments, waiting to see if he would appear. There had been an incident in PE involving another student's trainers that she needed to discuss with him before parents became involved.

It was half-way through the twenty-minute slot allocated for the tutorial and she had more or less given up on the prospect of Donkey's attendance, when the door opened, and Doggett stuck his dark, tousled head round. He had not yet acquired the knocking habit, but there was a detectable element of deference in his manner. She wondered if this was pre-emptive.

"Sorry I'm late, Miss. Is it still all right to see you?"

"Sure," she said. "Grab a seat." Donkey did so and looked at his feet for a few seconds. Kate was about to prompt him with a question when he lifted his head and looked at her directly. There was something quite startling in the gaze of his blue eyes.

"I wunna do this debating thing."

Kate was taken aback but did her best not to show it.

"You mean the inter-schools competition?"

"Thassa one."

"Right…well…that's great. I'm really pleased. Debating is a very worthwhile thing to get involved with."

"So can I do it?"

"Well possibly. It's not straightforward. It wouldn't be me who selects the team." Even as she said this, she knew it was something of a cop out.

"Who selects the team, then?"

"Mr Singleman."

"Well that's it then. I might as well forget it. Singleman don't like me."

"What makes you say that?"

"I dunno. We just don't get on."

In fact in last year's Shakespeare festival Donkey had half-inched an expensive replica pistol that one of Dave's class had brought in as a prop, after Dave had signed a promise in blood to the boy's parent that he would personally supervise its issue and retention each time it was required. Kate, of course, knew nothing of this.

"Well look," she said. "Let me talk to him. As you know I'm new at the school, and I don't know how many teams we're allowed to enter. Have you thought about who your partner might be?"

"I dunno. Maybe Pascoe?"

"Sammy?" Kate had noticed that there was little love lost between the two.

"Yeah, him. He don't look much but he's got a mouth on him. I bet he's good at debating."

"Well – it would really have to be somebody in your English group. So that you can practise together."

"Everyone's thick as shit in our group, though miss, aren't they?"

"Donovan…"

"It's true though, in't it? It's the thickos group. That's why there's only fifteen of us in it."

"It's for people who struggle with that particular subject. That doesn't mean they're stupid. Look – leave the debating thing with me. As I said, I think it's really great that you want to do it. In fact, I'm going to give you a merit just for bringing it up."

"And one for coming to see you?"

"Two merits, then. However, there is another matter we need to discuss."

"If it's about those trainers…"

"What trainers would they be, Donovan?"

She caught up with Dave in his classroom after lessons. He was picking up crumpled pieces of paper from the floor.

"Can I have a quick word? About the inter-schools debating?"

"Um, sure," Dave replied. "God my Year 10s were lively today." He completed his clearing operation and turned to face her. This was the first time the two of them had been alone together since the Opie Autocare Proposition, and he felt himself reddening a little. If Kate noticed, or if she had made the same observation to herself, it seemed to cause her no discomfort.

"Right. Long shot, but…how many teams can we enter?"

"You're allowed to enter up to three. Most schools enter one or two."

"So if I had a team I wanted to enter…"

"Are they likely to be any good?" Dave was well aware that Kate had the bottom set.

"Frankly, no. At least I don't think so. It's just I've got a student who's very keen to do it, and I want to encourage him. I don't even have a partner for him yet."

"Who is it?"

She paused. "Donovan Doggett."

Dave looked at her incredulously.

"*Donkey?* Donkey wants to enter the debating competition?"

"Yes. Is that a completely mad idea?"

"It's worse than mad. It's positively dangerous. The guy's a major incident waiting to happen. He can barely sit still. Or pass a shiny object without wanting to put it in his pocket. He'd be unable to make a point of information without calling his opponent a twat, or worse. And who's going to want to be his partner?"

"I acknowledge there are hurdles to overcome," said Kate. "But he came to me today and said he wanted to do it. Isn't that fairly incredible for a student like Doggett?"

"Highly suspicious, if you ask me," said Dave. "He's almost certainly planning something."

"I'm not sure that he is. He's actually taken a bit of interest in class."

"That's because you're debating drugs policy. It'll be a different manner when they're discussing…I don't know – euthanasia, or whether we're better off outside the EU."

"I want to encourage him."

"Well I'm sorry, said Dave, "but I'd be very reluctant to enter him. Apart from anything else I couldn't take responsibility for his behaviour out of school. You know it all takes place up at County Hall? The Leader of the Council, the Chair of the Rotary Club, the press, they'll all be there. I simply can't risk letting Donkey loose among all that lot."

"He said you didn't like him."

"Well he's right. I don't."

There was a pause. Dave turned away from Kate's steady gaze and began packing his briefcase. He was aware that he was not coming out of this well, and half expected Kate to flounce out, disgusted at his lack of compassion. Instead she pulled out one of the chairs and sat down.

"What if I took full responsibility for him? And for his entry. I'll do the paperwork. And I'll sit in the back of the minibus with the kids. You can concentrate on your high-fliers and I'll just have Donkey and whoever we can persuade to enter the competition with him."

Dave sat down too, in his own seat behind the desk. He thought for a moment.

"I don't know. It's still, in my view, a massive risk. Look, I'm sorry Kate. I know I probably seem really negative here, but I've been doing this competition for the last three years, and it's a great night out for our brighter kids – they rise to the occasion. And this year, with Sammy and Issy, I really think we might have a chance of winning."

"Does it always have to be the brighter kids that get the breaks?"

"Well you tell me. You're the one who's been teaching in a grammar school."

Kate looked stung. "I'm not teaching in a grammar school now."

"No. Sorry."

"Could you maybe not rule the idea out completely? Maybe think about what I suggested? I'll even do the risk assessment."

Dave paused again. The truth was he wanted nothing to do with Kate's plan, and didn't want Donkey Doggett within ten miles of the debating competition. But he felt trapped.

"OK. I won't rule it out…yet. The entries don't have to be in for a couple of weeks. If you still think it's a good idea, I'll enter two teams. Then we can wait and see what the topics are. If Donkey's still interested, and you've found a partner for him, we'll take a decision. If he's gone off the idea, I can probably put together another scratch team from my group."

"Thanks." Kate rose. "As you say, it may be a flash in the pan. But it would feel really wrong just to knock him straight back at this stage."

"Well quite," said Dave. "The male ego is notoriously fragile."

Kate looked at him, "Well maybe in adolescents. In my experience grown men can survive the odd setback."

She turned to leave, and he had the distinct impression she was trying not to laugh.

As Dave walked back to his car, he was accosted by Issy Brunel.

"Hello Issy, what are you hanging around for? "

"I've got the dentist in town in a bit," said Issy. "Have you got a couple of minutes, Sir?

"Well – yes," said Dave. "If you're happy to chat here?" There were still odd students and members of staff crossing the playground, but nobody within earshot. He noticed Kate's yellow Fiat, almost always one of the last cars remaining at the end of the day.

"It's just, um, it's about Sammy."

"Sammy Pascoe?"

"Yes. You see, I think he's not going on the London trip, because his family can't afford it, and Mum said she thought there was a fund that could cover the cost."

"Well your Mum's right. There is a fund. It won't necessarily meet the full cost, but it should make it affordable."

"So does Sammy just apply?"

"I can't really discuss another student's circumstances. But in general, it would be the parents who would apply."

"In this particular case, I don't think the parents will." Issy's face was serious, and Dave noticed with approval her effortless adoption of the lawyerly non-specific third person.

"I see. And would that be a result of lack of awareness or lack of inclination?"

Issy didn't bat an eye. "Possibly both."

"Right. Leave it with me."

She smiled her thanks and turned to go.

"And Issy…"

"Yes sir?"

"We haven't had this conversation."

Issy nodded, turned on her heel and loped off towards the school gates.

On the way home, Dave mused on the events of the previous hour. He felt he had been wrong-footed by Kate, and was still hopeful that the scheme to include Donkey in the competition would fall on its face well before the trip to County Hall. On the other hand a shared evening trip with her, even in the company of students, was not without its attractions, and might even advance his cause. But had that cause been dealt a blow by his strongly negative response to what was, admittedly, a noble idea? Noble, but deeply flawed, as anyone with experience of Donkey would be able to see. Had it not perhaps been his responsibility to gently and firmly kill the idea there and then? And would he not have done so, if it had been anyone other than Kate proposing it? Then there was Sammy. That would have to be dealt with carefully. And would need to involve Sammy's form tutor, who was Kate. Wheels within flaming wheels.

Chapter Eighteen

"About the other day..."

That weekend the surf looked good and the weather fair, and Dave decided he would have a day on the beach. On Saturday morning he packed a bag with towel, hoodie, cereal bars and various other necessary or precautionary items that would save him coming back up the hill before evening. He pulled on his wetsuit in the outhouse, picked up his board, and set off down the cliff path. It was nine o'clock and there was no sign of Kate, although her car still sat next to his on the drive.

There was a light offshore breeze with a hint of autumn in it, and the three-foot swell coming in from the southwest in corduroy lines made for near perfect conditions. Few holidaymakers were left now, and the handful of surfers already out were mostly regulars, known to him by sight or name. He wasted no time, stowing his bag by a rock at the foot of the cliff and crossing the stretch of sand, his board under his arm. He strode out into the green water, and the familiar cleansing chill crept up his thighs and seeped into the neoprene of his wetsuit. He knew that within minutes he wouldn't feel the cold. He waded out until he was waist deep, then launched himself belly down onto his surfboard and paddled out on the rip to where the larger waves were breaking.

For a few minutes he lay on his board, rising and falling with the swell, enjoying the view of the Engine House and exchanging the odd greeting with surfers he knew. He had all day and he was in no hurry. He let slip by one or two decent waves that he might have caught before picking out a dark curving comb of water, still forty metres distant, that promised much. He angled his board and began paddling as the vast lucent wedge approached, its top beginning to show white. Then, when the first rise began to lift beneath him he sprang up to a crouching position. By the time he was on his feet the wave was tipping him forward, and his board was running fast down its face. It was a great first run, almost half a minute of flexing and turning before eventually he ran out of water. He skipped nimbly off his board and scooped it up neatly as the water began sucking back around him. This was just what the doctor ordered.

He surfed for a couple of hours, enjoying the pleasure of both surrendering to and mastering the elemental power of the waves, then came out for a break. The sun was well up now, and he was warm from his exertion, so he unzipped the top of his suit and pulled his arms out of the sleeves, allowing the warmth of the sun to dry his brown, lean body. The tide had gone out a little in the time he had been in and he had a walk of a hundred yards or so back up the empty beach towards the spot where he had left his bag. He was some way off when he noticed a figure standing next to it that was both familiar and incongruous. Familiar because it was Kate, and incongruous because she too was wearing a wetsuit, conspicuously new and unscuffed. Without her glasses she looked even neater, but there was also something in her proportions that betrayed her swimmer's physique. She grinned at him self-consciously.

"Hello. I wondered if it was you. I couldn't see at first."

"Kate! Is this you launching your surfing career?"

"Well that was the plan. But the surf school's shut today."

"Yeah, Barry's competing in Devon this weekend. Nice wetsuit by the way."

"I feel a bit like a walrus – I'm not used to swimming in rubber. Is the water cold?"

"Not really. But a wetsuit's for protection as much as anything – jellyfish, rocks, whatever. Look I'm just coming out for a break. If you want to borrow my board for a bit you're welcome."

"Really? Isn't it very precious?"

"It's very ancient and very battered. But it's quite a good one. It's maybe a bit small for a beginner, but if you're just going to belly-board you'll be fine."

"You're not expecting me to get on my feet then."

"Well you might be a prodigy I suppose. I'll watch in case you do anything really spectacular. Don't forget the leash."

"Cheers."

Kate picked up the board, coiling the cord leash with its Velcro cuff round her arm, and set off down the beach. Dave pulled on his hoodie and rummaged in his bag for a cereal bar, then sat on a rock and watched her progress towards the water. The weekend was looking up.

Kate's distant figure waded into the shallows. She had some difficulty controlling the board when the waves broke, but once she was further out it was obvious that she was at home in the water. Twice he watched her pick a wave and paddle energetically, but her timing was off, and she failed to catch it. He saw her push out another twenty metres or so, so that now she was just a bobbing dark dot on the green of the water. She was well positioned, but she needed to get onto the board and start paddling. Now! he said, out loud, and as if in response she did, still lying flat, and glancing over her shoulder as the wave approached, paddling desperately to stop it from sliding beneath her. She caught it, or it caught her, and she begun accelerating shoreward, the green slope driving her forwards as it curled white above her. Dave set off down the beach at a jog to meet her as she came in.

"You caught that one nicely!" He took the board from her.

"Wooooh! I enjoyed that. I don't know how you get on your feet though. It's as much as I can do just to crawl onto the board and lie flat."

"Yeah, that takes a bit of work. It helps if you have long arms."

"I don't have long anything, unfortunately. Do you want your board back, or can I have another shot?"

"You carry on. I'm planning on being down here all day. Come to think of it, there's been an old longboard knocking about round the back of the cafe for a while now. I'll see if it's still there."

"Thanks!" Kate gathered up Dave's surfboard once more and began wading out towards the waves. Her evident enthusiasm for the sport that gave him so much pleasure further lifted his spirits, and he was smiling to himself as he jogged along the beach to the café.

He went round the back of the building and there, sure enough, was a battered green longboard, complete with a leash. It would be ideal for Kate. He returned to the front of the café and stuck his head round the door. There were a couple of customers drinking coffee. A slender man with a blonde ponytail and coat-hanger shoulders was working at the sandwich toaster.

"Morning Olly!"

"Dave! My man! How you doing. Looks nice out there."

"Yeah, it's peachy. Listen mate – that longboard out the back – does it belong to anybody?"

"It was left there at the end of the summer - dunno whose it is."

"Ideal. If anyone comes looking for it, I've borrowed it for a couple of hours."

He retrieved the board and set off back along the beach. There were more people in the water now, and it took him a while to pick out Kate. Eventually he spotted her, further out really than she needed to be, lying belly down on the board and facing out to sea in search of her next wave. He waded into the water, heaved himself onto the board, and struck out towards her.

"You've got a board!" she exclaimed when he reached her.

"Yep. It's seen better days, but you should find it easier to balance on than mine. Shall we swap?"

She slithered into the water like a seal and they exchanged surfboards. They were beyond the point at which most of the waves broke, and the swell moved beneath them, lifting them with its easy rhythm so that they could see the shore, the Engine House, and the distant ships, then dropping them once more into the dark green troughs between the waves. It was further out than was ideal for a beginner, but he didn't think she'd appreciate the suggestion that they move into shallower water.

"I'm enjoying this," she said. "It's great when you catch a wave, but it's kind of nice just sitting here too. Usually when I'm in the water I'm ploughing up and down the lanes."

"I do a bit of swim training in the winter," said Dave, "but I don't enjoy it that much. Shall we try and catch this next one?" Behind them a larger, darker fold was building, still some distance off.

"Do we need to paddle in a bit?"

"Yes I think so. Come on!"

They turned their boards towards the shore and paddled vigorously. Dave pulled away from her, and popped up just at the right moment to take the wave. Kate was lifted high on her board then dropped back behind it, and had to watch the top of Dave's head as he stood up and carved his way in towards the shore, dipping and swerving elegantly as he went.

She cursed in frustration and looked over her shoulder to see what was coming next. The following wave was a few metres away, the top just beginning to curl. She turned back to the shore and paddled as hard as she could. This time however she was too vigorous, and the wave began to break before it reached her. For a moment nothing happened, then she felt the board begin to nose-dive, and there was a roar as the wave broke on top of her, spinning her sideways and tipping her off, so that she and her board were bundled over and along in a boiling, shifting cauldron of white water that dumped them eventually in the shallows, a few feet from where Dave was waiting.

She shook herself, and rose a little unsteadily to her feet, the water sucking back around her where she stood.

"That's called a wipe-out," he said. "For obvious reasons."

"I'm going back out," she said. "Come on!"

They stayed in the water for another hour or so, Kate successfully belly-boarding on enough waves to feel she was getting somewhere, and Dave doing his best to demonstrate his mastery of the sport without giving the impression he was showing off. After one successful run that brought them both to shore at the same time and in approximately the same place she said,

"OK I reckon I've got the hang of belly-boarding, but I want to be able to surf like you do. How do I get to the next level?"

"Well mostly it's practice," he said, as they walked back up the beach. "But the tricky bit that you need to get over is the pop-up."

"You make it look easy."

"Well it is once you've got the technique. Why don't we grab a coffee. I'll explain the theory, then we can get in the water and put it into practice."

"Sounds good. My shout, seeing as I'm getting free tuition."

They walked back along to the café, Kate copying Dave and peeling back the top of her wetsuit to allow her shoulders and arms to dry in the sun. Her black one-piece swimsuit was functional rather than flashy, but wet as it was, it revealed enough for Dave to feel an odd sense of privilege. There was more of the tattoo on display too, but by no means all of it. It appeared to be the spiked limbs of some kind of reptile, the body of which presumably inhabited her back.

At the café they sat on the verandah with their coffees. Dave borrowed a pen and drew diagrams on a paper napkin to illustrate the correct angle at which to paddle, and the point at which the pop-up should be attempted. He taught her about rip tides, too, how if you did get caught in one you just let it take you out until it lost its force, then swam in further along the shoreline. They were more like children engrossed in an imaginary game than neighbours and colleagues with a history of difference and disagreement. I want more of this, thought Dave, but I'm not sure how to get it.

Later, back in the water, Kate did her best to put the theory into practice, pulling herself gamely on and off the board until her arm and stomach muscles ached. Dave left his own board on the beach and swam patiently alongside her, instructing and encouraging. Initially she had little success, but after six or seven attempts, she managed to get up to a crouch, caught one wave, and successfully balanced for two or three seconds, her arms out straight like a child's representation of a jet plane, before falling off again, laughing.

Dave retrieved her board and they went out once more, he swimming and Kate paddling, but she was tiring.

"I'm going to have one more shot, then I'm going in. But I want to just get my breath first. She rested with her arms on her board, dipping and rising with the swell.

"Yeah, I'm beginning to feel it. I'm getting hungry too." He swam slowly round in circles.

"Have a bit of board," said Kate, adjusting her grip to make room for him. He swam over to join her, leaning on the other side of the board to maintain the balance. She was facing the sun, and her eyes were closed against it. His cheek was inches from hers. For a short while they floated in silence. Most of the other surfers had gone in for lunch.

"I've been meaning to say," said Kate, "about the other day."

Oh God, he thought, what's coming now. He fixed his eyes on a container ship steaming slowly out of sight on the horizon.

"Mmm," he said in what he hoped was an unconcerned tone.

"I'm not sure if you're still interested in that kissing thing," said Kate, "But now feels like a much better time."

He turned slowly to look at her. Her eyes were open now, and she was looking at him. He took a moment to be sure he understood her correctly. He thought he did.

"Um….Yes – still interested," he said, and adjusted his grip on the surfboard so that his mouth could reach hers. She did the same, and behind the salt tang of their lips they found the fresh taste of each other's teeth, then the tips of their tongues touched briefly. The position, suspended in twenty or thirty feet of open water on either side of a surfboard wasn't ideal, and Dave raised himself up on the board.

Kate broke away.

"Now let's see if I get on my feet one more time. Surfboard, please!"

Reluctantly he released it. It felt like releasing Kate herself from his embrace. She flashed him a quick smile, pulled herself on to the board, and began paddling away from him in the direction of the shore.

Chapter Nineteen

"Candice was only mildly offended"

"Candice! How are you doing?"

It was Sunday morning, and Candice had caught up with Dave at last. He had meant to return her call, or message her, or something, but had never been quite sure what to say. Now he was mentally cursing himself for not having used the intervening time to prepare a strategy. He had been sitting with his coffee, thinking about Kate, trying to recapture that moment on the water when her lips had parted against his, when his phone rang. He answered it without thinking.

Candice seemed unoffended by his failure to return her messages.

"You're very elusive, Darling."

"Yeah, I'm sorry. It's been on my to-do list…"

"Well look, here's the thing. I'm coming down this Thursday. I don't intend to make a nuisance of myself – I'm very self-sufficient as you know. But it would be very helpful if I could stay over. We could talk about our writing."

"But Candice the flat's tiny. And my sofa's really not very comfortable."

"I wasn't imagining I'd be on the sofa!"

"Well the bed's not very big either, so one of us would be on the sofa. And another thing, I've got to be up at stupid o'clock on Friday for a school trip. Look, I need to be frank here. We slept together. And I'm sure it was a beautiful thing, and all that, though to be honest I can't remember a great deal about it. I take my share of responsibility for what happened of course, but realistically, we had both had a lot to drink..."

"I do hope you're not suggesting that you only made love to me because you were drunk..."

"Oh come on Candice. Look, you're a very attractive woman, and I'm sure that played a part. But I *was* drunk, as you well know..."

"Please don't keep saying that. It's offensive." She sounded, for once, genuinely put out, and Dave immediately felt remorseful.

"Yes of course. I'm sorry."

"Perhaps it's my age. I should warn you, darling, I'm sensitive about my age."

"Candice you're in great shape for...whatever age you are. But..." It came to him in a flash of convenience. "You *are* married."

"Henry and I are completely open with one another. There's no deceit involved, I can assure you."

"Well that's very creditable. I'm, um, a bit old-fashioned in that regard, myself." He attempted to steer the call to safer ground. "What brings you down here anyway?"

"I'm visiting my godmother. She's in a care home in Penzance. I could drive up and down in a day but that would be very tiring. I thought it might be nice for us to meet up, and have a little chat, and I could see this mineshaft or whatever it is you live in."

"It's an engine house. It's all above ground level."

"Well it all sounds frightfully romantic."

"I suppose it is when you're not used to it. OK look. I'm at work on Thursday, but I can be home by five. Drop by for a cup of tea, by all means. That would be great. We can have a walk on the beach if the weather's decent. But I really think when you see the accommodation you'll feel much more comfortable in a hotel."

"Oh darling, you are dull!" said Candice. But her good humour appeared to be restored.

After the call ended, Dave sat for a while in thought. He hoped he had done enough to get the message across to

Candice, kindly but firmly, that he was not interested in being her bit on the side. He couldn't really have been clearer without being downright rude. He felt he had done well to get away with a cup of tea. Supper might have involved wine, with all that wine could lead to. With a bit of luck he'd get her out the door before Kate got home. He didn't want to have to explain Candice to Kate.

Kate. Kate the gorgeous, the enigmatic, the elusive, smart and sexy woman of his dreams. This last adjective was a recent and exciting addition to his mental list, and was leant colour and force by the brief impression he had had of the contours of her breasts inside her swimsuit - neat, but round and firm, and almost certainly small-nippled. He had a bit of a thing about small nipples. What was Kate doing now? He had heard the Fiat's perky engine fire up an hour or so ago, and had gone out onto the balcony in time to see her drive off down the hill.

After her last run on Saturday, Kate had insisted she was through with surfing for the day, and despite his offer to buy them lunch, she had headed back up to the Engine House, without a backward glance, or a touch, or anything to indicate that matters between them had altered. Dave would cheerfully have followed her like a dog, but he had to return the longboard, and smitten though he was, he knew instinctively it was wiser not to show it. He had wandered back to the café in something of a daze, and after chewing half-heartedly on a cheese and tomato toastie, had returned to his surfing. That evening he had gone to the cinema. He had considered knocking on Kate's door to see if she was interested in joining him, but her car was gone, the ground floor of the Engine House in darkness. It was hard not to feel that she was avoiding him.

Now, his day of indulgence behind him, the weekend offered only schoolwork. He looked with something close to loathing at the pile of exercise books on the table, knowing that in each there was several pages of unmarked work – at least three or four hours' labour in total. His eyes moved to his laptop. *Mousehole!* had made little progress since his weekend at the Old Rectory. Could the prospect of Candice's visit be used as a stimulus to tackle Chapter Three? His novel, he recognised with a pang of self-knowledge, was at that moment of little more interest to him than the exercise books.

The laptop also held his application for the mentoring scheme. That too had to be in in a matter of days. He sat down at the table and opened the relevant file, scanning it a final time for errors, without any great enthusiasm. Then, not so much because he believed in what he was doing, but because it seemed in some small way to increase the chances of a future that involved Kate, he attached it to an email and hit the send button.

Kate was by no means indifferent to the brief moment of intimacy across the borrowed surfboard, but it hadn't pierced her heart, as it had Dave's. Certainly she was beginning to see him in a different light, but quite what the nature of the alteration was had yet to become clear. Self-contained by nature, it was not difficult for her to maintain her focus. She was happy for the undeniably pleasant memory of the kiss to linger as long as it was disposed to linger, but she was not going to be thrown off course by it. She was vaguely conscious that a situation of sorts was arising that might at some point require to be managed. She understood enough of her neighbour by now to sense that he might be inclined to view this latest development as encouragement.

Kate was not, at this point in her life and in this new situation, in a mood for any kind of committed relationship. A candid friend might have suggested that in that case she should not have led Dave on, but she would have replied that he had asked if he could kiss her, and she, having turned down the request at the time it was made, had simply acceded to it when the circumstances were more appropriate. A kiss, after all, was just a kiss. And so she went about her weekend's business and pleasure as planned, and thought little of the occupant of the upstairs flat.

In the tiny miner's cottage in Eglos, Sammy Pascoe was also seated at a laptop. It had been provided for him by the school, and it was the only one the family possessed. He was working on his speech for the class debate that was planned that week, as a kind of eliminator for the inter-schools competition. His mother, through her parish council connections, had furnished Sammy with an array of densely written documents about second homes policies and neighbourhood plans, and he was trying to work out how the material might be used. His parents were both sitting by the small, cheerful log fire, his mother sewing while Viv Pascoe picked out a tune on a battered banjo. Sammy's father had had a good week, and soon they would go to the nearby pub for the Sunday Carvery, an occasional treat and the only time the family ate out. Then Sammy was going to cycle over to Issy's house to compare notes.

"I had a phone call from the school, Friday," said Maisie, without looking up.

Sammy pricked up his ears but continued working.

"Sam been misbehavin' again?" asked his father with a wink.

"It's about that London trip."

"What London trip?"

"Sammy?"

"Uh-huh?"

"You didn't tell us there was a trip to London."

"I don't want to go."

Maisie let that settle and carried on with her sewing.

"It was your form tutor. She sounds like a nice lady."

"Yeah, she's all right."

"She said it would be good if you could go, because they'se doing loads of exciting things, and even though it seems like a lot of money, really it isn't these days, what with the price of rail travel, and hotels and everything."

Sammy said nothing.

"I done all right this week," said Viv, pausing in his playing. "Should be good next couple of weeks too. Brunel's pushing a bit more work my way. How much do they want?"

"A hundred and twenty," said Maisie.

Sammy looked up. "It's more than that. The letter said a hundred and eighty."

"That's why your Miss Porteous was ringing up. The school's prepared to give you a discount, on account of the progress you've been making the last couple of years." This construction was one that Kate and Maisie, realising the reason for Sammie's reluctance, had come up with between them.

"That's great," said Viv. "In't that great, Sam? Well done Lad!"

"Said I don't want to go."

"Well nobody's going to make you go, boy. But it would be a crying shame if you was to pass by the chance to see these plays, and museums and things, because you thought we couldn't afford it, when all the time we can afford it easy."

"Not that we could always afford it easy," said his father, "But as it happens right now it wouldn't hit us too hard, would it Maze?"

"I reckon we could do it no trouble."

Throughout this exchange Sammy was hunched over the laptop so that they wouldn't notice his discomfort at the conversation. Now he raised his head to face them.

"Will it mean there's other things you need that we can't afford?"

"No, boy. But if you was to miss out on good things that other kids was having, that would upset us sorely."

Sammy sighed. "Ok," he said. "I would like to go, if you're sure we can do it. Only…Dad?"

"Yes Sam?"

"This extra work you've had from Mr Brunel – when did you know about that?"

"Oh he's been talking about that for a while now."

"Oh. OK."

Sammy turned back to his laptop, and his shoulders slowly relaxed. His parents exchanged glances across the flickering fire, and the banjo picked up its melody once more.

That Sunday morning Anton Killick was at home as was his custom. The many outdoor attractions of Cornwall meant little to him, and normally this part of the weekend would be spent either reading self-help manuals, or producing his trademark emails to colleagues, which tended to arrive with multiple attachments, each composed of several sheets of data that were colour coded for ease of interpretation. At this moment however he was engaged with neither of these things, but was studying Kate Porteous's CV. The white rats were silent, curled up together in their bed of straw.

The previous week there had been a second meeting of the Appraisal steering group, and Kate had made a number of helpful suggestions. They were not one hundred percent aligned with his own thinking, it was true, but they had moved the debate substantially in the direction he wanted it to go, so much so that the troublemaker Robertson had looked decidedly put out. After the meeting Killick had felt no need to take out his frustrations on the punchbag in the corner, but had instead waited until Emily Flowerdew had gone to teach. He had then entered her office and extracted Kate's file from the cabinet. He returned to his own office and photocopied her application form and CV, then returned the file to its place.

There was little of substance to be gleaned from the documents – Kate's age (she was ten years younger than Anton – that needn't be a barrier); the details of her education, including the precise class of her degree, which was, as it happened, the same as Anton's own; and her stated hobbies and interests. He noted with approval that she had been a County-level swimmer. He read again her precise, cogent statement of application, with its outline of the responsibilities undertaken at the northern grammar school where she had begun her career.

He sat back in his seat and sought to marry this information with the sound of her voice, as he remembered it from the meeting, the flattening of certain vowels, and her habit of leaning forward slightly when making a point. He thought a little about her face, which was not strikingly beautiful, but which nonetheless was not unpleasing, and then he thought about her shape; that compact, neat figure kept toned by her morning visits to the gym.

He made a decision.

Chapter Twenty

"Please just say yes or no"

With just a fortnight to go until half term, the weather was fair again, but the mornings and evenings were cold. As long as the sky was blue however, Dave dropped the roof of the MG for his morning commute, his leather flying jacket zipped up to the neck and the legs of his wraparound sunglasses secured beneath a bright red beanie. It was a great look, but Kate, who invariably left the Engine House a good forty-five minutes before him, was never there to see it. It had occurred to Dave to suggest they share a lift, but he couldn't quite bring himself to alter his schedule, and he was pretty sure she wouldn't alter hers.

Their paths hadn't crossed since Saturday. In an odd way Dave felt that this strengthened his hand – he was fairly sure that any attempt he might have made to consolidate their relationship over the weekend would have met with a rebuff, and only set back his cause. It wouldn't do however to let things simply drift – the moment of intimacy had been so fleeting, so ephemeral, that it might easily evaporate to a mere imagining with the passing of time. Something had to be said or done within the next few days, and certainly before half term, when he knew Kate was heading north to see her parents. The London trip, set for the coming weekend, might provide the ideal opportunity to make some kind of move.

In the meantime he had taken one or two steps that might render him more acceptable in her eyes. He had submitted his application for the mentoring course – that was a tick in the box, and something he would drop casually into conversation with her at an appropriate moment. And, although it went strongly against his better judgment, he had decided he would go along with her plan to enter Donkey Doggett in the inter-schools debating competition.

He caught up with Kate as she was washing up her mug following the breaktime staff meeting. He was strictly professional in his tone – this was a work matter, and it was a Monday morning. There must be no sense in which his concession might be interpreted as part of a complex courtship game.

"I've been thinking about your idea, about Donovan Doggett." He thought the use of the boy's correct forename a particularly subtle touch, likely to appeal to Kate's sense of propriety. "I think I may have been a bit negative about it last week. Everyone deserves a break, after all. So – if you still feel it's a good idea, I'm happy to support it."

Kate was disappointingly off-hand in her response. She had slept badly the night before, troubled that her relationship with her neighbour had once more shifted into potentially awkward territory.

"Oh. OK. Thanks. Well – it was just an idea. I really don't know who I could find to be his partner. When do you need to know?"

"I'm doing the entries on Thursday. I'd like to get it done and dusted before we go to London. But I don't need to name names at this stage."

"Right. Well I'll see what he feels this week. You know what kids are like. He might have had a change of heart."

By some sleight of hand, it seemed that Dave had become the supplicant in the matter of advancing Donkey Doggett's debating career, and Kate the voice of cold realism. He wandered off to his lesson a little discouraged.

Subsequent interaction between them did little to persuade him that he was on the verge of any kind of breakthrough in their levels of intimacy. She was quiet in the departmental meeting, which Frances had brought forward to Tuesday to enable them to finalise the arrangements for London. On Wednesday she was unforthcoming when, over lunch, he attempted to draw her out on how her Year Eights were progressing with their Shakespeare Festival preparations. He had to ask her whether Sammy had, in the end, submitted his letter for London, and her confirmation that he had was unaccompanied by any acknowledgement that Dave had played a part in drawing the problem to her attention.

Dave found this all rather difficult, and he was short-tempered with his classes as a consequence. Driving home on Wednesday he found himself in a state of considerable confusion. Should he stick to plan and wait until the London trip, engineering the moment of crisis in some side-gallery of the Tate Modern? Or should he just knock on her door tonight and have it out with her there and then?

He ruled out knocking on her door. It was dark now in the evenings, and although a few weeks back, when his thoughts of her were uncomplicated by romance, it had seemed a small matter to appear on her doorstep and explain his dilemma with the MG, the situation was now quite different. Instead, when he arrived back at Wheal Prosper he sat outside in his car for half an hour, willing her to arrive back from school early for once. She didn't appear, and it began to rain, so that plan too was abandoned.

On Thursday however, a quirk of the duty roster brought them together. The convention was that when a staff member knew they would miss a duty owing to a planned absence such as a school trip, it was their responsibility to arrange a swap. With this in mind Dave had exchanged his own Friday duty for Robbo's Thursday stint on the bus queues. Although Dave didn't know it, Thursday after school was also when Kate had her duty. While Dave's job was to ensure good order and safety in the bus lines, Kate was required to patrol the school fields at the other end of the site to deter smokers and snoggers from congregating in the rhododendrons. Each duty finished at four o'clock, and the two met on their way back to the staffroom.

"Hi" said Dave, in as casual a voice as he could manage.

"Afternoon," Kate responded. "I don't normally see you here at this time."

"Yeah, I'm standing in for Robbo. Um…Kate – would you mind if we had a bit of a chat?"

Kate continued walking. They were almost at the staffroom.

"Sure. Shall we get a cup of tea?"

"Actually…I wouldn't mind a bit more privacy. Could we maybe take a turn round the fields?"

She stopped and looked at him. "Is this about last Saturday?"

He nodded miserably. This wasn't encouraging, but he was committed now.

"I just need to get one or two things straight."

She looked as though she might dismiss him out of hand, but then she said,

"OK. But I've not got long. I need to get to the bank."

They turned and headed back towards the playing fields in silence. When they reached the grassed area and were out of earshot of the few students still around, she said,

"Go on then."

Dave had intended opening with a delicate, nuanced appraisal of the situation as he saw it, making clear that he was sensitive to the difficulties of their professional and domestic constraints, but instead he said,

"I wondered if you would go out with me?"

There was a pause. They had reached the half-way line of the first fifteen pitch, and they both stopped, looking out over the empty field as if an intensely interesting but invisible game of rugby were in progress. After a moment Kate said,

"This is like being back at school."

Dave said nothing. He had asked a question, a reasonable one, and he would wait for his answer. But Kate had questions of her own.

"Could you define your terms? I mean are you just after a date? Or something more permanent? Or do we have a quick snog in the rhoddies and I give you my pink pencil sharpener as a love token?"

"Please don't be flippant. I want to…well I just want to be with you, really… I know it sounds a bit lame."

"No. Sorry. It's not lame. It's flattering, actually. I'm being flippant because, yet again, I find myself taken aback. I'm sorry. I don't really know what to say."

"Okay look, it's an awkward situation. I get that. We're living next door to one another and working in the same department. So if the answer's no, then fine, I respect that, of course, and I'll do my best to keep out of your way, and pretend this conversation never happened. But the thing is, I…well I think you're great, actually, and I know what happened on Saturday could be put down to a bit of a lark, unusual circumstances, gratitude even for a free surfing lesson, but…" He ran out of steam.

"Please just say yes or no. Preferably yes. We can work out the details afterwards."

There was another pause. Over on the astroturf a hockey practice was in progress. He picked out the leggy figure of Issy Brunel. Finally Kate spoke.

"Okay. So here's my take on things. Firstly, thanks for the compliment. You're a nice-looking, decent guy and I'm sure there are lots of girls out there who would jump at the offer."

"I'm hearing a but."

"You are, yes. I'm afraid the short answer to your question is no."

Dave said nothing, in the hope that the longer answer might offer more encouragement.

"The slightly longer answer is, not right now. I don't want to give you a big long story but basically my recent experience of men, particularly at my last school, has kind of put me off them. And my first impression of you was that you weren't very different."

"I know we didn't get off to a great start…"

"Well I hope we're over that. The point is I've come down here to advance my career, not to moon around on some bloke's arm. So I'm just not up for any sort of serious commitment."

"Casual sex, then?" He didn't actually say this, though it popped into his head, courtesy of Dave One. Kate continued, happily oblivious to the irreverent promptings of his alter ego.

"And also, thinking longer term, and trying to be realistic, you're maybe a bit laid back for me. I mean it's all very nice, the surf-dude lifestyle, but where's it leading? Any plans to buy a house? A car that you could undertake a serious journey in without wrecking your back or risking a breakdown?"

He bristled. "MG's are famously reliable. And parts are dirt cheap…"

"I'm sure they are. Look, don't get me wrong – I'm not being critical. Your lifestyle works for you, and it's probably good for the planet, too. It's just not where my ambitions lie. I want to achieve things. I want to get on, get promotion, aim for headship in due course. I know that's a long way off, but you need to start with the end in mind. I'm just not sure how getting involved with you would fit in with all that."

"Is that all you want?"

"Isn't it enough? To be going on with?"

"Yeah, it's plenty. But isn't it all maybe…a bit sterile?"

"I don't think so, no. What do you want out of life?"

"I'm not all that sure now. I was quite happy bumbling along. Meandering, as Frances would call it. And I do want to be able to surf, and do some good in the world, and leave it a bit cleaner than I found it. Part of me would like to run my own department or lead a year group, but to be honest I don't know if I can face the hassle." He didn't mention *Mousehole!* Probably a wannabe novelist wasn't Kate's ideal partner either.

"Sounds like we want different things, then."

"Maybe. I'm not dismissing your…ambition. You'd probably make a great Head, much better than me. And recently…well just this year, I suppose, I'm kind of questioning where I'm heading, and I'm thinking of taking a few steps towards tightening things up a bit. I've applied for this mentoring course, for instance."

"Great! Me too."

"Yeah, well, it's probably more your thing than mine. Look – I appreciate your honesty. Sounds like maybe I'm not the kind of guy you're looking for."

"I'm not looking for a guy, Dave, that's the thing."

"No. Sorry. You did make that clear."

"Look I've got to go. I've got to get to the bank and it's twenty to five."

"What? Shit! I've got a visitor coming at five. I really do have to run."

"Better get a wriggle on then. Early start tomorrow." She gave his arm a brief squeeze, and they both turned and walked quickly back towards the car park.

Over on the Astroturf, Issy Brunel watched them go with interest. Her uncharacteristic lapse of concentration allowed the team in bibs to score a goal and earned her a rare rebuke from her coach.

It was a few minutes after five when Dave pulled up at Wheal Prosper. Candice's enormous Audi was already there, and Candice herself, looking trim and cool in white slacks and a denim jacket, was leaning against the driver's door smoking a cigarette.

"Hi, hi," said Dave as he pulled up. "Sorry I'm a few minutes late."

"That's all right darling, I've been having a wander round. Nice spot."

"Yes, it's not too shabby," he said, getting out of the MG and receiving the two obligatory kisses before attending to the roof. "Now look, there's a couple of hours of daylight left, so would you like a cup of tea and then a walk on the beach, or shall we do the walk while the sun's still shining? Your call."

"I'm awash with tea as it happens darling, the care home seems to run on it. Let's have a walk first and you can tell me what you've been up to, and how your pirates are getting on with their pillaging."

"They're Spaniards, technically, not pirates, though I don't suppose it made much difference to the locals. Actually, would you mind sticking your car over there? It's just that my neighbour usually parks here and they'll be home from work any minute."

"Well there's plenty of space darling, is your neighbour frightfully inflexible?"

"Just mildly, on occasions. But you're right, it probably doesn't matter."

"So is he nice, your neighbour?"

Dave took a breath. "It's a she, actually. This way." They walked towards the beach path.

"A she? Tell me more. Are you just good friends? Goodness I'm not sure I can do this in these shoes. Give me your arm, darling."

At that moment Kate arrived back at Wheal Prosper, just in time to catch the briefest impression of a blonde head next to Dave's as they dropped out of sight down the path to the beach. She pulled up next to the Audi, and sat for a minute in the car, long enough to allow the pair to complete their descent. Then she got out and walked to where the path began and peered over. Sixty feet below, Dave was helping his companion down onto the sand. Kate watched as the woman, with a girlish motion, slipped off a pair of white shoes and began running towards the surf. Dave strolled after her. Kate raised her eyebrows and pursed her lips, then turned and collected her briefcase before entering the flat.

Chapter Twenty-one

"Sauce for the goose, innit?"

A light drizzle drifted down from an opaque sky as the London trippers began to congregate at the bottom of the St Petroc's hill. It was five-forty-five am, and the coaches had not yet arrived. So far Kate, Dave, and two members of the art department were the only staff members there, but Frances's car had just driven up the hill to the staff car park, with Edward Tremenhere in the passenger seat. That left Sheila Abbot, Head of Year 9, and Mr Mumford, the Head of Art, who was notoriously disorganised and impractical, and quite likely to be late.

The ghostly drizzle added to the atmosphere of muted anticipation – the students were still drowsy from their unusually early rise, a little excited by what lay ahead, but reluctant to show it for fear of being un-cool. They were attired in a range of outfits from the practical to the raffish. A number of girls were still in their onesies, a sartorial choice unlikely to survive the arrival of Sheila Abbot, who had fought hard against Killick's contention that they should all be in school uniform. Few students appeared to have waterproofs of any description, despite various written and verbal promptings. The advice that one small backpack should be sufficient appeared to have been similarly lost in translation, and the pavement was cluttered with a variety of luggage from roller-cases to Tesco bags. This was all par for the course.

A red Range-Rover pulled up and Issy and Sammy got out. Sue Brunel hugged her daughter, and waved goodbye to Sammy. As she drove off the two drifted apart, Sammy towards a knot of boys from the tech team, and Issy to join Lily Tregunna, who had clearly got up in enough time to apply her make-up, and was dressed as if for a party, rather than a six-hour coach journey.

Frances Fivey and Edward arrived, Frances with a sheaf of registers which she began to hand out to the staff members already present.

"Morning everybody! No coaches yet? Not to worry. So, the students are in form groups, two to a coach, and I've allocated two staff to each, keeping staff with groups they know well as far as possible. The kids will try to swap coaches but this needs to be sternly resisted, otherwise we'll never keep track of them."

Dave and Kate's forms were on different coaches. From the list he saw that he was with Sheila Abbot.

"We'll call in at Exeter Services for breakfast, then a brief comfort stop on the M4 late morning."

An ironic cheer went up as the first of the coaches appeared round the bend. The paved area was now crowded with students, and Sheila Abbot had arrived, though there was still no sign of the Head of Art. Frances began organising the students into form groups, while Sheila fielded the concerns of anxious parents and collected various medicines and special instructions. The girls in onesies were ordered to change at Exeter. Dave glanced across at Kate, who was studying her register list.

They had, by prior arrangement, both come in Kate's car. There had been little conversation, which might have been put down to the earliness of the hour, but had more to do with the unspoken acceptance that any attempt to pretend that everything was normal between them was doomed to failure. No reference was made by either of them to Candice – Dave had, thankfully, persuaded her that between the Spartan accommodation available at his flat and his early start in the morning, a hotel was the better option. He had felt no compunction at this - Candice could easily afford it, and the alternative was too fraught with potential complication and misunderstanding to be contemplated. Candice had left him just after seven, and aside from a rather over-enthusiastic embrace on the grassed parking area in front of Kate's window, nothing of a carnal nature had passed between them. This was a huge relief to Dave. He had not had time to re-assess how matters now stood between himself and Kate, but he knew that any further entanglement with Candice was to be avoided at all costs. Candice for her part had picked up some of Dave's discomfort, and decided not to press matters.

Kate had found herself mildly, and irrationally, unsettled by the appearance of this other woman. Clearly this was not something that Dave had conjured up by way of a defiant answer to her rejection, as that had only just taken place, but equally clearly it was not a visit from a maiden aunt. From the two fleeting glimpses she had had of Candice – one from the heights of the cliff top and one surreptitious view through her kitchen window of the final warm embrace before she climbed into the Audi and departed, Kate had the impression of a slightly older woman – difficult to say how old exactly - but also a woman of considerable allure who seemed to be assuming rights normally borne of a certain romantic familiarity.

Why this should bother her, she couldn't quite say, but bother her it did. Presumably Dave was not in any sense involved with the woman, or he would hardly have approached her as he had on the playing fields the previous day. His sincerity then had been evident – movingly so, in retrospect, and while she had been equally sincere in what she had told him, she had found it difficult to avoid replaying the scene in her head, and wondering whether she had done the right thing in closing the door quite so firmly as she had.

Anyway, there would be plenty of time to contemplate the immediate past and its implications for the future on the long drive ahead. She was sharing the journey with Frances, on the first of the four coaches that were now parked in line astern along the pavement. On the whole she was happy that the travel arrangements had worked out in this way - the thought that she might have ended up sitting next to Dave for six hours was a disconcerting one.

The doors were open now, and students from her own form and one other were gathering in an excited wedge on the pavement. The driver, a short, taciturn man in a grey uniform, had come out of his cab and was opening the luggage compartments to stow the larger cases.

"Shall we let them on?" called Kate to Frances, and Frances gave her the thumbs up. Kate climbed aboard and side-stepped into one of the front seats, watching the students as they filed past her. She took a certain pleasure in knowing half of them by sight and name, and the sense of ownership was reinforced by the way they greeted her.

"Hi Miss!"

"It's exciting, isn't it Miss?"

"Can I sit near the front Miss? I get sick otherwise."

Once all were onboard, she took the register. Between her own and the other form there were four still missing, including Donkey.

"Can somebody give these students a call please," she said, reading out the names.

"Here's Donkey now, Miss!"

"All right Miss?" Donkey swung his way up the steps of the coach, looking a little as if he had not been to bed.

"Good morning Donovan. Find a seat please."

He stumped past her up the aisle.

It was now nearly six. Across the four coaches there were only two students still missing. One turned out to be sick, and unable to come, and the other appeared after a few minutes, climbing on board to mocking cheers.

"Right," said Frances. "I think we're good to go."

The caravan of coaches ground down the hill and onto the main road that would take them up the southwest peninsula and eventually to the capital. The students settled to their chatter and their music and their bags of Haribo, and the staff to their novels and, for some, an optimistic plumping up of travel pillows and rolled up rain garments. By the time the coaches were speeding along the dual carriageway they were largely silent, and remained that way until Exeter.

The half hour at the service station passed without incident. Once back on the motorway there seemed to be an acceptance by all parties that, breakfast being out of the way, and it being now the hour at which they were normally on their way to school, conversation should resume. Frances and Kate chatted about novels and films, and while Kate had been prepared to fend off any questions about Dave with bland, non-committal responses, none were forthcoming.

Dave and Sheila Abbot had spent the first leg of the journey in the front seats on opposite sides of the aisle, but once the students had been counted back on at Exeter, Sheila dropped into the place beside him. The coaches were not completely full, and the students had gravitated towards the back, so that there were two or three empty rows of seats behind them, and they were able to talk discreetly.

Dave moved his jacket to make room for his colleague.

"I don't know if you'd heard," began Sheila, "But I shall be handing in my notice later this term."

Dave admitted he had, and said he was sorry to hear her husband was not well.

"Yes, I'm afraid the doctors are not terribly positive, so it's the only thing to do, really."

"That's really sad."

"Anyway, the point is that my job is going to be advertised, probably before the end of the Christmas term. Now obviously I have very little say in the matter, and it may be advertised nationally anyway, but as you know the Head has quite a strong record of making internal pastoral appointments."

"Yes, I suppose that's true."

"I've said to him that I'll willingly chat to any staff members who are interested in the post. I can think of several who might be, and clearly I need to be even-handed in the encouragement and advice that I give. I just thought, if you were thinking of throwing your hat in the ring, this would be as good a time as any to pick my brains. And strictly off the record, I would be delighted if you were to apply."

Dave took in this compliment.

"Thanks Sheila. I appreciate that. I think probably I am interested. It's about time I applied for something, and the pastoral route appeals to me more than the academic one."

"Good. Well, fire away."

"Okay." He thought for a moment. "You make the job look relatively straightforward, but I know that's the result of a lot of work behind the scenes, and I guess also all the goodwill you've built up over the years. Can you give me an idea of the workload? Where the pinch-points are, how much it encroaches on the holidays, that kind of thing?"

Sheila talked candidly about the pressure at report-writing time, the predictable peaks of parental anxiety that needed to be anticipated and managed. She explained that there was also a large part of the job that was unpredictable - responding to an almost limitless range of problems and incidents that seemed to be growing more complex by the year, as a consequence of the impact of social media and the widespread availability of drugs. In ninety percent of cases, she explained, it was better to under than to over-react, but the real knack lay in identifying the ten percent where swift and decisive action was required. She told him that in her view he had all the necessary qualifications to do the job well.

The conversation continued for the best part of an hour. Sheila returned to her seat, and Dave spent the next part of the journey pondering on what she had told him. The position would be demanding, there was no doubt about that, but wouldn't it also be rewarding? He was very aware of the challenges faced by students at this complicated period of their lives, and surely helping them to negotiate these difficulties would be immensely worthwhile? By the time they reached the M4 services he found himself quite excited at the prospect of applying, and buoyed by the confidence that first Frances and now Sheila had expressed in him.

At the service station, Sammy was mooching around in WH Smiths waiting for the call to return to the coach, when he became aware of Donkey Doggett standing next to him.

"All right Pascoe?"

"Yeah," said Sammy, without enthusiasm.

"Next bit of the journey, you and me's goin' to have a bit of a chat, like."

"Is that right?"

"A business discussion."

"Right. Business. 'Cause, I'm, y' know, really into all that kind of stuff."

"The future, innit?" said Donkey sagely, and moved off again.

WTF?, thought Sammy, gloomily.

Back on the coach, Hardeep had without explanation moved further down to sit with one of his cricketing mates, and Sammy was unsurprised when Donkey dropped into the seat beside him, and began fiddling with his phone. Sammy stared out the window and waited for the coach to leave, so that the business presentation could get under way.

On the coach carrying Dave's form, Issy was engaged in a *sotto voce* conversation with Lily Tregunna. It was an odd conversation. Projected forward a dozen years, it would find its counterpart in a junior barrister seeking advice from an expert witness on a subject that was distasteful and at the same time strangely fascinating. Issy found Lily interesting and likable. She was clearly one of the more precocious girls in the year group, rumoured to have a boyfriend in Year 11, but she wore it all lightly, and was catholic in her friendships, and cheerfully blunt with her advice. Issy had reached a point in her long-distance relationship with Enrique where she felt she needed some guidance, and Lily Tregunna was the obvious choice.

"So, the thing is..." said Issy, "...he's asked me to send him a picture."

"What, topless, like?"

"Um, yes."

"Up to you bird. Has he seen 'em before?"

"No! I mean, no. We didn't really...do much in that line."

"Have you had a dick pic off him?"

Issy admitted that it hadn't occurred to her to ask for one.

"Well there you go. Sauce for the goose, innit?"

This logic was so unanswerable that Issy felt that she could have reached the conclusion herself, but this is often true of consultancy, and Lily was dispensing her counsel for free. At the same time, the absurdity of the bargain that was being proposed struck Issy with some force, and by the time their coach was crawling through west London her thinking about Enrique had become considerably clearer.

Chapter Twenty-two

"One never really knew with abstract art"

It was Saturday morning, and the St Petroc's crocodile was progressing along the brutalist concrete terrace of the South Bank. They were bound for the Tate Modern, with the exception of Edward Tremenhere, who claimed to be allergic to modern art, and had been given dispensation to visit the National Portrait Gallery instead. Everything up to this point had gone smoothly, in as much as no child had been lost or injured, no shops looted and no Londoners mortally insulted. The Victoria and Albert museum had been satisfactorily grand, with enough variety and oddity to keep the students amused, and the visit to the Globe the previous evening had been a huge success. They had checked into the youth hostel without incident, and apart from one or two groups of diehard talkers who kept the duty staff up longer than they would have liked, the night had been quiet, the students exhausted by the travel, the early start and the novelty of it all.

They had been lucky with the weather, too, which improved as they drove east the previous day. This morning London was cold but dry, with a watery sun escaping from time to time from behind a thin blanket of high cloud. The sheer scale and iconic grandeur of the capital, the clean light on the broad river and the sharpness of the air combined to work a kind of magic, so that there was a general sense of wellbeing among the staff, a collective out-breath. There was an unspoken acknowledgement that the trip was probably going to be fine, now, given that they were operating almost entirely in pedestrianised areas, away from shops and traffic. The Tate Modern was vast and impressive enough that the students could be let loose to roam freely, and the coach would pick them up near the entrance at midday.

"So far, so good," said Dave, falling into step beside Kate. It was his first attempt at conversation *a deux* since the Playing Field Proposition.

"Yeah, the kids have been great," agreed Kate.

"What did you reckon to Macbeth?"

"A bit gimmicky in places for my taste. But that was good for the students."

"The ones I was watching looked completely into it. They were all talking about it on the way back, too."

"Well – you can't ask for more, really."

The crocodile slowed to watch the skateboarders leaping and grinding in the concrete undercroft of the Southbank Centre. Some students drifted over to the parapet to watch the river traffic, while others gathered round a group of buskers belting out afro-jazz on battered instruments. Frances came over to join them.

"Don't let them disperse too much. They can have a few minutes to watch the skaters, then we need to crack on."

"Sure," said Dave, and wandered over to the students by the river to pass on the message. When he looked round for Kate she was browsing a nearby bookstall arranged on a platform of wide tables. Their brief conversation had been civil enough, but nothing had been offered by way of encouragement. In the face of romantic disappointment Dave embraced duty, and began circling, sheepdog style, the outliers who showed signs of wandering off.

When they reached the Tate Modern the students were told they could wander at will within the confines of the building, provided they remained in groups of no less than three, with at least one mobile phone per group. Like animals released into the wild, they were at first almost reluctant to leave the security of the staff members, cowed a little by the vastness of the space, its bizarre angles and curves. Gradually, however, they began to disperse. It was only just after ten, and there were as yet relatively few other visitors.

The staff had agreed to work four shifts, with one pair having half an hour off for coffee at any one time, the rest patrolling randomly and keeping an eye on the exits. This arrangement left one member of staff orphaned as a consequence of Edward Tremenhere's absence, and Dave volunteered. He was in solitary and contemplative mood, and part of him did not object to the possibility that Kate might notice that he cut a lonely but indisputably conscientious figure.

Dave was allowed his coffee first by way of compensation, and he set off up the series of escalators to the highest level of the building, where there was a café overlooking the river. He ordered an Americano and took his pick of the empty bar stools in front of the plate glass window. He made a conscious effort not to think about Kate and contented himself instead with taking in the extraordinary vista of skyscrapers, cranes and waterfront bustle. Far below him to the right the thatched roof of the Globe Theatre sat incongruously, like a bird's nest fallen from a huge concrete tree.

One more week of the term to go. That would fly by. He would know by Friday whether he had a place on the mentoring course. Then there was the Sunday School Outing, which he was not especially looking forward to. They weren't cheap, these lads' weekends, what with the booze, and the golf, and the various silly competitions for which they all chipped in to buy prizes. For a few hundred more he could have had a week on the beach in Morocco or Portugal, riding some serious waves, and storing up Vitamin D for the coming winter. He decided this Sunday School Outing would be his last one, his idling swansong. It was all so Dave One, when you thought about it.

His mind drifted back to the Inset Day at the start of term. A lot had changed since then. He remembered feeling resentful at being back in harness, having to sit and listen to Killick and his absurd pedagogical pieties. He recalled Frances mentioning the Year 9 job, and how he had turned up his nose at it. Inevitably, he remembered Kate, his first sight of her, from high in the darkness of the Theatre, that half-ironic, half-deferential wave to the gallery. His feelings for her were no less strong for having been, for the time being at least, thwarted. He recognised that in a strange way she had been the catalyst that had caused this shift in his ambitions – the call to arms that had awoken Dave Two. It would be Dave Two that would embark on the mentoring course, Dave Two who would apply for Sheila Abbot's job, and who maybe – just maybe – would win Kate's favour as a result.

And here they were, in the heart of London with a hundred and eighty teenagers, students for whose wellbeing he might, before too long, be responsible, as Sheila was now. Students who were, as a result of their efforts, seeing things they would not otherwise have seen, and who were repaying their trouble in the best way possible, by being awed by the experience, by being grateful and responsive, and generally behaving themselves in a civilized manner. That was a fine thing in anybody's book. A career to take pride in. Why had he not seen it before?

He drank down his coffee and wandered back into the main gallery. He strolled through some of the side spaces on the higher levels, noting small groups of students, some of whom were clearly engaged and provoked by the oddness of the artworks. Others, it had to be admitted, appeared bored, more interested in their phones than the exhibits.

He smiled wryly to himself. It was probably as well to be reminded that his rosy picture of receptive adolescents gratefully lapping up high culture was not the whole story. He took a seat on one of the chrome and leather loungers on the balcony and surveyed the vast Turbine Hall, currently given over to a series of domestic appliances painted in dayglo colours and suspended from the roof at varying heights. A commentary, presumably, on the frivolous nature of consumer capitalism. Or possibly not. One never really knew with abstract art. He resolved to google some reviews. He spotted Sammy and Issy, his two ace debaters, sitting on one of the benches in deep conversation. They had at one time been inseparable, those two, but these days they seemed to be moving in somewhat different circles. It was nice to see them together again.

It occurred to him that he had not seen Donkey that morning. In fairness, the boy had been reasonably well behaved up till now – a bit loud at times, but that could be excused. They had all been registered on arrival at the gallery, so he was clearly around somewhere. Still projecting himself forward into his Dave Two role as future pastoral leader, he decided that even though he was off duty for another five minutes, he would set off in search of the lost sheep. No sense in slipping up through complacency in the final hours of the visit.

Down on the floor of the Turbine Hall, Issy was listening with incredulity as Sammy told her about Donkey's business proposal.

"Surely he's making it up…I mean even if his family has got connections with drug gangs or whatever, they're hardly going to entrust their affairs to Donkey, are they?"

"I dunno. I hope he is bullshitting. He says he wants me to be their guy in Eglos."

"In *Eglos*? That's completely mad. There aren't any drug addicts in Eglos. And anyway, your Mum's on the parish council!"

"I don't think that's going to put them off. And I wouldn't be too sure about Eglos. Someone found a needle in the swing park the other week."

"God, you're kidding."

"No, I'm not. My mum told me about it."

"Anyway, I hope you told him to eff off?"

"I said I wasn't interested. He said I might not have a choice."

"Well he's hardly going to burn your house down, is he?"

"I dunno. His Dad's already in prison for something or other. His bother's a complete headcase. They're not…I mean…they don't mess around."

"Are you going to tell someone?"

"He says if I breathe a word I'll be in hospital."

"Well you've told me, that's something."

"Yeah, but don't say anything to anyone, will you? I need to think about this. I'm hoping maybe it won't come to anything."

"OK. I won't. But look…I know I haven't been very...available this term. As a friend, I mean. I've had stuff on my mind."

Sammy looked up. "Yeah…I did hear something."

"OK but that's all over now. It was just a stupid holiday thing. I'm back, as your buddy. Team Pascel."

He grinned. "Team Bruno."

"Donkey though," said Issy, shaking her head. "What a knob."

Meanwhile, Dave had worked his way round the galleries on the upper level, asking any students he came across if they had seen Doggett. No-one had, or if they had, they weren't going to admit to it. He decided to switch tactics and cut back outside the building. He looked up and down the walkway that bordered the Thames but could see nothing. He walked back along the outside of the gallery in the direction of Westminster, then turned left so that he was standing at the top of the broad ramp that led down to the turbine hall. At the bottom he spotted Donkey, seemingly in conversation with a thickset man in a leather coat.

Who's he upset now, wondered Dave, and set off down the slope to investigate. As he did so, the man turned away from Donkey and set off back up to the exit, so that he and Dave passed one another at the midpoint of the ramp. Dave was keeping his eyes upon Donkey, who was starting to move off into the main gallery space, but he had a fleeting impression of a hard, expressionless face behind dark glasses as the man passed him.

Donkey was perhaps thirty yards ahead of him, walking quickly. There were no other students that he could see. Dave called after him and quickened his pace, catching up with him as they passed under the first of the fluorescent washing machines.

"All right Sir? – I didn't see you there," said Donkey glibly, "What do you reckon to this crap, then? I could do better myself."

Dave detected a degree of nervousness beneath the bluster.

"Come over here a minute, Donovan," he said. "I need to have a word with you."

Donkey allowed himself to be led over to one of the benches at the side, and they both sat down.

"So, first off, you're meant to be in threes. Where's the rest of your group?"

"I dunno, they kind of left me. I was looking at this…this really interesting sculpture thing – all metal hoops and that, and when I turned around they was gone."

"Who were you with?"

"Lily and Amy."

"I'll check that out. Now who was that you were talking to a minute ago?"

"Talking to?"

"Yes. When I came down the slope from the outside you were taking to a man. Dark glasses and a leather coat."

"Oh him! He just wanted directions."

"Really? Where to?"

Donkey looked momentarily thrown. "I can't remember. I mean, it wasn't a place that meant anything to me, not being from these parts."

"You hadn't done anything to upset him? He wasn't telling you off?"

"Sir you're well harsh. I been good as gold all weekend."

This was true enough.

"You know where we're getting the coach from?"

"Miss said to meet at the door we come in by."

"Correct. In…" Dave looked at his watch. "Just over an hour from now. Call Lily for me, please, and ask her where she is."

Donkey did so. She and Amy were in the gift shop.

"Right. Let's go and meet them."

Donkey reluctantly put his phone away, and they made their way to the shop. Dave extracted Lily before Donkey could say anything to her and asked her whether she and Amy had been with him, and how they had got separated. She was vague in her reply but said nothing that contradicted Donkey's account. He decided there was no virtue in pressing the matter further, warned them not to be late for the coach, and wandered off for a last contemplation of the day-glo domestic appliances.

Donkey watched him until he was out of sight, then succumbed to the temptation to check the inside pocket of his coat. The fat brown envelope the man had given him was still there.

By a quarter past twelve, more or less on schedule, the students had been registered and had embarked on the coaches. As a reward for the general good behaviour exhibited throughout the trip, rules were relaxed and they were allowed to travel back with friends from other forms if they wished, a head count at each stop being considered sufficient to ensure nobody was left behind on the way home. Dave noticed that Sammy had joined Issy on her coach. Some of the staff swapped too, and he wondered forlornly if Kate might choose to join him, but she didn't, and instead he found himself sharing the homeward journey with Edward Tremenhere, who fell asleep shortly after Hounslow.

Chapter Twenty-three

"He considered full disclosure, and opted against"

The journey home was uneventful, with one exception. While many of the students slept for the first part, a small group of boys on the back seat, who to their credit the night before had gone to bed early and slept soundly, were now wide awake, and rather bored. An hour into the journey, one of them returned from the toilet that was situated down a small set of stairs half-way up the coach in a state of great excitement. The conversation that followed was carried out in hushed tones.

"Guess what! There's a kind of panel thing next to the bog, and if you take it off, it leads into the luggage compartment!"

"Get off!"

"You're having a laugh!"

"I'm not, honest! Go and see for yourself. It's just on the right as you're pissing."

"I could do with a slash – I'll go."

The next boy came back and verified the story of the first. There was indeed a panel, less than a metre square, with two small silver handles that could be turned to release it. Once removed, suitcases and bags were clearly visible in the cavernous space behind.

"I dare you to go in."

"What'll you give me if I do?"

"I'll buy you a can of coke at the services."

"A can of coke and a mars bar."

"I've only got a quid."

"I'll buy the mars bar," said another.

Further down the coach, Dave's mischief antennae twitched. The toilet had not been serviced since they left Cornwall and had acquired an unpleasant odour that meant most students, unless their need was desperate, preferred to wait until the next Service station. Yet now there was an unusual level of activity and excitement around that area of the coach, and a degree of suppressed giggling. He rose from his seat and swung his way to the back to investigate.

"Right boys, what's going on?"

Toby Trott, who had made the initial discovery, decided to come clean, and establish himself as a responsible reporter of potential health and safety hazards before he was branded a transgressor.

"Sir there's a door in the toilet that leads to the luggage compartment."

"Is there?" said Dave. "That sounds unlikely."

"Sir it's true."

"Well if it is, it's probably some kind of emergency exit, and nothing to get excited about. It's also not to be meddled with. Now settle down and stop being silly. We'll be stopping at the services soon."

"Yes sir." The boys settled back in their seats in attitudes of resigned boredom, and Dave returned to the front of the coach. On the way he braved the malodorous atmosphere of the toilet compartment to check what he had been told. Sure enough, there was the panel. He checked that it was securely fastened, and resumed his seat.

Edward Tremenhere awoke on his return and raised an enquiring eyebrow.

"Just some lads being silly," said Dave.

Edward, being Edward, saw no need to enquire further, and returned to his slumbers.

They stopped for half an hour at the first services after London, where the students stocked up on food and drink. There was a further two and a half hours until the next stop, and a mood of unfinished business hung around the back seat of the coach.

"Suppose we all chip in some crib," said one, "and the person who gets furthest into the luggage compartment gets it all."

The competitive element of this had immediate appeal, and each considered what could be contributed to the prize. Soon an impressive jackpot of sweets, drinks and crisps was amassed.

"Singleman will go ape if he catches us."

"We'll have to be dead quiet then. Like those soldiers in World War One tunnelling under the enemy."

It was agreed that the evidence of the extent of each foray should be recorded on phones, with a picture built up of the geography of the terrain in terms of colour and shape of the luggage.

At the front of the coach Dave too drifted off to sleep. By the time he awoke at Exeter the back of the coach was quiet, the subterranean space having been surveyed in detail and the prize awarded to Toby Trott, who, fired by a sense of pride at having discovered the portal, had crawled the full length of the luggage compartment and touched all four walls, including the exterior access door, the emergency handle of which was clearly visible on his video footage.

It was early evening when the coaches arrived back at the school, and by the time the last of the students had been collected, it was beginning to get dark. Dave and Kate drove back to the Engine House in silence, which inevitably called to mind the silence of the journey the previous morning, and the reasons for that. Odd to think how far they had been and how much they had done in the interim. The London trip served as a border to the new territory in which they now found themselves, a wall over which they might look at the land they had left, a land to which they could not return. It was Kate who broke the silence when they arrived back at Wheal Prosper.

"Do you mind if I ask you something?"

"It's probably your turn," said Dave.

"Who was your visitor the other day? I mean, I know it's none of my business, but I'm curious."

"No, that's fine," said Dave. "Her name's Candice. She's a friend I met on a creative writing course in the summer. She was down visiting an elderly relative." This of course was all true as far as it went.

"It's just…and again, tell me if it's not my business, but…you seemed very…at ease with each other. I only ask in the light of our last conversation."

Dave sighed. He considered full disclosure and opted against.

"Candice is…I don't know, pushing fifty, maybe? I know she doesn't look it. She's an ex-pole-dancer and she possibly fancies me a bit, but I can assure you it's not reciprocated. I didn't particularly want to see her, but she can be quite insistent. There's nothing in it if that's what you're thinking. It has absolutely no bearing on what I said to you last week."

"No...goodness, I mean, whatever. She's an attractive woman, though."

"There's nothing in it, Kate."

"OK, thank you. I apologise for prying. I just wanted a bit of clarity."

"Of course. I'm glad you asked."

"God I'm tired. I don't think I've got any food in the house either. I'll have to go out to Tesco."

"I'm OK. I slept on the coach. I've got a cook-chill lasagne in the freezer that's big enough for two, if you're interested?"

Kate smiled. "Thank you. That's kind. But I've got a load of other stuff I need to get."

"OK," said Dave. "Well, thanks for the lift."

"No problem. It was a really good weekend." She leaned over and hugged him, a hug which meant nothing, which was no more than had been exchanged with other members of staff when they had parted back at the school. A hug that was a million miles from a kiss across a surfboard. He returned the pressure briefly, then got out of the car.

On the Penhale estate, behind St Petroc's school, Donkey pushed open the small metal gate that led, via a simple path of ten square concrete paving slabs, to his back door. He let himself in with his latchkey, and bent to scratch the ears of the

Staffy that waddled, growling, into the tiny hallway to greet him.

"Hey Spikey, hey there son. Guess where I been? Cross the Tamar, boy. Into England to visit the fuckin' Queen, so I 'ave."

Then he called "Yo!" and dropped his backpack to the floor.

Jason stepped into the hall.

"You got it, then?"

"Got what?"

Jason smacked him across the head in a swift movement.

"Ow."

"Hand it over."

Donkey reached inside his jacket and handed the brown envelope to his brother, who ripped it open, and briefly inspected the contents.

"Good boy. Did anybody see you?"

"Naw."

His brother looked at him hard.

"Better not have."

"Is there any food? I'm starving."

"Ma!" called his brother. "Donny needs food. Sort it out, will you."

The next morning Dave slept late. When he awoke, the sunlight was streaming in through the arched window, falling across the wooden floor of the mezzanine and climbing the stone wall behind his bed. He had been dreaming about Kate, an exaggerated, slo-mo re-imagining of the experience of the previous two days, where she was always within sight but never within reach, separated from him by a conspiring mass of students, or traffic, or fluorescent domestic appliances. At one point Candice had been there, on the stage of the Globe, possibly as Lady Macbeth – it was hard to be sure.

He desperately needed to get to the end of term. Not because he was exhausted by the teaching, although that had no doubt taken a toll, nor because the pile of marking was becoming impossibly large (which it was), but because he had a need to process the experiences of the past two months, and set the half-term to come in some kind of strategic frame that would lend it coherence and direction. He was not giving up on Kate. Something told him that was not over and done with, that the colours she had nailed to the mast the previous week were not the only colours under which she was capable of sailing. Her interest in Candice was noteworthy, suggesting something less than total indifference. He had little doubt that he would have to play a waiting game, but he was up for that.

In the meantime, it seemed obvious that Dave Two had to be given his head. The mentoring scheme, the debating competition, the Shakespeare festival – these were all things that, with a slight adjustment to the optics, would play strongly into the image in which he was now quite sure he wished to recreate himself. He wouldn't sell the MG – that would be a little too obvious, and would feel like a betrayal - but in all other respects he would become a serious career teacher. And the jewel in the crown would be his application for Sheila Abbot's job, whenever that was advertised. Let Kate draw her own conclusions as to the validity of her damning caricature. He would show her that he was more than just a surf dude.

He threw off the bedclothes and took his phone off its charger to check the weather forecast. Fine until late afternoon, when the rain was scheduled to return. He would have a morning on the golf course, lunch in the clubhouse and then home for a couple of hours of marking. A classic teacher's Sabbath.

Kate spent her own Sunday in planning and preparation. She was returning to Yorkshire for half-term to see friends and to celebrate her parents' ruby wedding anniversary, the party for which was scheduled for the first Sunday of the holiday. It would be the first time she had been home since starting her new job, and while she had always planned to go back for the October break, it had until now been a vague and unformed future intention, the detail of which she had barely had time to consider. Now, suddenly, there were only five teaching days and this precious, empty Sunday between her and her departure, and there seemed to be a mountain of small but important things to do: turn around the washing; fill the car with petrol and check the tyres for the long journey north; buy her parents' present and card – not to mention wrapping and writing them. The flat hadn't been properly cleaned since she moved in, and she didn't want to return to it in a grubby state. Then there was the marking, always the marking…

Kate would normally have been undaunted by tasks such as these. She would have made a list of what needed to be done, and by when, allocated each a length of time, and dug out her planner to see which might be slotted into gaps during the week. She would have put on some music and cheered herself with thoughts of home while she worked.

This morning, though she went through the motions, it was an uphill struggle. She knew she was tired, and understood why, but she was surprised to find herself tearful. At one point she stopped and dug out an old photo album that her parents had made for her when she left for Cornwall – pictures of the small, happy family as she grew up and her parents grew old, snaps of her as a teenager, on church outings, the last they took before embracing the digital era. She thought it would cheer her but the thought that her parents were now in their sixties, the mongrel, Midge, that had been her childhood companion, long ago buried at the bottom of the garden, and the one child they had nurtured so lovingly now living her own life three hundred and fifty miles away, seemed suddenly unbearably sad, and she pushed the album aside. She knew it was possible that the Dave situation played a part in her low mood, but she didn't have the time or the energy to turn over that particular stone.

She cleaned the flat in a mechanical way, but it seemed to take enormous reserves of energy. Marking was out of the question. By four o'clock she might easily have fallen asleep on the sofa, but she knew it would be better to stay awake, then get to bed early and sleep deeply, so she pulled on her waterproof jacket and her walking boots and headed out into the grey afternoon. She was down on the beach when the first raindrops began to fall.

Dave arrived home in cheerful mood shortly after Kate left. His golf, much neglected of late, had been pretty respectable. If he played like that on the Sunday School Outing then he might be in the money. He bounded up the wooden stairs to his flat, turning on a couple of lights against the greying of the afternoon. He made himself a cup of tea and opened his laptop to check his emails.

The only one of interest was from Emily Flowerdew, asking him if he could meet her briefly at eight o'clock the following morning to discuss a disciplinary matter arising from the London trip. He racked his brains to think what it might refer to, but came up with nothing, and presuming it related to something that had occurred on one of the other coaches, he settled, with better humour than usual, to his marking.

Chapter Twenty-four

"More than one way to skin a cat"

Dave left the flat the following morning in plenty of time for his appointment with Emily Flowerdew, noting with satisfaction that for once he was leaving ahead of Kate. He went straight to his classroom and made sure he was set up for his first couple of lessons, then checked his emails. The successful applicants for the mentoring course were due to be informed this week, though probably not quite this early. He dealt with a couple of minor items of parental correspondence, then set off for the SMT corridor, arriving at the same time as Sheila Abbot.

"Any idea what this is about, Sheila?"

"It's a bit bizarre," she said. "I'll let Emily explain."

There was room for them both to sit on the comfortable chairs designed for anxious parents and distressed children. Dave noted the box of tissues on the low table. Emily was seated behind her desk.

"Right," she said briskly. "Thank you for coming in early for this meeting. I don't know how much you are both aware of what's been happening, but the essential facts are these. There are a number of video clips circulating on social media that purport to show – indeed there is little doubt that they *do* show - St Petroc's students crawling around the luggage space on one of the coaches. I've had several anxious parents on the phone, and the initial intelligence suggests that this took place on the way back from London, on the coach staffed by you, Dave, and Edward Tremenhere."

There was a pause. Dave was aware that both the women were looking at him. Clearly he was expected to speak. He took a deep breath.

"Right..." he said slowly. "I may be able to shed some light on this. One of the students did say something about a door that led into the luggage compartment from the toilet. Which does seem a bit crazy when you think about it. I checked it, and it was closed. I was unaware that any crawling was going on."

"Well apparently," said Sheila, "something of a dare game developed, and at least three boys – all in your form – actually entered the space. One of the clips appears to show the exterior door by which the luggage is loaded, and the boy in question pretends he's about to open the handle."

"Let me guess," said Dave. "It wouldn't be...oh let me see now...Toby Trott?"

"You can't actually see who it is," said Emily, "but Toby's parents were among those who rang in. Now, my default position on all this is that the boys knew perfectly well that what they were doing was wrong, and indeed highly dangerous. They are at fault, and they will be disciplined."

"Absolutely," said Sheila.

"However, as you can imagine, the parents, particularly those of the boys in question, are trying to turn it into a staff supervision issue. The boys claim the staff were asleep down at the front of the bus while all this was going on, and that when they initially pointed out the existence of the door to the teacher he - and I quote – 'didn't seem that bothered'". She looked at Dave.

"That's ridiculous," said Dave, even as his mind raced to measure this partisan construction of events against his own recall. "Firstly, I went up to the back of the bus and quizzed Trott and co, precisely because I thought something was going on, and secondly, I specifically told them not to touch the door."

There was a palpable release of tension.

"Good man," said Sheila.

"You're quite sure about that?" asked Emily.

"Absolutely. I mean, I didn't jump up and down and yell about it, but I definitely told them not to touch it. I think if you press the boys on that they'll admit it."

"And what about the suggestion that the staff were asleep?"

"Well I won't deny we may have dropped off. It had been a tiring weekend and it was a long and tedious journey. Where is Edward, by the way? Shouldn't he be here?"

"We couldn't get hold of him," said Emily. "He's not on email – and it was your name that came up."

"Well it was me who dealt with it."

"Quite so," said Emily. "I think there's enough there to keep us all in the clear. I'm sorry about this Dave – it sounds as if you acted perfectly reasonably in the circumstances – but would you mind just emailing me a written account of what you've told me? And if you can be as specific as you can about what was actually said, that would help."

"You want me to make a statement? Signed and witnessed?"

Emily smiled tolerantly.

"Not at this stage. Look, it will probably all blow over, but at the moment I've got a load of angry parents out there, and Anton next door chuntering about how he's always said these trips aren't worth the trouble. The more shots I have in my locker, the better."

"Oh yes I'm sure Anton will love this," said Dave bitterly. "Now if there's nothing more, I need to go and register my form."

"That's all for the moment. And thank you. I understand that in all other respects it was a highly successful trip."

Dave rose and left the room. Emily and Sheila exchanged glances.

"He'll be worrying about his mentoring scheme application," said Sheila.

"Oh, has he applied? That's good. I didn't think it was his kind of thing. I always imagine Dave to be the kind of guy who'll still be doing the same job in thirty years' time."

"I think that would be a terrible waste, don't you? By the way, I'm pretty sure there were times when both the staff on my coach were asleep."

Emily smiled. "I'll pretend I didn't hear that."

The coach incident was brought up in the breaktime staff meeting. Emily Flowerdew gave a sanitised version, presenting it as purely a disciplinary matter, and asking colleagues to refer any enquiries from concerned parents to her. Anton Killick, however, who held overall responsibility for all curricular and extra-curricular matters, issued a heavy-handed reminder to staff about the school trips policy, which stated, amongst other things, that on coach journeys there would be one member of staff alert and on duty at all times, and that regular checks should be made on students. The Head wished everybody a pleasant and restful half term. Dave stamped off to his lessons in a black mood, ignoring the courteous greeting of Edward Tremenhere, who was returning his coffee cup after his breaktime duty, and who remained in blissful ignorance of the whole affair.

Kate and Frances caught up with Dave at lunchtime. Both were sympathetic and understood exactly how he must be feeling.

"It could have happened to anyone," said Frances. I was completely out of it for the whole of that bit on the M4."

"I don't see that anyone can blame the school," said Kate, "I mean you don't need a teacher to tell you that it's not a good idea to go crawling around the luggage space of a coach on a motorway journey."

"You would think so, wouldn't you," said Dave, gloomily. "It's just this supervision thing that worries me. Technically, Edward and I shouldn't have both been asleep at the same time."

"I can't see there being any comeback. You thought there was some mischief brewing, you checked it out and issued a warning. End of."

"It's not what the trips policy says."

Frances shrugged. "Policy shmolicy."

Dave excused himself and headed to the workroom to write up his statement. He appreciated their attempts to cheer him, but as ever in such cases, it was much easier for the disinterested spectators to be sanguine about the outcome than the potentially guilty party. He passed Killick marching self-importantly along the corridor in the direction of the Head's office. Neither of them acknowledged the other.

The senior management team convened at two o'clock to review the state of play regarding the incident.

"Right," said the Head. Where are we at? Any media interest?"

"I've had one call from the Clarion," said Anderson, who dealt with the press as part of his role as Director of Digital Strategy. "I think I persuaded them to hold off from running anything in Thursday's edition."

"I've responded to the parental emails," said Emily. "You've all been copied in."

"Any phone calls?"

"Three, but apart from Mrs Trott they were all from concerned parents of students who weren't directly involved."

"What do the culprits have to say for themselves?"

"Sheila's interviewing them just now. Their written statements are fairly consistent. All acknowledge that Mr Singleman said something to them about not meddling with the door, though there is a sense that it might have been more strongly expressed."

"My concern," said Killick, "Is that having comprehended that there was an issue, Mr Singleman didn't feel any need to monitor the situation as it unfolded. In fact he went back to his seat at front of the bus and fell asleep. If I were a parent…"

"I don't think we can blame staff for having forty winks on a long coach trip," said Emily. "Particularly when they've been up early the previous day, and, in all probability, up half the night before trying to keep students in their own rooms."

"The policy allows for staff catching up on sleep," pointed out Anderson. "Provided they don't both do it at once."

"I'm sorry," said Emily, a steely note creeping into her tone. "I absolutely refuse to allow this to become an issue of staff negligence. That would be doing a huge disservice to conscientious colleagues who have put themselves to considerable personal inconvenience for the benefit of our students."

"I'm not sure that in this case we are talking about particularly conscientious colleagues," said Killick.

Emily looked about to retort when the Head spoke.

"I agree with Emily," he said. "We're not going to pillory the staff. We need to decide an appropriate sanction for the students, then it's a case of limiting the reputational damage, and ensuring nothing similar happens again."

Killick said nothing.

"I think that's as much as we can do for the time being. We'll meet again at the end of the day and review the situation."

The meeting broke up, but Anton lingered in the doorway, anxious to re-establish himself as a manager who had his staff's best interests at heart.

"Anton?"

"Just to let you know there's been an excellent response to the mentoring scheme – fourteen applications for the eight places. And a good range too, across all metrics."

"Good," said the Head, who wasn't entirely sure what a metric was, but was aware that Anton had been snubbed a little, and should be mollified. "When will you have the shortlist?"

"On your desk Wednesday."

"Good. Thank you Anton. It'll be nice to end the term on a positive note."

Killick nodded and left the Head's office. It would have been satisfying to engineer a reprimand of some sort for Singleman, but perhaps it was too much to hope for at this stage. Still, there was more one way to skin a cat.

After lunch Emily had a meeting with Kate to discuss Donovan Doggett. Kate had raised concerns about Donkey's attitude around the subject of drugs, and Emily had been in discussion with Social Services, to whom the family were well known. As with many students with difficult and sometimes tragic home backgrounds, Emily, who was the schools safeguarding lead, knew far more than she might wish to, and certainly more than she could share with her pastoral staff. In this case however there were factors of which Kate needed to be made aware.

"So the general picture," said Emily, "Is that there are almost certainly hard drugs in the home from time to time, and the older Doggett boy – one of our less distinguished alumni - is known to be a dealer, but the police, for their own reasons, don't want to move on him yet. Does the phrase "County Lines" mean anything to you?"

"Something to do with the supply of drugs to rural areas."

"That's right. It's a tactic being used by the big city gangs to move Class A drugs, often recruiting and exploiting kids via social media. So far it hasn't come west of the Tamar, but it's only a matter of time."

"That puts Donovan at considerable risk," said Kate.

"It does," acknowledged Emily," but at the moment there's a reluctance to remove him from what is, in other respects, a stable home. Mrs Doggett, while she is not without her own issues, works hard to keep Donovan in school, and there are no indications that he's suffering either abuse or neglect. The drugs issue is the only real cause for concern and as you know resources are extremely limited. So for the moment Social Services are inclined to leave him where he is."

"So the school is going to be a really important player in all this."

"Indeed. We need to monitor him closely and support him as best we can. I hear he's expressed an interest in debating?"

"Yes. I – that is we, are thinking of letting him enter the inter-school competition. It's Dave Singleman's decision really."

Emily noticed this small show of support for Dave.

"Well that would certainly be brave. But in the context, I think, a really good thing. There's another factor I should mention."

Kate waited.

"The word is that the father may be about to be released from prison. Earlier than expected, though we're not sure exactly when."

"Right," said Kate. "How is that likely to affect the family dynamic?"

"Difficult to say. But the father was in for burglary – he was never in the drugs trade. And he's being released early partly because his behaviour inside has been exemplary. He's apparently started an OU degree."

"Really? That's got to be a good thing."

"That's what I thought. Anyway, one thing is sure, all this has the potential to unsettle Donovan."

"Does he know yet?"

"I don't know. Mrs Doggett has been informed. Anyway – that's about it. Sheila is in the picture, but otherwise this is all confidential."

"Of course."

There was a pause, and Kate was about to get up when Emily said,

"How has your first half term gone?"

Kate nodded. "Good, thanks. I'm feeling a bit tired right now, but… generally speaking it's gone well. The department's great."

"Yes, I wish I saw more of them," said Emily. "I miss the banter. There isn't much room for irreverence at this level. Anyway – it's very nice having you around. Enjoy the break when it comes."

"Thank you," said Kate. "You too."

Chapter Twenty-five

"I am delighted to inform you..."

Dave spent the next couple of days suspended between anxiety and a dull, weary anger. He was vaguely aware that Kate was doing her best to be supportive, smiling when she saw him, and sitting next to him at lunch, but he was largely unresponsive. He still hadn't fully processed his feelings about her rejection of him the previous week, and he was transferring on to her some of the unease he felt about not having been entirely honest about Candice, although logically it was none of her business. He also, at some sub-conscious level, suspected that she considered him to have been a bit slack in his response to the luggage compartment nonsense. He would have laid money that there would always have been at least one person awake on her coach.

Kate might easily have taken offence at this grumpiness and backed off, but she discovered in herself a considerable sense of responsibility and loyalty towards her colleague. Having initially rejected his overture, she was now conducting a private audit of his virtues, in a sort of inversion of buyer's remorse. She was determined to show that even if she was not ready to be a lover, she could at least be a loyal colleague and friend.

As the week wore on however, it seemed likely that the luggage compartment incident was closed. The parents of the boys concerned were persuaded that, given the seriousness of the offence, they would be wise to accept an after-school detention on the last day of term, and a tacit agreement on both sides to draw a line under the affair. When the Clarion came out on Thursday there was no mention of the school.

Donkey was unusually quiet in lessons during the week. Kate, who was now more keen than ever that he should enter the debating competition, had found him a partner in the not entirely enthusiastic shape of Lily Tregunna, and although for a time it appeared that the boy had lost his own enthusiasm for the project, she persuaded him to go ahead with his entry. The partnership with Lily had a certain anarchic logic to it, and when Kate, slightly hesitantly, raised the matter of their entry with Dave once more, he rolled his eyes in weary bafflement but raised no objections.

On Thursday night, as was the custom in the last week of term, the English department went out for a curry. Dave and Kate went together, in the MG this time, as there was no luggage to be accommodated. Kate was wearing a mini-skirt and dark tights and Dave couldn't help thinking that she was a splendid addition to his passenger seat. His left hand was inches from her thigh every time he changed gear, and he would have been quite happy if the restaurant had been in Plymouth, instead of ten minutes away in Penzance.

"This is fun," said Kate, stretching her toes forward into the long low footwell. She sounded as if she meant it too. "Like sitting on a skateboard."

On arrival Dave felt a brief pang of loss, and in the restaurant he made a point of sitting between Mark and Jenny Skinner.

Then, finally, it was Friday, the last day of the half-term. Kate, who had shaken off her tiredness from earlier in the week went to the gym as usual. Anton was there, his focus as always entirely taken up with the strange sequence of martial arts exercises with which he was invariably engaged by the time Kate arrived. The rowing and running machines that Kate used were off to one side and slightly behind the mat where Anton worked, so she never felt the discomfort of being watched, and if she chose to she could look straight ahead and more or less ignore him. Over the weeks, however, she had built up an awareness of the exercise sequence that he used, and had developed an appreciation of its strange, balletic beauty. On one occasion when she had forgotten her ear buds, she discovered that his routine was punctuated by a series of soft, primal grunts – not grunts of weariness or frustration, but low, tight expressions of controlled power.

Anton rarely spoke on these occasions, other than to wish her a polite good morning if they happened to be leaving the gym at the same time, but this morning, as she emerged, showered and changed, he was waiting for her in the foyer.

"Hello," he said.

"Oh, hello, Anton."

He looked briefly and uncharacteristically unsure of his ground. Then he said,

"I just wanted to say I hope that you feel your first half-term at St Petroc's has gone well, and that you've felt welcome here." There was an odd formality to the phrasing, but the sentiment seemed genuine.

"Yes, thank you, it has. And I have."

"And I wanted to say that I've appreciated your input to the appraisal steering group."

"Oh. Thank you." They were now both standing at the glass front door of the leisure centre. Kate didn't quite feel that she could just walk out. Anton had the look of a man who had more to say.

"On a less formal note, I wondered if perhaps next half term we might go for a drink sometime? Or a coffee, if you would prefer that. I'd welcome the chance to hear more about how this all worked at your last school. Appraisal, I mean. The lunchtime meetings are always so rushed…"

"Oh…well…Yes, sure. We could do that," said Kate, aware even as she said it of the slight oddness of the proposal.

"Good. Good. Well I hope you have a restful half term." He held the door open for her.

Kate thanked him again, and walked to her car a little nonplussed, unsure whether she had just agreed to a business meeting or a date. Anton set off briskly for his office, and she turned to see his broad back disappear down the steps to the SMT block. She put her gym kit in the boot and headed to the workroom to check her emails. In the discombobulation of her conversation with Anton she had forgotten that this was the day the successful applicants for the mentoring programme were to be informed, so that when she saw an email from him in her inbox she half expected it to be a list of instructions as to where and when they should meet. In fact it said:

Dear Colleague

I am delighted to inform you that your application for the Middle Management Mentoring Course has been successful.

The course, which is sponsored by the Marcato Academy Trust, will commence in the second week after half term and will run until October of the next academic year. A full programme is attached.

I look forward very much to working with you on the course over the next twelve months.

Kind Regards
Anton Killick
Senior Deputy Headteacher.

There was, not unreasonably, no indication of who the other successful applicants were. After her initial pleasant surprise that she had been successful, Kate's first thought was of Dave.

Dave opened his email from Anton in his classroom, at approximately the same time. His read:

Dear Colleague

I am sorry to inform you that your application For the Middle Management Mentoring course sponsored by the Marcato Academy Trust has been unsuccessful on this occasion. There were many well-qualified applicants for the limited places available, and I would encourage you to apply again in the future.

Kind Regards
Anton Killick
Senior Deputy Headteacher

Briefly, Dave took a bitter pleasure in this latest setback. It validated and reinforced his dark mood. Well good luck to you, suckers, he thought. Enjoy those bonding games. Then, almost immediately, his mood changed to one of resentment and self-pity. Why had he let himself be talked into applying in the first place? Reluctantly, at the prompting of others, he had changed into his Speedos and climbed the damp steps of the career development diving tower, only to find as he balanced on the end of the board that the pool, for him at least, had been drained. Now what was there to do but turn around and climb shamefacedly back down again?

And if he hadn't got a place, then who had? Who were the gilded eight whose applications were so markedly superior to his own? There was no way of knowing without making discreet enquiries, and that would only betray his own position. At present, only Frances and Kate among his peers knew of his application. A thought occurred. Had Kate got it? Surely not, when she had only been in the school a matter of weeks? And yet she was on that steering group, hob-nobbing with Killick in his office every two or three weeks. He remembered something Robbo had said, about Killick cultivating her, making her his creature. Almost immediately he concluded that she would have been successful – of course she would!

He was free first lesson, and after registering his form he signed out at the office and walked into town.

Frances Fivey had in the end been persuaded by Inga, somewhat against her better judgment, to put herself forward for the course, but had barely given it a thought in the intervening week. Her morning inbox was always full, and often included two or three emails from Anton, which as a matter of practice she never opened until she was in a frame of mind to deal with them. She therefore went through the morning blissfully unaware of the excitement, disappointment, and in some cases second thoughts that were the lot of the various applicants, including those in her own department. At lunchtime, however, Kate caught her in her classroom.

"Hello. In case I don't see you before I go, I just wanted to say thank you for everything these past few weeks. It's a lovely department and I've felt really supported."

"Oh. Gosh. No. It's been so great having you!" Frances rose and hugged her.

"And thank you for supporting my application for the mentoring course. Much to my amazement I've got a place!"

"Really? Oh that's terrific. Well done! I'd better check my emails."

"Did you apply, then?"

"Yes, I did in the end. Inga talked me into it. I really don't have time to do it."

"I think Dave applied too. I hope he's got it."

"Let's go and ask him." Frances set off up the stairs to Dave's classroom, Kate following somewhat reluctantly behind.

"Actually, I don't think…I'll head for the staffroom. I'm gagging for a coffee."

"OK," called back Frances.

Dave was at his desk, marking some exercise books. This in itself was somewhat unusual. He didn't look up when Frances entered, and she guessed the answer to her question before she asked it.

"Just wondering if you…"

"Nope." Dave put his pen down and looked up. "Not on this occasion. Although apparently I should not be deterred from applying in the future. They'd be wise not to hold their breath."

"Oh. Well I have to say that surprises me. I would have thought you were exactly the kind of staff member the scheme was designed for."

"Apparently not. Any idea who did turn out to fit that particular mould?"

"Well…I haven't really…you're the first person I've asked."

"I'm right in thinking Kate applied?"

"Yes, I believe so."

"I'll give you a tenner if she doesn't get it."

Frances crossed and sat on his desk. "Oh Dave, you're a bit disappointed, aren't you?"

"No, actually I'm glad. I would have hated it. But…nobody likes rejection, do they?"

"I guess not."

"Well look, I'm trying to shift the last of this marking before the break…"

"Yes of course. Sorry. And have a great half term if I don't see you." She reached over and hugged him.

"Thanks. And you." He returned once more to his books, and Frances returned to her office. She logged on to her emails, and found the one about the mentoring scheme. She had been offered a place. Frances, she told herself, you have not handled this well. The one member of the department who really needed this hasn't got it, while places have gone to the keen newbie, who could easily have waited another year or two, and herself, who didn't even want to do it. What a mess. She pursed her lips and thought for a moment. Was Anton's hand behind all this? Had the luggage compartment nonsense played into it? It certainly couldn't have helped. She got up and closed the door, then dialled Rona d'Allesandro.

On the way back to Eglos on the bus, Sammy and Issy were chatting.

"Did our coach have one of those doors in the toilet?" asked Sammy.

"I dunno. I managed to avoid going anywhere near it. It stank!"

"It's a bit mad, though, isn't it? I mean who wants to get from the toilet into the luggage compartment?"

"I bet you'd have had a go if you'd found it!"

"I'm extremely disappointed that you could even suggest such a thing. Toby Trott said his parents are going to sue the school for negligence."

"Is that before or after he does his detention?"

"Yeah, he's literally full of shit."

"Heard any more from Donkey?"

"Nope. He's been a bit quiet this week."

"Maybe the exposure to culture has…I don't know…redeemed him or something."

"I don't think even twenty day-glo dishwashers hanging up in an aircraft hangar would be enough to redeem Donkey."

"Nobody is beyond redemption Sammy. And talking of which, I've heard a weird rumour that Donkey and Lily might be entering the inter-schools comp."

"You what?"

"That's what I heard."

"But Donkey can…I mean I don't want to be harsh, but he can barely talk."

"Apparently your Ms Porteous has been coaching him. Anyway, you haven't said whether you're going to come to my Hallowe'en party."

"When is it again?"

"Next Friday. I did message you."

"Do I have to dress up?"

"Of course."

"I don't really like dressing up."

"Just put on a mask or something. It won't be the same if you're not there."

"Ok then. I'll come."

"Good!"

The bus swung into the Eglos layby and the two friends, the natural equilibrium of their relationship restored, stepped down into the autumn sunshine to begin their half term holiday.

Chapter Twenty-six

"These men, these mates"

The venue chosen by the Idlers for the Sunday School Outing was the latest incarnation of a slightly-better-than-budget hotel chain near the centre of Bristol, an anonymous low-rise concrete layer cake whose principle virtues were its location, and the fact that it possessed a swimming pool. Dave pulled into the car park a few minutes after eight. He had intended to leave straight from school, but on something of a whim he had gone back to the Engine House and picked up one or two extra items of luggage, including his passport. He hadn't enjoyed the journey. The MG wasn't great for night driving, nor for navigating the suburbs of large cities in the rush hour, and his mood was still low from the troubles of the week. The golf clubs that occupied the passenger seat were a poor substitute for Kate in her mini-skirt.

He had plenty of time on the journey to reflect upon recent events, and his feelings regarding his failure to secure a place on the mentoring course. It had become clear by the end of the day that he was not alone in missing the cut the list of winners and losers, although as yet unconfirmed, was the talk of the staffroom, and gradually a picture emerged – most of the places had gone to those who kept their mouths shut and their noses clean, with those who had joined the school in the past three years being particularly favoured. Women appeared to slightly outnumber men, which was interesting as the gender split on the applications, as far as Dave could gather, lay in the opposite direction. What was indisputable was that there were plenty of good colleagues who had been disappointed, and this went some way to smoothing his ruffled feathers.

He had kept out of Kate's way for the rest of the day, partly because he didn't wish to either tackle or avoid the question of whether she had been selected, (he heard later on the grapevine that she had) and partly because some instinct for the way things lay between them at that point told him that a little aloofness on his part wouldn't do him any harm. He did regret, however, that this meant he had not wished her well for her trip to Yorkshire, and as he drove east into the October dusk, his initial resentment towards the success of her application was subsumed by a more noble feeling that she quite possibly deserved it. He resolved that when they saw one another after half-term he would congratulate her cheerfully.

Where this latest setback left his Dave Two ambitions was unclear. There was still, of course, nothing to stop him applying for Sheila Abbot's job when it came up. And the mentoring course would barely have got underway if, as was the rumour, the Year Nine position were to be advertised before Christmas. Yet surely logic suggested that those favoured for mentoring would be those favoured for any internal promotion. And there were certainly one or two among the successful applicants who might fancy their chances of the Year 9 job. When it came to it, there was no reason why Kate shouldn't go for it herself.

For a while, somewhere between Exeter and Taunton, there bloomed within him a glowing generosity of spirit that enabled him to take comfort in the rising of her star. He had a fleeting notion that he might even sacrifice all his own ambitions to become her cheerleader, and that in turn slid into a fantasy of a future together where she would pursue her educational career while he baked bread, wrote novels, and collected the kids from playgroup. As the harsh lights of Bristol approached however, and the prospect of an evening in the bar with the Idlers assumed a more concrete shape, this cheering vision of a joint future faded, and Dave felt himself sliding once more into gloominess.

As he lifted his bag out of the boot and headed for reception he cursed himself for signing up to this weekend of juvenile nonsense. Right now he could be sitting in the departure lounge of Bristol airport, waiting for a flight to somewhere sunny with ten foot turquoise waves. He pushed his way through the glass doors into the bright anonymous foyer and took his place at the back of a small queue waiting at reception.

Eventually it was his turn.

"Your colleague's already here," the receptionist said brightly as she handed over the key card. "He said they would see you in the bar."

"Right, thank you," said Dave.

"You're on the second floor - the stairs are over to your left."

"Cheers."

He followed her instructions and found the room. He pushed the door open and turned on the light. The girl had clearly made a mistake – the room, which was a twin, was already occupied, an open suitcase on one of the beds, and a coat over the armchair. With a tut of exasperation he headed back to the foyer.

The queue had reformed in his absence, and it was another five minutes before he had the girl's attention once more.

"I think there must be a mistake," he said, brusquely. "There's somebody already in that room."

"Oh. Oh dear," said the girl. "One minute please. Let's just see what's gone wrong here."

She returned to her computer. "Ah – that's Mr Stubbs. He said you were in the same party."

"Well we are in the same party, but we should be in separate rooms."

"Let me check the booking….no the rooms were booked by a Mr Robertson, two twins. Robertson and Pengelly in 215, and Stubbs and Singleman in 216."

What the hell was Robbo playing at? He had specifically asked for his own room. And Robbo knew he had little time for Stubbsy.

"That's not what I was expecting," said Dave. "Perhaps there was an error at our end. Is there another room I could have?"

"I'm sorry but we are absolutely full to the brim tonight, Sir. It's the half term weekend, you see…"

"Yeah I'm aware of that," said Dave testily. "OK look, would you do me a favour? If you get a cancellation, give me a call. Here's my mobile number."

He waited just long enough for her to take it down, then spun on his heel and headed for the stair. As he crossed the foyer a chorus of greeting followed him.

"There he is!"

"Singleman! Hurry up – it's your round!"

"Did you break down, Mate?"

He glanced round. All three of them were standing in the door of the bar, pints of beer in hand. And not the first of the evening, to judge from the ruckus, which caused one or two of the new arrivals at the reception desk to turn and smile. Dave raised a hand in an unenthusiastic gesture of acknowledgement and set off up the stair. In the room once more, he sat down on the bed to assess the situation. It was farcical really. Unless the girl at reception came up with a cancellation, he was now doomed to spend the next two nights in Stubbsy's company. He contemplated leaving there and then. He even, for a mad moment, contemplated ringing Candice, whose accommodating rectory could only be half an hour away. He felt like crying.

He sat with his head in his hands for a full minute, then unpacked his washkit and filled the basin. He wiped his face with a hot flannel, and cleaned his teeth, then changed into a sports shirt. There was nothing for it but to look cheerful and join the party.

In the bar, to his relief, there was no talk of school. Instead they finalised the format for the following day's golf. There were to be two separate competitions either side of lunch – an individual stableford based on full handicap in the morning, followed by a greensome, played between two teams, the composition of which would be determined by the morning scores. There were to be prizes for the longest drive on certain holes, and nearest to the pin on the par threes, plus various other more obscure events, some of which had more to do with novelty than expertise. The idea was that nobody would leave the weekend empty handed.

They moved through to the restaurant, where there was a debate about Stubbsy's handicap. The others were all members of clubs and had official playing handicaps that determined the number of holes at which a shot could be deducted from the actual score taken. Stubbsy however was not a member of any club, and therefore had to be allocated a handicap for the occasion. Although given to inconsistency, he was known to be a fiercely competitive player, and very accurate around the greens.

"I think we'll put you on twenty-four," said Robbo.

"What?" said Stubbsy incredulously. "Surely you mean twenty-eight?"

This elicited a mocking rendition of a spaghetti western theme tune from Mike Pengelly – an old golfer's joke implying that Stubbsy was a bandit, a player who maintains an artificially high handicap in order to win competitions.

"We'll see how you get on in the morning round," said Robbo. "We can adjust it up if you're struggling."

The meal was surprisingly appetising, and Dave discovered that his best way through the evening was to enjoy the buzz of the alcohol, savour the food, and laugh at the jokes, poor though many of them were. He had considered raising the matter of the room with Robbo if the opportunity arose, but in the end it didn't seem worth it. It was only a couple of nights, when all was said and done, and tomorrow they had two rounds of golf at a championship course to look forward to. He could sit this out.

As the evening progressed he found himself assuming a kind of Olympian objectivity. He sipped at his wine and watched while the others grew steadily more animated. Really he should not judge them too harshly, these men, these mates, all striving to get round the great golf course of life without disaster or humiliation. The problem, he reflected, was their attitude to women. As long as they maintained this swaggering masculine disdain, this hunter-gatherer mentality, they were doomed to struggle. He, on the other hand, had made a discovery, experienced an epiphany, that offered a superior route to happiness and wellbeing. Sure, there were certain preliminary barriers to be overcome, but he was confident, in that moment, that he had the resources to overcome them. He would win Kate in the end, and there would lie his happiness.

It was well after ten by the time they finished dessert.

"Who's for clubbing, then?" demanded Stubbsy.

"Not me," said Dave, holding up a placatory hand against the disbelieving protests of the others.

"What's the matter with you, man?" said Stubbsy.

"To be fair," said Robbo, "Dave did make clear he wasn't interested in hitting the clubs."

"I'm here for the golf," said Dave. "And the company, of course," he added, a little disingenuously. "I don't get to play high end courses very often, and I want to make the most of it."

"Very wise," said Mike. "But I don't get to high end night clubs very often either, so…"

"That's the attitude!" said Stubbsy. "Lead the way!"

"See you at breakfast Dave."

Dave watched the three of them swagger off into the night, then went to reception and enquired about a spare room. There had been no cancellations. Although he was physically tired, he was not yet sleepy. He ordered a mineral water from the bar and sat in the corner scrolling through Facebook and Twitter on his phone, but could take little pleasure in the predictable bland ironies on offer. Eventually he went back to the room and channel-hopped until he found a film that would bear watching. Halfway through he felt himself falling asleep, but the ping of his phone roused him to wakefulness. It was a text from Kate.

This was unprecedented. They had exchanged numbers on the London trip for ease of communication, but as they saw each other every day the need to contact one another by phone never arose. The sight of her name on the screen now gave him a frisson of melancholy excitement, and he sat for a while just looking at it, prolonging the moment of anticipation and possibility. Then he opened it.

Hi Dave. Just wanted to say thanks for being such good company this term, and a great neighbour. I heard you didn't get the mentoring course and I'm hoping that's not too disappointing. To my surprise I was offered a place, but I'm not sure I want it! Looking forward to working with you next term on the debating, and maybe fitting in a bit more surf action? Have a great break. Kate xx

He read it through twice. On the whole it was an encouraging message, and he was touched that she had troubled to send it. She certainly didn't need to. No love, but two kisses. One could be dismissed as girlish convention, but two might reasonably be taken as encouragement. And the surfing reference. That, surely, was not there by accident.

He thought for a moment, then typed his reply:

Thanks Kate! Not too disappointed – it probably wasn't really my thing. You can always pass on what you learn. Have a good holiday and I'll see you next term. Dave x ps always up for surfing.

He left it on his phone unsent and went to the bathroom to get ready for bed, then he came back and looked at it again. He considered doubling up on the kiss, but in the end he let it stand. He felt the message struck the right note - warm, responsive, but undemanding. He hit send and settled down for the night comforted by the thought that possibly the proverbial fat lady was some way from mounting the stage for her final aria.

He dropped off to sleep for a couple of hours, but was awoken at 2 am by Stubbsy, who had forgotten his room key. There then followed what seemed like an age of his room-mate stumbling around without apology, trying to find his toothbrush and his phone charger, before eventually the light went off once more, and the room settled into a stillness that was broken only by steady snoring and intermittent flatulence from the next bed.

Chapter Twenty-seven

"I know who you're dreaming about"

The Idlers played the Saturday morning round in two separate pairs in order to get back to the clubhouse in time for lunch. The weather was dry, and the course in first class condition, but a stiff breeze blowing from the northwest presented a challenge. Dave was partnered with Mike, who, given his current mood, was the ideal golfing companion– a solid, capable, unexcitable player who kept his easy conversation to golf-related topics. As a result, he began to relax, and aside from a tendency to slice the ball off the tee, his game was respectable. In the bar, waiting for their bacon rolls, they compared scores. Taking handicap into account, Stubbsy had come out on top. Mike Pengelly whistled his Ennio Morricone tune once more.

"Just as well you weren't off twenty-eight," remarked Dave.

"Hey, cut me some slack," said Stubbsy. "I happen to be having a good day."

"So," said Mike. "That means me and Robbo against you two this afternoon."

"Looks like it," acknowledged Dave, without enthusiasm.

"All those shots – we'll have our work cut out," said Mike. By the agreed rules Dave and Stubbsy would receive the benefit of a one-shot reduction at fourteen of the eighteen holes.

The morning round had been a warm-up – each of them playing against the course, with the only competitive element being the comparison of the scores at the end. The afternoon match was to be a greensome - a lighter, more social form of the game, but one with a strong tactical element. In a greensome, all the players hit a tee-shot, and the better of these within each pair is chosen, with the rest of the hole played out by the members of each team hitting alternate shots, starting with the player whose drive was not used.

As the afternoon progressed Dave was surprised to find that he was beginning to enjoy himself. The sun broke through, and the match was close, thanks to their generous stroke allowance. There was little banter, but much *sotto voce* discussion of tactics. At the half-way point he and Stubbsy found themselves one hole up, largely thanks to the younger man's consistently solid performance from the tee.

He noticed with interest the intense competitiveness that his partner brought to the game. As the match progressed, and it became clear that it was going to be close, Stubbsy spent more and more time lining up his putts and pondering his club selection, gauging the wind by plucking a few blades of grass and observing them thoughtfully as he released them. This was in Dave's view a fatuous exercise, as the north-westerly breeze could be easily felt on their faces and seen in the direction of the flags. He was aware of Mike and Robbo exchanging grins and eye-rolls.

With five holes left to play, and the match finely balanced, Stubbsy hooked his tee shot into thick rough, meaning that Dave needed to keep his on the fairway.

"Take an iron, mate," said Stubbsy.

This was just the wrong side of the thin line between tactical discussion and unasked for direction, and Dave ignored it. He stepped up with his driver, took his stance, and faded the ball into the rough on the right.

"Well there's a surprise," said Stubbsy. "I didn't see that coming."

"Fuck off," said Dave, ramming his driver back in his bag. It was the first display of ill temper from anyone that day, and doubtless in part a result of the irritations of the previous night. Robbo and Mike maintained a tactful silence. They duly won the hole, which left Dave and Stubbsy one down.

This was still the situation when they reached the second-last hole of the match. The seventeenth was a short par three, down a steep slope of gorse and heather to a wide undulating green, with the flag set at the left-hand side. Mike and Robbo put their shots fore and aft of the pin, about ten feet from the hole in each case. Stubbsy put his on the green, but over on the right-hand side, leaving a tricky putt of about thirty feet. Dave pulled his into the bunker at the side of the green where the pin was set. Their opponents clearly had the advantage, with every prospect of a securing a par three, or even a birdie. If they won the hole, they would win the match two up with one hole left to play.

Dave's ball was sitting up provocatively in the middle of the bunker, on top of the freshly raked sand. Nonetheless the obvious choice was to play the shot that had landed on the putting surface. Dave picked up the rake and was about to use it to retrieve his ball when Stubbsy, who had followed him over, put his hand on his arm. This in itself was a provocation.

"What?" said Dave in irritation. "You're not suggesting we play it?"

"I think we should consider it," said Stubbsy. "I mean, how close do you reckon you could put that putt?"

"Well I'm not giving a guarantee," said Dave, but I ought to be able to get it within six feet." Six feet from the flag would give his partner a fighting chance of sinking the vital putt, but no more than that. "Maybe closer," he added, without conviction.

"I reckon I could put your ball nearer than that," said Stubbsy.

"What?" The proposal was unconventional to say the least. It was perfectly possible to take three or four shots to get out of a bunker.

"It's my signature shot. Remember how close I laid it on the seventh?"

It was true that earlier in the round Stubbsy had dropped a challenging bunker shot two feet from the pin. Even Dave had applauded.

"Maybe you just got lucky."

Stubbsy looked pained. "Do me a favour."

"Would you like us to putt out while you decide?" asked Mike mischievously.

"No, it's fine," said Dave, and pulled his ball back off the sand with the rake.

Stubbsy looked as if he'd been slapped. "Whaddafuck?"

"I'm making an executive decision as the lower handicap player," said Dave, pocketing the ball and wheeling his trolley round to the other side of the green. "We're playing your ball."

Robbo grinned at Stubbsy.

"Rank has its privileges."

The fact that they were now playing Stubbsy's ball meant that the long putt to the hole was Dave's responsibility. It was an awkward one, now that he looked at it, over thirty feet across a green that sloped first one way and then the other. For a brief moment it occurred to him that his partner's proposal, controversial though it was, might not have been such a bad one. He was aware that Stubbsy had not joined them on the green but was standing with his clubs by the path to the next tee, as if he regarded the hole, and the match, as already lost.

Dave took his stance and flexed his putter back and forth, trying to sense how much weight to give the shot. He had already determined the line, up to the right of the pin. He eased himself forward over the ball, drew the putter back and struck, following through gently.

Careful as the shot had been, he knew he had over-egged it as soon as he hit it. The line was about right, but as the ball approached the hole it was clear that unless it hit it dead on, it was destined to overshoot. It passed the hole an inch or two to the right, rolling on and on until it came to rest a couple of feet to one side of where Robbo had marked his own ball. They had now played two shots to their opponents' one.

"Nice line," said Mike. "Still just you, I think." It was now Stubbsy's putt, but he had still not come onto the green.

"You'd better go ahead mate," said Dave, "My partner's sulking." A slight movement of the younger man's head suggested he had heard the taunt. Mike shrugged and replaced the ball, then rolled his putt up to within a foot. Robbo tapped it in for a par three, meaning that Stubbsy needed to sink his putt to halve the hole and keep the match alive. He walked onto the green, his head down.

He marked Dave's ball and cleaned it ostentatiously, replacing it with the logo top dead centre.

"Bit more than six feet, I'd say."

"Yeah, well we'll never know what your bunker shot would have been like."

"I'll show you. Once I've sunk this."

But he couldn't sink it. It was a brave effort, finishing only inches from the hole, but in these cases a miss is as good as the proverbial mile. The match was over with one hole to play.

Dave turned to shake hands with his partner, as convention demanded, but Stubbsy was walking back to where he had left his bag. The other two looked on in amusement, Dave in irritation. Stubbsy drew out his sand wedge and strolled, with studied casualness, to the bunker where his partner's tee shot had landed. He dropped his ball approximately where Dave's had been, and shuffled his feet down into the soft sand. He took a couple of light, phantom swings, then brought the club through sharply an inch behind the ball. Ball and sand flew up, and rattled down onto the green together, the sand acting as an inhibitor to the ball's onward motion, so that it came to rest three feet from the hole.

Mike and Robbo clapped, as much as anything else to cover the embarrassment caused by this unnecessary and discourteous piece of showmanship. Dave looked on in silence.

Stubbsy raked the bunker carefully, then picked up his ball from the green, before walking towards the others.

"Thanks for the game chaps," he said glibly. "Sorry we couldn't take it to the last."

He held out his hand provocatively to Dave, who took it as if it were something found under a stone. They exchanged handshakes with the others and walked to the eighteenth tee.

Dave managed to play the last hole with a show of civility, but inside he was seething. On the return trip to the hotel, Robbo tried to make light of the pantomime on the seventeenth green.

"Likes to have the last word, young Stubbs," he observed laconically.

"They will be his last words if he doesn't keep his mouth shut," said Dave grimly.

"He gets up your nose a bit, doesn't he? Why is that?"

"God knows," said Dave. "Does he not annoy you?"

"Not really. I find him quite amusing. I'll tell you one thing though, I'm cutting him to twenty tomorrow. He's never a twenty-four handicapper."

"He's a twenty-four carat twat," said Dave. "It's one of the reasons I wanted a single room."

"Yeah sorry about that mate," said Robbo. I completely forgot when I was booking it."

When they arrived back at the hotel the three older colleagues went for a swim, but Stubbsy pleaded tiredness and retired to his room. By the time Dave returned to get changed for supper there was no sign of him, and when he arrived in the bar Stubbsy was sitting moodily on a stool, already on his second pint. Dave glanced around and was relieved to see that the other two were approaching across the foyer. He offered to get the round in, and by way of a goodwill gesture offered to buy one for Stubbsy too, although his glass was three quarters full. The reply was curt.

They had a couple of pints, which meant three for Stubbsy, who remained sulky and silent, then moved through to the restaurant. The atmosphere throughout the meal was muted, but they saw off a couple of bottles of wine between them, and managed to find things to say about the quality of the course and the state of things at St Petroc's. At ten o'clock brandies were ordered by the other three, though Dave declined.

"Not for me thanks, I'm heading for bed. He rose and said as he passed Stubbsy, who was rocking back in his chair,

"Got your room key tonight?"

"Don't worry," said Stubbsy without looking at him. "I know you need your beauty sleep. And I know who you're dreaming about too."

Dave paused. He was standing directly behind the younger man.

"Say what?"

"You were quite vocal in your slumbers last night. "Darling Kate," you called her. Very touching."

"You little shit," said Dave and yanked on the back of the chair so that Stubbsy overbalanced and fell to the floor with a crash. There was a gasp from nearby tables, and one or two other diners stood up to see what was going on. A waiter with a laden tray altered course to avoid the fracas. Stubbsy, impaired a little by the arms of the chair and the amount of alcohol he had consumed, took a second or two to scramble to his feet, but when he did, he came at Dave, swinging his fists. Dave dodged the blows and got inside the younger man's guard. By the time Robbo and Mike reached them they were locked in a comical embrace, and staggering towards a neighbouring table. The restaurant manager came hurrying across.

As quickly as it had begun the brawl was over. Robbo overpowered Stubbsy and frog-marched him towards the entrance, while Dave held his hands up to Mike Pengelly, who was prepared to do the same to him if he had to.

"It's all right Mike, I'm cool."

He collected himself, and turned to the diners at the nearby table.

"I do apologise most sincerely for that…I…I'm afraid I briefly lost my temper with my friend. I assure you it won't happen again. Please carry on and enjoy the rest of your meal."

He then addressed the restaurant manager.

"I'm leaving now. There will be no repeat of this unfortunate incident."

Then to Mike, "I'll settle up when we get back."

He turned and walked a little unsteadily towards his room. Once there, he gathered up his things, checked briefly in the bathroom and under the bed, and headed for the car park. There was no sign of the others. He sent a text to Robbo apologising and explaining that he was bailing out, and spent a sleepless night in the MG. At five the next morning, when he was reasonably confident of his sobriety, he checked Skyscanner for flights, drove to Bristol Airport, and caught a plane to Marrakesh.

Chapter Twenty-eight

"And if not Dave, then who?"

On that same Sunday morning that Dave left the Idlers and the country behind him, Kate awoke to the autumn sunlight brightening the familiar floral print curtains in her childhood bedroom. Her parents still lived in the stone cottage on the edge of Harrogate where she had been brought up, and to which she had regularly returned while teaching at the grammar school. Now, somehow, it felt different, as if neither her term-long absences during her University years nor her first proper job some forty miles away constituted such a decisive break with the past as her recent sojourn in Cornwall.

It was still only a little past eight, and she could hear her parents bustling around downstairs. There was lots of work to be done for the party, but she needed a few moments to come round before she went down to join the fray. She lay mummified beneath the duvet, reacquainting herself with the familiar bumps and declivities in the mattress, and thought back over the past thirty-six hours.

Friday had been such an odd day. Already vested with significance through marking the end of her first half term, it had been lent an unwelcome intensity by the announcement of the successful applicants for the mentoring course. Her own pleasure and surprise at being included had been undercut when it was clear that Dave, and so many other worthy applicants, had been overlooked. It was well known that Killick was the key member of SMT driving the project, and Kate was left feeling slightly uncomfortable by the memory of his approach to her outside the fitness suite. Was she being improperly favoured? Why, after all, should she, who was barely known to the school, and who had done little of note since her arrival other than make a reasonably professional and competent start to her new job, be chosen above more senior colleagues?

She had stayed at school until five, tidying her classroom and finishing some odds and ends of marking. When she left, the car park was virtually empty and the sky grey, a damp and early dusk in prospect. She returned to the Engine House feeling distinctly low, and was struck by a further pang of melancholy when she noticed the tyre tracks of the absent MG on the gravel. She had forgotten that Dave was also heading up country, and that evening as she packed and tidied the flat, she missed the sound of him moving around above her head. What if he, too, had been at home this evening? They might have gone for a drink down at the café, laughed, and relaxed, and put the half-term, with its strange rollercoaster of experiences, to rest in a civilized manner.

Even as she mused on this fantasy, Kate knew that it was only permissible because in reality it wasn't an option. There was, still, an uneasiness between her and Dave, arising from all that had passed between them in the course of the term, and crowned by this last complication of the mentoring scheme. Probably a clean break of a few days was a far better idea. Nonetheless, as she lay in bed that evening, sleep eluding her, she was moved to send him a text, spending longer on its composition than its recipient might have imagined. Only when Dave's warm reply came through did she drop off to sleep.

The journey to Harrogate through the half-term traffic had taken the whole of Saturday, but she had made it back for supper as planned. The meal had been cheerful, the conversation running predictably upon her anecdotes of Cornwall, the school, and her colleagues. Kate noticed for the first time that her parents, who were in their mid-sixties, seemed old; her father in particular a little slower and more careful as he poured the wine, or ducked his head to avoid the cottage's low wooden lintels.

This morning, however, they seemed lively when Kate joined them in the kitchen, animated by the prospect of the day's celebrations. There were to be twenty guests, mostly friends from church and a couple of close relatives, including a cousin of Kate's with whom she had always got on well, and who would be bringing her four-month-old baby. They were expected for drinks and canapes at twelve-thirty, with a generous buffet to follow. The cottage dining room wasn't large, but the weather was set fair, and they hoped to spill out into the long garden, with its ancient apple trees, whose fruit had already been efficiently harvested and stewed, or sold at the cottage gate.

"Happy Anniversary," she called cheerfully as she came down the stairs. "I have a present, and a card, but I thought I might save them till the hurly-burly's done."

"You're the present," said her mother.

Kate hugged them both, then set about pouring her cereal. The table was already covered with various components of the feast, so she leaned against the dresser to eat.

"Right!" she said briskly. "What's to be done?"

"Here's the list," said her mother, from whom Kate had inherited her own no-nonsense approach to organisation. "If you like to tell me what you fancy doing, we'll take it from there. The plan is to have the house and the table appointments ready by ten, then we'll move on to food prep." She passed Kate a sheet of printed A4 with a lengthy list of tasks.

"I'm on glassware and drinks," said her father. "Then I hope to get to the 9.30 service."

"What about you, Mum?"

"Too much to do here, I think. I don't want to feel rushed."

"Very wise. How about if I sort out the crockery, cutlery, and napkins, then move on to shifting the seating round? That shouldn't take too long. Then I'd be happy to prep the canapes. What is it, tomatoes stuffed with pesto?"

"Yes, and smoked oysters on crackers, and there's some tempura from M and S too, but that just needs to go in the oven."

"Nice," said Kate approvingly.

She put her cereal bowl in the dishwasher and set to work. At nine o'clock her parents put on Steve Wright's Sunday love songs – not one of Kate's favourites, but tolerable in the circumstances. The three worked cheerfully, navigating their way round each other, and the cottage's odd angles, with an ease born of long familiarity.

Her father arrived back from church at eleven to find Kate and her mother drinking coffee in the garden, feeling justifiably pleased with what had been achieved. Most of the preparation had been done, so that it was largely a case of clearing the debris before they changed into their smart clothes.

"How was the sermon?" inquired Kate brightly.

Her parents accepted that she no longer shared the faith in which they had raised her, but Kate knew enough of the modes and foibles of the church and its congregation to express a lively and not ungenuine interest. This allowed them all to believe that the family's shared experience of years of Sunday observance at St John's remained valued and in some way alive.

"Very nice," said her father. "Very nice indeed. Your mother and I got a mention, which was thoughtful. I felt a little guilty at the thought of you both slaving away back here…"

"I felt a bit guilty, staying here," laughed her mother, "Like Martha doing the housework when Jesus visited."

"It was probably the right compromise," said Kate, who had limited patience for biblical allusion. "Now unless there's anything else urgent, I'm going up to get changed."

Once the guests began to arrive, the party ran itself. They were all known to Kate, and she to them, from her childhood, and they all brought a genuine warmth and appreciation of the family, and in particular of her parents, whose long and indisputably happy union was being marked. The late October sun shone obligingly, and the garden seemed to expand to accommodate the guests, mingling its intoxicating autumn smells with the tempting aroma of garlic bread from the kitchen.

For all the pleasures of the occasion, it was a working day for Kate. There was a lot of interest in her new job, and Cornwall, and she found herself producing the same responses and anecdotes several times over. She was keen to take as much of the load from her parents as she could, so that they were free to mingle and chat, and along with Vicky, her cousin, she took charge of putting out the food, while Vicky's infant was passed around various willing matrons. Her mother seemed happy enough to trust her with this task and made only occasional proprietorial interventions.

Eventually the puddings were on the table, and two of her mother's friends from the WI took over serving the coffee. The baby was asleep in its pram, and Kate and Vicky were able to retreat to the bench seat at the top of the orchard.

"It's been a lovely day," said Vicky. "Which is no less than your parents deserve."

"Yes, it has," agreed Kate. "And they do. Marriage, eh? Do you think you and Ed will take the plunge?"

"I expect we'll get round to it. We didn't want to knee-jerk into it just because Oscar came along, but at the same time it does kind of feel different, now. Ed's quite keen, actually - it's me who's still holding back a bit."

"Oscar's very sweet. Is he always this good?"

"Yeah, he's a poppet. It's funny though. I thought I'd be super keen to get back to work, but now that it's come to it, I'm really happy just doing the new baby stuff."

There was a pause, and they listened to the chatter floating up from the garden, a little more muted now, in tune with the mellowness of the autumn afternoon.

"What about you?"

"What, kids?"

"No…just, you know. Love interest."

"Oh God, where do I begin," said Kate, then seeing Vicky's eyes widen, "No, I'm joking."

"What…nobody?"

"Well…there is somebody hovering. I'm keeping him at arm's length at the moment."

"So… what's he like?"

"Gosh, I don't know. What is he like? He's nice, basically. He's a genuinely nice guy. Quite good looking, sober in his habits…"

"Got any pics?"

"We're not really at that stage. Oh, wait a bit...there's a group one I took at our end of term do." She pulled out her phone and found the picture. "Dave's the one on the left."

"Let's have a look? Oh yeah...he's kinda cute. The Italian looking one's quite hot."

"He's taken I'm afraid."

"So what's the story? Has anything actually happened?"

For a moment Kate considered closing the matter off, dismissing it, as she could quite legitimately have done, as something and nothing. Or she could make her excuses and return to the party. But the party seemed to be running itself, her parents now happily passing round photo albums. Why not just talk the thing through, as she had been unable to do up to now for the lack of close friends on hand. Vicky was fairly sensible, and although the same age, was a bit further along the settling down track. Drawing together the disparate threads of her relationship with Dave, if one could call it that, fixing it in a narrative, might bring clarity of a sort.

She told the story, as best she could. The wing mirror incident, Wheal Prosper, accidentally locking him in the outhouse. The surfing, the kiss, the declined offer of a more serious relationship. And the latest complication of the mentoring course. She didn't mention the text exchange that had recently passed between them.

Vicky listened, smiling from time to time, but never interrupting.

"So that's where we're at," said Kate. "When he made his move, I was quite sure that knocking him back was the right thing. But now all the intensity of the term is behind me, and I'm out of the situation, I feel differently."

"In what way?"

"I kind of miss him. I think maybe I care about him more than I thought I did."

At that moment Vicky's mother came up from the garden, carrying the baby.

"Your son needs changing, dear. And we're about to have cake."

The cake was followed by speeches, including a brief one from Kate, who thanked everyone for coming, and her parents for getting together, because, you know, if they hadn't...and then she said some heartfelt things about how they had set her a great example about what a marriage could mean, though at the same time that set the bar high, and in case there was anybody present who hadn't yet asked her, no, she had not, amongst the Cornish, met a man who looked as if he might cut the mustard in that regard…

Those were the words she had prepared, and the ones she delivered, but even as she paused for the inevitable laughter, she wondered if the last bit was in fact true. At any rate, the speech seemed to fit the bill, and the cake was passed around, with a final glass of champagne, or elderflower cordial for the drivers. Before long it was getting a little chilly to remain out of doors, and the party started to drift inside, which in turn led to the departure of the less tenacious of the guests.

Later that night, the clearing up all done, and the presents opened and their provenance logged for the thankyou letters that would be written without fail the next day, Kate wondered, as she lay in bed, whether it were not possible that she and Dave, more than forty years hence, might match her parents for happiness and stability, and the secure home that her mother and father had provided for her? And if not Dave, then who?

Chapter Twenty-nine

"It's nice to come back to company"

Kate returned to Cornwall the following Thursday. She made the excuse of having lessons to prepare, which was true, but a deeper reason, one she could not easily have explained to her parents, was that Cornwall now felt like the place she belonged. Not home, exactly, but the place that held the key to her future, rather than her past.

A further benefit to returning early was that the roads were quieter, but nonetheless she took the journey slowly, making one or two diversions on the way – Stratford upon Avon to pick up some wooden swords for the Shakespeare festival; Wells, to visit the Cathedral. It was dark when she finally reached Wheal Prosper.

She had hoped that the windows of the upstairs flat might be lit, and had imagined that she might knock on Dave's door just to let him know she was back, and to ask him how his half-term had gone. She told herself that this would be nothing more than the natural behaviour of a friend and neighbour, but the disappointment that she felt in her stomach, when she saw that the drive was empty and the Engine House in darkness, suggested that the motivation for the impulse was more complex. She knew that the first weekend of his October break had been taken up with the Idlers' Sunday School

Outing, but had thought that he was spending the rest of it surfing and catching up on marking. It occurred to her that he had never mentioned his family, and she hadn't asked. How little she knew about him!

Friday came and went without any sign of Dave. It was colder now, but the day had been fine and the weekend was set to be sunny. There were no trees in the immediate area of the Engine House, but further along at Lamorna, where a deep wooded valley plunged down to the rocky bay, the leaves would be starting to turn. Kate thought how nice it would have been to be sharing at least some of these last few days of the holiday with Dave, walking on the cliffs in woollen jumpers and hats, or braving the surf for a final few times before the last vestiges of the water's summer warmth slipped away to the south. There was no reason why she shouldn't go down to the beach herself in her wetsuit, hunt out the spare surfboard and have another shot on her own, but her heart would not have been in it.

At moments she even found herself worrying a little on Dave's behalf, remembering the various setbacks he had suffered in the last few days of term, in one of which, at least, she had been complicit. On Friday night she composed a text.

Hi. Just wondering how your half term is going, and when you're expecting to be back? Bit lonely here on my own…

Then she deleted the last sentence and wrote instead *Nice weather here!* x

Then she changed it back to the original.

Then she deleted it altogether.

It was five o'clock on Saturday afternoon, the last day before the clocks went back, that she finally heard the crunch of the MG's tyres on the gravel outside the Engine House. She was preparing lessons at her desk by the window, her little oil-fired heater on against the autumnal chill. She jumped to her feet and went to the door, then paused, her hand on the latch. Where she stood she was out of the line of sight of anyone climbing the stair to the upper flat, but was still able to sneak a view of any such person from behind. She waited. She heard the familiar sound of the MG's rather creaky door closing, then the little boot being opened and shut again, followed by the sound of his footsteps as he crossed the gravel towards the stair. She watched as he passed the window, his brown hair, even more unkempt than usual, leather flying jacket, blue jeans, trainers. There was a pause while he fumbled with his keys, then she heard the door of the upstairs flat opening and closing.

Might she have opened her door? It would have looked odd. They were not in the habit of coming out to greet one another. But then it was odd that she was standing where she was, and not simply continuing with her marking. She realised that she badly wanted to see him, just to check in. That was all.

Then she remembered she had washing to get off the line. She put on her jacket, collected her basket and set off across the yard to the other side of the outhouse. She resisted the temptation to glance up surreptitiously while she was unpegging. She would be able to see all she needed to see as she walked back across to the flat. Perhaps he would be at the window, and she would wave, and he would come out and say hello.

But there was no sign of him, so she returned to her own flat and folded the washing. Then she went to the fridge. She had shopped that day, so there was plenty of food. She could easily knock something up to feed two of them. That would be a simple enough neighbourly gesture. She considered texting him, but told herself that his phone battery might well be dead after his journey. It made perfect sense to simply go up and knock on his door.

She climbed the stair, wrapping her jacket around her, a subconscious defence against imagined accusations of forwardness as much as a conscious one against the cold. There was no response to her knock. She waited for a moment, then she knocked again. All warmth had gone out of the sun now, and she shivered. She was about to descend the stair when she heard the creak of the floorboards, and the door opened. Dave stood in front of her, unshaven, and looking thoroughly confused.

"Kate. God. How long have you been standing there? Come in. I sat down for five minutes and I must have fallen asleep." He moved aside and she stepped into the flat. He had turned on the heating, and it was just starting to make an impact on the chill that his absence had left.

"Hi." She said brightly, feeling a little as if she had intruded. "How you doing?" She had thought she might give him a hug, but that moment seemed to have passed. It was good to see him though. So good.

"Look I'm sorry to crash in on you - I know you're just back. I just…I mean, I don't know how long a journey you've had…"

"About twelve hours."

"Goodness. Where from?"

"Morocco."

"What?"

"It was a spur of the moment thing."

"Morocco. Goodness. Well anyway, I was just wondering – do you want to come down to mine for supper? I'm doing this prawn curry kind of thing that'll easily stretch…so…"

"Oh!" he seemed genuinely taken aback by the offer. "Well – are you sure?"

"Yes, absolutely! Come down…say… about seven? You can tell me all about Morocco, and Bristol."

"Only if you promise to tell me all about Yorkshire."

"Wow…yes. Wild Ruby Wedding Action in Harrogate."

He smiled. "Seven will be fine. Give me a chance to have some shuteye. Not to mention a shower and a change of clothes."

"Great. I'll see you then."

They stood, looking at each other, and Kate realised that it was up to her now to leave, but that she really didn't want to, even though it would be only a couple of hours until he appeared again at her door.

She leaned forward and hugged him, briefly and tightly, then before he could respond she said,

"It's really great to see you again." Then she turned and went out the door, closing it behind her.

Dave stood, slightly bemused by this turn of events. In truth he was exhausted, disorientated by the strangeness of being back in his flat, having woken that morning to the crashing surf on Morocco's Atlantic coast; and by the many hours of travel by bus, plane and finally the MG that had brought him back to Cornwall to face the various unsatisfactory situations that he had left behind him. He set the alarm on his phone and climbed the wooden ladder to the mezzanine bedroom. Five minutes later he was sound asleep once more.

He was no less disorientated when he awoke to the beeping of his alarm at 6.30, assuming at first that it must be morning. By the time he had been under the shower for ten minutes he was beginning to feel normal once more, and able to think clearly about the evening. So much of what had happened over the past ten days had seemed to place further obstacles between himself and Kate, so that he had discounted any serious pursuit of a relationship with her until he had clarified his position on the various other matters, not least of which was the unseemly scrap with Stubbsy.

Yet here he was, out of the blue, about to join her in her flat for supper *a deux*. He dressed with a little more care than usual, and ran an experimental hand over his stubble. A shave would probably be overdoing it. There was a half-full bottle of red wine on the worktop, and another two or three to choose from in the pantry. He decided that bringing an unopened bottle was perhaps pushing the event a bit far up the formality scale, and he knew in any case that Kate took her alcohol in homeopathic quantities. The opened bottle, however, might just hit the balance between making a contribution and making a statement. He picked it up and checked his watch. Five to seven. No harm in being early.

When she opened the door he had the impression she too had changed, though he couldn't have said what she had been wearing when she called earlier. Maybe she'd just freshened up a bit. Anyway, she looked good. She had lit lamps against the encroaching darkness outside, and they picked up the bright colours of the cushions and the throws. He held up the bottle.

"I've brought this. It should still be OK."

"Oh, thanks. I probably won't, but you help yourself." She produced glasses from a cupboard. "Take a seat. I'm just finishing cooking."

He sat on the sofa and looked around. It was several weeks since he had been in her flat, and it had been made comfortable in a folksy kind of way - evidence of the lingering influence of the higgye fad that had swept the nation a year or two back. She spoke to him over her shoulder as she messed with pans and a colander.

"So…Morocco? I thought you were playing golf in Bristol."

"I was. I had an argument with my partner."

"Must have been a big argument. Did you end up wrestling in a bunker?"

"No. Just on the floor of the hotel dining room. It wasn't very dignified and I'm not proud of it. I was sharing a room with…the other guy, and it wasn't really sustainable, so I banged out and took a plane to Marrakesh. Which is probably what I should have done in the first place."

"And the other guy was?"

He paused. He had intended to say nothing about this incident, about which he was, genuinely, embarrassed. But the room, and the occasion, lent itself to confidences.

"Stubbsy."

"Excellent!" She was decanting rice onto plates she had taken from the oven. "And I'm sorry – I'll stop asking questions in a minute. But…why Marrakesh?"

"Well I was just passing through Marrakesh on my way to the coast. There's really great surf at a place called Magic Bay. I needed a proper break on my own, so I had five days of total chilling in the sunshine." He had also smoked some excellent quality Moroccan weed, but he didn't mention that.

"Wow. That sounds amazing." She turned to face him, two plates of steaming curry in her hands. "I think we're pretty much ready here."

The curry was delicious. Kate took half a glass of wine, but declined a top-up, which left enough for Dave to have two glasses. Over the meal she told him about her own trip home to see her parents, and the party, and what it felt like to be coming back to Cornwall again. She didn't say that this meal, this easy conversation with this man, was what she had wanted to come back to, although such experiences had barely existed up to this point, even as an idea.

She cleared the plates.

"There's some ice cream if you want it. I'm afraid you're not really getting my hospitality A-game."

"Actually ice cream would be great. And this is just lovely. The food, of course, but also…I dunno. Just being here, chatting. It's nice to come back to company."

Kate rummaged in the freezer for longer than she needed to. She was aware that the evening was at a crossroads. Up to now the conversation had been restricted to their holiday anecdotes. They hadn't mentioned their friendship, where exactly that stood after the ups and downs of the previous eight weeks. If the conversation took that turn, who knows where it might lead. She tried to recall what state her room was in.

She returned to the table and served out the ice cream. They began to eat. She was wondering whether to say something honest about the shift there had been in her own feelings, when Dave spoke.

"When does the mentoring scheme kick off then?"

"Oh, em, in about a fortnight, I think. There's an all-day session with some educational consultant guy."

"Do you think you'll enjoy it?"

"I hope so. I quite like getting fresh input, hearing other people's ideas. I'm sure there'll be plenty of nonsense in there, but there are bound to be a few things worth considering."

"I'd have hated it. I'm not just saying that out of sour grapes – it's just not my idea of fun."

"But you applied."

"Yes, I did. Frances talked me into it, and to be honest, your own attitude challenged some of my prejudices. And there's the possibility of the Year 9 job, which I would be interested in. But I don't see it going to someone who's not already been selected for this. So I was, I guess, a bit disappointed. You always wonder why, too. You know – why *not* me?"

Kate had no answer to this. There was a moment of quiet. The evening, which had seemed only a few moments ago to be rich with promise and possibility, was losing its energy. Dave looked sad and deflated.

"You look shattered," she said.

"Yeah, I am, actually. I need my bed. Let me just give you a hand with these dishes…"

He stood up, and she did too.

"No, seriously, there's no need. It's only a couple of things. You get back to your flat." That sounded dismissive, which was not what she had meant at all.

He made as if to protest, then gave way.

"Thank you. I think I will. But that was lovely. A real treat."

They were standing a few feet apart. Kate had the empty ice cream bowls in her hand. She regretted having picked them up but didn't feel she could now put them down.

"Maybe see you tomorrow." He stepped forward and in a gesture that had more in it of gallantry than romance, kissed her on the cheek. Then he turned and walked out the door. Kate heard the sound of his heavy steps as he climbed the outside stair.

Chapter Thirty

"Sir, I can't say this"

On Sunday morning, the last day of the holiday, Kate worked on her final preparation for the half term ahead, alert to the sounds of movement in the flat above. It was another fine day, and the chill in the air stirred the faint excitement that Autumn always awoke in her, a feeling that inevitably drew her out of doors. At eleven she put down her pen and closed her laptop. She contemplated calling on Dave again, but felt that would make her look a little too keen. She had, she reasoned, opened the door to a warmer relationship, and whether as a result of his tiredness, which had been evident, or through hurt feelings at her earlier rejection, or some other cause, he had held back. Well, that was fair enough. She decided she would make herself a coffee, which would give him another half an hour to put in an appearance, and then she would head off out. The weather was due to change and she didn't intend to waste her last free sunny day moping around the Engine House.

Dave had slept late, and woke to the sunshine streaming through the arched window in the wall opposite his bed. He lay for several minutes, thinking about the previous evening. He was aware that he might have let an opportunity slip past him, but his sojourn in Morocco had left him in fatalistic mood. His feelings towards Kate in person were as warm as ever, and he recognised that the signals she was sending out were more encouraging, but he saw her now as intimately bound up with the St Petroc's world. That world included the mentoring scheme, and Killick, and the Idlers, and the bus incident, and a range of burdensome things that for a few days, viewed from the white sand and the long green curling walls of water at Magic Bay, had seemed of no importance whatsoever. He had a deep reluctance to step back into any of that stuff.

There was another reason for his sense of dissociation. A chance encounter with a Moroccan he had met on the beach had given him food for thought. Amir taught in an English Language school in Agadir, some distance down the coast. They had shared a coffee one morning and Dave had taken great pleasure in the smiling, courteous company of this fellow surfer, who was around his own age. The man had talked with enthusiasm about his school, the willingness of the students to learn, and the simple, limited educational tools that they had at their disposal. He had said he thought there might be vacancies later in the year, and they exchanged contact details. Of course it might all come to nothing - but all the same it had planted a seed. There might, after all, be other ways of living.

He dressed, and found enough bits and pieces in the cupboard and fridge to construct a basic breakfast. It looked like being a great day, but he hadn't done a scrap of work all half term, and he knew that whatever his pipe dreams, he still had to face his classes on Monday. He resigned himself to the fact that he had had his fun, and that this day would be spent around the flat, turning round some washing - perhaps venturing out to the shops in the afternoon - and thinking about the term ahead.

So it was that by the time Kate had finished her coffee, there was still no sign of her neighbour from the flat upstairs. A little disappointed, she packed a day sac and some sandwiches and set off for the cliff paths and beaches to the west that she was yet to fully explore. Dave's laundry was washed and dried, and his brief, practical forays into town completed during her absence. The next time they saw one another was in the Monday breaktime staff meeting.

The transition to the second half of the autumn term is always a significant one. Like passengers on a ship that has passed the midpoint of a substantial stretch of water, students and teachers are no longer casting their minds back to memories of summer but instead looking forward, through a sequence of steadily darkening evenings, towards Christmas. Obstacles that had once been distant and hypothetical now loomed as realities. For the St Petroc's staff these ranged from parents' evenings and report writing to mock examinations, and for the English department the peculiar joys of the Shakespeare festival, now a matter of days away.

Dave had been pleasantly surprised to find his classes by and large compliant and focused, as if they too sensed that a destination of sorts was looming. By the time he was half way through the morning it was Magic Bay and the Moroccan surf that seemed like the ephemera of some past experience, impossibly distant and ungraspable, while in front of him lay the familiar series of challenges which he knew he could deal with comfortably if he kept his mind on the job.

Last lesson before lunch he had his first rehearsal in the theatre with his Year 8 students. In accordance with Raphael's strict rules they were waiting outside when he arrived, many clutching the lines they were supposed to have learned over half term, and all in a state of pent-up excitement. Dave reminded them of the rest of Raphael's rules – no swinging on the tabs, no students in the costume store, no running etc etc. It was, of course, the anticipation of just such joys that created the excitement in the first place, and while the warning was sufficient to quell the ambitions of the quieter spirits, the livelier ones simply ignored it.

The rehearsal, however, was largely successful. They choreographed the fight scene without anyone being injured, largely because Dave had not yet issued them with the swords, and the two highly sensible students whom he had cast in the lead roles had learned their lines, and performed the plighting of their troth with a rather touching dignity. The one slight setback was a minor rebellion from the lad playing Mercutio.

"Sir I can't say this."

"Say what?" In fact he had a good idea what the obstacle might be.

"This...about the bawdy hand of the dial being on the...you know what."

"The prick of noon," supplied one of the spear carriers helpfully. The chorus of townsfolk collapsed in mirth.

"Well what's wrong with that?" asked Dave. "It's Shakespeare. It's great literature."

"It's a metaphor," said Romeo.

"Well it's personification really, but that's a kind of metaphor, so you can have a merit."

"I'm still not saying it," insisted Mercutio. "My mum's coming to see this."

"Your mum will probably find it funny."

"Have you met his mum, Sir?"

"She's like proper-strict Methodist."

And so on. Eventually Mercutio was allowed to omit the offending line, and the rehearsal resumed.

At lunchtime he found himself in the queue next to Mike Pengelly and Robbo. He had been planning on eating with his English colleagues as he usually did, but at Robbo's suggestion he agreed to join them at the far end of the hall, feeling that perhaps it would be an opportunity to draw a line under the Bristol affair. He was not wholly surprised to see that Stubbsy was already seated at the table towards which they were heading.

In addition to the brief texts he had sent on the night of the brawl in the hotel, he had sent an email from Bristol Airport to all three of the other Idlers, apologising to them as a group for having broken up the party, and informing them that he would be withdrawing himself from Idlers Club events until further notice. He had received a short but not unfriendly response from Robbo, dismissing it as "just one of those things." While Dave didn't consider himself to owe Stubbsy any kind of personal apology, he was well aware that things between them had not been left on a satisfactory footing. He had no intention of spending any more time in the man's company than was absolutely necessary, but he didn't like the idea that there was bad blood between himself and another member of staff.

Stubbsy didn't appear to be eating. Dave nodded to him and was about to sit down when his young colleague stood up.

"Just wanted to say sorry mate. I was probably a bit out of order." His acned face was set in a serious expression, and he extended a hand towards Dave. "Hope we can put it behind us."

Dave put down his tray and shook Stubbsy's hand.

"Well I don't think either of us covered ourselves with glory. And…thanks. I appreciate the gesture."

"Right," said Stubbsy. "That's all good then. I've got to see a student." And he turned and walked away, his narrow shoulders back and his head high.

"He's not a bad lad, you know," said Robbo as they sat down.

"And to be fair," said Mike. "He is pretty handy out of the sand."

Dave said nothing, and the three friends began to eat, then to speak of other matters.

When he checked his emails after lunch, there was one from the organisers of the debating competition, acknowledging their entry of two teams and providing the topics. Between them they had to propose "This House would lower the voting age to sixteen", and oppose "This house would ban boxing." He forwarded it to Kate, adding a brief note to the effect that it looked like a no-brainer that Sammy and Issy should take the first, and Donkey and Lily the second.

There was also an email from Rona d'Allesandro, asking him if he could drop in to see the Head at the end of school. Dave found this unsettling. Surely word of the Bristol fracas had not reached St Petroc's? Robbo hadn't mentioned any comeback from the management of the hotel, and in any case there should be nothing to link their visit with their place of employment. And the luggage compartment incident had appeared to be sorted out before they broke up. It might conceivably be something about the Shakespeare festival, in which the Head, a keen amateur actor himself, took a lively interest.

A satisfactory afternoon lesson with his Upper Sixth put him in a positive frame of mind, so that he was reasonably relaxed when he knocked on the Head's door just before four o'clock.

"Come in, David, come in." The Head's tone was avuncular. Dave could never work out whether the Head's habitual use of his full name was a mark of respect or a means of reminding him of his place. He took the proffered seat.

"And how *are* you?" Goodness. At this rate he would be leaving with a pat on the head and a five pound note tucked in his top pocket.

"Fine thank you," he replied. "Did you have a good break yourself?"

"Oh yes indeed. We try to get to the Dordogne at this time of year. Wonderful colours."

Dave murmured an appropriate affirmation of the autumnal glories of central France.

"Anyway, look, the point is this. You applied for the mentoring course, as I hoped very much that you would."

Dave nodded.

"And you didn't get it. Which I'm sure came as something of a disappointment."

It seemed to Dave that his response to this ought not to be too glib.

"Well I understand there were a lot of well qualified applicants."

"Yes there were. Very many. And you were very close to making the cut. In fact you are top of the reserve list."

"Oh. Well. That's some consolation."

"And it turns out that a place has unexpectedly become available. So I wondered if you would still like to take it."

Dave was rather thrown off balance. Not only was this an unexpected reversal, but it was interesting that the Head was putting it to him in person. Why had he not simply received an email from Killick?

"Well…I don't know," he said. "I mean it's very nice to be asked…"

"Oh, I completely understand," said the Head. "You will have accommodated yourself to the disappointment, and perhaps made other plans. I don't expect an answer now. Please take forty-eight hours to think about it."

"Well – I probably won't need that long," said Dave. "I'm sure I'll be able to give you an answer tomorrow. Might I ask how the vacancy has arisen?" As he said it he knew that the question was probably not appropriate.

"Well you know how it is," said the Head. "People apply for these things on impulse, or because they feel they ought to, and in the cold light of day they think again."

Dave felt he had gone as far as he could. He was about to make his excuses when the Head spoke again, leaning forward in his seat a little as if to mark a change in tone.

"I also wanted to take this opportunity to say how much we appreciate your work here. We don't say these things as often as we should. There aren't always the opportunities. You may not be one of the more high-profile members of staff, but I have my ear to the ground, and you might be surprised how many parents – and students - speak highly of you."

Dave was now completely at a loss, but the Head stood up to signify the end of the interview.

"There you are. You might not hear it again for another five years. Do think about doing this mentoring course, won't you?"

"Yes, I will," said Dave. "Thank you."

He dropped by the staffroom to pick up his bag on the way back to the car. Through the open doorway he could see that Kate was in the workroom, on a computer, with her back to him. He was about to say something when a thought struck him. Surely…*surely* Kate would not have given up her place on the course for him? It was unthinkable, yet…somehow at the same time plausible. If she had, he certainly wouldn't take it. He wasn't a charity case yet. Still, the possibility intrigued him, and he decided that if she were alone he would tell her what had just occurred, and judge her reaction.

Kate, oblivious to his presence, continued tapping away at her workstation. Cautiously Dave peered round the corner into the workroom. There was one other colleague on a computer. The conversation would have to wait. He turned and walked quietly out of the staffroom.

Chapter Thirty-one

"Other possible futures"

Dave drove back to the Engine House through steady drizzle that had been falling since lunchtime. The suspicion that Kate had given up her place on the mentoring course for him was hardening into a conviction tinged with resentment. Why had she done such a thing? Sympathy at his run of bad luck? Embarrassment at being selected while a more senior colleague had been passed over? Perhaps it was simply as the Head suggested, that she had had second thoughts. But if that were the case, why had she given no indication during their supper on Saturday night, when the subject of the mentoring course had come up? He remembered that he had mentioned the Year 9 job and how that was almost certain to go to an applicant from the mentoring course. That might conceivably have prompted her to withdraw. He would need to tackle her about it, explain that he had no intention of accepting the place, and urge her to ask for it back before it was allocated elsewhere.

His thoughts then turned to the Head's other comments. Those had been, undeniably, pleasant to hear. The whole dynamic of secondary schools is such that teachers are rarely thanked. Students are there under duress, after all, and showing appreciation for even the most carefully prepared and stimulating lesson is not cool. Teachers don't get reports, so that appreciation from senior staff and governors tends to come in occasional, general and formulaic expressions at the end of term. Why had the Head chosen that moment to tell him he was doing a good job? Could he really care whether Dave did or did not apply for the mentoring course? And, once again, why had he not simply received a standard email from Killick. He did not doubt that Killick's perception of him as a member of the awkward squad might have played a part in him missing out. Was it possible that the Head had intervened? From this line of thinking he reconsidered his theory about Kate's act of sacrifice. How could she have known that the place she had vacated would go to Dave? The thing grew stranger and stranger the more you looked at it.

When he got back to the Engine House he texted Kate.

Wouldn't mind a quick chat this evening if you have ten minutes.

The reply came back almost immediately.

Sure. Come down around 9.

At eight he took a break from his marking to check his facebook and emails. There was one from Amir.

Hey Dave,

I hope your journey home was all to the good. As I promised I have mentioned your situation to my superior at the Language School, and he is most interested in hearing further from you. He thinks beyond shadow of doubt there will be two vacancies at Easter. He was most impressed when I said you came from the highly prestigious St Petroc's academy school. OK that last bit is my Moroccan sense of humour. But he said to send your CV.

Seize the Day!
Your friend
Amir

Dave pursed his lips. What state was his CV in? He hadn't looked at it in five years. He found it after a brief file search and spent fifteen minutes bringing it up to date. In a spirit of mischief he added the line "Recently selected for a prestigious middle and senior management mentoring course." It could always be deleted later. He saved it and returned to his marking until it was time to visit Kate.

The drizzle had eased by nine o'clock, so that he didn't arrive with the benefit of droplets of water on the ends of his long lashes. Nonetheless she seemed artlessly pleased to see him.

"Tea? Coffee?"

"No, I'm not staying. I just wanted to ask you something. You are going to take the place on the mentoring course, aren't you?"

"Well yes, I've said I will, but...why do you ask?"

"So you haven't dropped out?"

"No. Like I said the other night, I'm quite looking forward to it."

"Good! That's good."

"What's this all about?"

Suddenly he felt flummoxed. Why would he have thought she might surrender her place to him? For a moment he considered dissembling, but instead opted for the truth.

"It's just that the Head has offered me a place. He said somebody had had second thoughts. I just wanted to make sure it wasn't you."

She looked perplexed at this and hesitated before responding.

"Right. Because... you thought I might have asked him to give the place to you instead?"

Dave had the distinct impression the idea was in some way offensive to her, that the atmosphere had chilled.

"Well no, I mean, I thought it was highly unlikely." (This of course was not entirely true) "and I wouldn't have accepted it if you had." (This he could utter with greater conviction.)

Kate folded her arms, leaned back against the worksurface.

"Well it's not me, so you can accept it with a clear conscience. Was there anything else?"

"No. Please, don't be cross."

"I'm not cross. I'm just a bit taken aback." Where had he heard that before?

"Well so was I. It's come completely out the blue. OK, look, I'm sorry. I won't take up any more of your evening." He turned for the door. As his hand was on the latch, she said,

"Are you going to take it?"

"I don't know," he said. "I'll think about it."

She nodded, and he left.

Well that went well, he thought ruefully as he climbed the stair once more to his own apartment. But he had at least established that the Head's offer was now unrelated to any act of charity on Kate's part. Which was good if he were inclined to accept it. A pity he appeared to have upset her in the process. On the other hand, if he were going to seriously explore the Morocco option, perhaps upsetting Kate was unimportant.

By way of reminding himself of his other possible futures, he googled the Agadir language school. The website reminded him of what websites were like a decade ago, all sharp angles and clunky links. There was a group photo of smiling Moroccan kids, with the optimistic banner "Equipping the global leaders of tomorrow." On a sidebar he noticed a missing apostrophe. He explored a couple of pages, including the canteen menu, which was in French, but appeared to offer apple purée for desert on a Tuesday.

He sent Amir an email thanking him for remembering his promise, saying he'd be in touch. Then he thought some more about the offer to join the St Petroc's mentoring scheme, which, after all, brought the Year Nine job back into play.

Downstairs, Kate was regretting her response to Dave's question had not been more friendly. Really, there had been no need to take offence. The development was good news, on all counts. And the truth was, she *had* felt the tiniest bit guilty that she had made the cut and he hadn't. It had never crossed her mind, however, to offer him her place. What exactly did it mean that he should have thought she might? It struck her that while they now had a considerable familiarity with one another's domestic routines, they had still never had the kind of conversation that helped you to understand how a person's thought processes worked.

She dug out her phone and texted him.

Sorry I was arsey. You should definitely go for it. Kate x.

The answer came back almost immediately.

Cheers. Appreciate that.

No kiss.

Dave found that he was no clearer in his mind the following day as to what course of action he should take. He watched his emails in case the offer the Head had made should arrive in more tangible form from Killick, but there was nothing. After his Year 9 English lesson he broke the news about the debating topic to Sammy and Issy. Sammy pulled a face, but Issy merely nodded.

"You not too keen, Sammy?"

"I dunno – I'm not sure how much there is to say about it."

"There'll be loads of info out there," said Issy. "And for once, I agree with the motion. Shall we meet at mine after school one day this week?"

"If you guys can get together and thrash out some initial ideas," said Dave. I'll see what I can find and meet with you one lunchtime – say Wednesday?"

"I've got tech team," said Sammy.

"Thursday, then?"

They both nodded.

"Good," said Dave. "If it's any consolation, I think you're on the easier side of the argument."

At lunchtime he ate with Mark Armitage.

"Now listen," said Mark. "How are you fixed this weekend? It seems ages since we had a catch up."

"This weekend is free," said Dave. "Most of them are these days, if I'm honest."

"I would have thought by now you and Kate might have found something to occupy yourselves with."

"Oh – that relationship's all rather transactional I'm afraid," said Dave evasively. "Who gets to use the washing machine when, that sort of thing. I'll tell you about it in the pub." From time to time he had considered including Mark in the various ups and downs of the Kate thing, but somehow it had never happened.

"Then to the pub we shall go," said Mark. "Where do you fancy?"

Dave named a quiet pub on the north coast that they often used, and they agreed to meet at seven the following Saturday.

"Excellent," said Mark. "Now. How's Romeo and Juliet coming along?"

"We're getting there," said Dave. "I'm issuing weapons tomorrow lunchtime. What about you? Is it Henry the Fifth again?"

"No – we're taking a thematic approach this year. Ghosts and Spectres. Hamlet, Macbeth and Richard the Third."

"Nice. You going high-tech? Or method acting?"

"Lots of tech," said Mark in a pleased tone. "Back projection, sound effects, spooky lighting."

Dave sucked his teeth. "Good luck with that." Over-reliance on tech in the Shakespeare festival was a dangerous game.

"I've had several long conversations with Harrison," said Mark. "I think we've got it nailed down." He picked up his tray. "Anyway – I'll look forward to Saturday."

Kate also had her Year Nine that day, and she too passed on the details of the debating topic to her team.

"So, like, that means we're in favour of boxing," said Donkey. "Cool."

Lily looked unimpressed.

"That's right," said Kate. "So we need to get together and decide who is going to make which points."

"You also need to work out what the other side'll say, don't you miss?" Since committing to the competition, Donkey had shown himself to be surprisingly engaged with the tactics of competitive debating.

"Well they're going to say people get brain damaged, aren't they?" said Lily. "What do I say to that?"

"You can get brain-damaged playing rugby," said Donkey.

"S'pose. Then there's headguards and that."

"Exactly," said Kate. "You're thinking about this in just the right way. Now look, I'm really pleased that you two are doing this, so I'm prepared to give you a bit of time out of the next English lesson to prepare."

"Awesome!"

"So on Wednesday, you come and register as usual, then you can go to the library for half an hour. If you show signs of having achieved something, I'll know I can trust you. If you don't, you'll have to prepare in your own time. Deal?"

"Deal Miss!"

"My dad used to box," said Donkey.

"Yeah well your dad's not here, is he?" said Lily.

Kate shot a warning glance at Lily, but Donkey just said,

"You don't know nothing about my dad."

"Right!" said Kate brightly. Obviously if you two do want to get together in your own time to do some planning, that will be great, but we'll do some brainstorming with the class to help you think of points too. Lily – I need to chat to you. Donovan – I'll maybe see you tomorrow at our usual time?"

"Yes miss," said Donkey sullenly, and he shot an unfriendly look at Lily before sloping off. Kate waited until he had gone.

"I'd like you to explain your remark about Donovan's father."

Lily stuck out her lower lip and looked at her shoes.

"It's just…he's always bangin' on about his Dad. He never sees his Dad. His dad…"

"OK" said Kate. "Two things. One, I need you two to work as a team, so please try not to wind each other up. And two…whatever the reason for Donovan's father's absence, that's not an easy thing for a boy of his age. So a bit of sympathy and sensitivity might be in order."

Lily said nothing.

"Actually, we'll make that three things. Gum in the bin please."

Like a grand actress leaving the Victorian stage, Lily simultaneously rolled her eyes, spun on her heel, tossed her head and flounced out of the classroom, dispatching a bullet of chewing gum in the bin as she passed. Kate watched her go, and heard again Dave's words of dark prophecy regarding the wisdom of taking this pair to County Hall to represent their school.

At lunchtime she picked up an email from Anton Killick.

Would you care to join me for a drink this Saturday evening? There's a nice pub on the north coast where we're unlikely to bump into any Sixth formers.

Kind Regards
Anton.
Anton Killick
Senior Deputy Headteacher

Aside from the use of his Christian name, it was the familiar salutation he used for all his school emails. Kate was unsure whether she found this reassuring or un-nerving. She considered making an excuse, but she had the suspicion that

Anton would not easily be put off. A drink was just a drink, after all. And Anton intrigued her. She decided to commit.

Yes sure. 8 would suit me. Let me know the venue.

Chapter Thirty-two

"The pub on the north coast"

The rest of the week passed without incident. Still unclear in his head as to what the focus of his future plans should be, Dave opted to leave both doors open. He sent his CV to Amir's superior at the language school, and he emailed the Head to accept the offer of a place on the mentoring course. The Head's prompt response was business-like, and brief, the window for expressing fulsome gratitude having apparently closed once more.

The following day he received an email from Anton with the details of the course. It made no mention of the fact that Dave had not initially been offered a place, and read like the standard letter that would have been sent out to the first tranche of successful candidates, which in fact it was, complete with the assurance of kind regards. The course instructions gave him further food for thought – he was asked to give some consideration to the 3000 word dissertation to be produced on some aspect of his teaching practice, although that wouldn't be required until the end of the summer. More pressingly he had to select colleagues and students who would participate in the 360 degree feedback exercise.

After their brief moment of connection at the end of the holiday, Kate and he seemed to have reverted to the more functional co-existence of the previous half-term. He didn't tell her that he had accepted the place on the course, and she didn't ask. They were in any case all busy preparing for the Shakespeare festival, and this was the main focus of Thursday's departmental meeting, where Dave took the floor to talk everyone through the complex and detailed operational plan that he had produced.

"With the exception of Kate, you've all heard this before. But there were one or two points last year at which things didn't go quite as they should, so I've made some refinements. Two key points. Everyone needs to know when and where to meet and register their classes, and where to be at the start of the performance. That's all dealt with on the first page. The second thing is to follow the circular route when coming on and off stage. So you wait with your group in the drama corridor while the performance before yours is in progress, then move to the back stage area one minute before that group comes off stage. The off-going group goes back to rooms 43 and 44 to change, then they muster on the languages stair and wait for the Y9 prefects to tell them that the space they are to occupy in the seating area has been vacated by the next group to perform. The one thing to avoid at all costs, of course, is two groups meeting in the middle."

"Sorry," said Kate. "I'm a bit unclear. I thought the next group to perform were already in the backstage area."

"I mean the next group after that group," said Dave, a little testily. "At any given moment groups can occupy one of four positions in the theatre complex. They can be onstage performing, backstage getting changed or waiting to come on, in the changing rooms changing back into school uniform, or they can be seated in the auditorium. It's all clearly illustrated in the diagrams on the back of the handout."

"Ah," said Kate. "I must study these carefully."

"Careful study of the diagrams is essential," said Raphael, without looking up from his Moleskine.

Frances, who could see that Dave was delicately poised between ironic self-parody and genuine frustration that the elegant genius of his plan was not immediately obvious to everybody present, stepped in.

"The difficulty is," she said, "that there just simply isn't any slack in the system. Dave has done an amazing job in devising this scheme whereby there is a place for everyone, but it does rely on everybody following it to the letter."

"And when they follow it not, chaos is come again," said Edward Tremenhere.

"Now, there are, of course, some issues when we come to the interval," said Dave, "which you will find addressed on page four..."

Dave's briefing took up half the meeting. By the time it was over Kate was a little clearer about what she needed to do with her group on the night, but her chief impression was of the very long list of things that could go catastrophically wrong. It showed a different side to Dave, she reflected, revealing a teacher who cared deeply about getting it right, and an oddly endearing faith that things *could* be got right if everyone would just follow the plan. He would never see it, of course, but there was even, arguably, a little of the spirit that motivated Anton Killick in him.

The rest of the meeting covered the programme, which Edward Tremenhere was producing, and for which they all had to supply a cast list and brief paragraph about their group's piece; and the ticketing arrangements, which were Jenny Skinner's responsibility, and which were apparently another aspect of the venture that was invariably fraught with difficulty. By the time the meeting was over Kate could see why Shakeyfest was not universally adored by all those involved. Her own class's simple but, she hoped, poetic, rendering of The Tempest, which relied little on technical wizardry, and which had been taking shape nicely, was clearly only one small cog in a complex and rather temperamental machine.

She was aware that she hadn't asked Dave about his decision on the mentoring course. She also needed to speak to him about the debating competition. After the meeting she waited in the corridor, but it was clear that he in his turn was lingering in order to speak to Frances, so she made her way to the workroom instead, leaving Frances and Dave alone.

"How are you?," said Frances brightly as she gathered up her things. "I've barely seen you since half term."

"Yeah. I'm fine," said Dave. "Better than I was a fortnight ago. "Were you aware that I've been offered a place on the mentoring course?"

"Have you?" said Frances. "That's excellent news. Will you take it?"

"Yes," said Dave. "I was wondering – the Head said somebody dropped out. Any idea who that might be?"

"Well I wouldn't be surprised if one or two people had second thoughts over half term," said Frances. "I haven't actually seen a list of who was offered it first time round. But I had heard that there was a reserve list, so maybe they were anticipating this."

"Well of course it doesn't matter really," said Dave. "Maybe it's better not to know."

"I think you're right," said Frances. "I wasn't first choice for this job, you know."

"Really?"

"No. They offered it first to the guy who was already a Head of Department in Newquay. I was gutted. I thought I had it in the bag."

"I remember him," said Dave. "He taught my Year 8 for the observed lesson and they said it was just power-point start to finish."

"I think that's what they liked about him. I've seen him since at training days. He's a deputy head now, apparently."

"Looks like we dodged a bullet there," said Dave.

"Anyway, my point is, there's no virtue in dwelling on how these chances come your way or how they sometimes slip by. Best just to grab them when you can, and move on."

"Yes. I'm sure you're right," said Dave. "Thanks."

As he walked back to the car he wondered whether the language school job was one of the chances that would slip by, or be grabbed with both hands. Frances for her part wondered whether she should have been more frank about the meeting she had had with the Head just before half term, when she had told him she wouldn't be able to accept her place, and that she had strong views as to who should have it instead.

On Saturday evening Dave parked his MG on Mark's drive and the two of them caught the bus up to the Miners' Arms on the north coast. The pub had a number of different seating areas, and several small alcoves that were ideal for discussion of confidential matters – one of the downsides of living in the far west of Cornwall was that you could never be sure you would not meet, or be overheard by, people you knew. It was bonfire night, and outside, the intermittent popping of a distant fireworks display could be heard. They found a quiet table and Mark bought the first round.

"Cheers," he said, raising his glass. "And congratulations. Frances tells me you're on the mentoring course."

"Well I am. But I'm kind of hedging my bets. I'm actually thinking it might be time for me to move on."

Mark looked genuinely taken aback. "You mean, get a job somewhere else?"

"Yes. I'm wondering about teaching overseas."

"Wow," said Mark. "Well, I mean, obviously you've got to do the right thing for yourself, but you'd be a real loss to the department. What's brought this on?"

"I dunno. Turning thirty, I guess. And not really having put any real roots down here. I mean the department's great, obviously, and I'll be sorry to leave Cornwall, but I kind of feel I'm ready for something else."

He went on to tell Mark about Amir, and the job in Agadir.

"Of course, it might not come to anything, but it's made me think - why not teach abroad? Somewhere warm. Now's the time to do it, before I do end up meeting somebody and settling down. Assuming that's ever going to happen."

"So…joking apart, you're not interested in Kate? We all think you'd make a good match."

"Well…I thought there was something there for a bit, but she doesn't seem that keen. I think she's come down here to advance her career, and sees blokes as a bit of a distraction. I'm trying not to take it personally."

"I certainly wouldn't take it personally. I think she likes you."

"What would that be based on?"

"Oh, something Frances said. She said you had got off to a rocky start but that Kate was beginning to wake up to your true value, or some such thing."

"Well…maybe she was at one point. As I say I thought I was making some progress, but basically I asked her out and she said no."

"Maybe you should ask her again."

"Isn't that a bit desperate?"

"I don't think so, no. Look – Marriage and settling down isn't everybody's cup of tea. I get that. But I think to really thrive as a single person you have to be quite a particular type of individual. I'm not that type, and I'm not sure you are either. I know you've done it quite successfully up to now, but you have to ask yourself if it's really what you want for the next thirty years, and beyond. Remember Hardy – how rarely the time for loving coincides with the appearance of the one to be loved?"

"Or something like that," said Dave.

"Well, at the risk of flogging the analogy to death, you don't want to end up like Angel Clare, pining away in some foreign land, bitterly regretting that you let your Tess slip through your fingers. And all because you didn't want to appear desperate."

"Well…I take your point. How was it with you and Hermione? Was it love at first sight?"

"Not exactly," said Mark. "In fact we broke up twice before we finally got engaged. I think we both had to conclude that we were ready to compromise – you know, to shift a bit in the other's direction. Now look at us."

"Indeed," said Dave. "You are a positively Dickensian picture of domestic bliss."

He noticed Mark start slightly, and wondered if he had spoken out of turn. Then he realised that his friend was looking past him, towards the door. He began to turn round but Mark shook his head.

"What?"

"Well, oddly enough, she of whom we have been speaking has just walked into the pub. It's all right, they've gone into the other bar."

"They? Who's she with?"

Mark took a deep breath. "Believe it or not she's with Anton Killick."

"WHAT?" Dave nearly choked on his pint. "Are you winding me up?"

"No, honestly. Kate just walked in followed by Anton."

"Well did they look….I mean were they…?"

"No no, nothing like that. There was plenty of fresh air between them. Are you all right? You look a bit taken aback."

"It's just…I mean *Anton.* Has the girl no discrimination? Is she doing this to get at me?"

"I doubt it. Maybe he asked her out."

"*I* asked her out."

"Well maybe where you were concerned, the stakes were too high. Maybe she can go for a drink with Anton because she knows there's no danger of getting involved. Don't turn round, by the way, Anton's at the bar."

"Maybe I'll go and say hello to him. Thank him for his offer of a place on the mentoring course."

"Uh-huh…he's seen me." Mark smiled and raised his hand in the direction of the bar. "I think he's coming over. Best behaviour. Ties straight."

"Good evening, Mark," said Anton, with his customary stiff courtesy. Then, seeing Dave. "And Mr Singleman. A pleasant surprise."

"Evening Anton," said Mark. Dave made a noise that was intended as an acknowledgment of sorts, but which sounded more like a kitten trying to cough up a fur ball.

"Are you both well?"

"Yes, thank you. And you?"

"Yes indeed, thank you."

"Are you going to join us?" This was from Mark, and was of course pure mischief.

"Oh that's most kind, but I'm…I'm settled in the other bar. Well. Have a pleasant evening."

"You too," smiled Mark, urbanely.

"Is he completely mad?" said Dave, when a few seconds had elapsed. "What on earth did he come over for?"

"Goodness knows," said Mark. "Anton being Anton, he probably thought it would be impolite not to."

"You two seemed remarkably pally."

"Well I see him in town. We're often in Sainsbury's around the same time. He always says good morning."

"And now he's sitting through there making small talk with Kate. Can you imagine what that's like?"

"Well let's not be too unkind. Look, here's a suggestion. There's a bus in ten minutes. Why don't we bail from here and go back to my place. Hermione would be pleased to see you. There's probably enough supper left for both of us."

Dave nodded miserably and drained his pint. The two friends left the pub by the side door.

Chapter Thirty-three

"The intermittent winking of the channel buoys"

Anton and Kate had in fact arrived independently, though at the same time, in the pub car park. He had offered to pick her up, but she had politely declined. A drink to discuss educational matters was one thing, but she had no intention of encouraging the Deputy Head to find his way to the Engine House. Besides, there was a fireworks display in town earlier in the evening that she had wanted to watch. Conveniently, this resolved the issue of how smartly she should dress; Anton would have to be satisfied with her in a clean but notably scruffy jumper, and the jeans she had been wearing all day. Her only scent would be the faint whiff of cordite, and she reasoned that this would prevent him from falling into the illusion that she had made any great effort on his account.

She was amused to see when they met that Anton was wearing his usual dark suit and white shirt, albeit open at the collar. He looked like a political adviser, or perhaps, given his build, a bodyguard. She thought any attempt at a kiss of greeting unlikely, but kept her distance just in case.

As he had promised, the pub was quiet. They chose a table in the lounge bar, and she asked for a lime and soda. He was gone some time, and she took in her surroundings. The building was ancient, with the familiar granite blocks and timber beams that characterised the older pubs in the area. Framed facsimiles of Victorian posters on the wall told the story of some historical mining disaster.

When Anton returned she saw that he too had ordered a lime and soda. It appeared that the evening was unlikely to slide into drunken debauchery. He took his place across the small table from her but seemed a little distracted.

"Thank you," she said when he put the drink down. "Long queue?"

"Um…no. I met somebody I knew in the other bar."

They both took sips of their drinks, and Anton gathered himself. He looked briefly as if he were trying to recall a script. Kate decided to help matters along.

"You said you wanted to know a bit about how appraisal worked at my last school?"

"Yes indeed. Why don't you just tell me about it, in your own words, as it were." Now he sounded like a kindly magistrate.

"Okay," said Kate. If nothing else it might normalise what was already feeling like a slightly odd encounter. "Well, it was a boys' grammar school…"

"Yes – about 800 students?"

"That's right." She was impressed by his memory of the detail. The following forty-five minutes fell just short of awkwardness, largely through Kate pacing the delivery of the limited material at her disposal. Anton frequently interrupted with questions, and seemed most curious about the degree of resistance initially shown by staff, and how this was overcome, although Kate explained the actual introduction had happened before her time. He nodded vigorously when she explained that her previous head was a humourless, remote man who had played rugby for Newcastle, and who had in the end, so far as she understood, pushed the scheme through by sheer force of will. Eventually, she said, people got used to it.

"And you, Kate," he said. "If you don't mind me asking. How did you find it?"

"It seemed fair enough to me. There are some administrative irritations, but at least you get some feedback on your performance. And the opportunity to highlight any training you might want."

"Resources permitting, of course."

"Exactly."

It was by this time just after nine. Their glasses had been empty for some time. If she offered to buy the next round, as courtesy dictated, they would be there for another half an hour, talking about…what? She decided the evening had run its course.

"Well, look. Thanks for the drink. I hope that's been of some use. I'm going to head off now – I'm catching up with a friend later on." She stood up. Anton stood up too, looking slightly disappointed.

"Oh. Right. Yes, thank you. It's been most helpful. Are you sure I can't offer you another drink?"

"No, thanks. I need to get on." Then she added, a little clumsily, "I'd be happy to get you one if you're staying, though?"

"No, thank you. I have an early start in the morning. Well – thank you once again for coming out." He stepped back and held out his hand. There seemed nothing to do but to take it, and while his grip was gentle, she sensed that the power in his fingers could have crushed hers easily. He was smiling and nodding. She smiled in return and withdrew her hand.

"Enjoy the rest of your weekend."

There was more nodding on both sides, then she left the pub. The story about meeting a friend was partially true, in that she intended calling in on Dave when she got back. Half past nine felt like the watershed before which she could reasonably knock on his door without invitation. When she got back to the Engine House however, his flat was in darkness, with no sign of the MG. She hadn't spoken to him since school on Friday.

The night was less cold than it had been of late, and the rain from earlier in the week had passed through, so that the skies were clear, and the white disc of a full moon lit up the yard of the Engine House. Kate walked over to where the cliff path led down to the beach and peered over. The tide was out and the sand stretched away on either side, a pale silver against the sea and the dark anthropomorphic shadows of the rocks. There was little wind, but a substantial surf, residue of some distant sea-storm, rolled in steadily in long scores of white foam. She descended the first few yards of the path experimentally and found she could see well enough to find her way without stumbling. She zipped up her jacket and set off down to the beach.

She had never been on the beach at night. Once she was at the foot of the path there seemed to be less light than there had been when she stood at the top of the cliff. There was still the silver-grey band of the sand, but the cliffs behind her were darker than the sea, and at their base she could see nothing. She turned to check whether the beginning of the path back up to the Engine House was obvious. It wasn't, so she drew a large arrow in the sand a few yards out where she couldn't miss it on her way back. Pleased with this device, she set off towards the distant rocks.

So the drink with Anton was ticked off her list, and with it, she decided, Anton himself. There had been something very odd about the experience, as if behind the scrupulous politeness and the business-like manner there lay a darker purpose. What that might be was unclear, for he had given her no indication that he was romantically interested in her. She wondered if she was being made use of in some way.

Anton had never been any kind of rival to Dave for her affections – at least, not from Kate's point of view, but he had been a presence, a minor but not entirely irrelevant signifier, in that he represented something that Dave lacked. But if Dave were seriously about to take up a place on the mentoring course, perhaps his earlier lack of ambition was, as he claimed, something that he had outgrown. They had been out of kilter since her return from Yorkshire, although she felt that she had, on that first evening at least, done her best to make clear that she was open to something warmer. She could hardly blame Dave if, in the light of the events around the end of the previous half term, and the perspective offered by his sojourn at Magic Bay, he had in effect given up on her. She found that thought depressing, and was, unusually, inclined to blame herself. She could have done more. Perhaps she still could.

She reached the far end of the beach, where the rocks merged with a jutting corner of the cliff, preventing further exploration in any but the lowest of tides. She thought the tide was coming in now, but the water's edge was still sixty or seventy yards distant, and she felt quite safe. Her eyes had adjusted to the darkness, and now almost the entire vista - sand, rocks, cliffs, sea and sky - was laid out before her in curving lines of gunmetal, silver and slate. The firework displays were all finished, and the monochrome palette was relieved only by the red and green navigation lights of a pair of ships on the horizon, and the intermittent winking of the channel buoys. It struck her that ships that pass in the night must be, to one another, objects of considerable significance – compact communities of light and life in all that empty darkness.

She found a flat piece of rock and sat down, listening for a while to the slow rush and pull of the surf. Her thoughts turned to school, and a meeting she had had earlier in the week with Donovan Doggett. The boy was changing, there was no question of that. There was less swagger these days, more interest in what she had to say, particularly about the debating. In the last meeting he had spoken again, and without prompting, about his father.

"You know about my Dad, don't you Miss?"

She had admitted that she knew a little about the situation.

"Well, he's getting out. He's coming home."

She had acknowledged this, without making too much fuss. She knew that such changes could be disruptive.

"Thing is, I'm a bit worried. About him and me brother."

He had talked a little, without giving much away, about the fact that his brother was engaged in his own criminal enterprises, enterprises in which he wanted Donkey to get involved.

"And I used to really want that, 'cos, I, like, always looked up to him and that, and he's always got loads of dosh…but, my mum says Dad's going to put a stop to all that, and he wants me to focus on my education."

"And what do you want?"

"I want to please my dad. Mum says he was dead chuffed to hear about the debating. Miss, what's an Open University degree?"

"It's a way of getting a degree if you can't physically get to a University. People often do them when they're a bit older and have started working."

"So they're not just special easy degrees for folk in prison?"

"Not at all. In fact they're very highly thought of."

"My Dad's doing one of them."

"Then you should be really proud of him."

"I'm scared about what's going to happen though, between him and Jason."

"When are you expecting him home?"

"We don't know yet. They don't tell you exactly until just before."

"Will you keep me informed? There's a parents' evening in a couple of weeks. Maybe I'll meet him then."

"Will you give us a good report Miss?"

"If you keep doing as well as you are doing, I'll have lots of good things to say."

He had gone away reasonably happy with that.

It was this development that she had wanted to discuss with Dave. The mutual dislike between her colleague and the male half of her debating team was something that might need some managing if Donkey were to be kept on the straight and narrow over the next fortnight.

She realised she was starting to feel the cold, so she set off back along the sand. She was about half way along when a dark figure detached itself from the shadow of the cliff face at roughly the point at which the path from Wheal Prosper met the beach. Her first thought, oddly, was of lurid newspaper headlines – it was undoubtedly an excellent spot for a murder. And there was something odd about the silhouette, something unnaturally clean and clear in outline. Then the figure stepped into the moonlight and it was apparent that it was only a man in a wetsuit, carrying a surfboard. Surely it was Dave? They were fifty yards apart now. He must have seen her, but instead of greeting her, or waving, he set off at an angle, down towards the sea, but in the opposite direction, so that soon she was out of his direct line of sight. His head was bowed as he walked.

She was about to call out, but something told her that the intrusion would be unwelcome. Was it safe to surf at night? She had never heard of anybody doing so, though the appeal was obvious. And the surf didn't look dangerous. She moved back into the shadow of the cliffs, and watched as he paddled out, waiting until he caught the first wave and skimmed his way expertly down its moonlit face towards the beach, twisting and turning as he went. It was in many ways a romantic spectacle, but there was also something poignant, almost sad about the solitariness of the activity.

It felt voyeuristic to stay longer, so she turned and climbed back up the cliff path, an idea forming in her head as she went.

Chapter Thirty-four

"A Pictish sea-goddess"

The waves were not large, so that the surfing was effortless, requiring little more than Dave's muscle-memory and his innate sense of balance to keep him upright. It was tame stuff compared to Morocco, but nonetheless he knew he would miss it if he went. Right now it was his therapy.

They had caught the bus back to Mark's house, and there had been some macaroni cheese left over, which Dave had gratefully eaten, while gently fending off Hermione's enquiries about his love life. It would have been impossible for him to explain to them the complexities of his feelings around Kate, and the blow to the guts that the knowledge of her date with Killick had given him. He excused himself early and drove back to Wheal Prosper. His surfboard and wetsuit were waiting for him in the outhouse, and he registered dully that there was no sign of life at Kate's, although her car was back.

Then, at the bottom of the cliff path, she had appeared like a wraith from the far end of the beach. Even now he was not entirely sure he hadn't imagined her presence. As he paddled out and surfed in, it was the more vivid mental picture of Kate and Anton smiling at one another over their drinks that he was trying to erase. He surfed mechanically in this way for the best part of an hour, then carried his board back up the sand and began the ascent of the cliff path. It must by now be late, but he felt wide awake. He would find something on Netflix to fall asleep to. Another rip-roaring Saturday night for Singleman.

On her return from the beach, Kate put on some music. She switched on the heating to warm the room, then she turned on the oven. She had done some baking that afternoon, but it would be even nicer warm. She took clotted cream out of the fridge and set some bowls on the table. Then she sat down to wait. It seemed an age before she heard the crunch of the gravel and the sound of the outhouse door opening. She pondered. Would he change back into his clothes, or flit across the yard in his shorts? Diverting thought.

She opened the door, and leant against the frame with her arms folded, in the classic pose of the put-upon housewife waiting for an erring husband to return from the pub. A moment or two later Dave emerged from the outhouse, wearing his shorts and his jacket, and carrying the rest of his clothes. He stopped when he saw her.

"What time of night do you call this?"

The light behind her accentuated her figure. There was a note of provocation in her voice. He was confused. Confusion was rapidly becoming his default state.

"I'm not really in the mood for banter," he said, crossing towards the stair.

Kate changed her tone. "Oh. Right. Sorry. Has something happened?"

He stopped next to her, one hand on the rail of the staircase.

"You tell me."

"I don't understand."

"Look, I feel a bit stupid standing here half dressed, and it's too chilly for a long conversation. Who you see is up to you, obviously, but…Killick? I mean, really?"

He started to climb the stair.

"Wooah!" said Kate. "Hold on a minute. What's brought all this on?"

Dave sighed. Even to his own ears, he sounded distinctly small-minded.

"Mark Armitage and I were in the pub tonight. In the other bar. Mark saw you come in. Look, I'm sorry. I really do know that it's not my business. It just…upsets me a little. Given our recent history."

"I see." Kate, feeling that she had been in some way spied upon, felt her irritation rising. "Well you're right on both counts. I was in the pub with Anton tonight. And it is none of your business. Any other questions?"

Dave shook his head miserably and turned to continue his progress up the stair. Then he paused.

"Actually, I do have one. What's that smell?"

"What? Oh. That's just some parkin warming in the oven. At home we always have some on bonfire night. I had thought, well…it doesn't matter."

"You made it for me?"

"No, I made it for me, actually. But I was going to offer to share it. It goes nicely with hot chocolate."

For a moment or two they stood suspended. Forces that were both within them and beyond them were pulling them in opposite directions, back into their respective quarters, into the unhappy security that self-protection and resentment offered. Only the smell of the warming parkin, hanging between them on the still, cold, November air, held out the promise of something better. Dave spoke first.

"Is it, um, ready now? This parkin?"

"It wants another couple of minutes."

Another pause, then,

"Would you still consider sharing it? If I try to be a bit more grown up?"

She nodded. "I would consider that."

"Let me get my jeans on." He set off back up the steps two at a time.

"You could come as you are," she called after him, then she turned and went back into the flat.

When he returned a minute later the door was open, and Kate was perched on the edge of the sofa. The room was lit only by candles and some soft piano music was playing. There was a low coffee table in front of her and he sat on that, so that his knees were touching hers. He took her hands gently. It didn't seem necessary to ask permission.

"I've made a bit of a pig's ear of this, haven't I?"

She smiled. "It's not all you. It seems we either trip over one another, or we pass each other going in the opposite direction."

"We could talk about the reasons for that," he said.

She gazed back at him, her beautiful dark eyes steady on his. "We don't think that highly of talkers where I come from."

She moved her face towards his and kissed him slowly and deliberately. Then her hands were on the buttons of his shirt, and his hands were reaching round her firm swimmer's body as he shifted across to join her on the sofa. They didn't speak because there was nothing to discuss. For perhaps the first time since they had met they were in complete accord, and soon the jeans he had so recently put on were tangled on the floor with hers. The intense animal pleasure of the minutes that followed combined in a heady synaesthesia with the music and the candlelight, and something other - a deep, sweet, faintly carbonised aroma from the oven. It was some time before they were in a condition to notice this.

"Oh my God, the parkin," squealed Kate, and disentangled herself from Dave's embrace to affect a rescue operation.

The parkin was not beyond redemption. They put on just enough clothes to not feel ridiculous, then Kate made the promised hot chocolate and they sat, entwined once more on the settee, and ate it with clotted cream, as a final distant volley of fireworks from the direction of Newlyn announced the midnight hour.

"There's so much I don't know about you," said Dave, when they awoke in Kate's narrow bed in the quiet hours of the night.

"Ask away," she said sleepily.

"I want to know about your tattoo," he said, tracing its periphery with his fingernail, an artistic exercise that induced some satisfactory wriggling on the part of the canvas. The tattoo covered much of Kate's back, and appeared to be a species of two-tailed mermaid. "I've been wondering about it since the day I met you."

"It's a Pictish sea goddess."

"Wow. I love it."

"You don't have tattoos, then?"

"I do have one," he said. "But it's very small and you have to look quite hard to find it."

It took a pleasurable twenty minutes for Kate to find the outline of a honeybee, only two centimetres long, that was etched on the inside of his left ankle. Then they slept some more. When they next awoke it was early morning, and the first sunlight was striking the back wall of Kate's apartment. They could both have slept longer, but the day seemed too precious to waste, their altered world too full of questions, and things to be said and settled before Monday intruded. They dressed, wrapping themselves warmly against the chill breeze, and walked down to the beach, where the tide was out once more. It was if the sand had been washed and swept for their pleasure, and they walked barefoot along the empty strand just above the point at which the breaking waves settled and receded.

"Tell me about yourself," he said.

"There's not much to tell. I've led a quiet, self-contained and sober existence. Which I've no wish to change."

"We can be quiet and self-contained for ever, as far as I'm concerned," said Dave. "And sober most of the time, if you absolutely insist."

"Will you teach me how to surf? I mean properly."

"If you teach me how to bake."

"Seriously?"

"Seriously. I've always wanted to bake. My mum started to teach me, then she got ill."

"Did she get better?"

"She died when I was fifteen."

Kate was silent, absorbing this, and how it might have affected the boy that was still somewhere to be found in the man who walked beside her. Then she said,

"But you still have some family left?"

"Not much," said Dave. "My father re-married, and lives in Spain now, with his partner's kids. We're not as close as we should be. I've got an older brother in London, he's an investment banker. We don't have a lot in common. You?"

"I'm an only child. But I never really minded. I had a dog. And I had my nose in a book most of the time."

"And your parents have just celebrated their fortieth? That's an achievement."

"Yep. So far as I can tell they're pretty much still in love. It's quite intimidating sometimes."

"They must have been together a while when they had you?"

"Yes – mum had several miscarriages, so they kind of gave up on a family. Then I came along."

"I think I quite like it that there's only one of you."

She smiled.

"Why the bee?"

"Symbol of industry."

"Right." She looked at him sceptically.

He didn't feel ready to tell her that it had been the abbreviated form of his mother's name.

They reached the end of the beach, and they stood and hugged one another against the chill morning breeze.

"This is for real, isn't it, Kate? I mean – it's not just a one-off?"

Still holding his hand, she turned and pulled him back along the beach.

"You do like to know where you stand, don't you?"

"Please don't tease me. Not today."

She sighed. "Well, I hope it's for real. I want it to be. But, like I said before, this wasn't my game plan. I need to get my head round it."

"But your game plan – that's basically to work hard, get promotion, build a career, yes?"

"Pretty much."

"Well I'm down with that. I mean that's pretty much my game plan too these days. Good grief, I've even submitted myself to being mentored!"

"Yes, I heard. And that's great. But Dave – when I said a few weeks back that I thought you might be a bit laid back for me, I wasn't trying to make you into a different person."

"I don't think I am becoming a different person. I'm just kind of… changing my direction of travel." She stopped, and he did too.

"You're so sweet," she said, and kissed him softly. Then, as, he moved to gather her to him, she slipped out of his arms and looked quickly up and down the empty beach.

"Let's go in! Just a quick dip!" and suddenly she was peeling off her top layers, crabbing sideways up the beach towards the drier sand with her jumper over her head.

He followed her, collecting her clothes as she discarded them.

"You're just going to strip off?"

"Why not? There's nobody about." Now she was stepping out of her knickers. "You coming?"

And the Pictish sea-goddess ran past him down towards the freezing surf.

"Wait up!" called Dave. Dropping the bundle of Kate's things on the sand, he pulled off his own clothes, and ran after her.

They didn't stay in the water long, which was just as well, as the first of the dog walkers started to appear at the far end of the beach as they came out. They dried themselves as best they could and pulled on their jeans and jumpers and ran back along to the footpath to get warm. Back at the Engine House they had breakfast in the upper flat because Dave had some bacon and eggs in his fridge, then the knowledge that they wearing only rough denim and wool against their skin proved too provocative and they climbed the ladder to the sleeping deck, and made love again, then fell asleep until midday.

"I'm going downstairs to have a shower," said Kate, when they awoke. "And get properly dressed, then I'm going to do some work."

"You're not serious," said Dave.

"I am." Then seeing his crestfallen expression, "Look, if this is going to work – and I really want it to work – we're going to have to keep business and pleasure separate."

"So…what about tonight?"

She was silent for a moment.

"I'm sorry, but I think sleeping together is going to have to be a weekend treat. It's Monday tomorrow and I need to be in the right frame of mind."

"Bloody Hell," said Dave. "You're a hard woman."

She softened.

"Look – I need to do about three hours' work. And I need some head space. But I'll cook us supper if you like, provided you're out the door by nine."

"*Nine?*"

"I need my beauty sleep." She was pulling on her clothes now.

"You really don't."

"Flattery will get you nowhere."

He jutted his lip, then acquiesced.

"OK. Fair do's. I like to do some lesson preparation myself on Sundays, as I'm sure you're aware."

"Of course. Industrious Mister Singleman. I'll see you at seven." Then she was descending the ladder, her dark serious eyes fixed on him until she dropped out of sight. He flopped back onto the bed, and listened to her leaving the flat, then he lay in thought for a further half hour before taking his own shower.

Chapter Thirty-five

"The smack of firm government"

They travelled to school on Monday morning in their own cars, at their own habitual hours of departure. Like many men who achieve what they think will make them most happy, Dave found himself confronted with a range of previously unimagined sources of anxiety. Supper the previous evening had not been an unmitigated success.

True to his word, he had spent Sunday afternoon in marking and preparation, though his mind was not entirely on the task. He had a sense of how the evening's discussion might go. He was convinced that he and Kate wanted the same things, or at least that the things that he wanted were sufficiently close to those Kate aspired to that there need be no serious obstacle to this relationship becoming what he deeply and instinctively wanted it to be. He also understood that Kate's feelings were not quite so unequivocal as his own, and that to keep her he would need to be careful to respect her boundaries. He had turned up on the dot of seven with the very best of intentions.

It had started well enough. They embraced warmly, and Kate seemed to be as pleased as he was that the hours of voluntary separation were at an end. She had found time to shop for one or two ingredients that allowed her to produce something nice – a warming casserole with apple pie to follow

- that he had the good sense to recognise would not have been her normal Sunday evening fare. Then they had sat across the table and talked in an oddly business-like manner about what implications the weekend's events had for the busy weeks that lay ahead. Kate had done her thinking while she cooked, and she knew precisely what she wanted.

The relationship was definitely a thing, she said. She was excited about it and she wanted it to work. But it would have to be carried out strictly off school premises, and she didn't, for the time being, want it broadcast. She made an exception of Mark on the basis that she judged him to be discreet, and Dave insisted that he needed someone to confide in.

"I'm not sure how realistic it is to expect to be able to keep it a secret," he said. "This is Cornwall, remember. The five degrees of separation thing reduces to two at the most down here."

"Well if something gets out, it gets out," she responded. "Unless they hear it from one of us, it's just gossip and rumour. There's probably a bit of that anyway."

"Is this is all because you're not very sure about it? About us, I mean."

"I wouldn't put it quite like that."

This was not entirely reassuring, and Dave's despondency showed in his face, so she added, more patiently.

"The thing is - unless you count the understanding I had for a while with Darren Butterworth in year five, I've never actually been in a relationship. It's just always made more sense to me to steer clear of entanglements. I like to be in control of my life and I'm not really much of a romantic, if I'm honest."

He said nothing, hoping there was more to come, hoping it might be more encouraging.

"Having said that, this feels…different. Last night was kind of lovely. And…I think you're great. So I am ready to explore it farther – see where it takes us. That's actually a really big step for me. I can see you want us very much to have some kind of fixed idea about the future, and maybe we'll come to that. I'm not ruling it out. But – you know…nice and easy does it."

A little reluctantly, Dave agreed to her proposal that they should spend weekends together, but that Monday to Friday would continue exactly as before. The carrot was that if it was all still going smoothly, they would spend some time together over the Christmas break. Then, in the New Year, when Kate had a complete term at St Petroc's behind her, they would go public. It seemed like a plan, and one that held open the possibility of a future, but by the time they got to the apple pie, it was clear that Dave's vague hope of ending the evening in Kate's bed would have to be abandoned as unrealistic. They kissed briefly when he left as agreed at nine o'clock, and he climbed the stairs to his flat unsure whether the evening had cheered or depressed him.

Now it was the week of the Shakespeare festival, and quickly it became clear that Kate's insistence that their school relationship should continue unaltered was, at least in the short term, the only sensible way forward. On Tuesday each Year 8 group had an hour in the theatre to rehearse with technical support, and Dave, in his role as co-ordinator, was taken off timetable to oversee and troubleshoot as required.

It was evident by the end of the day which were likely to be the problematic pieces. Kate's *Tempest* would be fine – she had wisely taken his advice and kept tech to a minimum, relying instead on choreography and an extremely well-cast Caliban to carry the piece through. His own *Romeo and Juliet* was solid enough, and while the sword fight needed a bit more rehearsal, and the Nurse (a local trawlerman's son in drag) was a bit shaky on his lines, the groundwork was all there. Frances had opted this year for an abstract piece on Shakespeare's imagery in which he had complete confidence because Frances, so far as he could see, had never screwed up anything in her life, and Edward Tremenhere's group were taking his rather cerebral *King Lear* with touching seriousness. He had some residual worries about Mark's over-reliance on the tech team for his ghosts and spectres piece, but his greatest concern was reserved for Jenny Skinner's *Henry V*. It was well known that the drama department had an impressive store of WWI props and costumes left over from a sixth form production of Oh What a Lovely War some years previously. Jenny, with her unerring instinct for complexity, had decided to capitalise on this by transposing her production to the trenches of the Somme. This meant that much of the backstage area would be taken up with a howitzer and a papier-maché reconstruction of a dugout that the students had made in DT, both of which were to be wheeled on for the performance. He cursed himself for not putting her piece at the end of the programme.

At lunchtime he texted Kate:

Fancy sharing a quick beer at mine at 6? We could discuss Shakeyfest…

The reply came swiftly back:

Slippery slope. Open to suggestions for Friday though. Xxx

He grinned ruefully. The smack of firm government was bearable when it came with the promise of better times to come. Perhaps on Friday he would cook for her. Or should they just bunk off out of County for a dirty weekend in a provincial hotel? Reluctantly he rejected that idea. His bank balance was low after his unplanned trip to Morocco, and Christmas was coming. Deferred gratification was something he was going to have to get used to.

He had his top set year nines in the afternoon, and at the end of the lesson he asked to see Issy and Sammy to check on progress with their debating speeches. He was pleased to find that they had clearly been working together in their own time, and that the two draft speeches, while a little muddled in places, each had some strong points that would form the basis of a solid argument. The competition was the following Tuesday, and they agreed to meet again later in the week for a run-through.

"Actually, guys, there is one other thing I need to talk to you about."

They looked at him with blank expressions. Generally, such an opener was the prelude to something awkward or unwelcome.

"I'm involved in a course that the school is running – a kind of professional development programme, preparing teachers for management positions. One of the quite interesting aspects of this thing is that I need to get feedback from a whole range of the people I come into contact with in my job – so colleagues, parents, Senior Management and so forth. They also want input from pupils."

"That's a really good idea," said Issy. "Nobody ever asks us what we think."

"Do we get to write a report on you, Sir?"

"Well, in effect yes. I think it mostly takes the form of a questionnaire. It'll need your parents' permission, of course, but I thought I would ask you both first if you'd be happy to do it."

Issy nodded enthusiastically.

"Don't worry," said Sammy. We won't write anything bad about you."

"Well actually it's important that you're honest. The idea is that I get a realistic picture of what people actually think of me. Anyway, talk to your parents about it. There'll be a letter in a few days."

The two friends disappeared to catch their bus, clearly animated by this new development. It struck Dave that while it was certainly a little risky asking your students to comment on your performance, it also felt right, somehow.

Despite the constraints that Kate was putting on the relationship, and her apparent hesitancy, she too was excited about it. The memory and the anticipation of the sex was something she carried with her like a warm secret during the week, and when Dave's text came through at lunchtime there was pleasure in knowing that he was thinking about her. But she knew the course she was setting for them was the right one. If they could just get through the next few weeks, she was confident that by Christmas she would be able to reassure him that that the relationship was something she was prepared to invest in.

At the end of school there was an email from Anton in her in-box.

Thank you for meeting me on Saturday. I did enjoy our evening. Would you be able to drop by my office at 4.30 this afternoon?

Anton

This was odd. Something about appraisal, possibly, but equally, possibly something more. She noted the abandonment of his customary salutation. Dave had not mentioned Anton again, but Kate had put two and two together and realised that however slender the evidence, Dave saw the deputy head as a rival. The term ahead was going to be a difficult balancing act as it was, and the last thing she needed was Anton turning up at Wheal Prosper with a bunch of roses. She checked the time.

She would be a little early, but she might as well get it over with.

Anton's door was open when she arrived at his office. She tapped and stuck her head round.

"Ah Kate – thank you for coming. Come in." He got up from his desk and came round to the cramped seating area. "Please sit down. I'll just…"

He reached past her and closed the door. She took a seat as requested, and he sat opposite her.

"There was something else I wanted to ask you."

Kate waited, her face composed into what she hoped was a bland expression of mild professional interest.

"I very much appreciated our meeting on Saturday. Of course that was an entirely professional matter, and it would not have been appropriate to…that is to say…I wondered if you would be willing to meet me again on a more…social basis?"

"I'm sorry," said Kate, affecting more confusion than she felt. "do you mean you're asking me out?"

"Yes. I am."

"Well…thanks for the offer, but actually I'm in a steady relationship at the moment."

"I see." He sat a little more stiffly in his chair, and his tone became more like the one he used in staffroom briefings. "May I ask if this is somebody from Yorkshire, or someone…more local?"

"No."

"From somewhere else then?"

"You misunderstand me. I mean no, you may not ask. It's none of your business."

Killick whitened. He looked as if he had been slapped, and for a moment Kate wondered if she had overstepped the mark. But she had the moral high ground. It was pretty outrageous for him to invite her to a meeting at the end of the school day, and on school premises, via school email, for the express purpose of asking for a date. She stood up.

"I'm glad you found our conversation at the weekend useful. I'm happy to continue to serve on the appraisal working group. And I think, provided we keep our relationship entirely professional, I can quietly forget about this meeting, if that would be helpful."

Anton recovered his composure. He stood and walked past her to the door.

"Yes, that will be entirely satisfactory." He opened the door for her, and she felt the heat of his body through his freshly laundered shirt as she passed him. The door closed again, and she walked, a little unsteadily, along the SMT corridor past Emily Flowerdew's office. Behind her she heard an odd sound – a series of muffled smacks as if a carpet were being efficiently beaten in the old-fashioned way.

Chapter Thirty-Six

"Proper job, wunnit? Proper job!"

The theatre was buzzing. The main auditorium was filled with mums and dads, for the reputation of Shakeyfest preceded it, and even the most disengaged parent, who might rarely be seen at a parents' evening, was not insensible to the significance of their offspring uttering (or, as was sometimes the case, stuttering) the immortal words of the bard on stage. The lighting box was also packed, principally with the considerable bulk of Harrison Roche, but with excess space occupied by his minions, peering anxiously at their tech scripts, going over the sequence of the first few cues in their heads. The various form groups in their differing states of readiness were disposed around the theatre block according to Mr Singleman's legendary battleplan, copies of which were sellotaped to walls and pillars in the hope that this might ensure compliance. It never had in the past, but Dave lived in hope.

Issy and Sammy were both there, Issy in her school uniform as Dave's form prefect, invested for the evening with the responsibility of marshalling the various groups from changing room to backstage area and back to their allotted space in the auditorium when their hour upon the stage had been duly strutted and fretted. Sammy was in black, his job tonight being to run the backstage area, troubleshooting any prop or set issues, and supervising the setting and clearing of the stage by the Year Seven techies. This small army of stagehands, who were too junior to be employed in anything more complicated than scene-shifting, were a troublesome team of theatrical goblins who did not entirely respect Sammy's authority, and who from time to time had to be encouraged with a sharp word or the threat of physical violence. Raphael D'Allesandro was flitting around with a serious expression on his face, and Kate had the impression his principle concern was not the success of the evening but the security of his departmental real estate.

Kate was backstage with her cast, already changed into their minimalist costumes of black jeans or leggings and brightly coloured tee-shirts, though at present these looked rather odd in the soft red glow of the backstage lights. They were a gentle crew, with the exception of Caliban, who was being played by Lily Tregunna's cousin, and who revelled in her role as an earthy spirit given to colourful cursing and snarling gesture. Kate herself was growing anxious that, as the hour of curtain up approached, a collective glazed look was starting to appear across their faces. She realised that all the obedient rehearsal, the creative choreography and the diligent learning of lines, could be wiped out in a moment by stage fright. She sought out once again the boy who was playing the Bosun and checked that he was in good shape to belt out his opening line as soon as the storm effect subsided a little, as she had briefed Harrison that it should. She cast a concerned glance at Ariel, delicate and diaphanous, and at this moment crouched in a corner with her head in her hands. She hoped this was actorly preparation, and not blank terror.

Dave's head appeared round the door.

"All ready, Ms Porteous?"

She smiled and gave him the thumbs up, and amid the nervous tension felt a flutter of a different kind of excitement. She rather liked this secret that they had.

An adjustment to the house lighting quietened the hubbub of the audience, and she knew that Frances would be stepping out of the wings. She listened as her Head of Department, with her customary gentle confidence, welcomed the parents to the theatre, and explained the format of the evening. It seemed to take an age to get through the fire evacuation procedures, the arrangements for interval refreshments, and the list of do's and dont's that were deemed necessary to ensure a smooth show, and her cheeks ached from dispensing encouraging smiles to her now clearly petrified cast. But then suddenly Frances was saying,

"So, without further ado, please put your hands together for 8G, who are presenting The Tempest!"

Under cover of the applause, and with the help of Sammy, she ushered her group out onto the darkened stage, and watched anxiously from the wings as they took up their positions, most sitting cross legged in the shape of a boat, while others struck pre-rehearsed frantic mariner attitudes. She was relieved to see that Ariel was in position and looking alert.

"They'll be fine, Miss," Sammy whispered kindly, "So long as they know their lines."

Up in the lighting box, the sound guy on one desk, and the lighting guy on the other, glanced up at Harrison, got the nod, and hit their respective buttons. There was an almighty crack of pre-recorded thunder, the blue wash came up and the strobe kicked in, and the Bosun bawled at the top of his voice "Avast me hearties!" This was not of course the opening that Shakespeare wrote, but one that Kate had imposed upon her adapted script in the interests of getting the play off to a strong start. The tactic worked.

In the time available they could only scratch the surface of the Bard's enigmatic and magical swansong to the English stage, but they rattled in some style through abbreviated renderings of the storm, the Ferdinand and Miranda log-carrying scene, the rude bits with Caliban under her gaberdine and finally, and rather impressively, Prospero's grand renunciation of his magic. Then the stage emptied to leave only Caliban, temporarily forgotten in a corner, whose final flourish was to pick up Prospero's staff, shamble downstage centre, and cackle obscenely at the audience as the lights faded to black. There was a moment's silence, then the theatre burst into enthusiastic applause, nobody clapping more excitedly than Kate in the wings.

"Nice one, Miss," said Sammy. "Can you get them back to the dressing room quickly please. Next group's waiting."

Kate was so delighted with the fact that her group had performed so well, that she barely noticed Sammy's casual assumption of authority. In any case he was preoccupied by this time with assisting two goblins in the task of manhandling the howitzer onto the stage.

Meanwhile a bizarre scrum was developing as the massed rifles of Jenny Skinner's Henry V cast met the rainbow tide of Kate's spirits in the corridor beyond the drama room, but somehow she steered them through and to their allotted changing rooms where she dispensed Haribo and praise in equal measure. Issy peered round the door.

"Awesome show Miss. Well done guys!"

"Oh, thank you. Yes, weren't they brilliant? Do you need us out now?"

"You've got five minutes, then you wait on the stair until the next piece is over."

"Right you are. I'm glad somebody knows the plan."

"Mr Singleman makes us learn it by heart," said Issy, and disappeared to execute some other prefectorial function.

"Five minutes everybody!" called Kate. "Then all wait on the stair in *complete* silence."

She stepped out in the corridor, where she nearly ran into Dave. He gave her a quick hug, which he reasoned could be put down to collegiate congratulation.

"That was really lovely, Kate. A great start to the show! You happy what your lot do next?"

"Of course," she said coolly. "We wait on the stair, then we occupy the seats left by 8K. All in the battleplan, isn't it?" Over his shoulder she could see Issy waiting on the stair, looking rather theatrically in the other direction. That one didn't miss much.

Her group filed back into the auditorium in time for the next changeover, so she missed Jenny Skinner's rather ponderous Henry Vth, which, critical opinion agreed the following morning, had been more than a little upstaged by its own howitzer. King Lear and his courtiers were now filing on from the wings, and while the show might have been considered a little dull, she had to admire the precision with which Edward had coached his cast – the diction was excellent, and the piece received a warm round of applause.

At the interval she was approached by several adults, some with tears in their eyes, all anxious to thank her for the effort she had put in. She was moved by the genuine appreciation and warmth that they showed. One weather-beaten man with the look of a fisherman about him seemed reluctant to approach her directly, but stood a few feet off, saying to whoever would listen. "Proper job, wunnit? Proper job!" She discovered later that it was Caliban's father, who worked for the council, and who felt chronically sea-sick if he so much as ventured onto Newlyn harbour wall.

It took a full half-hour to administer refreshments, then the seats began to fill up once more. According to the battleplan, which it had to be acknowledged was running like clockwork, Kate could relax for the rest of the evening. She settled down with her group and checked the programme. It was Dave's Romeo and Juliet up next, and she could see him in the wings, looking reasonably relaxed.

This was a good choice of piece with which to start the second half: a less polished, but much more rambunctious production than Edward's measured King Lear. There was plenty of swash and buckle, and the wooden swords she had brought back from Stratford were put to good use. The nurse's scene provoked much hilarity. Having been excused the utterance of lines he thought might embarrass his mother, Mercutio inexplicably re-introduced them, declaiming them with a lewd waggling of his eyebrows, and rolling the letter "r" on the phrase "prick of noon" in a manner that would have done justice to Kenneth Williams. In contrast, the simple hesitant dignity of the young Romeo and Juliet, who were not great actors, but who had, in the course of rehearsal, fallen genuinely and dumbly in love with each other, quietened the theatre and brought the piece to a moving conclusion.

Kate could see why, for all the difficulties, the Shakespeare festival was a jewel in the English department's crown. She felt proud to be a part of it, and that moment at the interval when parents had thanked her somehow sealed her place at St Petroc's, and convinced her that this, for the foreseeable future, was where she belonged. She was quietly pleased too that this event was something in which Dave played a crucial part.

Up in the lighting box, Harrison Roche decided that his fledgling operatives had demonstrated their worth and could be left in charge while he nipped out for a quick ciggy. The consequence of this was the only major technical glitch of the evening, as somehow the effects for Mark Armitage's Ghosts and Spectres piece became digitally displaced by those for Jenny Skinner's WW1 extravaganza. The result was that for the first five minutes any apparition was accompanied, not by the clanking of chains and creaking of doors that Mark had selected, but by muffled explosions and the rattle of machine gun fire. It is possible that the audience, dazzled as they were by the menu of delights and occasional oddities that the evening had so far thrown up, didn't notice that anything was amiss, but the young actors did, and were at that early point in their thespian development where the default response to anything unexpected happening on stage is to giggle. Mark, who had no technical knowledge at all, could only fume helplessly in the wings, but fortunately Raphael was in the auditorium and was able to make his way to the box to reset the programme before the show was hopelessly compromised.

Frances's clever, lyrical, elegant piece on Shakespeare's language, which consisted of several short vignettes linked by a witty commentary, brought the evening to a suitably scholarly conclusion. The audience stood as one to applaud the students and their teacher directors, then the Head himself stepped onto the stage, held up his hands for silence, and delivered a short but clearly heartfelt speech in which he paid tribute to St Petroc's "wonderful English department, whose work so clearly illustrates that real education is not a matter only, or even principally, of league tables and tests, but of stretching students' minds and developing their self-belief."

Anton Killick was not in the auditorium.

It was after ten by the time the theatre had emptied and the last piece of costume had been picked off the floor of the back stage area. The English department, exhausted though they were, went for a drink in town afterwards – where Kate's debut production and Dave's organisation were both roundly praised. The secret lovers, seated scrupulously across the table from each other in the Admiral Benbow, resisted the temptation to exchange a mutually appreciative glance. At one point Kate slipped off her shoe and extended a tentative foot beneath the table, but withdrew it when she realised that she couldn't be sure of stroking the correct limb – Dave being flanked by Edward Tremenhere on one side and Frances on the other.

Nobody felt like staying late, and Dave and Kate left the car park together, driving back to Wheal Prosper in a convoy of two, with Kate leading. Each in their own vehicle was thinking the same thing – that really it would be very, very, nice just to curl up together in the same bed, possibly just to sleep. Dave for his part however was determined not to be the one to broach the issue, and after a lingering goodnight kiss at the foot of the stairs to his flat he peeled away with the intention of making good on their agreement. It was Kate, as he put his foot on the first step, who trailed her fingers down the sleeve of his jacket until they entwined with his own, then held them in the lightest of grips while she fished out her key.

"It's near enough Friday," she said, and drew him into the darkness of the ground-floor flat.

Chapter Thirty-seven

"The glorious plumage of the parrots"

The first session of the St Petroc's Middle-Management Mentoring Course took place the following Monday. Killick opened proceedings with a few pompous words about how lucky they were to have this opportunity, then introduced them to the man he described as their facilitator. He lingered at the back for a few minutes until he was happy things were running smoothly, then withdrew. If he had secrets to impart regarding his own rapid ascent of the greasy pole of education management he was keeping them to himself for the time being.

The delegates had been told that they should dress in comfortable clothing, which might have felt like a bonus of sorts. Dave suspected, correctly as it turned out, that it meant some "everybody-up-on-your-feet" ice-breaker games of the kind Year 8 drama students quite enjoy. This preliminary was achieved without anybody storming out in indignation or pulling a muscle, and now the eight aspiring middle-managers were seated in an attentive semi-circle around the interactive whiteboard, all eyes on the man who would be leading them through the day.

Les Leggett was a sharp-suited, sharp-featured consultant from Wolverhampton, a man in his early forties who still had something of a barrow-boy look about him. He had apparently spent "several years in a variety of mainstream schools", before he left to set up his own consultancy, which was as much detail as they were given on the educational component of his CV. As no-one was rude enough to say out loud, that might neatly summarise a short history of pedagogical failure, not to mention disgrace. Even Dave recognised, however, that there was no point in expending all one's cynicism on the first day, and like his colleagues, he assumed an expression of open-minded attentiveness as Les began his spiel. Kate (his Kate!) was seated across the semi-circle from him, which allowed him to gaze in her direction from time to time while contributing to the smoke screen they were maintaining around their relationship. As long as he kept up the same open, alert expression, an observer might conclude that he was mulling over Les's words of wisdom, when in actual fact he was occupied with altogether more earthy considerations and remembrances.

"I'd loike you each to take few mowments," said Les in tones more appropriate to a dolorous black-country Vicar than to a market trader, "to consider the point you've each reached in your careers to dight. And I'd loike you – now please indulge me here - to picture yourselves as stranded on an oyland…a tropical oyland, if you loike, a bit loike one of those paradise oylands they used to have in the bounty adverts if your old enough to remember those. You can foind them on Yowtube if you look. You can foind all sorts on Yowtube if you look, but that's another stowry." Here the Vicar gave way to the barrow-boy briefly, before he collected himself. "So there's a bit of jungle on this oyland, and maybe a few wild animals, and though you don't see much of these in the day time, you can hear them howling at noight, and it puts the fear of death in you… yes, by all means close yer oyes if it helps…"

This scene setting was the prelude to a complex metaphor for the educational workplace, and their next task was to categorise themselves as one of five allegorical types of castaway, namely a Swimmer, a Searcher, a Striver, a Singer or a Systematiser. Dave couldn't decide between swimmer or singer, but he suspected the swimmer might be shorthand for those who were always trying to get out of their situation, rather than work within it, so he plumped for singer. Kate, obviously, would either be a striver or a systematiser.

After a few minutes of playing around with this idea, which involved them each coming up with a word that described in more detail their character, along with a prop or tool that character might use on the island, it was time inevitably to feed back to the group. Dave was faintly alarmed to find that most of his colleagues saw themselves as strivers or systematisers, with the only other singer being the Head of Music, who could be excused on professional grounds. He felt slightly exposed, and indeed his idiosyncratic selection earned him Les's vicarly attention.

"Now that's very interesting," said Les. "I down't want to put you on the spot, but would you care to share with the group, some of your thinking around that choice?"

Dave felt momentarily trapped. He hadn't intended, this early in the course, to mark himself out as the most unambitious delegate. He considered for a moment, then said,

"I feel that in a workplace situation, we are, of course, all striving. We are all seeking to systematise, because otherwise there would be complete chaos. And I am sure this would also be true on an island." He paused, and judged that the group were all with him. Les was nodding slowly, encouragingly. He continued. "Yet often our eyes are on the ground, and we lose sight of a higher reality – I could call it the *numinous*, were that not perhaps too grand a word. To put it in plainer terms, we are scratching around for nuts on the jungle floor, when really we should be appreciating the glorious plumage of the parrots. I would see my role as being to point my fellow castaways towards beauty, and for this, singing seemed the best metaphor." There was silence, and he lowered his eyes. Then from further round the circle, a colleague from the mathematics department, not known for his appreciation of the numinous, intoned earnestly,

"That's beautiful, David."

Across the circle he was aware that Kate was looking at him intensely with an expression that was not entirely benevolent. He didn't dare meet her eyes. Their facilitator was silent for a few seconds, and something told Dave he knew that possibly he was being ridiculed. Fortunately a ripple of applause, which may or may not have been ironic, spread around the circle, and Les decided the safest course was to treat the contribution seriously, and move on.

In due course they broke for coffee, and Dave had a slight sense of being in the doghouse. Kate certainly seemed to be avoiding him, and was instead notably friendly to Les, who appeared to enjoy the attention. His satirical colleague in the maths department sidled up to him and asked him what his all-time favourite parrot was. He felt a little chastened, and made a mental note to rehabilitate himself after the break.

The second half of the morning was spent considering some general principles of team management, material that had more obvious basis in the real world, and relied less heavily upon risible extended metaphor. It was mostly common-sense stuff, or at least ideas that he had come across before, but he listened attentively, and even took some notes. It still seemed to him that these were strategies designed to maximise the efficiency of teams of widget producers, and that the idea of applying them in an educational context was doomed to failure. Teachers are an odd breed - part nanny; part repository of knowledge; part performance artist, and the raw material they work with is endlessly varied and unpredictable in its behaviour. Once the classroom door is closed, what you have is an hour of complex human interaction, the full consequences of which are impossible to measure, and will inevitably not always be entirely benevolent for those involved. The value added is cyclical and gradual. But presumably Les Leggatt, with his several years of experience in a variety of maintained schools, knew all that.

At lunchtime a table had been set aside for the delegates in the dining hall, although Les was doing his own thing with some Tupperware boxes. Dave contrived to sit next to Kate, feeling that he had endured enough purdah to have earned a little proximity. She was still, he felt, being a little cool, and would engage only in small talk of the kind you might make if you found yourself sitting next to the Head. He decided there was no point in pursuing the matter, and when lunch was finished took himself off to the playing fields for some fresh air.

November had chosen this week to signal its damp and chilly presence, and the sky was a pale and uniform grey. It wasn't raining, but the dew had not lifted from the grass, so that his trainers began to let in moisture, and he was forced to shift to the artificial hockey pitch. He pondered on the morning. Perhaps he had been a bit flippant. Perhaps it would be wise to give Les the benefit of the doubt. If only the whole thing had not been such a parody of touchy-feely management-consultancy gobbledygook. And he had been put on the spot. Really, it didn't merit being sent to Coventry. He took out his phone and texted Kate.

Please don't be cross. I was provoked. Send me a nice text back and I'll be on best behaviour this afo. xxx

The reply came almost immediately.

*I could just about cope with *numinous* from an English teacher but *the glorious plumage of the parrots* was outrageous. I have my eye on you, Mr Singleman xxx*

Clearly he was forgiven. He slipped his phone back in his pocket and continued his strolling with a lighter heart.

The afternoon session was spent going through the structure of the course and the accompanying paperwork. They looked at the questionnaires that would be completed by colleagues and students, and considered what might make a valid subject for the short dissertation that would form the principle academic component of the course. Dave thought he could do something on the value of debating in the English curriculum. Les referred them to a book he had written and, as far as Dave could tell, self-published, entitled *Lessons from Leggett – Twenty Ways to Turbocharge your Teaching Career.* He resolved to order it from Amazon as a penance.

The day finished a few minutes earlier than formal school lessons would have done, and he and Kate walked together back to the staffroom. They passed Killick on the way, who accorded them the curtest of nods.

"You know the funny thing is," said Dave, "after only six hours in Les's company, I feel as if I've known him all my life."

"He never did say what his subject was," said Kate. "What would you go for?"

"Geography," said Dave without hesitation.

"Yeah, I'd go for humanities," agreed Kate. "Maybe business studies? Anyway, that's the last we'll see of him this term."

On the staffroom noticeboard, the advertisement for Sheila Abbot's job was up, advising interested colleagues to email the Head's secretary for details.

On the bus back to Eglos, Issy and Sammy compared the letters and the accompanying questionnaires they had been given about the teacher appraisal.

"Blimey, there's quite a lot of it, isn't there?" said Sammy. "Shall we do it together?"

"It says you're not supposed to."

"Makes sense I suppose. Look at this bit though. "On a scale from one to ten, how do you rate your teacher's personal presentation?" Does that mean the way he dresses?"

"I guess. He won't be getting top marks from me on that one. He's had the same jacket since we were in the first year."

"And his ties are a bit dull, don't you think?"

"Dreadful."

"So…maybe a four?"

"A bit harsh. We don't want to discourage him. Anyway, I predict an imminent improvement in that department."

"How's that?"

"I'm fairly sure they're an item."

"What Singleman and Porteous? How do you work that out."

"They were looking very loved up at the Shakespeare festival. Only, you know, trying not to show it? It was quite funny."

"To be fair, you predicted this from day one."

"I did, didn't I. I'm only surprised it took so long."

"That's Singleman for you."

"You're right. He is chronically laid back. I'm not sure I could give him more than a six for energy and dynamism."

The bus swung into the Eglos layby, and they stuffed the papers into their ruc-sacs.

Chapter Thirty-eight

"My name is Donovan Doggett"

If someone had told Dave back in September that he would be driving up to the West Cornwall inter-schools debating competition with Lily Tregunna and Donkey Doggett in the back of the minibus, he would have laughed in their faces. Yet here they were, bowling along the A30 with Kate riding shotgun in the back as she had promised. The dynamic was distinctly odd. In his rear-view mirror he could see that Kate was concentrating on some final coaching points with Donkey, who was listening with a furrowed brow, while Issy offered quiet encouragement to Lily Tregunna, who was, possibly for the first time in her life, experiencing a bout of nerves. Sammy on the other hand was looking moodily out of the window. It had been evident as they gathered by the bus for the pre-departure checks that the two boys still did not get on.

Cornwall's New County Hall is a vast rectangular structure of dark grey concrete which, like many brutalist seventies constructions, is much more impressive viewed from the inside. As they stepped into the cavernous foyer with its cantilevered balcony and clusters of bright lounger chairs, Dave was pleased at the evident impression that the place made on both Kate and the students. Even Donkey seemed struck by its scale.

"This is bleddy massive. What goes on here?"

"This is where Cornwall's run from," said Dave. "In the very chamber you will be debating in tonight, men and women take decisions that affect our daily lives."

"My mum comes here for meetings sometimes," said Sammy.

They made their way up the wide stair to the debating chamber, where the teams and their coaches were gathering. The audience, who were beginning to filter in, was made up of parents, teachers and a few Rotarians. Viv and Maisie Pascoe were up in the public gallery, where there was room for Maisie's wheelchair. A reporter from the Clarion in a leather jacket was seated to one side, fiddling idly with his phone.

The chamber itself was semi-circular, large enough to seat comfortably Cornwall's hundred and twenty councillors. It was steeply raked like an amphitheatre, with the debaters speaking from behind a long rectangular table on a platform at its centre. Kate cast a glance at Dave.

"I didn't realise it was going to be quite so grand," she said. "I hope my two don't completely freeze."

"Well it does happen," said Dave. "Fortunately, we aren't first up." Sammy and Issy had been drawn second, with Donkey and Lily in the final debate.

Dave was rather enjoying inducting Kate into this corner of his educational world, one that he had quietly cultivated, and in the value of which he fervently believed. He had also, eventually, come round to her view that students like Lily and Donkey deserved to be given a chance. It was odd to remember that they had nearly fallen out over it a few weeks previously.

Now the Leader of the Council, complete with chain of office, was on his feet, welcoming everyone to the venue and reminding them that this was *their* County Hall, the seat of *their* local democracy, and assuring them that nothing gave him greater pleasure than seeing young people, who might one day in the future represent their communities on these very benches, cutting their teeth in a competition such as this one. Without further ado he was going to hand over to the Chair of the Rotary Club, who would get matters under way.

A well made-up women in her fifties with a plummy accent and an expensive cardigan stood up and briefly explained the rules, before calling the first two teams to the front for the opening debate.

The four St Petroc's students sat in the second row, flanked by their teachers. Issy and Sammy spent much of the debate looking at their notes – they were up next, against the independent school that they knew was their main rival. Donkey leaned forward attentively, the same look of intense concentration on his face that Dave had noticed in the bus. Lily Tregunna stared blankly ahead.

The opening debate was not of high quality, and one of the four speakers dried completely after only a minute. The Rotarian in the chair was gentle and reassuring, however, and the student eventually found his place and finished the speech, to an encouraging round of applause from the audience. Kate was relieved that she had allowed Lily to type her speech out in full – reading from a script wasn't a great look, but it was better than total breakdown.

The open period that followed offered opportunity for redemption, with the nervous speaker demonstrating that he could in fact deal well with questions from the floor. On the whole, however, there was a feeling that the competition had not got off to a flying start, and that the second debate could only offer an improvement.

Sammy and Issy took their seats and arranged their notes, Sammy glancing briefly up at the balcony where he knew his parents would be sitting. He was glad they weren't directly in his eye-line. More people were coming on to the gallery now, a thin, slightly haggard looking woman in a tracksuit and a thickset man, who exchanged a greeting of some sort with his father as they manoeuvred past the wheelchair. Then the Chair was introducing the motion, and the auditorium fell into respectful silence once more.

The main speeches went smoothly enough. They had done their homework and the points made by the opposition were the ones they were expecting. Of the two openers, Sammy thought Issy at least the equal of her opponent. He was pleased to get in a couple of incisive points of information, one of which was slightly technical, and wrong-footed the opposition speaker. Then it was his own turn.

His style was quite different to Issy's. Where she was polished, clear and confident, he was prepared to improvise. Issy would have rehearsed every phrase several times, and timed herself to perfection; Sammy on the other hand had transferred his main points to cue cards, which allowed him to adopt a more rhetorical style, making plenty of eye contact with the audience, including the judges. He picked on details of the opposition's argument and attacked them in a witty and incisive manner. He could see Singleman nodding approvingly, and when he sat down there was enthusiastic applause. By the end of the debate the audience were clearly energised, and when the pair resumed their seats, he and Issy allowed themselves a congratulatory fist bump. Whatever the outcome, they hadn't screwed up.

"That was fuckin' good, Pascoe," said Donkey, not entirely under his breath. Kate glared at him.

"Yeah but it was though, Miss, to be fair."

"Well done you two," said Dave. "I'd put you ahead on that one."

There was a short interval between the second and third debates, during which Lily disappeared to the toilets. This did not go unnoticed by Kate, and she called Issy over.

"Issy would you keep half an eye on Lily? I think she's a bit anxious."

Issy nodded and set off after the other girl.

The third debate started before the two girls returned. It was a lively discussion of civil disobedience between two well-matched but poorly-balanced teams – each had one very impressive speaker and one much weaker one. Such pairs rarely carried off the honours, and Dave felt that of the teams he had seen so far, Sammy and Issy deserved the top place.

Issy and Lily slipped back in at the side door during the summing up, and Kate was relieved to see that Lily was looking more relaxed. They waited until the applause died down, then Issy returned to her seat as Lily joined Donkey on the rostrum. Kate caught her eye.

"Everything OK?"

Issy nodded.

"All good miss."

She had found Lily in the toilets, bent over her bag in one corner.

"Lily? You OK? What are you doing?"

"I'll be fine in a second bird. Just got to take me medicine."

"What medicine's that?"

"Vodka. You want some?"

"Um, no – I'm good thanks. Lily, I don't think you should have too much of that."

"One more slug and I'll be right as rain. I don't mind telling you, bird, this debating lark scares the crap out of me."

She screwed the top back on the quarter bottle and returned it to her bag.

"Give me a hug and wish me luck."

"You'll be awesome," said Issy, holding her tightly. "You *are* awesome. Now let's go."

Now Lily and Donkey were in their seats, and the Chair called the house to order.

"Our final debate this evening is on the motion, "This House would ban boxing. Proposing we have Simon Taylor and Sneha Kumar from St Austell School, and opposing we have Donovan Doggett and Lily Tregunna from St Petroc's Academy."

The usual polite applause was augmented by some particularly deep and loud clapping from the back of the chamber. One or two heads turned. Donkey looked up and his mouth opened in astonishment. Up in the gallery the stocky figure of Isaac Doggett, newly released into the community with the first two units of his OU degree under his belt, nodded his approval and gave his son the thumbs up.

The first proposition speaker was well prepared, and made his points clearly, but they were exactly the points that Kate and her team had anticipated, and provided Donkey kept to the script, he would be able to rebut them effectively. Kate was disappointed though that he missed one or two opportunities to make a point of information, seeming to be more interested in the spectators in the gallery than in what his opponent was saying. It was in fact Lily who, midway through her opponent's speech, jumped up with a confidence that had been far from evident before the debate, and punched her hand in the air,

"On that point!"

The challenge, delivered at volume in her broad Newlyn accent, would have been hard to dismiss, and the speaker gave way.

"You're sayin' right, that boxing's dangerous, but it ain't any more so than rugby, or skiing, or Formula One. Are you gunna ban them too?"

Her opponent attempted a response, but the point had been well made, and the judges bent over their notebooks.

The first proposition speaker moved to his closing remarks, clearly a little rattled by Lily's rhetorical assault. Now it was Donkey's turn. Kate was relieved to see that he looked more focused, though he still glanced nervously up to the back of the chamber as he pulled his notes together. Then, as if on a whim, he pushed them to one side, and began to speak, hesitantly at first, and a little mechanically, but clearly enough.

"Chair, Ladies and Gentlemen," (they had been well drilled in the formalities).

"My name is Donovan Doggett, and tonight, with my partner Lily, I am opposing this motion. We do not think that boxing should be banned. It is a noble sport. It pits men and women of equal size and weight against one another in a *gladiatorial* contest," he negotiated the word a little slowly, but successfully – he had practised it a hundred times, "a gladiatorial contest that is ancient and fundamental to human experience. It brings excitement to millions of fans around the world and it provides a route out of delinquency for many troubled youngsters."

Kate was impressed. The text was familiar – she had helped them to draft their speeches - but she had never imagined Donkey would actually learn it and be able to deliver it in this steady, deliberate manner. She stole a glance at Dave, who was nodding approvingly. Then came a line that was new to her.

"I have a particular, personal reason for opposing this motion. My dad," here Donkey paused, cleared his throat, and collected himself, "My dad, who is in this hall tonight, did a bit of boxing in his day, and while it didn't always keep him out of trouble," here he paused, and the audience, assuming this to be an attempt at levity, laughed politely, "it gave him a sense of honour and fair play, that he has passed on to me. And I'm proud of him for that."

Here he paused, looked up to the gallery once more, and gave his father the thumbs up.

"Thanks Dad."

The hall was completely silent. Only those on the platform, and Viv and Maisie in the gallery, could see that Isaac Doggett was beaming from ear to ear. Dave and Kate exchanged glances. Dave in particular was struggling to recall obvious examples of this ingrained code of honour from Donkey's past conduct. Donkey returned to his speech, and to Kate's relief, to the script. He seemed to relax a little, and the remainder was delivered competently enough, though none of it matched the power of that earlier moment of speaking from his heart.

The rest of the debate ran along the predictable lines one would expect from such a standard topic. Lily was less confident with her script than she was with her points of information, stumbling over her words in one or two places, but during the opposition's final speech she made two more interventions with the same intimidating gusto. The open period threw up nothing unexpected, and minutes later Donkey and Lily were returning to their seats, their ordeal over, to respectful and genuine applause.

"Well done, guys!" said Issy. "That was really great."

"Yeah, nice one," said Sammy. "Good work with the POIs."

Dave and Kate added their praise, as the judges retired to begin their deliberations. The audience, anticipating a lull of several minutes, got up to stretch their legs. Sammy chatted to Issy for a bit, then wandered up to the gallery to see his parents. Donkey was already there, standing next to Isaac Doggett, who Sammy was surprised to see was chatting amiably to his own mother.

"Hello Love, well done!" said Maisie.

"We was just saying you all did St Petroc's proud," said Viv. 'Specially that Lily with her interruptions. I wouldn't want to argue with that one."

"Seems our Dads know one another," said Donkey.

"Apparently so," said Sammy, totally disorientated by this unexpected love-in between the families.

"Oh Viv and I go back a long way," said Isaac. "We was on the same cricket team for a while, wasn't we Viv?"

"Right," said Sammy. "Um…I think we should get back, Donk…ovan. That's the judges coming out."

"Whoever wins," said Maisie, "We're all very proud of you."

In the end, it was Sammy and Issy who, to Dave's delight, carried the trophy back to St Petroc's that night, in a decision that nobody could really argue with. The judges praised their mastery of their material, their fluency, and the way they combined their differing styles to powerful effect. As the two friends went up to collect the handsome shield, Kate, who was now sitting next to Dave, could see that he was brimming with quiet pride as he applauded, and she leaned into him a little, to show that she understood what this meant, and recognised its value. Unobserved, Lily nudged Donkey and pointed.

"They's shaggin' you mark my words."

Then the applause died down, and the Chair of the Rotary Club was speaking again.

"This year we were fortunate to receive a small bequest from a long-standing Rotarian who did much to get this competition off the ground. This member wanted the money to be used to encourage participation in the competition, and so we have inaugurated a small cup, which will be awarded each year to a speaker not from the winning team, who is felt to have made a particularly notable contribution to the competition. Now I have to say this was a difficult decision, for there were a number of such speakers tonight, but the judges are agreed that the inaugural award of the Penhaligon trophy should go to Donovan Doggett of St Petroc's School."

More clapping, doubled almost in volume by a powerful, enthusiastic contribution from the gallery. A boxer's applause.

Sammy extended his hand to Donkey, who looked utterly bemused.

"Well done mate. Well deserved."

Chapter Thirty-nine

"Love you, whatever xxx"

It was a Friday, a week before the end of term, and Dave was sitting in the St Petroc's staffroom in a new suit, the first he had bought since leaving university. Kate had ruled his existing ensemble unfit for purpose, (she had held back from giving her honest opinion of his tie collection) and had insisted that they spend the previous Saturday in Plymouth, where there was a wider range of shops. Dave had always admired Kate's dress sense – without being in any way showy she seemed to know what she was doing with colour and cut, and he cheerfully submitted himself to her tutelage. An exorbitantly priced haircut had been added to the shopping list, and while he wouldn't want to be turned out like this all the time, there was a certain pleasure in feeling he was, in all probability, the smartest interview candidate the Governors would see that day. One of the secretaries had whistled softly as he passed reception.

There were five internal candidates for Sheila Abbot's job, including Robbo. Dave knew that his friend was well respected in the school, but Robbo had always been a sixth-form tutor, which was a different ball game altogether. Of the others, one might be regarded as a long shot, but the other two were perfectly competent colleagues who could in all probability do a decent job. Whatever. He tried to forget that he really wanted this.

In the course of the past month, matters with Kate had moved forward considerably. They were still trying to keep school and home life separate, but the unofficial bringing forward of the weekend to Thursday evening that had been initiated after the Shakespeare festival had become an institution. Without much being said, the relationship was moving from the condition of a delicate seedling in need of nurture to that of a healthy young plant that looked likely to thrive. They had talked a bit about Christmas, without making any decisions – Kate was expected at home, and Dave had a half-formed intention to go out to Spain to spend at least some of the time with his father's new family.

He had not told Kate about the Morocco job offer, and while he had no intention of taking it up if their relationship continued to thrive, he wasn't quite ready to close the door on it. He had however emailed Amir to explain that there was the possibility of promotion, and that he would be able to tell him after Christmas if he was in a position to take the matter further.

Kate was still not in favour of making any formal public declaration of their relationship, and while Dave would have happily employed a sky-writer to emblazon it on the heavens for all to see, he was content to play it her way, given that everything seemed to be heading in the right direction. Unofficial word was in any case getting out. Mark of course knew, which meant that Hermione knew (both were pleasingly enthusiastic), and he had also, with Kate's agreement, told Frances. She had seemed pleased but unsurprised, and when he asked her to keep it quiet for the moment, she said she thought it was possibly a bit late for that – rumours had been circulating on the sixth form social media networks for at least a fortnight. There had also been more traditional speculation in the form of some graffiti on a desk at the back of her classroom, but she kept that to herself.

The staff room door opened, and Rona stuck her head round.

"Your turn, Mr Singleman." And as he rose and followed her out, she said quietly over her shoulder,

"Ah'm lovin' the suit by the way."

Up in her classroom, Kate had just dismissed her Year 8 group, who since their triumphant performance at Shakeyfest appeared to have changed character completely, and were now quite demanding. She had not had the heart to crack down on them, but something would need to be done if they didn't settle soon. Now she had a free lesson, as her Year 11s had their mocks in the assembly hall. She glanced at her watch and wondered if Dave had been seen yet. They had been up early that morning, and she had surprised him with a special breakfast of warm croissants and some new coffee she had bought the previous day. Then he had gone back upstairs to his own flat to shower and change into his new suit. When he returned she told him he looked far too handsome for a schoolteacher. She herself was only partially dressed, and for a brief moment there was a tussle between the conflicting demands of business and desire, and the need to avoid the crumpling or otherwise degrading of Dave's new outfit. The dull forces of good sense triumphed.

She wandered round her classroom, tidying up, enjoying the feeling that term was as good as done, that she was settled here and happy. She hadn't told Dave, but it would make no difference to her whether he got the Year 9 job or not. She knew in herself she was committed. They had had three weekends now of spending time together, travelling many miles to explore parts of Cornwall where they would be unlikely to bump into St Petroc's folk, and they had done a lot of that romantic stuff that she had always rather looked down on – hand-holding, sharing cake in coffee shops, sitting back to back on benches reading books. Somehow, with Dave Singleman, all these things made perfect sense.

She assumed that all this was obvious to Dave, but she realised that she wasn't actually articulating it. Why, for instance, had she not told him before he went in for the interview that the outcome was unimportant to her? What if he felt that failure to secure the promotion, which was perfectly possible, meant she would reject him? She returned to her desk and took out her phone.

Dave was already in the Head's office, being introduced to the governors and advisers who would conduct the interview, when he felt the vibration of his own phone through the thin fabric of his suit trousers. There was only one person who would text him during a school day. He barely heard the names of the panel as he wondered whether he could legitimately check the phone. He waited until the introductions were complete, then he said,

"Actually, before we start, I'll just check that I've turned my phone off."

There were smiles and nods. One or two of the panel took the opportunity to check their own devices.

Dave pulled the phone from his pocket and made a show of pressing buttons. The text was brief, and displayed in full on the screen.

Love you, whatever xxx

He settled himself into a relaxed but alert posture and awaited the first question.

After school they met up in a bar in town with Frances and Mark. It was damp, but the Christmas lights were up across the main streets, so that the puddles flashed green and red and silver.

"So tell us all about it," said Mark. "What did they ask you?"

"Well the usual," said Dave. "Why I wanted the job, what I thought I could bring to it. They seemed quite switched on to the challenges of social media - wanted to know what I felt were a pastoral head's responsibilities in that regard. Thankfully Sheila gave me a bit of coaching, so I was up to speed on the safeguarding side."

"Did the debating come up?"

"Yeah they were very excited about that. Donkey is apparently going to be the poster boy for the new aspiration and achievement programme for lower school. To be fair – it's really Kate who should take credit for that."

"It wouldn't have happened if you hadn't been pushing debating in the school for years," said Kate.

"Well that's what I thought," said Dave, "so in the circumstances, I didn't overstate your contribution."

The others laughed.

"Any idea when you'll hear?"

"They were a bit vague about that. I imagine, unless it's a difficult decision, that they'll sort it out before they go home tonight, and the lucky winner will be notified over the weekend, or maybe on Monday."

"Well…here's to a good outcome," said Frances. "You know you'd get my vote, even if it'll give me a timetabling headache for next year."

They drained their glasses.

"Right, well I think we're off," said Dave. "We're both driving."

"I'm not," said Frances. "I'm feeling quite festive. What about you, Mark?"

"I'll have another, said Mark. I'm meeting Hermione and the kids in a bit. We're going to do some Christmas shopping."

Dave and Kate left their colleagues and threaded their way through the thickening press of Friday evening drinkers towards the door. The rain had stopped. As they stepped into Bolitho Street, Kate slipped her arm through his.

"You sure this is wise?" said Dave. "The place will be heaving with kids."

"I'm sure it's wise," said Kate. "And I'm sorry I've been funny about it. I meant what I said in that text. Did you get it before you went in?"

"Just about," said Dave. "I was so chuffed I nearly showed it to the governors."

She pulled him close.

"I'm not in a rush to go back, are you?"

"Depends what's on offer."

"Well you're cooking tonight," she said.

"That wasn't quite what I meant."

She ignored this.

"I'd quite like a look round the shops first."

"I like the sound of "first"."

And the pleasure of having her on his arm, of being publicly together, was such that he was quite happy to defer yet another bit of gratification. As if by way of a reward, there were complimentary mince pies and mulled wine in Waterstones.

They browsed the bookshop for twenty minutes or so, then dawdled back to where they had parked. On the way they bumped into Raphael D'Alessandro and Rona. It occurred to Dave that Rona might have an inside track on the result of the interview, although she would be too professional to say anything, and he would not have dreamed of asking. Her manner however seemed entirely relaxed.

"Hullo you two – getting ahead with your Christmas shoppin'?"

"Just soaking up the atmosphere really," said Dave. He and Kate were arm in arm once more, and while Raphael quite possibly thought nothing of it, he was fairly sure that Rona would clock it.

"How did the interview go?" asked Raphael.

"Yeah, OK, I think."

"They were all still deep in discussion when I left," said Rona.

"Sounds as if they're not in agreement then," said Dave. "I can't see them wanting to string it out longer than necessary on a Friday night."

"Anyway – here's hoping."

"Cheers," said Dave. "Have a good weekend."

"I like Rona," said Kate, when they had moved on. "I spent quite a cheery evening with her at Frances's once."

"Was there gin involved?"

"Well now you mention it…"

They reached the car park, where they had found spaces a few yards apart. There was a moment of touching confusion as they realised simultaneously that they had no blueprint for how to part after a shopping trip – a kiss seemed a bit excessive, so they made do with squeezing each other's arms before moving to their separate cars. Kate started up the Fiat and looked across to check that Dave was not pulling out simultaneously. They could do without another bump. He was still standing beside the MG. Had he lost his keys? Then she realised he was on his phone.

She turned her engine off again and wound down her window, trying to catch the conversation. He was nodding, but his face was serious. Then he was talking again, but he had his back to her now and she could hear nothing of what was said. She got out of her car as he came off his phone and turned to look for her. She tried to read his face, but he looked more puzzled than anything else.

"That was the Head," he said. "They've offered me the Year Nine job."

Chapter Forty

"Mousehole!"

It was the last day of the Christmas term. Dave and Kate had given up independent commuting and instead took turn-about to drive to school. Now, wrapped up against a bitter northerly wind, they were packed into the MG, the cockpit cramped with the roof up and the two occupants both in warm coats. "They're forecasting snow for tonight," said Kate, as they pulled out onto the Newlyn Road.

"Yes but it won't be real snow," said Dave. "You only get real snow in Cornwall about once every ten years. There'll be a few wet blobs and everybody will get very excited and decide they can't possibly go to work."

"We used to get two or three snow days a year in Yorkshire. It was a real bonus provided you weren't stuck at school. One year a whole bunch of us had to bed down in the gym."

"Maybe there'll be snow when we're up," said Dave. "I can't remember the last time I made a snowman."

It had become clear to Kate that there was little point in waiting until after Christmas to make themselves "official." Rona, who was clam-like in her refusal to disclose any of the school business to which she was privy, was less inhibited when it came to spreading good news. Combined with Dave's success at the interview, which nobody seemed to begrudge, it had made them something of a celebrity couple in the final week. Then, to Dave's surprise, Kate announced one evening that she had told her parents, and that he was invited up to join the family for Christmas.

"Are you sure? I mean, bringing me home to meet the parents – that's a bit of a deal, isn't it?"

"Yes, it is. I think you may be the first since Darren Butterworth was invited to tea on my tenth birthday."

"Well, I'm honoured. By the way I'd like to meet Darren. I'm sure we'd have a lot to talk about."

"That could be arranged. He's the manager of the Harrogate Co-op."

Dave had been quietly delighted at this evidence of Kate's commitment, and emailed Amir to explain that his circumstances had changed, and that he was now no longer in a position to follow up on the job at Agadir. He promised however that he would come back to Magic Bay as soon as he could, and that Amir was welcome to visit him in Cornwall any time he chose.

They worked a shortened day, with an early lunch and an assembly in the afternoon. There was little formal teaching, and the morning went by in a cheerful and only occasionally riotous blur of DVDs, quizzes and games. There were Christmas cards in the pigeon-holes. Bottles of wine, tokens of appreciation for various favours done in the course of the term, changed hands throughout the morning.

Kate had a free lesson mid-morning and had arranged for Donkey to come out of his class for a final tutor interview. After the initial excitement of the debating competition, Donkey had kept a low profile, and when Kate asked him casually how things were going at home he was non-committal. He had missed the previous week's appointment, but she was hopeful that he would turn up to this one, which didn't involve him sacrificing his lunch hour.

He appeared ten minutes later than scheduled, decked with tinsel and sporting one Christmas tree earring. This might be acceptable in a classroom given the occasion, but not to move around the corridors of the school, and Kate gently suggested he remove the ornaments before they began. Donkey did so with reasonable good humour.

"So," said Kate. "Tell me what's happening at home."

Donkey shifted in his seat, and looked out the window.

"Well…there was a bit of bust up between Jason and me dad."

"Was anyone hurt?"

"Naw. Just a lot of shouting and swearing. I can't tell you all the things Jason called him, Miss, you'd have to suspend me."

"That must have been upsetting."

"Yeah it was a bit. It's not as if they haven't had rows before, but this was different somehow. Like it was Jason who was in charge of the house and me old man was coming back to take over. Jase didn't like that."

"So what happened?"

"Jason's gone. The old man stood his ground. Jase wouldn't dare lay a finger on him."

"You mean Jason's moved out?"

Donkey nodded. "He's gone to Bristol."

Kate said nothing. She had some idea of what Bristol signified. Donkey went on.

"I'm glad to see the back of him if I'm honest. He knocks me about when he feels like it. But the old man's dead worried. He thinks he's lost him now."

"Jason will have to find his own path, Donovan. Just as you'll have to find yours. It's all about choices and consequences."

"That's what me Dad said. He said he learned that in prison. That's why he started the degree."

"What's his degree in, do you know?"

"Crimin…something or other."

"Criminology?"

"Thassa one. Makes sense when you think about it."

Kate smiled. "Yes I suppose it does. Well look, Donovan, I just wanted to say that I'm dead chuffed with how you've done this term, and I've said so in your report. Not just the debating, but the good things I'm hearing from your other teachers. I hope you have a really good Christmas with your Mum and Dad."

"Thanks Miss, And, you know…thanks for encouraging us, and believing in us, and all that crap…"

"It's really not crap, you know."

"Well whatever. And I hope you and Mr Singleman have a nice Christmas too."

Kate opened her mouth to protest at the impertinence, then she realised that for once, no impertinence was intended, so instead she just said,

"Thank you, Donovan. I'm sure we will."

And he shambled out, clutching his tinsel and his Christmas tree earring.

After school they went to Mark and Hermione's for an early supper, then they all headed along the coast road to Mousehole for the turning on of the Christmas lights. Even in Yorkshire Kate had heard about the Mousehole lights, and she was looking forward to the treat. It was already dark by the time they arrived and the parking spaces were filling up rapidly.

The town, which nestled at the foot of a steep hill, was an unexpected higgledy-piggledy cluster of granite cottages with one or two grander properties, set around a small circular harbour, whose tiny entrance must surely have given it its name. They worked their way through the thronging crowds until they reached the centre, where the frames of as yet unilluminated lights floated silently and it seemed a little sombrely on their rafts, as if in remembrance of darker days. It was possible in one or two cases to make out the outlines of what they would become when brought to life. There were other displays, at present quite invisible, on the dark hill behind them, and on the flat rocky island that lay a few hundred yards offshore.

The small Armitages were agog with excitement, and Dave took one on his shoulders so that all had a good view. As the moment approached the crowd counted down, 10-9-8… they reached the appointed hour of illumination and for a moment nothing happened, then a collective "Aaaahh!" rose from the hundreds of watchers as silently, hesitantly, magically, the displays came to life in shapes and patterns of old-style red, green, blue and white fair-ground bulbs – an octopus; a lighthouse; a Christmas tree; a starry-gazey pie. Best of all was a whale with an eye that winked and an intermittent water-spout of white light. The displays illuminated not only themselves but gave a magical half-light to the real business of the harbour – the fishing boats that floated shyly beside them, and the stacks of lobster pots on the harbour wall. Up on the hillside more displays flickered to life. Giant letters spelled out HAPPY CHRISTMAS.

Dave nudged Kate.

"Isn't that our champion debaters down there?"

Kate looked and sure enough, thirty yards ahead of them and a little further down the hill were Sammy and Issy, gazing out together at the magic of the display, Issy's long mane of fair hair falling out from under a woolly hat. Sammy, still a good few inches shorter than his companion, had his arm round her waist.

"I didn't know they were an item."

"Well who knows with kids. It's all very summer-of-love, these days, isn't it? I think something might have happened at the Year 9 disco."

They stayed at the harbour for a while, but the wind was beginning to bite, the forecast of snow looking more realistic. Mark and Hermione said their farewells and took the children back to the car, and Dave and Kate wandered into the town, where pubs, shops and art galleries were all open to catch the festive trade.

They wandered in and out of the galleries then they went into a pub and ordered some mulled wine. They toasted the term that was behind them, and Dave's new job, and the Christmas to come. Then they sat quietly for a while amid the chatter and warmth of the crowd, snug on a settle a few feet from the open fire, until they noticed that new arrivals were talking of snow, and shaking out coats and scarves as they came in. Sure enough, through the window, small dry flakes could be seen tumbling down out of the darkness, their density increasing perceptibly even as they watched.

"Perhaps we ought to be thinking about getting back," said Dave. "I've never driven the MG in snow before."

They left the pub and walked past the harbour once more to enjoy the novelty of the tumbling white flakes turning to green and red as they floated down past the lights of the displays, before disappearing into the dark water. On the way back up through the town they passed a compact, granite double fronted property with a rather grand stone portico set on four pillars. Despite its modest size it stood out against the tiny cottages that surrounded it - a manor house in miniature. On the wall was a plaque and Kate took off her glasses to read it.

"Goodness!" she said. "Apparently the Spaniards invaded in 1595 and set fire to the town. I had no idea."

"Incredible, isn't it," said Dave. "I've always thought it would make a great subject for a novel."

"You should write it!" said Kate.

"You know one day, when I'm done with this teaching lark, I might just do that."

And he held her close to his side as they walked in step back up the hill through the steadily falling snow.

THE END

Thank you very much for reading *Mentoring Mr Singleman.* If you enjoyed the novel, please leave a review on Amazon – just google the title and click on the Reviews icon. You can read the further adventures of Dave, Kate and their St Petroc's colleagues in *The Unbinding of Edward Tremenhere*, also available on Amazon as a paperback or download.

KS

Printed in Great Britain
by Amazon

24806597R00172